'An absorbing meditation on marriage, masculinity, parenting and the general anxieties of the middle class ... Bolger approaches these variegated lives with a wisdom that contrasts sharply with the benightedness of those he depicts. On every page, insight and illumination are found, as might be expected from one of Ireland's most perceptive writers.'

The Times Literary Supplement

'Only a writer of Bolger's precision and suppleness could wade back through the nation's self-loathing into that mess and mine new truths, treasures to be heeded and learned from ... Bolger isn't meditating on regret, love, moral fibre, greed and carpe diem – he's setting the record straight on them ... This is storytelling that flows deep and soundly, and brims with a hard-earned wisdom ... sublime.'

Sunday Independent

'Well-wrought, considered, layered and evocative.'

Irish Examiner

'Bolger is a witty and sensitive writer ... who has always been attuned to social issues ... Bolger writes about love and grief particularly well, and it is refreshing to see such an open portrait of the sexual lives of each of the characters, from menopausal Alice to lesbian Sophie, from sexually shy Chris to sexually rampant Ronan ... *Tanglewood* makes a critical contribution to contemporary Irish fiction of the post-boom period.'

Sunday Business Post

'Bolger is a gifted storyteller and prose stylist ... a gripping, well-observed examination of the corrosive effects of greed on love, relationships and families.'

Hot Press

'*Tanglewood* is an impressive feat by an author fearlessly interrogating one of the most traumatic moments in recent Irish history. It's a mirror to an age when the party ended.'

The National UAE

Praise for *The Lonely Sea and Sky*

'It is a full-bodied barnstormer, a coming-of-age tale of wanderlust ideal for readers aged 12 to 92. It is an ocean-going epic of sacrifice and derring-do against the backdrop of war-torn Europe. It is a paean to a fledgling Ireland trying to find its feet as the ground moves beneath it. It is all these things and yet it releases submerged thematic buoys to the surface in that effortless Bolger manner. You can only do this if your craft has been carved to precision by time.'

Irish Independent

'Bolger's rendering of the transformation of ordinary men, who have chosen a risky way of life, into truly heroic figures makes for engaging reading.'

The Irish Times

'Bolger's unforced style sings with colour, humour and excitement. But it's the way he smuggles "the bigger themes" into the narrative hull that grants this historical fiction "modern classic" status.'

Irish Independent

'An old-fashioned heroic yarn told with spirit and compassion and stoutly made like the characters aboard the voyage.'

Irish Examiner

'Bolger creates a personal, heartrending and atmospheric tale of the lives of these Irish sailors during a period of great international conflict … Dermot Bolger has done them justice in producing such a finely crafted and extremely readable tale which brings their story to life.'

Lonesome Reader

'That mother of life, that coffin of death, the ocean will continue to compel writers to their task. *The Lonely Sea and Sky* is a beautiful novel that will suit all ages.'

By the Book Reviews

Also by Dermot Bolger

Poetry
The Habit of Flesh
Finglas Lilies
No Waiting America
Internal Exiles
Leinster Street Ghosts
Taking My Letters back
The Chosen Moment
External Affairs
The Venice Suite
That Which is Suddenly Precious

Novels
Night Shift
The Woman's Daughter
The Journey Home
Emily's Shoes
A Second Life
Father's Music
Temptation
The Valparaiso Voyage
The Family on Paradise Pier
The Fall of Ireland
Tanglewood
The Lonely Sea and Sky

Young Adult Novel
New Town Soul

Collaborative Novels
Finbar's Hotel
Ladies Night at Finbar's Hotel

An Ark of Light

An Ark of Light

Dermot Bolger

NEW ISLAND

An Ark of Light
First published in 2018 by
New Island Books
16 Priory Hall Office Park
Stillorgan
County Dublin
Republic of Ireland

www.newisland.ie

Print ISBN: 978-1-84840-697-1
Epub ISBN: 978-1-84840-698-8
Mobi ISBN: 978-1-84840-699-5

Typeset by JVR Creative India
Cover design by Kate Gaughran
Printed and bound in Great Britain by TJ International Ltd. Padstow

New Island received financial assistance from The Arts Council (*An Chomhairle Ealaíon*), 70 Merrion Square, Dublin 2, Ireland.

New Island Books is a member of Publishing Ireland.

In memoriam

For Sheila and for those whom she loved.

Prologue

Tonight I dreamt that I was back in The Ark, my small caravan rocking in the tides of the wind. A scent of turf lingered from the iron stove where I had been toasting bread on the antiquated fork that I could barely still hold between my stiff fingers. The skylight was ajar to allow for secretive nocturnal journeys by my three cats, but Johnny, my collie dog – his bones almost as arthritic as my own – was content to sleep curled on the cushions beside me.

Mildewed books salvaged from nine decades of my life lined the crammed shelves. Old pictures and paintings hung above the long window, beneath which I sat, bent over a candlelit table littered with folders. So many letters to still write, friends to remember, causes to campaign for. Book reading is best kept for winter when no visitors come and I can let each layer of meaning filter down to the bedrock of my soul. But I had grown so absorbed in re-reading Mother's ancient copy of Maeterlinck's *The Treasure of the Humble* – her favourite chapter about how silence awakened the soul – that I'd forgotten how a last guest was due to call at this late hour. It was someone precious to me, but I could not remember who. The book so distracted me that I was unprepared for any visitor. I desperately tried to recollect his name and if he would mind sleeping on the window seat, with Johnny draping himself companionably against the crook of his knees. I am amazed at the number of people who track me down to this small ark I've made for myself and a few stray creatures amid the fields: friends from a half century ago mingling here with young visitors on my wavelength, young people who instinctively grasp truths it took me decades to learn.

A white cat descended through the skylight to land on the table. She shook herself and stood still, observing me with unblinking eyes. Jumping down onto the rush mat, she affectionately brushed against my brittle leg, then sprang up onto the window seat to ponder the possibilities of my lap. Instead she settled down on my left side, head nestling against my thin hipbone. On my right side Johnny rested his head possessively on my knee. He whined slightly, his eyes trying to convey something. Poor old Johnny. I stroked his head and he settled back, knowing it was not yet time for his last biscuit. Sitting there between the peaceful cat and dog, I knew I could never live with humans again. I have grown to prefer the companionship of animals: they have not lost their way; they know what they want and possess the rare gift of being content when they attain it. A sod collapsed with a soft thud inside the stove. The turf basket was almost empty. If I intended to sit up all night reminiscing with my visitor, I would need to go out and fetch more turf from my store under the concrete blocks that lead up to this caravan.

I glanced at the photographs above the window. My gentle father: a composer and dreamer who went to church but only to sing. My headstrong daughter, Hazel, gold hair streaming out from beneath her hat as she cleared a jump at the Dublin Horse Show some fifty years ago. My beloved son, Francis, eyes always lit with laughter. Alex, my only grandchild, who inherited Hazel's golden hair but not her impetuousness. My troubled husband Freddie, happiest when wading alone through a Mayo bog with his Holland ejector 12-bore gun and a retriever dog at his heels.

The night breeze was cool through the skylight, betraying a foretaste of rain. I patted the dog's head, then rose slowly to fetch more turf. Normally Johnny stirred if he saw me lift the turf basket, tail wagging at the prospect of a midnight sniff and a last chance to cock his leg. Instead he whined as if he didn't want me to venture out, his ears going back as they did whenever he heard somebody open the gate into the field. Even the white cat raised her head and, on the far side of the caravan, the old mother cat stirred herself from the comfort of the solitary armchair, which the other animals respected as her domain. All three observing me in the night silence that has been unbroken by any ticking for years – ever since I removed the hands from the last clock I owned and wrote the word '*NOW*' in black marker across the clock-face.

The moment was indeed now. The animals could sense it. When I threw open the caravan door my guest would be striding up the starlit path, framed by an arc of light spilling out from the doorway. But I paused – my fingers grasping the door handle – because, suddenly, I could not recall where my caravan was parked. Was I still in the field behind the Round Tower Bar in Mayo, near the remote road that twists across the mountains to Pontoon? Or back at Curracloe Strand in Wexford, where Alex used to joyously visit me for weekends away from boarding school? Or had I been transported back to that apex of grief in which I paid a stranger to tow my caravan up the overgrown avenue through Glanmire Wood and park it in front of the ruined house where my children were raised?

Or would an ever-changing vista await me once I opened the door? Would I discover my caravan perched amongst carved wooden horses on a fairground merry-go-round swirling in circles through time? Would I find myself briefly peering in through the window of my child art studio in Dublin, where children stood at easels, painting whatever shapes emerged from their imaginations? And then spin past the windows of the White Eagle Lodge where a medium relayed words from the dead, and past the open doorway of a basement flat where I cradled a corpse in my arms? Perhaps the merry-go-round would flicker past the bunk bed in a Spanish hostel in which I lay in grief for days, only surviving by losing myself in the pages of *The Glass Bead Game*, while hostellers half my age left fruit on my bunk but did not attempt to console me, knowing I was beyond being touched by any words except those by Hermann Hesse. Maybe the numerous places I've called home would merge into one blur of colour until the merry-go-round halted, toppling me forward to land as a toddler on my nurse's lap in my childhood garden in Dunkineely, intoxicated by the scent and colour of the fresh daisies I had picked as I waddled excitedly across the tennis court to share them with her.

But I reined in my imagination as I tightened my gnarled grip on the door handle. I felt certain I was still parked in the field in Mayo, where – after all my travails – I finally earned the right to be happy. When I opened the door I would see the fence separating my caravan from the adjoining field. What I didn't know was the identity of the visitor patiently waiting outside.

'Open the caravan door, Eva,' an inner voice urged me. 'You do know who he is and he hasn't come alone. Hundreds are waiting for you out there alongside him: faces stretching back almost a century. They haven't come to visit; they've come to take you with them. Focus, Eva, think hard, regain your senses. Seven years have passed since poor Johnny died. You searched every ditch in Wexford for him, inconsolable with grief. Your cats are long dead too – to your relief. You no longer need to fret about them being neglected after you die in this nursing home where you are trapped.'

I glanced around my caravan, aware now that everything I was seeing was a dream. But The Ark felt more real than the purgatory of the nursing home I would wake up within. Neither Johnny nor the cats moved as they watched me. Johnny's eyes cautioned against opening the caravan door. I could sense him trying to say: 'Wait one more night, Eva. Your love is still holding us firm. Before we disappear from all human memory, remember us just one last time.'

I couldn't open the door, although I desperately yearned to. Johnny's ghost was right: the silent host of faces had gathered outside my caravan not to claim me into their ranks yet, but to be remembered. I was their last link to this earth. When I died their faces would truly disappear. I knew my visitor's identity, the man at their head; the man with whom I most longed to be reunited. I imagined him climbing the concrete blocks beside my stacked turf. So close to me at last, just the width of an aluminium door away. But he was smiling and I knew he had the patience to wait one night more.

Chapter One

The Leave-Taking

Co. Mayo, Easter Monday, April 1949

Freddie had entered her bed at some late stage during the night, or entered what might still be referred to as *their bed*, at least until Eva left this Mayo woodland house for the last time this morning with her two packed suitcases already placed at the hall door. In fairness to Freddie, he must have drawn back the bedclothes quietly so as not to wake her. But the knowledge of this final intimacy perturbed her as she woke and turned over to see his features revealed in a solitary sunbeam shining through a gap where the dilapidated wooden shutters, warped by damp and neglect, could not fully block out the dawn light. Not that any physical intimacy had occurred, no matter how much Skylark whiskey Freddie had consumed before a distant echo of an extinct desire surely caused him to stir from the billet he had made up of old army blankets piled on the stone flags of the kitchen floor, and walk up the bare staircase to this bedroom where – in what seemed like another life – their two children were conceived in love and passionate haste on his part.

However, perhaps it was not a memory of past affection which lured him upstairs to where he now slept on the furthest extremity of their old horsehair mattress, but a forewarning of the loneliness possibly awaiting them both in their separate unknowable futures apart. Whatever Freddie's flaws (after twenty-three years of marriage Eva could enumerate them as easily as he could enumerate hers), he remained too much of a gentleman to force his unwanted attentions on her. Indeed she suspected that too much history and bad blood existed between them for him to feel any remaining stir of desire. So the disconcerting intimacy that may have occurred as she slept was not some final claiming of conjugal rights but the fact that – after drawing back the bedclothes in whatever moonlight filtered into the bedroom – Eva had no way of knowing how long he had spent staring at her sleeping body, curled up in a white cotton nightgown. Nor had she any sense of the legal status of the woman whom his eyes had studied for one final time.

For twenty-three years Eva had known who she was in the eyes of the law. But this morning she was seizing the chance to resume her journey to discover just who truly she was in her soul, while accepting that she was ceasing to exist in any officially recognised category in Ireland. Today was not just her independence day. In Dublin crowds would gather in O'Connell Street for official celebrations to mark the Irish state severing of its final tenuous ties with the Commonwealth by formally declaring itself to be a republic. But no matter what new title the state bestowed upon itself, Eva could not imagine a future Ireland prepared to recognise that a woman possessed any status if she willingly – or, some people might say, wilfully – left her husband. Divorce was possible if she and Freddie applied for it in England, but neither lived in England and even if they went through the motions of securing such a divorce it would not be legally recognised in Ireland. Today's leave-taking would change nothing about the limbo that she was about to enter, of still needing Freddie's permission to open a bank account or apply for a passport. Yet everything would change in her mind because this morning felt imbued with the possibility of freedom. No row about her decision would ensue when Freddie woke. They had endured enough rows and while there was no prospect of reconciliation, both were reconciled to this separation.

Eva stretched out a hand, anxious not to touch or wake him, but wanting one last time to feel something of Freddie's essential, if sometimes obscured, goodness: a quality which once caused Eva to imagine herself in love with him. Her hand hovered inches from his face, close enough to feel his breath on her fingertips and take away some faint resonance of his warmth. Despite their recent history of harsh words and the knowledge of how little value Freddie would place on such a blessing, her outstretched fingers also tried to bestow a tiny benediction of goodwill in this silent room: a wish that would be impossible for her to express if they were both awake. She hoped that perhaps he had expressed a similar silent hope for her when drawing back the bedclothes, but like so much else kept locked in his heart, she would never know his true feelings when studying her body last night.

Silently she slipped from the bed. Even though Freddie was asleep, she turned her back modestly when stripping from her nightgown to stand naked beside the sensible clothes she had laid out on a chair last night for her journey. Pouring ice-cold water from a tall jug into the china washbowl, Eva paused as she caught sight of herself in the dressing table mirror. At forty-six she could easily pass for a decade younger. Her diminutive size and elfin-like face leant her, in certain light, the appearance of being a girl. Yet an arthritic ache in her wrists on cold mornings like this brought home the actuality of her situation: a grown woman, closer in age to fifty than to forty, even if in her heart she felt childlike with joy at being granted this second chance at life. Forty-six was an age when most married women settled for the sour compromise of safety, retreating behind a protective wall of cigarette smoke, silence and piety. In even the most loveless unions she had seen women cling on grimly to convention and outward respectability, like she had done when her children were growing up. But if she delayed her departure any longer she would grow too cowed to ever take flight.

For over two decades Eva had given up her own happiness to make other people happy, beginning when she rashly agreed to marry Freddie during the emotionally tempestuous summer of 1927. Throughout that summer a succession of potential suitors had arrived for leisurely stays with her family, the Goold-Verschoyles, in the Manor House in the Donegal village of Dunkineely, seeking to woo Eva and her older sister, Maud. Her parents had hoped for both sisters to find love amid the heady courtship rituals of tennis on the lawn, picnics to Inver Beach and long walks up the cliffs of Slieve League where discreet opportunities presented themselves for young men to grasp Eva's hand while negotiating the steeper paths to the summit overlooking Donegal Bay. Amid this heady atmosphere her parents' hopes were realised, but not as they would have wished. While Eva and Maud both fell in love, unfortunately it was with the same young man – a Dubliner who arrived at the same time as Freddie: two rivals amicably competing in the outwardly playful, yet inwardly serious, courtship of the Goold-Verschoyle sisters.

Eva had admired her future brother-in-law's easy wit and athleticism, his tacit disinclination to pass judgement on her mother's unconventional beliefs in spiritualism and his encyclopaedic knowledge of Walt Whitman. This emerged whenever Eva's father got lost amid some Whitman quotation and discovered that, by glancing towards him for guidance, the young Dubliner could invariably continue the quote and modestly fall silent again, allowing her father to pick up the thread of the poem. She had also admired his Quaker-like moderation on political issues, in contrast to the dogmatic advocating for the communist cause engaged in by her oldest and youngest brothers, Art and Brendan: whose proselyting divided the dinner table whenever they were both present.

Eva sensed how this young suitor also admired many of her qualities. Unfortunately he admired her sister more. Eva's impulsive acceptance of Freddie's unexpected proposal came only after being forced to feign happiness while watching Maud walk up the aisle of Killaghtee Protestant Church to be given away by their father to the suitor Eva secretly yearned for. Afraid of being seen as an old maid left on the shelf at twenty-five, Eva felt sufficiently panicked to let herself fall in love, not so much *with* Freddie as with the illusion of *being in love* with him. Freddie's personality was different: abrupt, plain-spoken and with an explosive temper which Eva and her mother were shocked to witness from an upstairs window when Freddie encountered two local village children playing tennis in the garden and, in a fit of imperious fury, ordered them to clear off and remember their place. Eva had previously overheard her father explain to Freddie how the family allowed the village children to use their tennis court or visit the stables, which Eva had converted into an artist's studio, if they wished to try their hand at painting. But Freddie had not been listening or was simply unable to conceive of barefoot urchins being allowed such fraternising liberties.

This was the only time before their marriage when she saw Freddie's temper. She had let herself focus on his hearty love of the outdoors; his bravery in never allowing the impediment of a club foot prevent him from engaging in any activity and the way in which – as a mathematics teacher in a prep school – his mind seemed able to focus on practical matters in contrast to her own quixotic thoughts. Unlike some richer suitors that summer, with mannerisms groomed by privileged educations in elite boarding schools, she had found something endearing in Freddie's rough and ready nature, in how his clothes never quite properly fitted and his accent had not lost its provincial Mayo cadence – no matter how haughty his manner at times. Her decision was sealed when she overheard two Dublin visitors mock Freddie's accent and his club foot. Her heart went out to him, like to any underdog, with Eva mistakenly believing that if he could change her unworldliness, then she might also soften his mannerisms and outlook.

Accepting his proposal seemed the practical thing to do as that summer came to an end. Eva hoped that marriage to this seemingly decisive man of action would add a sense of purpose to her dreamy nature. When helping her to dress on her wedding morning, Eva's mother betrayed her unease by taking Eva's hands and earnestly whispering: 'There is one thing you must never lose sight of. No matter what life deals you, promise me that you will strive tooth and nail for the right to be happy.' Eva had ignored such warnings, anxious to leave behind her impractical yearnings for enlightenment and failed dreams of becoming an artist. At no matter what cost, she had determined to mould herself into a practical, attentive, provincial Protestant wife in Mayo. The problem was that Freddie's people – the landed Fitzgeralds of Turlough – were not like the free-spirited Goold-Verschoyles. Eva was barely settled into married life before she overheard Freddie declare that one half of the Goold-Verschoyles were daft and the other half dangerously certifiable. Freddie viewed her family as classic examples of the soft Home Rule liberals who let Ireland slip from the Empire's grasp; hapless idealists too immersed in literature and theosophy to know how to deal firmly with servants. Freddie had held his tongue during the discreet negotiations conducted as part of their courtship, but once back in Mayo he claimed that Eva's brothers only became communists because her father was too mild-mannered to ban dangerous political arguments at his table.

Just how dangerous those arguments were only became clear in the 1930s when her older brother Art grew so enthused by Stalin that he moved to Moscow, marrying and fathering a son while working as a propagandist on *Izvestia*, the official government newspaper. Her father never questioned his son and heir's political choices: neither of them alluding to their differences in the often delayed postcards exchanged between Dunkineely and Moscow; each card conveying greetings and an instruction for the next move in one final chess match played out over several years on two chess boards set up in two contrasting rooms, each containing the same slowly diminishing alignment of carved chess pieces. Her middle brother Thomas was less forgiving of Art, blaming him for influencing their youngest brother Brendan to proffer his services to the Soviets. While visiting Art in Moscow in 1937, Brendan volunteered to become an English-language wireless operator in a tightly monitored Soviet contingent that was sent by Stalin to assist in the fighting in the Spanish Civil War. Even today Eva did not know his exact fate: only that his Soviet superiors took Brendan prisoner in Spain after he quarrelled with them. He was lured onto a ship in Barcelona Harbour and transported back to Moscow to be imprisoned for counter-revolutionary Trotskyist activities. Her mother had bombarded the Soviet Embassy in London with pleading letters, but only shortly before her death did she receive a terse Soviet reply. This four-line communiqué claimed that Brendan died during an attack by a Nazi plane on a train taking him and fellow prisoners to a new camp for their own safety, after Germany's unprovoked invasion of the Soviet Union in 1941. If this story were true, then her youngest brother never saw his thirtieth birthday, but truth was never certain in the Soviet Union.

No dangerous political discussions were tolerated at dinner by the autocratic Fitzgeralds, who once owned seven thousand acres around Turlough. Successive Land Acts had forced them to sell their estate to the Congested District Board to be parcelled out and resold on favourable terms to former tenants. But the Fitzgeralds remained gentry, cognisant of their place in Mayo's social hierarchy and expected former tenants to know their place also. The fact that Freddie was virtually penniless when he brought her to Mayo as his bride never altered his sense of status as one of the proud Fitzgeralds who drank hard and bargained even harder. Eva still remembered the afternoon – a month before her wedding – when she entered the Manor House in Dunkineely, after spending a blissful afternoon outdoors sketching, to hear raised voices from her father's study. It was Freddie and their family solicitor haggling over her dowry. At that moment Eva suddenly felt like one of the thirteen-year-old waifs she once saw shivering in thin dresses at the hiring fair in Strabane, their limbs being prodded by farmers seeking cheap agricultural labour. Her dowry needed to be sufficiently generous because Freddie had based his plans for their future on it allowing him to pay for the renovation of his ancestral home, Glanmire House, which Freddie's father – as younger brother to the main Fitzgerald heir – had been bequeathed, and which was bequeathed to Freddie in turn after his father's death when Freddie was only fifteen.

This left Freddie the poor relation in the Fitzgerald family compared to his uncle who owned Turlough Park: a majestically imposing Victorian Gothic limestone mansion with a high-pitched roof whose wrought-iron gates dominated the solitary street in Turlough village, which was little more than a cluster of small shops and pubs. Located in a wood a mile away, Glanmire House – consisting of just one storey over a basement – surely looked small even at its heyday when compared to Turlough Park, which Freddie's uncle frequently closed up when preferring to live in exile in France, where the weather and politics better suited his temperament and pocket. At least this gave Freddie the status of being the most senior member of the wider Fitzgerald family to live in the locality, when Eva moved into Glanmire House in 1927 to find it already past its prime, with its roof leaking and the bedroom walls prone to mould. Still, back then Freddie was convinced that her dowry could transform Glanmire into a comfortable family home and a profitable business, as he abandoned his teaching career to oversee converting the house into a shooting lodge, with Freddie assuring her that guests from what he termed 'the mainland' would flock there for the authentic experience of taking part in a West of Ireland shooting expedition. It had been a revelation to Eva that a man as seemingly practical as her new husband could possess dreams as disconnected from reality as anything conjured up during her mother's séances.

Having dressed in silence, Eva was now ready for her journey. With her coat loose over her shoulders she quietly crossed the floorboards to place one hand on the brass bedstead and stare down at her sleeping husband's face. Even before their marriage, a weathered ruddiness in Freddie's features had made him look older than his years. While a trace of this former heartiness remained in the leathery complexion of a man happiest outdoors, it was impossible not to observe how years of heavy drinking were catching up with him. It was apparent in the web of spider veins protruding down his neck and the flushed redness around his nose; the enlarged blood vessels giving his face a bloated expression. Eva did not know how Freddie would fare on his own, no more than she knew how she would survive. All she knew was that no matter how bad things got, he would never seek help from her or anyone. Bad things had occurred between them, but if Eva took away any animosity towards him when departing, she would never truly leave her marriage behind: part of her remaining trapped within these walls like the ghost in the wine cellar.

The Second World War had acted as a buffer, keeping their marriage artificially alive by granting them an excuse to respectably live apart: Freddie serving in the British Army while Eva returned to Mayo to raise their children. But the stark actualities of peace – with Freddie's rank of Lieutenant Colonel insufficient to save him from being demobbed after one drunken outburst too many in the Officers' Mess – left them no option but to confront their incompatibility. All last night she had been saying goodbye in her silent way to each room in Glanmire House, storing up the feel of door knobs and sash windows; the touch of the mahogany walnut sideboard that had stood in the same spot since the day she arrived; the oval table where she once loved to sketch at night when the children were small and Freddie was off conducting drinking sprees in the discreet seclusion of the Imperial Hotel on the Mall in Castlebar. Now she touched the bedroom furniture one last time before descending the back stairs and stopping outside the disused wine cellar off the kitchen for one last farewell.

There was no glass in the tiny window in the cellar because no pane ever survived a night without being found smashed in the morning. The cellar was said to be haunted by the ghost of a butler who hung himself here – after being falsely accused by Freddie's grandfather of stealing a five pound note – his flailing legs smashing the window as he swung to his death. Eva had never managed to persuade any local girl working in the house to enter this cellar. In her first winter as a young bride she had felt an overwhelming sense of loneliness emanating from this narrow space and at first mistook it for the loneliness she felt at being separated from her family in Donegal who understood her. But Freddie's aunt – a kindly woman who tried to help Eva adjust to married life – insisted one night on Freddie telling his new bride the story of the butler, which he had previously avoided mentioning for fear of scaring her. Freddie was right in that it did initially frighten her, especially during the following spring when carrying their first child. Then she realised how she could not bring a child into this house if imprisoned by fear and that the butler's spirit – if it existed – was more frightened than frightening, trapped here in limbo and any manifestations of coldness were pleas for help amid the depths of his loneliness. Rather than shy away from the cellar, she had taken to standing in this doorway as the spring evenings of 1928 disintegrated into dusk: a young pregnant woman reading aloud from the psalms by the light of a paraffin lamp.

Finally one evening, soon before her precious first-born, Francis, arrived, Eva had sensed a vast, yet imperceptible heaviness lift from within this cellar and come toward her. Her hands shook as she tried to keep her reading voice steady but the trapped loneliness in that man's soul had so dissipated that, when passing through her in the doorway, it felt as light as a flutter of butterfly's wings. After that the same coldness never radiated from this caller where her two children happily hid during games of hide and seek without any apprehension. Yet Eva always sensed that some echo of that ghost remained trapped there and all that she had done was to lighten his burden by showing him he was not alone. She had no book of psalms this morning but she entered the cellar to press her palms against the cobwebbed brickwork in one final gesture of fidelity and farewell to an unseen presence who had come to feel like a companion. She was leaving him behind, along with so much else, because she could not imagine any occasion when she would stand under this roof again, unless she was still alive when the time came for Freddie to bequeath it to the son with whom he shared almost nothing in common beyond their passion for this isolated house and the remaining few acres of woodland surrounding it.

She turned now, feeling foolish for having stood so long in that cellar and entered the kitchen which held so many memories: Francis and Hazel's laughing voices during the war years when this house became a sanctuary with their father away in the army, the bustle at this kitchen table in the early 1930s when she and Freddie struggled to make a success of Glanmire House as a shooting lodge. Eva could recall labouring with the cook to pluck and singe each slaughtered wild bird that Freddie and his guests proudly displayed on the front steps: standing over them like overgrown toddlers anticipating exaggerated praise for having successfully deposited turds in a chamber pot, before they adjourned to the drawing room for whiskey.

By then Eva was already a vegetarian. Her overwhelming sense of compassion made her feel the plight of each bird with the same agony as if the shotgun pellet had pierced her own flesh. She remembered the awful nausea when – pregnant with Hazel – she would grasp the legs of each slain woodcock and golden plover to pluck upwards from the tail to the head, before plucking the legs and breast, knowing this needed to be completed while the bird was still warm. Having to enter the cool north-facing larder used to perturb her more than any haunted wine cellar because she could offer no gesture of atonement to the pale carcasses hanging by their bound feet for several days until rigor mortis had passed, with Eva needing to regularly check for any greenish tinge if a bird became over-hung. In the month before Hazel's birth, the cook took pity on her when the evening meal was being prepared, banishing Eva to prepare colcannon or a casserole of vegetables. The cook would cut off the neck of each bird being prepared for dinner, wiping away congealed blood before removing their windpipes and inserting her fingers to catch hold of the gizzard and extract it carefully so that no entrails spilled out. Deftly removing the lungs she would separate the liver from the gallbladder with a sharp knife and then, only when the bird was trussed for roasting would she allow Eva to help with the main preparations for those dinners, where Eva always served herself the smallest possible portion of fowl – just enough not to antagonise Freddie – and spent the meal discreetly concealing it under an uneaten pile of mashed potato.

Not that such lavish meals occurred every night. Despite Freddie's plans, relatively few paying guests were lured to make the long trip from England by his small advertisements placed in *Wildfowler's Shooting Times & Country Magazine*. The handful who came invariably praised his ability to find the best cover to shoot woodcock, his wisdom regarding the relative merits of retrievers over red setters, his generosity in pouring post-dinner measures of whiskey and his indefectible energy in guiding them across seemingly inaccessible bogs despite being impeded by the club foot which prudent guests learnt never to mention. They enjoyed his fireside stories about his most notorious ancestor, George Robert Fitzgerald, who once caused mayhem in Mayo by riding roughshod with his own lawless militia, who caged his father inside a cave with a live bear, and haughtily placed the noose around his own neck to jump to his death after the first two ropes broke during his public execution for murder in Castlebar in 1786.

As the guesthouse sank deeper into debt, every shooting guest left with a hearty handshake for Freddie, praising his prowess as a storyteller and a damn fine shot and vowing to return. Few kept their promise, but it always surprised Eva to see how her husband basked in such praise, while appearing to brush off all compliments. Maybe when growing up as the poor relation in the Fitzgerald family, Freddie had needed to develop his gruff *hail-fellow-well-met* persona as a shield against an Ireland in which he felt increasingly out of kilter. It hurt him to watch Mayo County Council gleefully demolish Big Houses when rate bills, death duties and the Wall Street Crash made it impossible for old families to sustain them: the walls of once grand houses being deliberately ground down to fill potholes. Eva remembered public tears in Mayo train stations during the 1930s: impoverished parents bidding farewell to children fleeing poverty by emigrating to Boston and Chicago. But she also recalled elderly Protestant couples sitting quietly in the single First Class carriage, anxious to pretend they were unnoticed, as they slipped away from decaying ancestral homes to spend their final years – like Eva's own parents eventually needed to do – in exile in drab English seaside towns.

As Freddie's dreams of a successful shooting lodge collapsed, this new social order of the Free State kept encroaching on his childhood domain: Freddie needing to sell off small parcels of land to local farmers to stay afloat. She remembered him spending most days in 1936 wandering the bogs alone with only his Holland ejector 12-bore gun and a dog for company and most nights drinking his way deeper into the debt of every Castlebar publican. This left Eva struggling with mounting bills, two small children and the realisation that – apart from her joy at being a mother – she was living a lie. Glanmire House was only saved from the bailiffs by their decision to emigrate in 1937 after Freddie secured an unlikely job as manager of a Culpeper Herbal Shop in Winchester.

Leaving the kitchen now Eva walked back up the stairs to the main house, careful to tread softly when passing their bedroom door, although his snores reassured her that Freddie was still sleeping off the whiskey he had drunk alone in the kitchen last night after they completed any final business needing to be conducted between them. She had come here this weekend not just to say farewell to a house that had been her home but also to secure Freddie's agreement not to make any claim on a small legacy which Eva had recently been left in her late mother's will. Eva would need every penny to purchase the two-storey red-brick Victorian house on Dublin's Frankfort Avenue which she had bid on, because no bank would offer a loan to a woman in her unregulated circumstances. She hoped to support herself there by taking in art students as lodgers and teaching child art classes, although she had not risked Freddie's ridicule by mentioning this second aspiration. But such a home would allow her to create a nest for her children for as long as they needed her. She had not sought, and nor had Freddie offered, any financial support for her new life: Freddie obviously feeling he was showing restraint and decency in allowing her to retain all of her mother's legacy, while he continued to pay Francis's Trinity College fees.

It would be hard to survive but after today she wanted Freddie to have no claim over her so she could live on her own terms. However, just now as she stepped over her suitcases in the hallway and opened the tall front door one last time to walk out onto the front steps, she did not feel strong. The daffodil lawn in front of the bay windows was overgrown, the gravel on the path so choked by weeds as to be barely visible. Up the wooded slope behind the house there were three oaks in a clearing, to which she used to secretly run as a young mother to press her arms around their trunks, trying to draw comfort from their inner strength during moments of utmost despair when she felt utterly trapped. But she felt no need to revisit those oaks this morning because after today she would no longer be trapped on these steps which had been the scene of so many departures.

She recalled their first departure in 1937: Francis and Hazel crying at leaving behind the only home they had known and Eva apprehensive because Freddie knew nothing about herbal medicine or managing a shop, and they both knew as little about Winchester as Winchester knew about them. Perhaps this was the secret of the unexpected happiness they had enjoyed together during their eighteen months in the small live-in flat above the Culpeper shop on Jewry Street, where Eva worked as the unpaid assistant that Culpeper's expected the wives of all managers to become. To Freddie's credit, he stopped drinking during this period and knuckled down in that provincial English city, no longer burdened by needing to keep up the appearance of being a Fitzgerald because nobody in Winchester recognised the weight of that famous surname. This was when Eva remembered him at his happiest: an anonymous Irish emigrant; albeit an educated, Protestant freemason, unlike the majority of Irish emigrants back then.

But his Fitzgerald pride never went away. When war broke out in 1939, Chamberlain warned of an imminent blitzkrieg, predicting a hundred thousand civilian deaths before Christmas. With factories working all night to stockpile cardboard coffins, Eva and Freddie decided it would be prudent for her to bring the children back to Mayo while he stayed on in Winchester. But when Freddie phoned the Culpeper regional office, the local manager shrilly told him that no English public school man would permit his wife to flee dishonourably in time of war. She further suggested that if Freddie could not control his wife, he should also hand in his notice and flee like an Irish coward, leaving her to find a responsible married couple to manage the shop. That same afternoon Freddie received a deeply apologetic phone call from the head office in London. The managing director – aware of how Freddie had increased turnover threefold in Winchester – begged Freddie to ignore this outburst, explaining that the local manager came from Coventry where a no-warning IRA bomb had recently killed five innocent passers-by.

But Freddie's pride was insulted by her inference of cowardice and the reference to him not having attended a good English school. He had barely waved Eva off on the long journey to Mayo before he attempted to enlist. As a middle-aged man whose club foot prevented him from serving on the front line, he was initially only accepted in the Royal Artillery embodied Territorial Army, although he would willing have stormed any Normandy beach or hacked through any Burmese jungle. But his ability to shoot, his imperious manner and his genuine desire – and uncanny ability – to drum the rudiments of marksmanship into even the rawest recruit attracted the attention of the Army Education Corps who commissioned him into their ranks as a Second Lieutenant.

By the spring of 1943 Freddie had attained the rank of Lieutenant Colonel, hobnobbing with hard-drinking fellow officers in Hyde Park Barracks in London, where he was tasked with overseeing security at several royal residences. His role and salary gave him the social status he had yearned for all his life, but it came at a price for Francis, when Freddie insisted on uprooting their son from Ireland to attend a harsh English boarding school where many of Freddie's fellow officers sent their sons. By then Eva had abandoned her attempts to educate the children here in Mayo and was renting a house near Dublin to allow Francis to attend the progressive Aravon School and Hazel to become a popular day girl in the nearby Park House. When Freddie summoned his teenage son to England, Hazel insisted on remaining in Dublin as a boarder at Park House. But Eva reluctantly went to live with Freddie in the Officers' Quarters at his barracks, sensing that it was important to stay close to Francis. Eva had not minded living through what newspapers called the 'Baby Blitz', when Hitler made one final, comparatively ineffectual attempt to bomb London in January 1944. She had felt an empathy with the ordinary Londoners who stoically sheltered in underground tube stations. What she found more stressful was mingling with the officers' wives at awful cocktail parties, although Freddie adored such gatherings, regaling people with colourful West of Ireland tales closer to the pages of Somerville and Ross novels than to the Mayo she knew. He had seemed incapable of not working in some reference to the prestigious school which he claimed their son was greatly enjoying.

Francis's weekly letters from the boarding school were censored by his headmaster – a man whose petrifying rages were supposedly caused by headaches brought on by the steel plate that was inserted in his skull during World War One. Reading between the lines, Eva sensed how Francis was being viciously bullied there. When she visited the school behind Freddie's back, Eva discovered her fifteen-year-old son to be so distraught that he seemed close to a nervous breakdown. Her marriage had never recovered from the furious row when she announced her intention to remove Francis from that school and return to Mayo to nurture him back to health here. Freddie finally consented after she insinuated that it would be only a matter of time before the sons of his fellow officers told their fathers about Francis's fragile mental state, damaging Freddie's newfound status in the Officers' Mess.

This status was now gone, with Freddie released from military service to try and find a new niche in an Ireland that had stayed neutral throughout that war and remained indifferent towards it. Just like Eva, Freddie was having to restart his life. Recently he accepted a positon as mathematics teacher in a boarding school in Wicklow: the same job he had held in 1927 when travelling to Donegal to seek a wife. He would undoubtedly still rattle around these empty rooms during school holidays, but once the school term resumed after this Easter break and he took up his new post in Wicklow, Glanmire House would cease to be anyone's real home.

A cough disturbed her thoughts. She turned to find Freddie standing behind her in the doorway: an old greatcoat thrown over his pyjamas. Neither would mention how he ended up sharing the same bed as her last night. They wouldn't properly mention anything because there was nothing left to be said. Even if there were, it was not in Freddie's nature to discuss what he truly felt.

'You're off,' he remarked after a moment.

She nodded. 'I thought I'd catch the early train.'

'Whatever it is, it certainly won't be early. The blasted train is always late, even though it only starts in Westport. You're all packed.'

'I am.'

'Are your cases heavy?'

'I'll be fine. I'll wait at the crossroads and flag down the early bus into Castlebar. It will save me walking through Turlough village.'

He nodded judiciously. 'Wise. Not that too many folks will be stirring in the village at this hour. They'll be too busy squinting out at you from behind their curtains.'

'I don't tell people our business, Freddie.'

'You don't need to. There are eyes everywhere. Even when you tell them nothing, they still think they know it all.'

'I'll meet no one on my walk down to the small crossroads,' she assured him. 'If I did, they'd just presume I'm home for the weekend.' He was almost standing to attention, yet she could see an agitation in his fingers: nerve ends screaming for one shot of whiskey. 'Will you be all right, Freddie?'

'Me?' He rubbed his chin as if surprised by the question. 'All I need is a shave and I'll be grand. I'd better set to, closing up the house properly or tinkers will break in and lift everything. Their own laziness is the only reason they haven't swiped the lead off the roof.' He glanced back into the hallway. 'It's not beyond repair. Too big a task for me, but Francis has his heart set on restoring it one day when he comes into his inheritance. Don't ask me how a horticulturist will make a living in Mayo, but there again, ask me nothing about that boy. Maybe he'll marry a rich American or make a fortune when he moves to London. In my last summer in London a lot of officers took their wives to the Chelsea Flower Show now that it's being staged again. I was amazed at the stories they brought back about this craze for garden designers and the fees they charge. A fool and his money are easily parted. If the boy is looking for fools, there's no better place than London.' He stopped, realising he was talking too much, trying to bridge the awkwardness of their farewell. 'Tell him the spare key is in its usual spot if he wants to bring down any Trinity pals.'

'I'll tell him,' Eva said softly, knowing how difficult her husband and son found it to communicate directly.

'Good. That's settled. Well, if you want to catch that bus, then I guess…'

'I know.'

He reached behind him for the two suitcases and placed them on the outside steps. Eva walked back to pick them up and stopped a foot away from him. Close enough to reach up and plant one last kiss on his check or for him to reach down and embrace her. Too close for Freddie though who stepped back and glanced up at the sky. The sun had gone in and it felt colder. His eyes stared out past her across the vista of his diminished domain. 'There will surely be rain later but I'd say it should stay fine till you get the train at least.'

'Hopefully so. Goodbye Freddie.'

Freddie took another step back, a step closer to enforced bachelorhood, a step nearer to the cure of that first Skylark whiskey. He gave the sky a final caustic glance. 'Hopefully so is right. The weather is changeable. You just never can tell how things will pan out.'

Chapter Two

Painting and Character

Dublin, April 1951

In this new life Eva was making for herself as a separated woman her motto was to always be prepared. During her marriage Freddie always claimed that she permanently lived *in the ether*: too naïve a dreamer to organise anything practical. Her unregularised status as an estranged wife made her the topic of talk among her middle-class Dublin neighbours on Frankfort Avenue in Rathgar. Eva had lost any last vestiges of financial security by leaving Freddie but found it a relief to be without a husband. What she found lonelier was the realisation that her two children were starting to no longer need her like they once did.

Both were here this afternoon but neither saw Frankfort Avenue as their true home anymore. Even Francis – whom she loved more than anyone on earth – had moved out in January to commence a clandestine love affair with Colville, an older fellow student in Trinity College. The sound of his joyous laugh came from upstairs, through the open door of the bedroom Hazel used on her increasingly infrequent visits. Eva longed to be upstairs joining in this light-heartedness but it was important to give Francis and Hazel their own time alone. Personality wise they were utterly different, yet even as small children Eva never knew them to quarrel. Each harboured such a protective instinct towards the other that it was often hard to tell who was the older: Francis being the most carefree, while Hazel – two years his junior – saw herself as the most mature. More mature than Eva, as Hazel's raised eyebrows often made clear.

Hearing Hazel's bedroom door close, Eva entered the hallway and was rewarded by the sight of Francis descending the stairs, smiling at her. Eva instantly forgot her preparations for the art class. In that moment she was consumed only by Francis's happiness: her heart buoyed into a tumultuous state of joy by simply being in his presence. Francis laughed as he reached the bottom step.

'You look positively radiant, Mummy,' he teased. 'Like you have a dashing young man stashed away, waiting for Hazel and I to leave.'

Eva smiled, amused. 'I'll soon have a house full of dashing young men – dashing about knocking over paintbrushes and easels: all eight years of age.'

He towered over her: so boyishly, strikingly handsome at twenty-three that girls regularly fell in love with him, though Eva had long abandoned hopes of any girl physically arousing his interest.

'Sounds like I'm leaving at the right time, before I'm knocked over by a stampede of miniature Picassos. I hope they appreciate how lucky they are to have you. I remember you teaching me to paint during the war, the fun we had creating cave paintings on the cellar walls in Mayo, and then panicking to whitewash them again whenever Daddy sent a telegram to say he was arriving home on leave. We'd even need to drag Hazel indoors off her pony to help us make Glanmire look respectable again. Our little secret.'

Eva couldn't resist reaching up to brush his unruly hair back into place.

'We never had secrets,' she said softly, being rewarded by Francis stooping to lightly kiss her forehead.

'Do you know how rare and lucky that makes me?'

Their relaxed intimacy was broken by a car horn beeping on the street.

'Lucky in love,' Eva teased.

'Lucky and late. Colville can be impatient. Since he got his new Aston Martin he loves showing it off. We're taking Max for a spin to Howth. Three may be a crowd, but it's damn good camouflage. Now open the door before Colville takes out his hunting bugle too.'

Eva opened the heavy oak door to wave down at Colville, a twenty-six-year-old Westmeath man leisurely finishing off his degree at Trinity with the somnolence of an affluent diner dawdling over an opened bottle of vintage port. Since the age of fifteen Francis had been honest with Eva about his sexuality – an open secret among his small coterie of Trinity friends. Colville was becoming Francis's entrée into the circles Freddie would love to see his son mix within, regularly taking Francis to dine in the Kildare Street Gentleman's Club – Dublin's last bastion of Protestant Ascendency privilege. But it would be impossible for Francis to be open with Freddie about his relationship with Colville, who now had Francis squirrelled away in a discreet love nest flat on Fitzwilliam Square, used by his family – whose fortune came from distilling – for occasional trips to Dublin. Freddie only knew what Freddie wanted to know. He deliberately avoided inquiring into their son's life, although he sometimes made a point of speaking approvingly about how, after the Allies liberated the concentration camps in 1945, they re-interned all homosexual prisoners found there.

Francis's friend, Max – a shy young American painter also studying in Trinity – waved at Eva from the back seat as Colville beeped the horn of his open-topped car again, more from playfulness than impatience. Francis pointedly ignored him, lifting Eva up to swing her around on the front step as he kissed her goodbye. He put her down and laughed as Eva playfully pushed him away, even though her protective instincts longed to draw him back inside where he would be truly safe.

'Run down or Colville will be mad at me for delaying you.'

'Colville mad at *you*?' Francis smiled. 'He's mad about you. All my friends are – Alan and Max especially, although Max is mad for everything Irish. He's dying to find someone who wants to attend a play in the Gate Theatre. You should go: you always say you've no one to visit the theatre with.'

Eva laughed. 'I'm old enough to be his mother.'

Francis squeezed her waist. 'My friends say you're more like a sister to me. Or maybe they'd prefer if you were my sister, because Hazel puts the fear of God into half of them. I'm unlikely to get introduced to Colville's mother, but I gather she can be a right dragon: snobbish in that insecure way new money always feels it needs to be. Colville says I'm lucky to have you as a mother.'

'Being lucky is good.' Eva couldn't resist kissing him one last time before he raced down the steps. 'Being careful is even better.'

She wasn't sure if he heard her as he leaped into the passenger seat without opening the door. Colville said something in mock reproach and both young men laughed, although Eva was relieved to see no display of over-affection, nothing to set them apart from any college pals on a jaunt to show an American around Dublin. Neighbours would not be suspicious. Indeed the appearance of such a car lent her house an air of prosperity that she plainly did not possess. Freddie needed to scrimp to pay Francis's college fees, which to his credit he did. He remained baffled by Hazel's anger at discovering that no savings existed to also allow her to attend college. Freddie had told Hazel that no woman with her looks or breeding needed to waste time setting foot in Trinity to find a suitor, while Hazel had called her father a dinosaur. Eva and Francis both left the room during this row, knowing that – as Freddie and Hazel could be mirror image Fitzgeralds to their core – both were incapable of backing down in any argument.

Colville beeped his horn one last time as he sped away: Francis waving back, the epitome of happiness. Eva loved seeing Francis at his most radiant like this. Yet she knew that his happiness was as fragile as the bubbles Hazel used to blow from a jam-jar as a child: luminous, wondrous and always only a microsecond away from bursting in mid-air. Even with discretion, two young men could not indefinitely live as lovers in Dublin without eventually letting the mask slip, even just once. One indiscretion was all it might take to attract hostility, ostracism, blackmail or physical assault.

But Eva could not worry about such dangers now because, as she closed over the door, she reminded herself of her new motto to always be prepared. She had other responsibilities: her art class starting in half an hour's time being one of them. Once again she checked the jam-jars of paint in the large south-facing front room she used as a children's art studio. There was white, vermilion red (which Mother always called cinnabar), orange, chestnut brown, crimson, lemon yellow, turquoise blue, purple, black and leaf green. Her oldest brother, Art, had urged her to mix only two jars of each colour so that the children would unconsciously learn the revolutionary collective principle of co-operation by needing to share the jars. Eva placed lids on the table for older pupils to mix their colours on: the previous dabs of brown, blue, white and yellow in them having congealed into a soft grey. When she began two years ago Art had built her a dozen miniature easels, refusing the money Eva tried to pay him and insisting instead on billing her at the official union rate of a jobbing carpenter. The easels were sturdy, although after she told one parent they were constructed by her brother, Art Goold, Eva was amused to see the woman furtively sprinkle holy water on an easel before letting her child use it. The incident taught her to be cautious about how much she told her new neighbours about her family's tangled past. To hold communist beliefs in this city was akin to being seen as the Anti-Christ and Art's frequent arrests were making his name notorious.

As the door knocker rapped now and she opened her front door, Eva sensed that it would also be prudent to say very little to the senior civil servant who stood on her top step with his twelve-year-old daughter. Donna from Rathmines was among her most eager pupils. Eva always let her arrive early to help out before each class, knowing the child craved a sense of responsibility.

'Hello, Mrs Fitzgerald,' Donna said brightly. 'Can I light the fire?'

Eva smiled and handed her a box of Maguire and Patterson matches, watching the girl run into the front room to kneel down and light the tightly coiled sheets of old newspaper beneath the kindling and stacked turf in the fireplace. Eva liked to have a fire blazing when the other children arrived. Donna's father followed his daughter into the studio, proceeding with self-assured circumspection while studiously ignoring the children's paintings on every wall. Normally Donna's mother brought her but her father seemed eager to reassure himself that nothing disreputable was occurring beneath this roof. He watched the flames spread in the fireplace and nodded approvingly, as if needing to pronounce judgement.

'I'm glad to see you have one symbol of my national culture here, a turf fire.'

'I always think that no child who stares into its flames will get stuck for inspiration.'

Donna's father pondered this last word, scrutinising it for any trace of subversion.

'It's hard to get good turf,' he pronounced. 'Those fellows selling it door to door try to swindle you on the weight. If the sack feels unusually heavy it's because they've filled the bottom with wet turf. Turf needs to be dried out.'

'I know. My father's cousin carried sacks of it up long flights of tenement stairs.'

The civil servant turned to study her, mildly amused. 'Your father's cousin was a coalman?'

'She was a countess: Countess Markievicz. In her final years she regularly drove to Wicklow to fill her car with turf and logs, delivering it as a gift to freezing families. My father always claimed it wasn't the spells in jail that destroyed his cousin's health, it was those bitterly cold flights of tenement stairs.'

Donna's father's expression became guarded. Dublin's poor had loved the Countess for turning her back on a life of privilege to fight for them, but her revolutionary activities earned less respect here in Rathgar among her middle-class neighbours, especially among those who voted for the Treaty. Eva rarely mentioned this family connection, but had felt slighted by the veiled insult in his comment about the turf fire: his implication that someone like Eva could not regard herself as truly Irish.

'My wife tells me that Jack Shanahan's son attends your classes,' Donna's father said. His tone was cautious, his words left hanging as if they carried an inference that Eva should be able to decode.

Eva lowered her voice, watching Donna use the tongs to rearrange sods in the grate.

'Do you know Mr Shanahan? I don't like to ask him directly but I hear his wife's cancer is bad. She's five weeks in hospital. I'm not sure how much his son knows, but you can sense the terror buried inside the boy.'

The man digested this information as if it were news to him. He shook his head. Eva mistook this for an expression of sympathy, then realised the gesture implied that she had misunderstood the import of his remark. He chose his words with even greater care. 'I don't know the gentleman personally, but my father was once interned in Frongoch with his father. I'm not criticising the choices other families made later on: I'd just prefer if Donna and Jack Shanahan's son don't get too close. To avoid any awkwardness, inappropriate birthday party invitations or suchlike.'

Eva couldn't prevent herself smiling. 'Donna is a very grown-up twelve-year-old girl and John Shanahan is an immature eight-year-old boy. I can't imagine anything inappropriate occurring…'

Eva stopped, realising from his askance glance how she had misinterpreted his remarks and the purpose of his visit. The silence with which he greeted the Countess's name could only mean that Donna's family took the Free State side during the Irish Civil War. She now realised that the Shanahan family must have supported de Valera. For the last three decades the families who took opposite sides in the Civil War had devised ways to avoid having to socialise, but because nobody had previously taught this type of child art in Dublin, Eva's house was unaffiliated territory. Eva sensed how Donna's father would be happier speaking to Freddie or Hazel because he would know exactly which social class he was dealing with. Eva's déclassé state discommoded him.

'Oh, I understand now,' she said.

The man sighed, visibly relieved. 'Then you'll understand that it's nothing personal. I've never spoken to Jack Shanahan but I'm dreadfully sorry to hear about his wife.' He glanced towards the fireplace, anxious to change the subject. 'Donna's doing a great job with that turf.'

'It's good turf,' Eva said, 'I'm from Donegal so I know. I can give you the name of the man who supplies me if you like.'

Donna's father buttoned up his black coat. 'That's hardly necessary: we only burn Newcastle coal in my house.' He hesitated, then added awkwardly, feeling the necessity to make a conciliatory remark. 'I don't know what you do in these classes but you're bringing Donna out of herself. She can make her own way home.'

Donna seemed too absorbed in the fire to notice him leave, but she was conscious of some unspoken undercurrent in the conversation because when Eva closed the front door she turned to find the girl holding a box of charcoal sticks in the studio doorway.

'Can I still come here?' Donna asked anxiously.

'Of course.' Eva smiled. 'Now would you like a task?'

'Yes, please.'

Eva set Donna to work slicing up lengths of cheap wallpaper. Boys loved to draw complex sets of train tracks on these long strips, inventing hazardous viaducts for engines to cross. Eva began to cut up strips of white butcher's wrapping paper, which was cheaper than the paper sold in art shops that Eva could not afford. During her first year of running the studio she was so poor that she had sometimes enlisted her great friend and kindred spirit, Esther O'Mahony, to help secretly raid local dustbins at night for old copies of *The Irish Times*. The two friends would sit up, chatting and laughing as they whitewashed each sheet of newsprint to give her pupils a flimsy white canvas to paint on. Her finances were now less precarious and Esther rarely needed to join her in moonlight bin raids but Eva still constantly needed part-time jobs to keep this studio afloat.

Eva didn't care how menial such jobs were if they helped her fulfil her dream of being a teacher. She had been equally poor in the early war years, when Freddie could only send a little money back to her and the children in Mayo, until his promotion changed everything. Yet even amid her poverty she had still been viewed in Mayo as part of the gentry: afforded the automatic respect which so infuriated her brother Art. In contrast Art spent the war years frequently imprisoned for agitating for revolution in the Dublin slums, organising rent strikes in new working-class estates in Cabra and Crumlin, and refusing to accept his inheritance as the eldest son after their father died. People in Mayo and Donegal always made allowances for Eva's ethereal nature. In Frankfort Avenue she fitted into no social caste: her new neighbours unsure what to make of her. But Eva knew what she wanted to make of her life. Freddie's disdain had helped kill any dream of becoming an artist, but – inspired by the joy she remembered from painting as a child – Eva was fulfilling a new dream in running this studio devoted exclusively to child art.

Art might wish to change the entire world, but Eva could only affect change at her own snail-like pace. Dublin echoed to the tramp of young footsteps heading for the boat to seek work in England. Those who stayed had little money or prospects: anyone in a job cowed into conformity for fear of losing it. In a society where creativity was considered deviant and self-expression frowned upon, she wanted to offer a sanctuary where children's imaginations were allowed unchecked freedom. When starting her studio two years ago she used a sunless back room, because Freddie – on an awkward visit from his Wicklow boarding prep school – maintained that it would be a disgrace to see her front room destroyed by paint.

Despite having left him to gain her independence, Eva had followed his advice back then when her self-confidence was low. In fact she might never have found the courage to persevere with her plans if Freddie had not brought with him a visitor that evening: an impeccably dressed, stern-looking poet who taught at the same prep school. Eva was unsure if Monk Gibbon's abrupt manner stemmed from arrogance or extreme shyness. Dublin people were wary of Gibbon's tongue. He said little during their visit as she babbled on about her plans, scrutinising her so piercingly that Eva wondered if Freddie had brought him along to make her realise how ridiculous her dream seemed. But as he was leaving, Gibbon surprised Eva with the gift of a book, *Child Art and Franz Cižek*, by Dr Whilhelm Viola, an art teacher who once studied under Professor Cižek when allowed to work in Cižek's famous children's studio in Vienna.

Since then this book became her bible, a beacon of encouragement when her initial hand-written notices attracted only two students. She loved Cižek notion that children drew what they thought and not what they saw, that naturalistic expression was unnatural in a child and any teacher with a rebel in their class was blessed. She savoured the story of the Austrian girl who, after painting a purple elephant, logically explained to Herr Cižek that grey was too dreary a colour for such an exotic animal. But what inspired her most was Monk Gibbon's inscription on the flyleaf: '*To Mrs Fitzgerald, from a fellow teacher.*' Eva still recalled her shock at seeing the words '*fellow teacher*' in his copperplate handwriting. Gibbon's inscription lent her confidence to grasp that this was who she might become: an evoker, drawing forth children's latent radiance. She had reached an age when many women felt marooned and obsolete: their designated task of child raising done. But maybe her true life was only starting. For years she had reined in her dreams to do the right thing for others. Now each art class seemed like a tiny declaration of independence, an assertion of her right to be herself.

The bright youthful clothes she wore were part of this same quiet assertion, although they caused further gossip on this street where many women dressed as if already in premature mourning or imprisoned by the need to look respectable. Hazel urged her to charge higher fees to stop slipping deeper into genteel poverty. But her art class was not about money. While most parents were well off, others who travelled from outside Rathgar found it hard to afford even the meagre amount Eva felt forced to charge. Eva provided smocks, but encouraged parents to send children along in their oldest clothes. Most mothers felt too inhibited to do so: passing on these inhibitions to their children. It worried Eva if any child was constantly tidy. Each pupil was allotted their own wall space in the studio or in the hallway. This perpetually changing exhibition space ran down the back stairs and around her kitchen walls, leaving her house ablaze with colour. Donna had now finished cutting up the wallpaper. Eva watched her stand at her easel, savouring a sense of importance at having the studio to herself. It was impossibly cruel to imagine this girl burdened by being on one side of a civil war, which had ended but never gone away, with eight-year-old John Shanahan forced to grow up on the opposing side.

'What will I draw today?' Donna asked, catching Eva watching her.

This was a trap Eva knew to avoid. Suggesting themes inhibited a child's ingenuity when all they needed was a blank canvas and the unlimited possibilities of their imaginations.

'I'm sure your ideas are more interesting than mine.'

The child grimaced. 'What if I have no ideas?'

'We all have ideas.'

'Was what I painted last week any good?'

Donna's work stood out amongst the other children's vibrant free-flowing paintings. Her propensity was to paint isolated objects in a subdued way, terrified of risking a mistake or straying from reality.

'It was what you see in life. But what do you see in dreams?'

Donna laughed nervously. 'You can't paint dreams. They would be like ... I don't know ... modern art.'

'And do you like modern art?'

'My father says nobody can understand it.'

'Why do you need to understand it?'

Donna smiled. 'You're silly sometimes, Mrs Fitzgerald. Not like a proper teacher.'

The girl blushed at her sudden impertinence, but Eva only laughed.

'I wish I had a penny for every time I've been called silly. Draw whatever you like.'

'Maybe I will try and paint a dream.' Donna scrutinised the blank sheet on her easel with perplexed anticipation.

Eva slipped away so as not to disturb her, venturing upstairs to see Hazel. Two canvases belonging to Camille, her latest art student lodger, were placed on the landing to dry in the sunlight. Eva paused to admire the richly subtle colours in the landscapes that merged abstract with realism: the lodger's signature, Souter, was barely visible unless you knew where to seek it. Camille had worked as a nurse in London before attending art school, gaining an experience of life which Eva had lacked in her youth when failing to cope as a student in the Slade School of Art. Eva loved her late-night talks with Camille, and Francis enjoyed her presence on his visits home: he loved the company of girls, and girls loved how he was utterly relaxed in female company, sharing their sense of fun. She walked past the paintings and entered Hazel's bedroom.

Hazel sat reading on her bed, her blonde hair recently towel-dried. Her feet were bare, the room filled with cigarette smoke. The music of Glenn Miller came from a Bakelite wireless set. For the last year Hazel had been living in at a Meath stables, having met the owners during a Horse Show Week hunt ball where Captain Barry's London victory on *Ballyneety* in the George V Gold Cup was still being raucous celebrated. Her wages were low, but Hazel would not feel fulfilled by earning more as a receptionist in some dreary solicitor's office. Eva suspected that her numerous male admirers in the strata where Hazel mixed would find it slightly vulgar if she earned too much. Hazel's wages made her job seem more like a hobby, which afforded her the entrée to jump at horse shows and attend hunt balls.

While Hazel still resented how Freddie had made no financial provision for her to attend Trinity, everything about working at the Meath stables suited her: exercising horses at dawn, patiently coaxing them through dressage deportment, rubbing them down with a serenity which only came to the fore when she was in close proximity with animals. The owners spoke about her having the seat of a young Iris Kellett, but Eva could not imagine her daughter possessing the steadfast dedication to master any single discipline. Hazel was only staying in Frankfurt Avenue tonight because she intended driving a borrowed car in tomorrow's Irish Motor Racing Club's annual Phoenix Park run. Last year the *Evening Mail* photographed her at the wheel of a Chevrolet-engined Lola, under the caption, '*Ireland's speeding blonde bombshell.*' Eva loved hearing about Hazel's exploits at championship trials, but her daughter greeted Eva's talk about the cruelty of fox hunting with the same look that Freddie used to convey affectionate exasperation with his bride early in their marriage. She threw up her eyes now when Eva suggested that she lower the wireless.

'What will jazz do?' Hazel teased. 'Poison their little souls?'

'I love jazz,' Eva said, 'but my classes are about expression, not impression. If the children want to hear music they can make it themselves.'

'Let those brats loose with drums and tin whistles like the last time I stayed here and I assure you I'll play Glenn Miller at full volume,' Hazel warned. 'If you taught them to draw a straight line you might have more chance of producing artists.'

'I don't want to produce artists.'

Hazel shook her hair, amused. 'What do you want to produce, Mummy?'

A memory returned from Eva's childhood in Dunkineely. Her youngest brother, Brendan, then aged only twelve, defining character during a chaotic family dinner: '*Character is what you are, it's what you do every day.*' She felt the familiar stab of pain whenever she thought about Brendan, even though thirteen years had passed since her brother's disappearance shattered whatever harmony had remained within her family. Eva might never uncover her brother's fate, but knew that if Brendan had grown disillusioned with Stalin's intentions in Spain, he would have possibly signed his own death warrant by voicing his honest objections, because it was in his character to do so.

'I want to produce character,' Eva replied.

Hazel sprang off the bed to lower the wireless, displaying the restless energy that was so much a part of her nature. 'Mummy, you sound positively Victorian,' she laughed. I wish Francis was still here to hear you. What on *earth is character?*'

'You possess it.'

'In what way?'

'By never agreeing with anything I say. Or with anyone else for that matter. I worry for you.'

'That I'll get myself into trouble with some Not-Safe-in-Taxies Trinity student?'

'I don't worry about you losing your virginity; I worry in case you lose your character.'

Hazel looked so hurt and unexpectedly vulnerable that Eva immediately regretted the remark.

'Like you've lost your character,' her daughter retorted.

'How have I lost mine?'

'Think about it, Mummy. What was it that awful stuck-up R. C. on Garville Road called you when you answered his ad for someone to walk his dogs while he went on holidays? *'A funny little creature.'* That's how people here see you: A church-mouse, living hand to mouth. You call yourself a teacher, but you earn more from child-minding, dog walking and checking on empty houses when folks go away.'

'You're confusing status and character,' Eva replied. 'You are born *into* the former, but born *with* the later. Art retains his character despite choosing to live as a labourer. Likewise, I've shed my class and religion. I couldn't do it when you and Francis were small. But now you're both finding your way in life and I can do the same.'

'So what exact social class are you now, Mummy?' Hazel asked.

'None. I'm simply myself.'

Hazel's tone was infused with world-weary sophistication, as if explaining home truths to an infuriatingly silly younger sister. 'You may wish to think that, but you'll always be the daughter of a Protestant barrister who was too rich to practice law, except for representing a few Dunkineely corner boys arrested for being drunk and disorderly. Uncle Art calls his slum neighbours 'comrades', but I doubt if many call him 'comrade' in return. To them he's a dangerous eccentric smelling of money, even if he gave away your family's fortune. Getting your name in the newspapers for being fined for trying to sell *The Daily Worker* on O'Connell Street doesn't enrol you into the working class. The policemen who keep having to arrest him only do so for his own protection, to save him being torn asunder by hostile, actual working-class mobs who have no interest in buying any communist newspaper unless it has Jane Russell in an underwire bra on the cover. Uncle Art may hang on his cross as a self-appointed martyr, but one cannot trade one's class like a cigarette card. A screwball like Art fools nobody – especially the poor – by trying to blend into a tenement.'

Art is no screwball. He simply believes in his principles.'

'Even though his principles tore your family apart? Even if the families on the Donegal land he inherited need to keep paying rent into a bank account that Art refuses to touch to pay for basic improvements to their living conditions?'

'Art never asked those tenants for a penny since Father died,' Eva argued, weary of having to defend her brother. 'He would prefer them to stop paying rent and run their tiny farms in tandem, like a collective.'

Eva heard a knock at the front door.

'Grant me patience,' her daughter said. 'Uncle Art's tenants are not collective farmers in Ukraine, happily singing revolutionary songs while starving to death. And if they were Ukrainian, they'd secretly want what Art's tenants want: to be let buy their farms or at least have their landlord acknowledge they are still paying rent to give them some security of tenure.'

'Art will hardly evict them when he doesn't even consider himself their landlord.'

Hazel regarded her quizzically. 'And do you think they know that? Country people have reason to fear evictions. Your grandfather tried to protect the Goold-Verschoyle wealth by creating a trust fund bequeathing those lands only to the eldest son of the eldest son. I wish I'd been born an eldest son. Instead I'm meant to flutter my eyelids at any attractive young man with a few thousand shares in British Petroleum. Art is the eldest son and heir, whether he likes it or not. Therefore what else is he, if he is not their landlord?'

The knock was repeated more loudly.

'Art has told those tenants that he refuses to recognise the acquisition of wealth by inheritance.'

'So why not enter a solicitor's office and sign over the land to his tenants?'

Eva sighed, caught as ever between Hazel's logic and loyalty to her brother.

'Don't you think I've begged him to a hundred times? He claims it's a matter of principle. He can only legally sign over the land if he accepts that he's the legal owner. But it's against his principles to recognise any system of primogeniture inheritance.'

Hazel snorted. 'So, the people Art claims to champion suffer for his principles while he passes himself off as a Dublin labourer? If Art wants to blend in with the poor, the first thing he needs to lose is conscientious objections. They are a petit bourgeois luxury the poor can't afford. But Art never thinks things through. The Soviets kidnap and probably murder his brother, yet Art still acts like Stalin's lapdog.'

Eva heard the knock at the front door a third time. 'Art says he knows nothing about Brendan's fate.'

Hazel walked to the window, watching another mother bring her child up the path. 'Despite living in Moscow when Brendan disappeared? I saw Art's picture in the newspaper the last time he was arrested for preaching revolution. His eyes had the haunted look of a man doing penance, even if he can't bring himself to recognise it. Notice how guarded he gets when Brendan is mentioned? I mean, why did the Soviets revoke his visa to live in Moscow, despite him having a wife and child there?'

'He says the NKVD told him he could better serve the revolution by returning to Ireland to re-energise the struggle here.'

'That's his way of saying they kicked him out like an old sheepdog. Still, he was lucky. When most foreign zealots in Moscow get visited by the NKVD it ends with a kangaroo court and a bullet to the head.'

Eva sighed, growing increasingly agitated from this feeling of being perpetually torn in two, trapped here upstairs inside her old life when she was needed downstairs in her new one.

'Criticise him all you like, but he's still my brother. The reason I didn't revert back to my maiden name after leaving your father is so that people wouldn't associate you with Art. To your friends in Meath you're just one of the Mayo Fitzgeralds.'

Hazel laughed. 'For God's sake, Mummy. Don't you know how small Ireland is? They keep two stud books at the stables – one for horses and *Burke's Irish Peerage and Landed Gentry* to trace the rest of us back for three generations. Besides I'm not ashamed of Uncle Art. I'm fond of the old fanatic.'

'And I am not ashamed of being poor,' Eva replied. 'I've never envied anyone their wealth or looked down on anyone's poverty.'

The knock came a fourth time, loud and impatient. Eva was relieved to hear Donna open the front door. For the next two hours, she owed it to her pupils to have nothing on her mind except inspiring their imaginations. Eva had hoped that her relationship with Hazel would become easier after her daughter left home, but an edge remained to their conversations that neither seemed able to avoid. They would never have had this conversation if Francis were here. He had a knack of injecting light-heartedness into any situation.

'Funny little creatures can hardly afford to?' Hazel lit another cigarette and turned off the wireless.

'I must go downstairs.' Eva was unable to disguise her hurt when turning to leave.

Hazel touched her arm apologetically and held out the lit cigarette. 'I'm sorry, Mummy. You know I fly off the handle. Have a ciggie: a peace offering.'

Eva allowed herself to indulge in the rare treat of a cigarette and inhaled deeply. 'That's in your character,' she said. 'You speak your mind no matter what. Never lose that trait.'

'Men don't like that trait. It scares them, especially in Ireland where women aren't meant to have opinions. Maybe you should have given me the odd going-over with a stick as a child: it might have made me less opinionated. But you were never great for discipline.'

'I could never have struck you.'

'Or struck Francis, you mean.'

The jibe was light-hearted but pointed. As a child, Hazel was tough enough to survive any 'going-over', but one slap from Eva would have destroyed Francis, who could never cope with unkindness.

'I love you both equally,' Eva replied, although the truth was that she loved them both intensely, but differently.

'I know you try to.' Hazel smiled, as if pardoning her mother as she combed her hair one last time. 'Look after Francis for us both. I don't trust Colville. Was it him I heard earlier, tooting the horn on his latest toy?'

'An Aston Martin,' Eva said. 'Very impressive.'

'It would be if he didn't drive like an old lady.'

'I like him,' Eva said.

'Do you trust him?'

Eva couldn't answer. It would mean addressing the fear in her heart.

Hazel nodded, understanding her silence. 'Colville's not the worst, but he's such a wet provincial. I saw him acting outrageously at a dinner dance last week, so desperate to prove his manhood that he pawed every girl he danced with.'

'Was Francis there?'

Hazel nodded. 'My brother has blossomed into quite the social butterfly. Francis was the exact opposite of Colville, relaxed in his chair surrounded by the most beautiful, unattached girls. I have the big brother every girl in Dublin wants, although they want him as more than a big brother. Valerie had her head resting on his shoulder. They were sharing private jokes like lovebirds, every girl giving her dagger eyes, thinking the best matches aren't made in heaven but in Trinity.' She paused. 'There is nothing going on between them, is there?'

Eva shook her head, noticing the barbed reference to Trinity. Eva had first met Esther O'Mahony among the meagre attendance at a meeting of the Dublin Vegetarian Society. When she introduced Hazel to Esther's niece, Valerie, an initial coldness developed after Hazel discovered that Valerie was able to attend Trinity. But it was not in Hazel's character to hold resentment, and the two young women were now close friends.

'If any girl could turn Francis, it would be Valerie,' Eva said. 'But they're just soulmates. They're too close to have secrets, but Valerie is discreet. I hope Colville is. He didn't do anything at the dinner dance to...?' Eva was too anxious to finish the sentence.

Hazel lowered the hairbrush and shook her long hair loose. 'Rest assured, Mummy, Colville did nothing to indicate he even knew Francis. Only a few people know and that's how to keep it. Now, your hallway sounds as crowded as a lifeboat from the *Titanic*. Run down and enjoy your brats spilling paint.'

Leaving the bedroom, Eva hurried down into the hallway where some mothers whom Donna had let in were being shown around the display of paintings by their excited children. Sunlight streamed in through the open doorway. The youngest child whispered to Eva, 'Can I have a hideaway?'

'Of course, Evelyn.'

The girl smiled shyly. 'I want nobody else to see what I paint. But you can.'

Eva left the front door open as more parents climbed the steep steps: mostly mothers lingering to chat to one another. But when she turned around Eva saw that Mr Shanahan had arrived and was studying his son's most recent pictures – violent images in dark colours stabbed onto the paper. Mr Shanahan looked drained and gaunt. For a moment Eva wished that Donna's father could see the anguish of this man whose son he did want his daughter to consort with, but then she was relieved that the two men's paths hadn't crossed. Civil War bitterness was too deep. Eva had never grasped all of Sigmund Freud's ideas, but she understood enough to comprehend what he called the narcissism of small differences. Behind their rhetoric, so little divided these two men in outlook that they could never be reconciled. They needed to cling to perceived differences or lose their identities. All she could do was create a free space for their children. John Shanahan strained at his father's hand, anxious to join the others.

'I hope he isn't a handful,' Mr Shanahan said. 'He is when he is at home these days.'

'Run along, John,' Eva said. 'Play in the garden if you like.'

They watched the boy stomp off towards the garden.

'Can you get him to paint something cheerful?' Mr Shanahan asked. 'I'd like to bring a picture into his mother in hospital.'

'I'll try. But it's no harm to let John get out what he's feeling inside.'

'Maybe so.' The father sounded doubtful. 'He clams up if I try to talk to him. Can you mind him next week? I can't afford to take any more time off work. The new minister and I are not exactly bosom pals ... our fathers took different paths.'

Eva didn't know which government department Mr Shanahan worked in. Could it be the same building where Donna's father worked? Perhaps the two men regularly passed each other in the corridors, studiously avoiding eye contact.

'I'll mind John whenever you want,' Eva promised. 'And don't bother coming back for him this evening. I'll make sure he is dropped home safe.'

The man nodded his thanks and left. The Shanahan house was on Donna's route back to Rathmines and the girl would savour the responsibility of bringing the boy home but Eva knew better than to step across these numerous hidden fault lines. The prudent thing would be to walk the boy home herself. She entered the studio where children were attaching sheets to easels, although smaller students preferred to use the floor. Eva placed one easel in a corner to let Evelyn have her hideaway. She walked over to Donna, who had completed a realistic picture of a child peering over a wall at a ball in an adjoining garden.

'I thought you were going to paint a dream?' Eva said.

'Last night I dreamt that our ball got thrown over the wall by mistake. I remember feeling *so* frustrated that I couldn't ask for it back because Daddy says we're forbidden to talk to the family next door.'

Donna impulsively layered the picture with a layer of stone grey paint that obscured everything.

'What is that?' Eva asked.

'The colour of frustration.' Donna looked at Eva, shocked by the irrationality of her remark. 'That makes no sense, does it?'

'It does,' Eva assured her. 'Remember you're painting a dream.'

Walking around to check on her other pupils, Eva realised how at times these classes felt like a dream for her. They could be exhausting if things got out of control, but she was always caught up in the children's excitement. Her final pupil arrived, looking around eagerly for a free easel. He was the grandson of old Mr Durcan who owned the main pub and grocery shop in Turlough village, a mile from Glanmire House. The shop was split in two: drinkers hidden away behind a wooden partition. His two daughters who ran the shop were always cautiously respectful towards Hazel but made a great fuss of Francis, who loved to spend hours at their counter gossiping with them. Eva never knew their brother well, but remembered him delivering messages up the long avenue to Glanmire House: a highly intelligent but reserved boy – the first of the Durcans to attend university. Eva remembered the excitement in Turlough when he qualified as a barrister: locals stopped using his Christian name and began calling him 'Mr Durcan', just like they addressed his father. On her final visit back to Mayo the Durcan sisters had hinted at talk of their brother being made a judge. Eva greeted this man's wife now – another Mayo woman – and leaned down to address his nine-year-old son.

'Hello, Paul.'

The boy smiled. 'Hello, Mrs Fitzgerald.'

His smile radiated a sense of wonder, not just because he loved the freedom of these painting sessions but because he was addressing one of the mythical Fitzgeralds of Turlough. The boy spent his summers sleeping above the pub run by his aunts in Turlough village and had told Eva about how scared he once felt for his soul when tempted to step inside the small Protestant graveyard on the side road leading to Glanmire House. The Durcan family had hauled themselves up within two generations. Paul's grandfather, old Mr Durcan, was born on the roadside in the 1890s, following his parents' eviction from their cottage by bailiffs employed by the Fitzgerald family. This was something the Durcan sisters never mentioned during all her years of buying groceries in the shop. The Durcans' social rise echoed the Goold-Verschoyles' journey in reverse. She didn't know if Paul's father, the judge-in-waiting, would have much time for things as impractical as art, although the boy's mother seemed very in tune with his sensitive nature. But the fact that the class was conducted by a Fitzgerald – even if only through marriage – would make it acceptable.

'What will you paint today, Paul?' Eva watched the boy stare around the studio.

'A scream,' he replied.

'And how will you paint that?'

'Zigzag, zigzag.'

Both Eva and Paul's mother laughed at his enthusiasm.

'That sounds marvellous,' Eva said, knowing it would be. From his first painting of a stick-like figure surrounded by furious dabs of colour – which he entitled *Match-Man Breaking Clouds into Cotton Wool* – she had rarely known a child with such a vivid imagination.

Hazel's jibe about Eva earning almost no money was true, yet Eva felt rich simply by being among these children. John stormed in from the garden, trying to pick a fight with a boy playing with modelling clay on the floor. Eva led John to the easel beside Paul, suggesting that he pin up a blank sheet. In reply John raised his brush and painted a long red trail across Eva's face. The boy stepped back defiantly, expecting to be slapped for boldness. Eva wondered if he longed to commit a similar outrage at home and gain his father's complete, if angry, attention. Eva decided to respond by laughing. Taking John's brush from him she painted the same line across his face, imagining Freddie's apoplectic expression if he could see his wife now.

'We're two of a kind,' she announced. 'Indian braves.'

'You're only a squaw,' John replied, but his tone had mellowed.

'Will you draw us a wigwam?'

'Draw your own.'

'I'll make mine as black as possible,' she said.

'Then I'll paint mine in bright colours that you've never even heard of.'

'I dare you to,' Eva challenged him.

The boy shrugged, but she saw how he was intrigued by this turn of events. 'Pin me up a sheet so, because you never do proper teaching anyway.'

Paul lowered his brush to address the boy. 'I can't work if you're going to be a cranky pants.'

John Shanahan disdainfully examined the zigzag streak across the black background on Paul's sheet. Eva knew that for these few moments at least he was forgetting his unspoken fears about his mother.

'What's that squiggle meant to be?'

'A scream.'

'You wouldn't know a scream if it bit you.'

'So what is the squiggle then?' Paul asked and Eva realised how acutely sensitive he was to John's pent-up emotions.

'A train, silly. Look, I'll show you.' John snatched up Paul's brush, dipped it in paint and drew two tracks that encased the zigzag. 'Rushing at night through the mountains.'

'You're right.' Paul stepped back to examine the picture. 'Isn't he right, Mrs Fitzgerald? Why didn't I see that?'

Other children stopped their work to gather around. 'If it's night-time,' Donna asked shyly, standing at John Shanhan's shoulder, 'how can we see the tracks with no moon or stars?'

'The stars are blocked by clouds,' John said, 'but a half moon is about to peep out. Look, and an aeroplane is passing as well.' He began to paint, losing his gruffness as he enjoyed being the centre of attention. He added in the aeroplane and glanced back at Donna, anxious for her approval. She rewarded him with a smile. 'You're not good at finishing these, are you?' he told Paul. 'I'll help you make another one if you like.'

'All right,' Paul agreed. 'We'll call it *Dragon Being Chased by a Flying Octopus*.'

'You do the dragon,' John said. 'I'll draw the octopus.'

The whole class became caught up in painting, exchanging ideas aloud as Eva walked around. Donna returned to her easel to add a piercingly blue eye besieged by black eyelashes in the sky above the garden where the girl yearned for her ball. 'I don't know why,' she confessed, 'but if ever I do anything wrong I get caught, so maybe this eye is God watching me.'

'Or your inner voice,' Eva suggested. 'Your conscience.'

The girl went quiet and Eva knew she had probed too deeply. Donna quickly painted two red high-heeled shoes in the space below the eye. 'It's finished now,' she announced.

'What are they?'

'The sort of American shoes I'd like to own one day, if my father ever let me.'

A shout alerted Eva to a spillage. She fetched the mop as Evelyn sang to herself, painting quietly in the corner. Paul and John chatted excitedly, cramming ever more colourful objects into their picture. Eva hoped that the hospital would allow John's mother to hang it over her bed. She approached Evelyn's corner, asking permission to enter the hideout and examine the girl's painting of a cluster of small figures gathered around a huge woman who loomed over them.

'Is that me?' Eva asked.

'Don't be silly, that's a real teacher with a stick. This is you.' Evelyn drew in someone standing among the small figures. 'You're just like a child yourself. That's what my mammy always says.'

Other voices kept demanding her attention, wanting to mix colours or play in the garden now that their paintings were finished. One toddler found a drum and marched into the hall, banging it and singing at the top of his voice. He stopped and stepped back, disconcerted by the look he received from Hazel who was descending the stairs. Hazel peered in at the mayhem and laughed, picking her way through the children to kiss Eva.

'Goodbye, Mummy. You look absolutely ridiculous with that streak of paint on your face.' Hazel smiled affectionately as she hurried towards the front door, anxious to embrace her burgeoning life. 'Then again, that's exactly in your character, so I suppose you look exactly like yourself.'

Chapter Three

Making an Exhibition

Dublin, September 1951

If Eva didn't hurry she would be late for the theatre. All day she had been rushing, first into town to check the gallery space, then out to a small printer in Drumcondra to collect the catalogues and now back into the city to eat here in one of the few cafés where she wasn't considered a crackpot for ordering vegetarian food. But even here the waitress who had just served her a plate of overcooked vegetables did so with a glance that conveyed either sympathy or condescension, as if anyone ordering a meal without meat surely only did so out of poverty. The Dublin Vegetarian Society had recently proclaimed that its membership was doubled, putting a positive spin on the fact that – apart from Eva and Esther O'Mahony – it still only possessed twenty-two other registered members. But at least this evening's meal was palatable, although Eva would need to eat quickly if she was to meet Francis's friend Max outside the Gate Theatre before the curtain went up.

These past six months felt like one headlong rush, until three weeks ago when duty engulfed her again, anchoring Eva back into an orbit of concern for her son. But this morning Francis rose from his bed in Frankfort Avenue of his own accord, which meant he had at least slept – perhaps fretfully and probably not all night – but long enough to gain some respite. Certainly he was sleeping peaceful on the three occasions last night when Eva had opened his door to sit by his bed, watching over Francis like when he was a boy, resisting the compulsion to stroke his hair lest she wake him. He needed rest to recover from the trauma of lying awake, night after night, face to the wall to try and prevent Eva glimpsing his tears. But Francis was beginning to recover because the human heart miraculously always recovers. The heart is not propelled by pure economics, though Art would undoubtedly describe what happened to Francis as another example of how Marx correctly preached that human activity is essentially governed by economic greed. Or, to put it more traditionally, that money always marries money, even when an actual marriage, or any public display of affection, is out of the question.

This summer it had finally felt as if Eva could get on with her own life, until three weeks ago when she received a distraught dawn phone call from Francis, a plea for help in removing his possessions from Colville's Fitzwilliam Square love nest. Colville had abruptly given him an order to be gone by noon. Everything Francis owned had fitted into one suitcase and two cardboard boxes, easily shunted back to Frankfort Avenue by taxi.

But that taxi journey had marked the end of this brief summer of respite where Eva had allowed herself to stop worrying about her son, so lulled by his joy at living with this slightly older lover that she had become conscious of a weight lifting: a burden of responsibility lodged deep in her subconscious ever since Francis first confided in her about being homosexual.

Thankfully, Freddie had never discovered Francis's relationship with Colville, though he would have dismissed Colville's family as social upstarts compared to the mighty – if mightily impoverished – Fitzgeralds. But a great family name only got you so far, even in affairs of the heart. Eva had always sensed that it would only be a matter of time before Colville dumped her son for a more socially appropriate 'special friend' who was as wealthy as himself. She felt so close to Francis that she experienced any anguish he endured just as keenly as he did. The past three weeks had been a nightmare, sitting up to console him and trying to create a space where he could feel safe. Yet, even amidst her pain, one part of her was relieved that this liaison was over with its constant dangers of exposé, arrest for gross indecency and certain expulsion from Trinity College.

She had offered to cancel the exhibition of work by sixty of her students that was due to open tomorrow night. But Francis was insisting that it go ahead, like he was insisting on her continuing to teach her classes and to go to the theatre with Max. Her decision to attend tonight's play was made easier by the fact that this morning Francis announced he would not be sleeping at home tonight. This suggested the possibility of a new man in his life. While Eva worried for his safety, she was relieved to see him strike out once more for happiness. She recalled her mother's words as Eva left her childhood bedroom on her wedding morning: *'No matter what hand life deals you, promise me that you will strive tooth and nail for the right to be happy.'*

It was Esther O'Malley who first suggested staging an exhibition in the basement gallery of Brown Thomas department store. They had been attending a debut exhibition there by Robert Ryan and Tony O'Malley, two young Munster and Leinster Bank officials, when Esther pointed out the store's owner, Senator McGuire, who often made his gallery available to new artists. Because the Senator was in conversation with Victor Bewley – whom Eva knew from Quaker meetings – she found the courage to approach him and the Senator immediately offered his gallery for free. For the past two months her excitement was matched only by that of her pupils. Eva noticed a subtle change in how neighbours addressed her after *The Irish Times* – Rathgar's bible and barometer – ran an article about how Dr Whilhelm Viola of the Royal Drawing Society, whose book on child art was her bible, had agreed to travel from London to launch what would be

Dublin's first exhibition of child art, brushing aside any question of a fee in his reply to Eva's timid letter of invitation.

The reporter, smelling of peppermints and self-importance when he visited her studio, wrote a condescending piece about how children in Rathgar were as good or – as he phrased it – as bad at art as Jackson Pollock. But he missed the point. For a start Pollock was a great artist whom the reporter was too prejudiced to appreciate. But child art was not meant to imitate adult art. It was a journey of blossoming. Eva was not attempting to produce artists, but rounded individuals with creative imaginations. She wanted to prevent what Wordsworth called the 'shades of the prison house' from closing off their minds, to set them free by giving them a belief that everything was possible. *The Irish Times* reported that Dr Viola would speak about how child art aimed to develop free and independent personalities: a statement which – as Donna's mother wryly informed Eva – would certainly ensure that the Department of Education boycotted the event.

Eva didn't care who attended, she simply wanted to celebrate the oasis of creativity she was trying to create. But now even this exhibition felt in danger of being overshadowed by Francis's breakup. Hazel's romantic life was equally complex and often as volatile as her daughter's own character. But in so much as Hazel let Eva see into her world, it was Hazel who generally dumped suiters for being what she would call insufferably wet. On the one occasion when Hazel had been jilted, her friends were able to flock around and fuss over her, to Hazel's growing irritation, as Eva recalled. But with homosexual love affairs there could be no public sympathy lest it attracted comment. You grieved alone, keeping your pain below the radar. So far Max, Alan and Valerie O'Mahony were the only Trinity friends to visit Francis since the breakup.

Alan, who had first befriended Francis when they were both schoolboys at Aravon School, came from a prosperous but undistinguished Glenageary Protestant family. His bedside manner was as stoic and discreet as his everyday persona, as if

Alan had made a conscious decision to render himself invisible in public. His sole distinguishing feature was a neatly trimmed beard, which leant him a nautical appearance, but Eva slowly realised that even his beard had been grown to deflect and disguise. As day boys in Aravon, Francis and Alan had recognised their shared secret in being homosexual. They had also recognised – with an initial disappointment and then relief – that neither was attracted to the other and they would never be lovers. Being both drawn to very different types of men meant that they would never be rivals ether. This made their friendship strong and unstrained: no jealous tantrums or lovers' tiffs, just mutual support when needed. Alan's visits helped to calm Francis, but Max's more lively ones drew Francis out of his despondency and, even if only for short periods, restored her son's gregariousness. Max had started to visit Frankfort Avenue so frequently that Eva initially wondered if the American was a closet homosexual positioning himself to become Francis's new lover. But Max seemed too overtly heterosexual and had started to speak about harbouring clandestine feelings toward some girl. He was too shy to reveal her name, but Eva was glad that Max had found someone special because he seemed slightly lost in Dublin.

The thought of Max waiting outside the Gate Theatre made her pay for her unfinished meal and hurry from the restaurant. It was at Francis's instigation that she and Max had started to attend Gate productions together, attracted by the more innovative drama on offer there than at the Abbey Theatre. Max's conservative parents in Ohio would possibly be horrified at some plays they saw and perhaps baffled that Max enjoyed attending them with such an older companion. But Eva had reached an age when she felt sufficiently free of convention to make friends without reference to age, sex or creed. What she loved about Francis's college friends was how quickly they became her friends also.

She needed to hurry now, weighed down by the bag containing the catalogues for tomorrow's exhibition. But rushing about kept

Eva feeling young. She might be penniless but marital separation granted her enough consolations to make life exciting again. The richest consolation was friendship. In Dublin she kept finding her own kind: free spirits, even if some were initially cautious about revealing their private beliefs. Friends so varied that they occasionally clashed if brought together; impassioned young artists and seemingly staid middle-aged civil servants whose idealism was camouflaged behind the conservative appearances they needed to publically project.

Eva was convinced she had known some of these friends in previous existences, whereas others were kindred souls she was meeting for the first time. Max felt like one such soul. Eva possessed no sense of having shared a past with him, but – from how they instinctively felt at ease together – she suspected that in a future life they would be more closely linked. He was waiting outside the Gate Theatre, when she appeared, slightly out of breath. He waved two tickets to show that – despite her protests – tonight was his treat.

'No pickets this time,' he laughed. 'It won't be as exciting.'

When they first attended the Gate some months ago protesters were picketing the theatre, distributing a pamphlet entitled *Red Star over Hollywood* because the actor Orson Welles was attending a performance of *Tolka Row*. The mob from the Catholic Cinema and Theatre Patrons' Association shouted such abuse at Welles as an alleged communist that the author of *Tolka Row*, Maura Laverty, sang 'The Red Flag' from the greenroom window above their heads to further provoke them. When Eva told Art about the jostling Max and she had received her brother scornfully proclaimed that Welles was no Marxist, merely a failed capitalist masquerading as one. But if Max's parents knew that their son occasionally fraternised in her kitchen with an actual communist like Art, Max would almost certainly be on the next liner home from Cobh.

Tonight only a small crowd were in to see a revival of Denis Johnston's *The Old Lady Says No*. Eva and Max took their usual cheap wooden seats at the back. He was often mistaken for her son until people heard his American accent. Eva loved the play's ending – with Robert Emmet's ghost gazing down on Dublin from the Wicklow Mountains – partly because it conjured up Esther O'Mahony's Wicklow cottage where she planned to spend this coming Saturday, if Francis seemed well enough to be left alone. After the final curtain Eva lingered in the narrow foyer to watch the courteous director, Hilton Edwards, stand with one hand on the shoulder of his lead actor, Micheál MacLiammóir, who delighted in looking conspicuous with extravagant hand gestures and a refusal to remove his makeup. The two men fascinated Eva for being Dublin's only openly homosexual couple, tolerated as exotic theatrical creatures because they seemed so utterly true to themselves.

Afterwards she strolled leisurely with Max down O'Connell Street: its atmosphere so different from the war years, when cowling had dimmed the streetlights and everything was rationed. Window shoppers gazed at the fashions in Clerys. Bicycle minders smoked, standing sentry over the piled-up ranks of bicycles parked beside the statues. Because Max had paid for their seats and deposited a coin in the collection box held by Lord Longford on the theatre steps, Eva treated him to a knickerbocker glory in an ice-cream parlour opposite the Metropole ballroom. A dinner dance was taking place, girls arriving in billowing dresses topped with sequin-studded lace netting. They discussed how Francis was recovering from his heartbreak; her exhibition tomorrow night; the White Stag art group show where – to his joy – Max's first paintings were soon to be shown; and how different Dublin was from Ohio. They never discussed their age difference: there being no need too. Max was simply a friend in his twenties who found in Eva a sympathetic ear who took his dreams of being a painter seriously. Theirs was a meeting of minds until, as Max escorted her to her bus stop, Eva unselfconsciously linked his arm. Then as her bus arrived it became a brief and – for Eva – utterly unexpected meeting of lips, initiated so quickly by Max that at first Eva didn't fully grasp what was occurring. His kiss was followed by an intense whispered request.

'Can I come back with you? Please.'

She was a mature woman, yet in that moment she felt as flustered as any inexperienced girl. She didn't know what to do or say, so she said, 'Not tonight. Not with Francis there.'

Max stood on the pavement staring in at her as the bus pulled away. He was trembling so much that his desire was unmistakable. Eva didn't know what other passengers were thinking or what to think herself. She was too embarrassed to look up at the strangers around her. Her emotions were a cocktail of guilt, dread and confusion. But she could not contain an unexpected gush of girlish joy: a painter half her age had kissed her and asked to stay the night. Eva now realised that when Max had dropped hints about harbouring clandestine feelings towards someone he was referring to her, although Eva had been too much in the ether to recognise the signs. What did she feel for him? She didn't know, having never given herself time to contemplate such things. When the bus reached her stop she deliberately stayed on it: the double decker almost reaching its terminus before she got off. She needed the long walk home.

As a girl she loved walking alone at night in Donegal. Now, walking back towards Rathgar, she felt like a confused girl again. The problem was that she was no girl. Forty-eight was a dangerous age: her hormones flaring up one last time. Friends claimed she only looked half her age: the illusion of youthfulness aided by her slender figure and passion for causes that her contemporaries had grown too cynical to believe in. Yet no matter how young she looked, Max was only a year older than her son. Eva fretted that she might have led Max on by linking his arm as they left the theatre. This was the relaxed way she walked with Francis, but perhaps Max had sensed a latent desire she was not conscious of. Eva had enjoyed friendships with men since separating from Freddie, but nothing physical ever arose, because life was simpler with her sexuality suppressed, seeing as her separation had no legal basis in Irish law.

Francis was not at home tonight: this was merely the first excuse to occur to Eva at the bus stop where it felt like all of Dublin was watching. If she had acted impetuously and allowed Max to accompany her home, she might now be experiencing sensations that she had only ever read about in Obelisk Press editions of Henry Miller books which daring friends smuggled home from Paris. Not that intimacy with Freddie had been unloving, at least in the early years, but even in her naivety she had recognised it as perfunctory and one sided. In the past the men for whom she felt genuine desire were always snatched away from her.

In 1920 she lost the first man she loved through her own immaturity: a young New Zealand officer who was staying with her family while still recuperating from wounds following the Great War. He had wanted to marry Eva and take her to the other side of the earth, away from the atrocities gripping Ireland as it lurched towards independence. A new life might have beckoned in New Zealand, a sense of light and freedom as she painted in the studio he promised to build for her on his family's land in Hawke's Bay on the North Island. But at seventeen Eva was not ready to leave behind the safety of Donegal – never realising how porous that sanctuary was and how quickly her family would be riven apart by politics. Her inexperience and hesitancy about embracing adulthood held Eva back when the officer set her a test: a midnight boat trip out to an island where they could finally be alone. Eva would never know how life might have panned out if she had not dragged along her youngest brother at the last minute as an unwitting chaperone. But without Brendan's presence Eva would never have summoned the courage to traverse the narrow road to the jetty where the officer waited. Only when it was too late had Eva realised how desperately she longed to be alone there with that officer who could not delay his return home until Eva sufficiently grew up to recognise that she was blossoming into a woman with desires as strong as his.

Seven years would pass before another visitor to Donegal captured her heart. This time she was ripe with longing but this suitor chose her sister instead, panicking Eva into an unsuitable marriage. Eva recognised that she was not blameless in the slow fracture of her marriage: after her children were born she became too emotionally preoccupied with being a mother to make time to try and please a husband who was happiest drinking with cronies or out shooting on his beloved bogs. During her marriage she needed to suppress any yearning for love to protect her children. But in the summer of 1944 Eva almost made a fool of herself over another young officer recuperating from a different war.

This was after Francis could not cope with the regime of casual cruelty and bullying considered essential for character building in that prestigious English boarding school where Freddie disastrously enrolled him. Returning with Francis to Glanmire House, Eva tried to turn their woodland home into a refuge for her son. But an unexpected surge of desire caught her off guard in this isolated sanctuary when Freddie sent over a young army officer, Harry Bennett, recuperating from his wounds, to act as a tutor who would, in Freddie's unfortunate phrase, 'stiffen up' Francis. Harry Bennett's arrival caused emotional mayhem, with Eva recognising Harry as a soulmate; a fellow idealist who loved to sit up by the fire and read French poetry aloud to her at night. An unspoken rivalry for his attentions even simmered between Eva and Maureen, the young maid. But once again this brief glimpse of personal fulfilment was snatched away when Eva realised – why was she always so slow to read signs – how the sanctuary her son truly craved was secretly being provided by this officer who shared his bedroom, tutoring Francis in ways Freddie could never have imagined. Indeed Eva spent a month sheltering her son's lover before becoming aware for the first time of Francis's sexuality. After Francis confided in her,

Eva's role yet again became to act as the bridesmaid to other people's happiness, the keeper of a secret during that summer when Francis blossomed into manhood and she found herself burdened by a new worry for the son whom she worshipped.

In the six years since then no man had entered her life in any physical sense. But tonight, when she finally reached Frankfurt Avenue after her long walk, Eva lay awake for hours, haunted by how easy it would have been – finally with no need to put other people's happiness first – to have said 'yes' to Max. 'Not tonight. Not with Francis there.' Those hasty words had not entirely spurned Max, but had bought her time to examine her confusion. If the roles were reversed, Eva would find nothing wrong in a young girl seeking an experienced older lover. Yet no matter how alluring this temptation felt when confronted by the loneliness of her bed, she knew in her soul that the notion of an older woman and a younger man did not feel right.

Yet she still lay awake paralysed by indecision until she rose at dawn, too perturbed to eat breakfast, and began stacking paintings in the hall, ready to be loaded into Esther O'Mahony's car. When Esther arrived she seemed surprised by Eva's unusual quietness. The top-coated doorman outside the Brown Thomas department store helped them to carry the artworks down into the basement gallery. Esther offered to stay and help but Eva had an exact sense of how she wanted the walls to come alive with colour and it was simpler to achieve this vision alone. Some parents had wanted to buy proper wooden frames but Eva opposed this, knowing that not every family could afford the expense. Frames and mounting boards would also disrupt the seamless vista of colour Eva was striving for. Pinning up every painting individually was exhausting work but Eva welcomed how this task required all her focus, leaving no time to think of anything else.

As the exhibition slowly came together, Eva grew so intoxicated by its vitality that she allowed herself to believe in the credo above her studio door: *With a blank canvas everything is possible.* Was it possible that a brief radiance of love could light up a middle-aged woman's life? The time was gone when anyone truly needed her. Freddie had settled into life at his prep school as if a life-long bachelor. Smart admirers besieged Hazel. Francis needed her during this present crisis, but youth was resilient. As his horticulture degree would be of little use in Dublin he was already seeking work in London. When he finished college and emigrated she would be truly alone.

Finally content with the display of paintings, Eva stepped out into the sunshine of Grafton Street at three o'clock, knowing that if Max repeated his question in the right circumstances she might find it hard not to be tempted.

She believed in signs and it seemed like fate was sending her one. After chatting to the elderly doorman outside Walpole's and pausing in Lipton's doorway to breathe in the musty reek of rich cheeses, Eva saw Max approach among a cluster of college pals, including Valerie O'Mahony. They were passing Woolworths, strolling down the less prosperous half of Grafton Street. Eva stopped outside Vine's antique shop to greet Max, then realised that he intended to stride past. His companions seemed taken aback by his uncharacteristic snub. Valerie waved as if to compensate for his rudeness and Eva waved back. But she felt so crushed that she needed to lean against the plate-glass: it was as if somebody had struck her.

The students reached Brown Thomas and stopped to study a poster for her exhibition. One young man offered around a packet of cigarettes, but Max shook his head, patting his pockets as if searching for his own. He liked to smoke an American brand that few Dublin shops stocked. He muttered to the others and turned back as if heading for Noblett's tobacconists at the top of Grafton Street. Hurt and confused, Eva walked quickly up the street. But once his friends turned the corner, Max must have started running because she heard him approach. He slowed down, maintaining a discreet distance so that no casual observer would think them together. It felt like being trapped inside a Hitchcock spy film.

'I have to see you,' he whispered. 'I can't stop thinking about you.'

'Then why pass me by without a word?'

'We don't want people talking. It would look bad if they knew.'

Knew about what? He made it sound like they had reached an understanding. Max slipped a folded sheet of paper into her hand.

'You're a free spirit,' he said. 'The freest spirit I've ever met.'

Without another word, he veered into Noblett's doorway so quickly that at first Eva didn't realise he was gone. She stopped to stare beyond the display of sugary canes in the tobacconists' window and watched Max address the assistant. Then she walked on, feeling stupid as she realised that he didn't want her to wait. It felt as if people were watching: Grafton Street filled with prying eyes. She had known this feeling before, when walking through Castlebar in the 1930s with Freddie in debt to every shopkeeper. It was not a feeling she liked. Reaching St Stephen's Green, Eva sat on a bench to open Max's sheet of paper. It was a love poem, addressed to her though she was unnamed. She could not prevent a flush of joy at imagining him writing these lines late at night. The poem made Eva feel special, but also furtive. An artist's mistress, a secret locked away like Francis had been in Colville's flat. That was who she would become if she let Max share her bed. He was offering a clandestine affair that she would be crazy to embark on, but maybe it was more than anyone else was offering.

Eva placed Max's poem in her bag where she kept treasured possessions and returned to Brown Thomas. She reread Monk Gibbon's introduction to the catalogue. As paintings were not for sale there was no chance of making any money. Nor was there any question of an entrance fee, because Eva wanted as many shoppers as possible to wander in. She could not even attract additional pupils, as she was already stretched to her limit. What she wanted was for others to follow her example and open studios for children whose imaginations were stifled by conventional education. Hazel would scoff at some of these pictures, claiming that any child could do them. But this was the point, to show what any child could do if given imaginative freedom. Eva nervously re-hung an entire wall, just to prevent her thoughts from wandering back to Max.

She needed to stay focused: Dr Viola was due to arrive on the mailboat. Eva was paying for his accommodation in the Royal Hibernian Hotel and had offered to take him for dinner in Jammets of Nassau St. It was Dublin's most expensive restaurant, but in his letter he fondly recalled eating there once before. Eva took a bus back to Frankfort Avenue to get changed. She sat alone in her bedroom, wearing her dead mother's rings and praying to her mother's spirit for guidance. '*Strive tooth and nail for the right to be happy.*'

Esther arrived to take Eva to Dun Laoghaire pier. When his boat docked Dr Viola put them at their ease, expressing admiration for her pioneering work in Ireland. He made her feel valued in a way that held no furtive undertones. She waited in the lobby of his hotel while he freshened up. Two men passed whom she knew to be Freemasons. Freddie attended meetings at the Masonic headquarters in Molesworth Street. But she suspected that he was probably black-beaned from rising too high in the Masons: his fondness for drink going against him.

The exhibition space was already packed when she arrived with Dr Viola. Children ran to greet her, wanting Eva to meet aunts and uncles. Evelyn waved shyly, holding her mother's hand. Even Donna's parents were present, her father standing in the furthest corner staring into the distance as if studiously ignoring the vibrant colours on the walls. Then Eva realised that he was gazing across the room at the black-suited figure of Mr Shanahan. This was the first time Eva had seen Mr Shanahan since his wife's death two months ago. His son stood beside him, a black armband denoting his observance of the appropriate mourning period. The boy no longer attended Eva's classes:

his unmarried aunt who arrived from Clare to mind him had described such classes as nonsense. But Eva had requested Mr Shanahan's permission to display his son's paintings, because their dark emotions were an integral part of the work conjured in her studio. She watched Donna's father hesitate and then cross the gallery to shake Mr Shanahan's hand in an act of silent condolence. Both men nodded, no words needed or exchanged before Donna's father returned to his wife.

Eva turned to see Mr Durcan stand beside his eager son, scrutinising each painting with a Jesuitical gaze. Her Quaker friend Victor Bewley was there to show support, with Sean Keating and several other established artists whose presence surprised her. Some newspapers were lured along by the novelty that a professor had travelled all the way from London to talk about these unframed children's paintings. The room hushed when Dr Viola began to speak, his tone quietening even the smallest child. His words seemed a validation of her struggle and every principle she lived by. A part of her – the generally dormant virago aspect – wanted every neighbour who slyly mocked her hand-to-mouth existence to be transported here and forced to listen. Francis appeared among the latecomers, attracting admiring glances with what Valerie O'Mahony called his Rupert Brooke looks. Hazel had wanted to get time off from the stables, but horses needed to be prepared for a jumping competition in Kildare tomorrow. Dr Viola finished talking and called upon Eva to speak. Freddie always claimed that she rambled too much. It was important to be succinct. Eva noticed a nervous young woman among the crowd who seemed to know nobody there. She aimed her remarks at her.

'Some of you may wonder, as I did, are you fit to teach if you possess no qualifications or certificates or outward signs of being valued. But what you truly need is love. If you love children and love life and sincerely believe in the unspoiled child, you are fit to be a teacher. Begin with your own child and how you wish to prepare them for life.'

Eva glanced at Francis who smiled back. He would survive this latest heartbreak because she had taught him confidence. He would blossom and leave her behind: the cruel reality of how life should be.

'Let your child's inner radiance flow into every task they undertake,' Eva continued. 'Equip them with imagination so that, later on, they will handle every difficult situation life throws at them like they solved a problem on a canvas. They will learn to use whatever colours are available, unafraid to make mistakes when mixing them. If you produce a Monet this is a bonus. But the true teacher and parent equips a child for life, for the time when nobody can stand at their shoulder to offer encouragement, so that when they find themselves among strangers they will still be able to hold true to their character and beliefs.'

The warmth of the applause surprised Eva. People surrounded her after the speech, parents anxious to enrol children, one man seeking private lessons for his son. She had to tell him this would be impossible, although the fee he offered was more than she would earn from teaching an entire class. But money was not the point. Her work only made sense when children learned about life by discovering how to share as a group.

Francis's friend Alan appeared at her elbow and squeezed it slightly. One silent nod was all he needed to convey his delight for her. Then he slipped away as silently as he came and Senator McGuire stood in his place, inquiring if he might bring two additional guests to Jammets and insisting on his department store paying for the meal. Monk Gibbon passed by and smiled, then frowned as the Durcan boy bumped into him in his eagerness to greet Eva. Francis chatted to everyone, holding court. But just then a sudden ache threatened to overwhelm Eva. Someone was missing.

Decades ago, on the night before she left for the Slade Art School in London, her brother Brendan promised to one day stand in a top hat and tails to greet crowds flocking into her first exhibition. But the more that art teachers in London tried to instruct her, the quicker her dream of becoming a painter died. Her intuitive talent withered under the Slade School's competitive scrutiny, where every night she slept with a sprig of Donegal heather under her pillow to remind her of home. Maybe fate never intended her to be an artist, but to be an evoker of talent within others. This sounded absurdly grandiose, but the thought wouldn't go away. Because if so then this was Eva's debut show, even if she hadn't painted a single picture. She could not prevent a memory of Brendan's comic expression as he mimed lifting a top hat with mock seriousness to welcome imaginary exhibition goers. She felt a stab of buried pain as she wondered if her youngest brother really did die on a prisoner train or if this was just another lie propagated by the Soviets. It might be wishful thinking but Eva prayed to whatever God she could still believe in that Brendan was alive in some remote gulag, his existence concealed from the outside world. She felt so overcome by the unknowability of Brendan's fate that she didn't notice Max until she heard his voice beside her: he had slipped into the gallery unnoticed.

'Your exhibition is wonderful. Did you like my poem?'

'Very much.'

'You're not annoyed by it?' Max sounded like an anxious child.

'No.'

'Then when can I see you?'

'I must have dinner with Dr Viola,' Eva said, buying herself time. 'Then tomorrow I've promised to visit Esther O'Mahony's cottage in the mountains.'

'I know the way; I cycled past it once. Beyond Enniskerry, near the waterfall'

'Max, listen: I need to tell you…'

Max didn't want to listen. He vanished into the crowd. A sour-faced mother appeared in his place, complaining about her daughter's paintings being hung too low in the corner. Eva tried to appease the woman but her mind was whirling. She had not invited Max to join her in Wicklow, but had he accidentally or deliberately misunderstood? Eva glanced towards Francis's friends who were leaving. Francis turned to wave; his companions shouting their congratulations. Only Max kept his back turned, so intent on maintaining their secret that his attitude seemed contemptuous. Valerie O'Mahony obviously thought so and scolded Max who reluctantly granted Eva a curt nod before they disappeared.

So this was his offer. To be cherished in private and snubbed in public; made feel precious when they were alone and worthless in public. It was not a fair choice but perhaps at her age life ceased to be fair. Esther O'Mahony pushed through the throng. She was staying with Eva overnight. Dr Viola congratulated her and as the gallery cleared Senator McGuire gathered up his party, giving Eva no more time to torment herself about Max as she was swept up in the huddle of confident men strolling around the corner to Jammets where the doorman respectfully bowed to them.

It was midnight when Eva and Esther reached Frankfurt Avenue. She was exhausted. But images of Max disturbed her sleep. Max as she once saw him unselfconsciously stripped to the waist, when Eva called to his Trinity rooms before the theatre. Max kissing her unexpectedly at the bus stop. Max snubbing her on Grafton Street. Eva woke at three a.m., convinced that any humiliation was worth the chance to seize one moment of love. But when she woke at dawn she knew that, while Max's youth could explain his naivety, Eva had no excuses for making a fool of herself. After breakfast they drove into the Wicklow hills: Esther remarking on Eva being uncharacteristically quiet. Eva kept imagining Max's bicycle leaning against Esther's cottage, with Max awaiting her decision. On the narrow approach to Enniskerry village Esther pulled over to allow a private ambulance speed past in the opposite direction. Esther laughed, watching it disappear.

'I'd fear for your exhibition,' she said. 'That may be the poet Sheila Wingfield from Powerscourt going shopping in Brown Thomas. The doorman told me that she travels there by a private ambulance that must be parked directly outside the store in case she falls ill. If there was a Nobel Prize for hypochondria she'd win it. Maybe if she likes your paintings she'll buy them all.'

'They're not for sale,' Eva reminded her.

'She's the Viscountess of Powerscourt. Do you think such a trifling detail would stop her?'

Esther laughed again and then, more seriously, studied Eva's face, reaching out to touch her shoulder. 'I'm jesting, dear heart. She's unlikely to want to festoon the walls of Powerscourt House with child art. Are you sure you're okay?'

'I'm just flustered,' Eva assured her. 'All the fuss these last few days.'

They drove on in companionable silence. Yet when the car crested the steep lane up to Esther's cottage the scene was exactly as Eva had dreaded: a black bicycle rested against the whitewashed window ledge. Esther exclaimed in surprise: 'Whoever can that be?'

'I think he's...' Eva began.

Esther's laugh cut across her. 'You truly are flustered if you think it's a man, dear heart. Even with your rose-tinted glasses surely you can still recognise a lady's bicycle?'

Eva recognised the bicycle now. It belonged to Hazel. Esther parked the car. They walked around to the side where Hazel lay sunbathing in white cycling shirts and a pristine white top. She smiled up at them.

'What slow coaches you pair are. I managed to slip away after we got the horses over to the show in Kildare. I thought I'd cycle up and get all your gossip. So, come on, Mummy, tell me everyone who was there last night and everything that happened.'

It was Esther who filled in the details, describing the lavish French menu in Jammets. Hazel noticed how quiet Eva was and, while Esther laid the table, she quizzed her mother about whether anything was wrong. Eva didn't know how to answer. On the journey here she had dreaded confronting Max, yet now that he wasn't here she felt oddly deflated. She began to discuss last night, laughing with Hazel as she described the sour-faced mother surreptitiously trying to move her child's paintings into a more prominent position. Hazel was the best of company at times like this when their true closeness came out. She made Eva forget about Max until they heard footsteps approach, just as they were about to eat. Hazel looked up as Max appeared in the open doorway in a pair of white cycling shorts.

'I've seen you among Francis's Trinity chums,' she said. 'You're the American chappie whose fingernails are always covered in flecks of paint.'

'That's right.' Max blushed and glanced at Eva. 'I was out for a cycle and saw the car. I didn't know if you folks saw the picture in today's *Irish Times*. I just wanted to say how good the exhibition was.'

'It was absolutely smashing from what I've heard,' Hazel said. 'Well, don't stand in the doorway like a gasping fish, come in and take a seat.' Hazel glanced at Esther and laughed. 'I mean, we had better feed this poor chap in case the crows pick his bones clean if he hasn't enough strength to cycle back down the mountain.'

Esther joined in the teasing. 'Oh, I'd say he has energy to burn. Look, at the muscles in his legs and he must have fierce energy stored up inside him because his cheeks are flaming red.'

Max sat down awkwardly between Eva and Hazel. He smiled once at Eva, then looked at Hazel and never looked back. The young American did not mean to be cruel, but he was obviously so mesmerised by her daughter that he had no choice. Eva tried to flatter herself that he saw a younger version of her in Hazel. But within moments she and Esther might not have existed. Hazel seemed equally mesmerised by Max's American mannerisms, quizzing him about Ohio and about Trinity which for her retained the mystique of the unattainable. Esther indicated to Eva that they leave the young people alone. The two older women carried their tea out into the afternoon air.

'They make a striking couple,' Esther remarked. 'Isn't he the boy you sometimes go to the Gate Theatre with? It seems strange him just arriving. Do you think he knew that Hazel was planning to come here?'

'I suspect Hazel told Francis and Francis told him,' Eva replied.

She hated lies but the truth was too silly. She opened Max's *Irish Times* to examine her photograph beside a report on the exhibition. Maybe it was the cruel flashbulb but she looked old in that photograph, standing between Dr Viola and the artist Sean Keating. How could any woman at that age allow herself – even if only momentarily – to get swept up in an illusion? Her thoughts were interrupted by the young couple emerging from the cottage. Hazel and Max announced their plan to keep each other company on the long freewheeling spin back to Dublin. The pattern of Eva's life was repeating. Her sister had taken her beau from her in Donegal; her son had claimed Harry Bennett in Mayo and now her daughter was taking Max. But Eva knew that Max and Hazel would turn heads for the right reasons, with Max never ashamed to take Hazel's hand in public. On the cycle to Dublin, Max would ask Hazel if he could see her again and Hazel would agree. The relationship would not last, when Hazel eventually tired of a perceived lack of traits of dangerous machismo to make her feel that she was living life on the edge. But for now, they would feed off each other's vitality and differences. Hazel went inside to wash her hands. Eva found herself alone with Max.

'It's been nice to see you,' he said awkwardly. 'It's lovely up here.'

'Yes,' Eva smiled. 'I'm glad you came.'

Max smiled back in relief. He had not made a fool of himself or said things that might haunt him. His poem had been coded and so although Eva would treasure it, its implicit plea was unclear to anyone else. They would never attend the theatre together again, but if they met on Grafton Street they could chat without him glancing fearfully over his shoulder. Eva had stolen nothing from him. Nor had she lost her dignity or made an exhibition of herself, even if she was left with the renewed ache of being alone.

Hazel emerged from the cottage. The young people mounted their bicycles, the white cycling shorts emphasising their tanned thighs. Eva kissed her daughter and with a last shout the couple set forth, laughing as they each dared the other to cycle faster, with Hazel's golden hair blown back. Esther O'Mahony went inside to wash up, leaving Eva to sit alone on the low stone wall and watch their twisting descent until they became two white specks, darting and fluttering down the hillside like a pair of butterflies, veering apart and then coming together as they left her far behind.

Chapter Four
Wedding Bells
Dublin, 1954

Eva had forgotten what it felt like to sleep in the same room as a man. How long was it since she last woke like this to another person's breathing? Five years – that last morning in Glanmire House when she discovered Freddie in bed with her. Since then there were temptations, aside from the mercifully averted foolishness with Max. She had grown close to several men more suitable in age: kindred spirits who instinctively understood – like Freddie never could – her belief in another sphere of existence, parallel to our physical world, yet beyond our grasp. Men who recognised how Eva's moments of contemplative reverie made it difficult for her to always stay immersed in the minutiae of whatever crisis preoccupied Ireland's latest insipid Inter Party government, comprised of grey men held together only by a shared hatred of de Valera's Fianna Fáil party.

Eva liked that these male friends were not dogmatic like Freddie or crusaders like Art – both of whom were always convinced they knew every answer, even if their proffered answers would be utterly divergent. Recently Art had mentioned a term to describe the fate of Soviet citizens who fell afoul of their government. Soviet justice was not about retribution but re-education, he assured her: enemies of the people were not

74

sent to jail but into internal exile for periods of reflection and readjustment. Although she loved Art – who had been her great protector when they were small – Eva rarely paid attention to what he said. But his expression, 'internal exile' stayed with her because, while unsure what it meant in a Soviet context, it described the covert world in Dublin where she and her friends felt it wise to only converse freely behind closed doors.

Last June one such friend – by day a bookkeeper in the exclusively Protestant management in Dockrells and by night an impassioned devotee of the Austrian-born Jewish philosopher Martin Buber – invited her to his house with such secrecy that Eva suspected him of having seductive intentions. Instead she discovered how he had purchased a television and spent the previous night positioning an aerial on his roof so that, amid snow threatening to overwhelm the screen, they could watch shadowy images of the young Queen's coronation in London. The man seemed disappointed by her lack of excitement but the ceremony's pomp grated against her belief in the need to strip away the veneer from every experience to reach the kernel of truth found only in simplicity. Eva was surprised at his decision to stand up during the playing of 'God Save the Queen' and by his surprise at her disinclination to do likewise. But Eva never remotely considered herself British, even as a child before independence. She might not fit into this Dublin whose Catholic archbishop could summon a hundred thousand citizens to rally against the imprisonment of a Yugoslavian archbishop for collaborating in Nazi war crimes, but this didn't mean she would feel more at home elsewhere. Home was wherever somebody needed her and for the past two months this somebody had been Hazel who required her help to meticulously arrange today's wedding.

Part of these arrangements meant that – after wondering if she would ever share a bedroom with a man again – the face she now observed gently snoring was not that of a passionate follower of Martin Buber, but of the man whom she had given up her security to separate from. In fairness to Freddie, he made no attempt to physically share her bed last night. He even declined her offer to take down the spare single mattress from the attic in Frankfort Avenue, which could have been discreetly made up on the bedroom floor. All he had sought was the right to share her bedroom one last time so that, on the morning of their daughter's wedding, both could emerge from the same bedroom, maintaining the illusion of still functioning as a family. He had only requested one blanket to place on the floorboards under him and one blanket to cover him, telling Eva that this was how he always slept beside the kitchen fire in Glanmire House on some weekends when he took the train to Mayo to be alone in his crumbling childhood home.

This dawn light showed her that Freddie was not ageing well. His love of the outdoors still leant him a robust appearance, but as he slept now she saw how the broken capillaries around his nose were far worse than five years ago. His complexion looked flushed: a yellow tint around his eyelids suggesting that his liver was struggling with his alcohol consumption. During the night he must have grown cold because Eva saw how he had risen to spread his greatcoat on top of his blanket for warmth. But she felt certain he had not ventured downstairs to where a well-stocked ornate burr walnut drinks cabinet with cabriole legs, borrowed from Esther O'Malley, occupied pride of place in the redecorated front room which once served as her art studio. Knowing how difficult it would be to resist the temptation if he woke, Freddie had asked Eva to lock the drinks cabinet and hide the key. She wondered how long it was since he had last gone forty-eight hours without alcohol. But Freddie knew that Hazel's great fear was of him being drunk when walking her up the aisle of St Ann's Church in Dawson Street. Staying dry was a private fight he would not shirk from. Although every nerve ending must have been screaming for alcohol, he had remained sober for two days to ensure there would be no shakes in his fingers when he linked his daughter's arm and walked Hazel up the aisle to ceremonially give her away into the care of the man she was to wed.

Sitting on a Wicklow hillside three years ago, Eva had watched Max and Hazel begin an affair that had lasted eighteen months. Max had been good for Hazel. Eva recalled the headmistress of her Winchester school warning that Hazel's weakness lay in how, behind her stubborn, iron-willed appearance, she was vulnerably impressionable, susceptible to having her opinions disproportionately influenced by whatever company she mixed within. Max soon broadened her horizons beyond hunt balls and automobile rallies, with Hazel revealing an unexpectedly sharp eye for comprehending the concepts behind modern art while still retaining a no-nonsense disdain for whatever felt bogus or unnecessarily esoteric. Hazel in turn gave Max a sense of self-assurance and maturity, with them making such a striking couple that photographs of them had regularly appeared in the newspapers when social diarists reported on the openings of exhibitions.

But Eva always sensed that Hazel needed an older man, supremely confident, with a spark of danger and an imperious glamour to equal her own. These were qualities that Geoffrey Llewellyn possessed. He made the men whom Hazel had previously dated seem like boys. Geoffrey was studying in Trinity at the same time as Francis, but while their paths never crossed Francis did remember complaints about the rattle of Geoffrey's two-seater MG Morris TF Midget across the Trinity cobbles late at night when Geoffrey occupied rooms in the Rubrics. His summers were spent back on the Kenyan coffee plantation which he had recently inherited from his father, who had left Ireland amid a flight of landed gentry after the Irish Civil War. His upbringing in the Kenyan outback gave Geoffrey a muscular exuberance and a capacity for hard living which Hazel's vivacity fed off.

They met the previous summer when both separately attended one of the parties thrown by the socialite Oonagh Guinness in

her Luggala castle in the Wicklow Mountains: riotous soirees
that could last for days, the only thing banned being clocks to
let guests keep track of time. Geoffrey, whose tendency was to
drive too fast, had misjudged a bend on a steep twisting road
when returning to Dublin at dawn and busted his radiator when
colliding with the dry stone wall. Hazel – a passenger in a next
car – got out to inspect the damage, telling her friends to go ahead
as she took charge of the situation by purchasing two freshly
laid eggs and a mug of warm buttermilk at a nearby farmhouse.
They shared the buttermilk while she cracked open the eggs and
poured them into the leaking radiator, knowing that, as they
bubbled in the heat, they would congeal over the crack, forming
a coating that would hold long enough to get the MG Morris
down the mountain to Roundwood village, with Hazel insisting
on driving at a speed that even unnerved Geoffrey. While a local
mechanic repaired the car, Geoffrey had inveigled a publican to
open early and find a dusty bottle of champagne, so tepid that
Hazel only agreed to share it if the publican added a double
measure of brandy to each glass. While the publican served
customers in the grocery half of his premises, Geoffrey had
raised his glass as they sat on stools behind the wooden partition
to toast Hazel as his saviour, joking about having finally found
an Irish woman capable of thriving in the Kenyan outback.

He had not been joking: since then their romance was a
whirlwind, with the engagement announced in the *Trinity Times*
college paper last September – Hazel's first time to get into
Trinity, as she wryly remarked. Today's wedding was arranged
to facilitate his return to Kenya after dallying long enough to be
conferred with his degree. Freddie – to his credit – was insisting
on paying all the wedding costs, though Eva didn't know where
he had borrowed the money. She was helping to keep the
costs down by hosting the wedding party here, after Hazel had
supervised the redecoration of her house. Eva tried to discuss
Freddie's finances with him, suggesting that perhaps he sell a few
acres of Glanmire Wood. But Freddie would not entertain this

idea. Glanmire was Francis's birthright, he explained, just like today's wedding was Hazel's due.

Freddie claimed to have always put aside money for the day he gave away his daughter: for the church and photographer; for the dresses and flowers and the honeymoon in Wexford; for today's food and drink and last night's lavish meal at the Shelbourne Hotel, where Fitzgerald relations assembled to meet their future in-laws and Freddie stoically endured the torment of watching everyone drink their fill. But Eva knew he was lying for her sake. He must have swallowed his pride and approached every acquaintance to borrow this money. The wedding notice in *The Irish Times* social column stated how 'Lieutenant-Colonel Frederick Fitzgerald, M.B.E., of Glanmire House, Turlough, County Mayo was delighted to announce his daughter's engagement'. But thankfully no Llewellyn visitors had time to visit Hazel's childhood home, where such thick creepers lay siege to the dwelling that Francis told her he had needed a machete to reach the back door on his last visit. A shared passion for the solitude of that decaying house was perhaps the only thing still uniting Francis and Freddie – although thankfully the occasional weekend trips that each took to camp out in the basement never overlapped.

Putting on her dressing gown, Eva stepped over Freddie's sleeping body to open the bedroom door and slip down the two flights of stairs to the kitchen. She made tea and toast and boiled an egg the way she remembered him liking it done. Carrying the tray upstairs, she knelt beside him, studying his ageing features again. Perhaps his hunter instinct made him stir, instantly aware of being closely observed. He sat up awkwardly in his vest, his back resting against the wall beneath the window as he let her settle the tray on his lap. He gestured as if to signify annoyance at her having gone to this fuss, yet was unable to disguise how touched he was. His expression hinted that it was a long time since anyone had done him such a human kindness. Eva felt slightly ashamed of her prime motivation, which was to prevent the awkwardness of Francis and his father needing to share a breakfast table.

'You shouldn't have,' he scolded.

'It's only a small thing.'

'As you get older it's the small things that matter.' His tone mellowed, as if he felt able to relax his guard despite the awkward sleeping arrangements. Pouring a cup of tea, he spilled some onto the saucer so it could cool quickly before he raised the saucer to his mouth and swallowed, then smacked his lips in relief. 'I was parched all night. There's a dryness in the air.'

'I can add more water to the pot and bring it back up,' Eva offered.

'No, no. I can't stand weak tea. Back in the army the tea in the Officers' Mess was always thick enough to trot a mouse across.'

'You miss the army,' she observed quietly.

He smiled ruefully. 'There are a lot of things I miss.' For a moment she thought him about to reach out and lightly brush her bare arm. She didn't know how she would respond. Perhaps he thought better of such an acknowledgement of past affection. 'There again, there are a damnable awful lot of things I don't miss.'

She sensed it was time to go downstairs and give him space to shave and dress.

'Is your back stiff? Those floorboards are hard.'

He used the teaspoon to open the egg with a brisk tap. 'I've a perfect trick to ensure that I never endure back pain. It's called a dicky leg. Lately this leg gives me so much gyp that I never have time to feel pain anywhere else. Are any stray Llewellyns mooching about downstairs, calling in with their tongues hanging out?'

'It's too early for callers,' she assured him.

'Still and all you'd better run down and open the drinks cabinet. The wine merchant thought I was a Name in Lloyds when he saw my order, but we'll give nobody an excuse to say they called in to a dry house. I'll finish this and be down shortly. He waved a hand airily to terminate the conversation, seemingly unaware of how this gesture came across as utterly dismissive. 'If anyone calls, pour them a stiff measure and say I'm donning my finery in the master bedroom.'

Eva went downstairs to find that Hazel had risen from bed and was pacing anxiously about in the kitchen. She gave her mother a quizzical glance.

'Is he...?'

'Sober as a judge.'

Hazel smiled. 'As against drunk as a lord.'

'Freddie is not finding this easy.'

'Nor are you, I'm sure. Carpetbaggers sleeping where there isn't even a carpet.' Hazel touched Eva's shoulder in appreciation and laughed at this absurdity of playing at happy families. 'I don't know why Daddy is being such a stickler for the appearance of respectability. Geoffrey's parents drank with the Happy Valley set in Kenya. Things can get so louche in Kenya that Oonagh Guinness's parties look like Temperance Society meetings.'

'He just wants to give you a good send off.'

'I know. It just feels odd having him here. Make sure to kick him out the moment Geoffrey points his car towards Greystones. He has a boarding school to return to, though I hear he's in the last chance saloon there, mainly because he spends his time drinking in every other saloon within ten miles of Bray.'

'Freddie won't linger,' Eva assured her. 'He just wants everything done properly for you.'

'I appreciate all he's doing. But you can't rewrite the past just to make appearances look right. I remember riding my pony around the daffodil lawn in front of Glanmire House, freezing with cold but not wanting to go indoors. I was talking nonsense to my pony so my voice would drown out him hectoring you in the drawing room. I was only eight, but I remember thinking I had a duty to love him because he was my father, but you should have a choice: being only his wife. Be honest, Mummy, was there ever a time when you loved him?'

'Today isn't about Freddie or him.' Eva was anxious to change the subject. 'It's about you.'

'In a few hours I'll be a married woman,' Hazel said. 'When our honeymoon ends it will be the boat train to England and a liner from Southampton to Africa. You and I may not get too many more chances to talk, woman to woman. So answer me.'

'I love how he gave me two precious children. How could one part of me not still love someone who gave me such a gift?'

Hazel threw up her eyes impatiently. 'That's typical of you, Mummy, to avoid answering a straight question. If he hadn't given you children, could you have loved him?'

'Love is an odd thing,' Eva said. 'Both simple and complex. I did love a man once but I hadn't the words to articulate what I felt to myself, let alone know how to tell him.'

'Are we talking about Daddy?'

Eva shook her head. 'Woman to woman, this was long before Freddie.'

'You never mentioned any other man before.'

'I hadn't thought about him for a long time. Not until I saw you and Geoffrey together. Geoffrey reminds me of him.'

'Physically?'

'No. And the resemblance isn't in temperament either.'

'Then what is it?'

'When I was seventeen a young officer challenged me to step into the unknown. But to admit that I loved him would mean leaving behind everything I knew. He wanted to bring me to the other side of the world, like the journey Geoffrey is bringing you on. In my case, not Kenya, but New Zealand. A cattle reach on the North Island, with a lake where he promised to build a studio with huge windows where I could paint.'

'It sounds wonderful.'

'I'll never know because I didn't find the courage to go. New Zealand just seemed too far away from Donegal and I was too young and scared to want to grow up. Sometimes we let life's big moments pass by, thinking they'll come around again.'

'But they don't.'

'No. The officer asked me to go out alone on a boat with him one night, to prise me away from the cocoon of my family. I stood outside my house, holding my bathing suit and a towel because we planned to go swimming together. I kept looking back at the drawing room window where my family and our guests were gathered around the piano, people singing the party pieces they always sang. My mother who was tone deaf saying 'that's lovely, Tim', like she always did whether Father played Chopin or 'Pop Goes the Weasel'. And I was paralysed with fright, torn between wanting to be a child back in that drawing room and a young woman meeting a handsome officer who was waiting by a pier to propose marriage to me.'

'What did you do?' Hazel asked.

Eva took her hand in hers.

'I didn't do what you're finding the courage to do. I wasn't brave enough to walk down that lane on my own. My brother Brendan found me standing outside and I took him with me, pretending it was a midnight adventure. I can still hear his twelve-year-old voice singing as we walked through the dark. When the officer saw me arrive holding Brendan's hand he knew I wasn't ready to be anyone's wife. But the thing is that it was his hand I wanted to hold. I wanted it so badly when it was safely out of reach. I hadn't the courage of my convictions when I was young. But even before you took your first step, from the determined way you moved your mouth to seek my breast at just two weeks old I could see you had steel inside you – not in any bad way – but you knew what you wanted and I knew that when your chance came you'd take it. I'm not telling you about the New Zealand officer to make you feel sorry for me but so you'll understand how overjoyed I am for you. You always had sheet-lightening courage. Even as a girl riding to hounds with riders three times your age, there was no ditch you shied away from jumping, and whenever you fell off you wiped off the mud and clambered back on. Maybe there are times when you and I sparked each other up wrong, maybe because I had a sense that you'd never accept help from me or from anyone. But even though I hate fox-hunting, I want you to know that I stood in the fields in Ballyvary and Behola to watch you gallop past: my heart filled with fear for you but also bursting with pride. Geoffrey is a good man, and I'm overjoyed at this voyage you're embarking on.'

'That's the nicest thing you ever said.' Eva saw that Hazel needed to blink back tears. She looked away, knowing that this was not the moment to be overcome. Neither of them felt comfortable with fuss. Hazel leaned forward to kiss her forehead.

'You were a poor little chick who wasn't ready to fly,' she said. 'You know there's always a place for you in Kenya if you ever want to come. I can't promise you a view over a lake but we would happily build you your own small house and studio. It's the least I could do, seeing as my wedding plans destroyed your old studio in the front room.'

'There is a season for everything,' Eva replied. 'My studio was wonderful while it lasted but that chapter is closed.'

A knock on the front door disturbed them.

'Your bridesmaid,' Eva said. 'You need to get ready. Isn't life exciting? This is going to be a great day and it's your day.'

'If that's Valerie, she's early,' Hazel said. 'It took us days to hunt down her blue grosgrain dress. I have it hanging in my room so we can get changed together.' She paused, listening to footsteps crossing the hall overhead and opening the front door. 'That's hardly Daddy up and about, is it?'

'Freddie won't appear until he's as spick and span as a new penny. He's convinced we're going to be invaded by Llewellyns, attracted like bees to honey by the drinks cabinet.'

Two sets of footsteps descended the stairs toward the kitchen.

'I suspect Geoffrey's family don't need to turn up on doorsteps looking for free anything. His pals were planning to drive out to the Forty Foot Men Only bathing cove to shake off any cobwebs. If you're used to the heat of Kenya there's a novelty in swimming naked in the freezing Irish Sea. Still, if you have the key, I could use a Dubonnet and soda to stiffen the nerve before I get dressed and you could go mad and have a gin.'

'It's too early for Dubonnet and too early for gin.' Francis's voice chided them good humouredly from the kitchen doorway. He was barefoot and tousle haired, his dressing gown tied loosely over his pyjamas and his arm draped around the shoulder of Valerie O'Mahony who held aloft a proffered bottle of champagne. 'It's champagne or nothing to toast my sister.' He glanced around. 'Is the coast clear?'

'He's upstairs getting shaved,' Hazel assured him.

'It's too early for champagne,' Eva said.

Francis rolled his eyes in mock reproach. 'Mummy, this is no time to start acting your age. It's never too early for love or champagne. Am I right, Valerie?'

The bridesmaid laughed. 'You're always right. I left it out on my bedroom windowsill all night: the Rathgar version of the ice bucket. We'll all have a ciggie to cloak the smell on our breath.' She smiled at Hazel. 'Well, dear heart, are you ready to have and to hold, from this day forward?'

'According to God's holy ordinance,' Francis added. 'To love and to cherish, in sickness and in health, in Ireland or in Kenya.'

'We can't say, "for richer, for poorer",' Valerie teased. 'Not after you told me the size of Geoffrey's plantation.'

'It's hardly Meath pasture land,' Hazel protested. 'It's volcanic red dirt, perfect for coffee and only if the monsoon rains come.'

'I feel a monsoon coming here.' Francis was using his thumbs to edge the cork off the bottle. 'If you don't want it to shower the entire kitchen then can somebody have a mug ready?'

'Wait,' Eva protested, laughing. 'I have proper flutes.'

'Champagne waits for no one,' Francis warned. 'Besides any fool can drink champagne from a champagne flute. Let's be decadent.'

'Absolutely.' Hazel scooped up four earthenware mugs and reached him just after the cork popped and champagne began to spill out in fizzing bubbles. She handed around the half-filled mugs and raised hers in a toast.

'To those we love,' she pronounced.

'To voyages ahead,' Francis added. 'And happy landings.'

All instinctively paused to listen out in case Freddie's footsteps were descending the stairs and then they clinked mugs and drank. Today would be a succession of speeches and elaborate toasts, but Eva knew that this was the one she would always remember, made truly special by being so simple, surrounded here in this kitchen by those she most loved.

Hazel downed her mug in one go.

'Now I've a dress to put on,' she announced. 'Make-up to do and a bridesmaid who is meant to be helping and not trying to get me drunk. The photographer will be here soon and my hair is a mess. It's all hands on deck and do promise, Francis, to turn up in church in something more fetching than those pyjamas that make me you look like Michael Darling in Peter Pan.'

'I shall look immaculate,' he promised with a laugh. 'We shall all be immaculate. Now I'll race you upstairs and bring the rest of that bottle for luck. I want to get into that bathroom before you lock the door and refuse to come out.'

The three young people ran, joking and chattering, up the stairs. The aura of their warmth, vitality and optimism still filled the kitchen. Eva knew that the two girls would burst into Francis's bedroom during every stage of the preparations, seeking his opinion and approval. Eva wanted to help, but her main duty was to keep Freddie out of their way. She carefully washed any remaining champagne from the mugs so that the smell would not torment Freddie. Then she entered the passageway, which six months ago had been a kaleidoscopic blaze of colour. Hazel had chosen new tasteful wallpaper after Eva removed the children's paintings that previously covered every inch of wall. The total redecoration was not just done to get the house ready for today's wedding but because the display of paintings were too big a reminder of how Eva's dreams of running a child art studio were over.

As she walked up the stairs and crossed the hallway to enter the bright front room, Eva remembered how a row of small easels once stood there. Her moment of apparent triumph – the acclaim that had greeted the Brown Thomas exhibition – had sown the seed of destruction. Perhaps her naivety was equally to blame; she had failed to grasp the socially competitive nature of parents in the goldfish bowl of Rathgar and Rathmines. Eva's classes were about allowing children to develop their individual personalities through art, and she had presumed that the parents understood this. But after the extensive newspaper coverage, the parents became obsessed with the next exhibition. Public exposure of the magic occurring within the room had tainted the process. Every parent began to have opinions on what should happen next. Children began to compete in class: some older pupils complaining that the younger ones were holding the class up to ridicule.

Donna's father had demanded that in future a rigorous selection process be employed before any painting by a member of his family was publically displayed again. He suggested bi-annual shows with independent judges and prizes and rosettes for winning entries. Most families who had taken his family's side in the Civil War felt automatically obliged to take his side in this argument also. Nobody seemed to understand that Eva had never planned to hold a second exhibition; she merely wanted to introduce Dublin to Franz Cižek's radical ideas in the hope of inspiring other art classes to spring up. Some parents were appalled at her refusal to countenance a second show, although a few mothers like Mrs Durcan, who were on the same wavelength as her, signalled their relief. But

Donna's father became an unstoppable force, determined not to be thwarted by a woman and especially by a Protestant woman. He tracked down a retired school principle with impeccable credentials: her late husband having been appointed to the Senate by W. T. Cosgrave in 1931. She was prevailed upon to start a conventional art class, training children to mimic dull pastiches of what adults expected art to look like – mainly Paul Henry style West of Ireland landscapes. No parent who voted Fianna Fáil would allow their children to join this breakaway class. Indeed most did not want their children to desert Eva's cosy studio, but, as one parent explained, they could hardly be publically seen to be 'bested by a Blueshirt'.

For a few weeks their children rattled about in Eva's half empty and now joyless studio, until a young widow – an accomplished Sunday afternoon painter with strong Republican ties – was prevailed upon to open a studio in Ranelagh. Eva appreciated how this young mother, struggling to raise two small children, found the grace to visit her one evening. Originally a typist in the Department of Education, she was forced to resign from the Civil Service after her wedding, due to the ban on married women. Two years ago her husband had drowned swimming off the Galway coast, during a visit to the Gaeltacht to improve his Irish and his job promotion prospects. The woman was embarrassed at stealing away most of Eva's remaining pupils but she explained her inability to resist the pressure put on her to start this class. She simply couldn't continue trying to financially survive by spending each evening churning out sentimental paintings of the Ha'penny Bridge for sympathetic neighbours to purchase when she displayed them at the local church fête. Eva had felt nothing except empathy towards this woman, who although twenty years her junior felt socially obliged to dress as if she were several decades older, and whose fingers kept nervously twisting the ends of the headscarf she removed once inside Eva's house. Eva's art studio might have limped on with the support of progressive mothers like Mrs Durcan, but the arguments with ambitious parents complaining that their children learnt nothing practical in her classes had tainted the innocent joy of it. That night Eva not only gave the young widow her open-hearted blessing, but presented her with the twelve miniature easels Art once built, along with brushes and half used tins of paint, refusing the woman's entreaties for Eva to accept some payment. All Eva had asked was that the new teacher never leave out more than two jars of any colour, to let the pupils experience the joy of learning how to share. Eva permitted herself a white lie in pretending that this advice came from her old tutors in the Slade School and not from Ireland's most notorious communist.

Despite Freddie's strenuous objections, Hazel had posted an invitation to today's wedding to the attic flat Art now occupied off Mountjoy Square. It was up long bare flights of stairs, where so many spindles had been smashed for firewood, that on the few occasions Eva visited him, she was afraid the handrail would collapse. Art wouldn't attend the church or the party but Eva suspected she would glimpse him standing among the pedestrians thronging Dawson Street, so inconspicuous in his workman's clothes that no Llewellyn would have any clue about his identity or his impassioned articles in the *Irish Worker's Voice* supporting the Mau Mau Uprising against white rule in Kenya. Max also planned to be in Dorset Street, having told Francis of his intention to watch the bride's arrival from behind the tall art nouveau stained-glass windows of the National Bible Society of Ireland bookshop across from the church.

Her Frankfort Avenue neighbours – far friendlier after growing used to Eva – would be less discreet. It was only a matter of time before the first onlookers arrived: local women pouring into this front room to admire the wedding gifts laid out on a long deal table covered with a velvet cloth. These women would smoke and gossip and reminisce about their own weddings; declining sherry but drinking endless cups of tea from the fine bone china tea service (also borrowed from Esther O'Mahony), ready to flock out into the hallway and clap Hazel when she finally descended the stairs, clutching her posy of mixed flowers and red carnations.

Eva needed to focus on getting dressed. She unlocked the drinks cabinet and went upstairs to her bedroom. Freddie had carefully shaved. She didn't know if his suit was purchased or borrowed but it looked brand new; the trousers and waistcoat fitting him perfectly, the jacket lying on the bed waiting to be donned. He was putting on the same silver cufflinks he had worn on their own wedding day, cufflinks that once belonged to his father. He saw Eva glance at them.

'Some things you don't sell,' he said, 'even when stony broke.'

Eva knew better than to ask why he placed such sentimental value on them. It would be easier to break out of Alcatraz or Robin Island than find a way to see into Freddie's heart. He patted his checks with aftershave, luxuriating in the stinging sensation and humming to himself. He was in such good form that Eva judged this a good moment to produce the form she had in her drawer.

'Freddie, while you're here, you might just sign this for me.'

He glanced at the official document that she placed on the bed.

'A passport? You know you don't need one to travel to the mainland.'

'England isn't my mainland, Freddie. Besides, it's not where I want to go.'

His look was quizzical. 'Then where? The newlyweds won't be keen on you bunking in on them, despite whatever balderdash they say out of politeness.'

Eva heard a knock at the front door and knew that her window of opportunity was closing.

'I'm not thinking of Kenya either: I don't think I'd like it there. I don't know where I'm going or if I'll go anywhere. I just know that if I decide to travel I'll need a passport and to get an Irish one I need your consent. Just sign the form, please. Let's have no unpleasantness today.'

He gazed at her bluntly. 'Do you think I'd want to stop you? I've never stopped you doing anything, even if I never understand half the things you do.'

Francis had gone down to open the front door. Eva heard excited laughter now as two of Hazel's closest friends trooped upstairs to help with Hazel's preparations. The chatter grew louder as Valerie opened Hazel's door and welcomed them in. Freddie was scrutinising the passport application form.

'Look, you haven't even filled out the damn thing properly. You've left half the questions blank – age, occupation, everything.'

'I found it confusing: every second sentence in Irish. I'll fill it in properly later.'

His glance contained a sly scepticism. Despite not really knowing Eva at heart, he knew her well enough to know when she was holding something back.

'Hand me a pen. If you don't want to tell me where you're going, that's fine.'

She watched him sign his name and add M.B.E. after it. He handed it back. Eva nodded her thanks.

'I don't even know if I'll go anywhere, Freddie. But I like the notion of being free to travel. When I was young I was too scared.'

Freddie shrugged and donned his jacket. 'I'll just warn you. Foreigners aren't like us.'

'That's what I'm hoping.' Eva placed the form back in her drawer. A knock came on the bedroom door. Esther O'Mahony entered without waiting for a response and surveyed them both. 'Freddie Fitzgerald, you look like a handsome devil. You also look like you are currently in the way. And needless to say Eva hasn't even started getting dressed. I'm banishing you to the scrutiny of the dozen women waiting to be entertained downstairs. Be gone. This room is requisitioned by females only.' Esther waited until Freddie shut the door behind him before turning to Eva 'You're a terror. You make a terrible mother of the bride. By now you should be fixing your hat as the icing on the cake of your outfit. I hope Freddie never strayed from the floorboards. I only inquire to know if a woman would be safe with him in a taxi.'

'If she were his wife, yes.'

Esther laughed. 'Let's get you looking beautiful.'

Eva didn't mind Esther jollying her along. It prevented her from thinking about how far away Hazel was moving and her sense that all the coordinates of her life were starting to drift apart: not violently but in that natural way in which dandelion spores allow themselves to be blown apart. After today, this house would cease to be Hazel's home. She knew that Francis was planning to move to London as soon as he graduated and was already inundated with offers of work, from old college friends and acquaintances who had started new lives over there and were looking for someone to design their gardens. She had already witnessed his work on old Dublin houses, where a younger generation who drank in Bartley Dunne's wanted their parents' old formal gardens replaced by the spontaneity and colour that Francis brought. Establishing himself as a landscape gardener would be a difficult challenge but one he appeared to relish. London was waiting for Francis to conquer, whereas – once he took the boat – only silence would soon await her in the rooms downstairs, which, from what she could hear through her bedroom door, were rapidly filling up with boisterous well-wishers downstairs. Eva was glad that Hazel and Francis were setting forth on voyages that offered the prospect of happiness. It was the natural order for her to be left behind.

Her financial position in Dublin was perilous but not yet precarious. She had good friends and causes she passionately believed in, no matter how unpopular and misunderstood those causes were. She had a book she secretly dreamed of writing. She had the anchor of a house which nobody could take from her. The nest she once tried to make for Hazel and Francis was now empty but she could easily fill it with more art student lodgers, thrilled to find a landlady who understood the importance of space and light, and who would allow them to treat their rooms as studios. Such vibrant lodgers would help to keep her young. But perhaps the moment that a house became an anchor it not only gave you security but weighed you down: becoming a terminus and not a stepping stone. She needed to seriously consider her future but not today. This was Hazel's day. Hazel had cautioned her against causing a fuss by weeping in church, but Eva was more likely to shout aloud in joy when the minister told the groom he could now kiss the bride. Maybe those earlier few sips of champagne were going to her head but Eva felt giddy with sudden excitement. Esther obviously felt this vibrancy surge through her body because she smiled, looking down as she fussed over the final touches to Eva's hair.

'How are you, dear heart?'

'I'm positively glowing.' Eva reached up to touch Esther's hand resting on her shoulder. 'Aren't we lucky? Isn't life exciting?'

'It is, dear heart.'

'This is going to be a great day.'

Esther laughed. 'For everyone except poor Freddie, determined to stoically sit through it sober. Or at least until Hazel throws her posy over her shoulder on the steps here in her going-away dress. When Geoffrey's car turns the corner I fear for anyone caught in Freddie's path to the drinks cabinet. Now here you are at last, shiny as a new pin. Do you think we are allowed into the bedroom of the bride-to-be to see what the young people have done to her?'

'She will be radiant,' Eva said. 'Even in a baggy jumper, Hazel looks radiant.'

'She'd better not be planning to walk downstairs wearing a baggy jumper to greet the crowd waiting to see her off, or Freddie will take to the drink early.'

They knocked three times on Hazel's door: voices warning them to stay out until everything was ready, and they were finally admitted. The room smelt of flowers due to the bouquets of flowers that had been arriving for days. Francis had left the guests downstairs in Freddie's hands and come back up to join

Valerie and Hazel's other friends in this inner sanctum. All looked flushed and giddy with excitement. Only Hazel looked calm as she turned to face Eva, wearing a white organdie wedding gown with white nylon veil and a headdress of white violets and lily of the valley. She took a last puff of a cigarette, which Francis then lifted away from her lips to ensure that nothing stained her satin white gloves.

'Will I do before I enter the parade ring?' she asked.

'You'd make any man proud,' Eva assured her. 'You make me proud. You always did.'

Eva didn't know if someone gave a signal or everyone instinctively knew to withdraw, because suddenly there was just Eva and Hazel in the room: the murmur of the well-wishers waiting at the foot of the stairs growing ever more vocal as if they sensed that the moment had arrived.

'I'll be back and forth every few years,' Hazel said. 'Kenya isn't as far away as it was once.'

'All I'll need to do is put Beethoven's Moonlight Sonata on the gramophone and you'll be close,' Eva said. 'Every night you'd ask me to play it in Mayo during the war.'

'They were happy days.'

Eva softly touched her gloved hand. 'Your truly happy days are still to come,' she promised. 'It's funny, this moment reminds me of my own wedding. Just before I walked down the stairs I ended up alone in my bedroom with my mother and she made me promise something.'

Francis was tapping at the door, indicating that the wedding car was here, the crowd impatient, the moment unable to be put off any longer.

'What did she make you promise, Mummy?'

'No matter what hand life deals you, promise me that you will strive tooth and nail for the right to be happy.'

Chapter Five

Gather Ye Rosebuds

Spain, 1957

From the moment Eva left her *posada* for the short walk through the winding streets to the shop that doubled as a post office, an inner voice taunted her: *there will be no letters today: no replies ever*. Eva ignored this voice, because even if her dreams of being a teacher were gone, she had fresh dreams to realise in this remote Pyrenean village. Over recent months the locals had grown accustomed to Eva and were less curious about having a foreigner in their midst, but no less courteous. The afternoon heat was abating. Old men halted their conversations at the outdoor café in the square to lift their hats as Eva passed. The uneven pavement was speckled with stray petals strewn in a religious procession yesterday, led by a guitarist walking through these shabby laneways. That atmosphere had felt exhilarating, unlike religious feast days in Ireland where the streets remained forlornly deserted if the pubs stayed closed. But behind yesterday's gaiety Eva had sensed the same sadness she often witnessed in Mayo: parents – and sometimes grandparents – raising children who would have no option but to leave, because only the old and the very young still populated this tiny village.

She reached the post office. Every afternoon when she came to inquire about letters, Maria's father, an elderly man with a limp, looked pained at sensing her disappointment, as if feeling personally at blame for the non-arrival of post. But this evening he spread out his arms wide and smiled when she opened the door. Maria was upstairs, attending to her three children. He pointed at the wooden rack behind the counter, his gesture reminding Eva of a magician having just pulled off a conjuring trick. Three envelopes lay there, each with British postmarks. The man seemed perplexed by Eva's initial hesitation to take them. She smiled to disguise her nervousness, thanked him in broken Spanish and placed the letters in her canvas bag. Saying that she would return to visit Maria when the children were asleep, Eva left before the man could notice how she had started shaking. She wanted to return to her *posada* and open her letters in the privacy of her room, but needed time to compose herself for what news they might contain. The voice in her head was silenced, but it would soon begin. Anticipation and terror consumed her. News of her long-anticipated post had probably reached the old men sitting outside the café, so it was important to appear calm. Therefore Eva kept walking, leaving the village to commence her daily trek up the dirt track into the hills, refusing to contemplate the contents of these envelopes until she reached the isolation of the small lake there.

These washed-out, pale Pyrenean skies would have provided her with a source of inspiration if her childhood dream of becoming a painter had come true. But Eva was not here to paint. Her old neighbours on Frankfort Avenue – most of whom never set foot on the continent unless on diocesan pilgrimages to Lourdes – would be perplexed as to why she gave up her old life to be here. Hazel called it 'making up for lost time'. Others might call it wanderlust, seeking a change of direction while going through the change of life. But Eva's journey to this village felt more like a realigning of her life to allow the resumption of a lifelong quest. Even when she had been a child in Killaghtee Church, she had sensed how some ministers who preached sermons there were more concerned with elocution than with any love of Christ. She had only truly felt close to God when out amid the fields around Dunkineely. Her quest for a spiritual home had continued during her art student days. While Ireland was preoccupied with seeking independence, Eva had been preoccupied with seeking a creed to belong to, sampling and savouring every religious service on offer while an intuitive inner voice always warned her to move on and not mistake each stepping stone for a summit. By the end of her student days, Eva had come to feel that she was simply a sepal to be blown about at her creator's will, although she once needed to hide such unorthodox beliefs when on display beside Freddie in the designated Fitzgerald family pew in the Protestant church in Turlough during her marriage. Now that Francis and Hazel were leading independent lives, Eva had feared succumbing to feeling old and sorry for herself. But since her arrival in Spain, Eva realised that she still remained a tiny sepal in her core, content to be blown about in her quest to discover what purpose God intended for her on earth. Today's letters might finally reveal the answer.

The air here was drier than in Ireland, the unpaved roads coated in dust. Eva stared ahead as she walked. Her soul was coming to love this landscape and so did her arthritic bones. The villagers kept expecting her to tire of the extreme remoteness, but Eva had no intention of going anywhere – at least not until her meagre savings ran out. Besides, where was there to go when she no longer possessed a home? In her recent letters from Kenya Hazel had scolded her for selling Frankfurt Avenue for such a low price. But Eva could not imagine any house in Dublin ever being worth much money: the night boat so constantly crammed with departing emigrants that it was easy to envisage a time when there would nobody left in Ireland except the young and very old. Hazel claimed that Eva never planned ahead, but she had prudently safeguarded her future by using the proceeds from the sale of Frankfurt Avenue to purchase an annuity with Standard Life. From now until her death Eva would receive a twice yearly dividend of one hundred and thirty pounds. She would never be rich, but with five pounds a week to exist on, she could not envisage starving either. If today's letters brought the news she was desperately waiting for, it would justify her decision to sell her home and stake everything on this dream of a new life.

This village seemed the perfect place to nurture that dream, allowing her to live cheaply in seclusion. Five months ago Eva had feared that Spain would prove a disaster when a white-gloved border guard at the crossing from France examined her meagre luggage, while armed soldiers scrutinised her standing beside a wall dominated by a picture of Franco. The frontier guard minutely studied the details on her passport. *Height*: five-foot, two inches. *Colour of eyes*: grey/green. *Face*: oval. *Colour of hair*: light brown. *Maiden name*: Goold-Verschoyle. Sensing the official reach her maiden name, Eva half-expected him to bark orders to the soldiers: her luggage thrown back at her feet amid taunts of '*Comunista!*' as she was refused entry into Spain. But the Goold-Verschoyle name meant as little to Brendan's old enemies who had triumphed here as it meant to those who fought against Franco in the International Brigade. Brendan's fate didn't conveniently fit into either side's narrative of the Spanish Civil War, leaving both sides equally indifferent and content to erase him from history.

Therefore the frontier guard had snapped shut her passport with a final glance of wary suspicion – caused, she suspected, by the stated occupation listed on the passport – and waved her through into a country dominated by uniforms. She found Franco's staring eyes everywhere: on café walls and hotel foyers and the front page of newspapers sold by barefoot urchins along the Ramblas when she reached Barcelona. The newspapers showed the Generalísimo making one of his curt high-pitched speeches; the Generalísimo receiving flowers from grateful children, playing at being the ascetic, austere father of an impoverished nation; a sage-like saint who favoured the humble food of the ordinary labourer and never flagged in his vocation to formulate bold steps to enrich his seemingly grateful flock. What Eva noticed about every photograph was how Franco's eyes never smiled even when his lips pretended to.

She could not even visit old churches with being reminded of Franco's victory by seeing young Falangists devoutly praying at shrines to José Antonio Primo de Rivera at side aisles decorated with flags and flowers. When booking into a cheap hotel on her first night in Barcelona – on a pilgrimage to retrace Brendan's final known steps – a squadron of the Falange marched with ramrod precision across the lobby, led by a stern-faced young chaplain. Watching them stomp out the door, Eva realised that she was witnessing an incarnation of the sort of Ireland which the Blueshirt movement had fantasised about creating in the 1930s.

These fascists were the antithesis of everything her youngest brother believed in; the embodiment of a tyranny Brendan railed against. Yet for all their grandiose uniforms and reprisal killings, Franco's thugs were never even afforded the chance to harm Brendan during his months fighting against them here in 1937. His fate was so abrupt and secretive that Eva suspected that his name probably never even had time to make it onto the lists of enemies of the state still kept by Franco's secret police. From their divergent perspectives, both Art and Freddie had often complained that Eva didn't understand politics or history. Undoubtedly from their black-and-white perspectives they were right, but even if her grasp was hazy, she understood that history and politics were never black and white. There had not been one civil war here but a dozen wars simultaneously combusting inside each other like a set of burning Matryoshka dolls, with Brendan ending up trapped inside the smouldering, inner rings of carved wood. What little she knew about Stalin horrified her, but she suspected that he never had any real interest in helping Spain's government, beyond looting its national gold reserves, in their war against the fascist coup to overthrow them. Brendan had been a naïve enthusiast, as much in thrall to his big brother as to Stalin. By dispatching Brendan to Spain in a tightly monitored unit, Stalin could use Brendan as a proxy in his war against what he perceived to be his real enemies there – not Franco's forces but any independent-minded socialist members in the International Brigades who expressed reluctance to swear unwavering loyalty to Moscow.

Eva would never know how quickly Brendan realised that he was not sent here to fight fascism. But she knew enough of Brendan's character to know how vivaciously he must have objected after realising he was being given no chance to fight for the Spanish people and allowed no contact with ordinary volunteers in the International Brigade unless he was willing to spy on their conversations. During the three days Eva spent in Barcelona, she had walked for hours along the dockside wharfs, halting at each mooring bollard, unsure if she was standing on the stretch of cobbles which Brendan had taken his final steps across as a free man. Sensing that she was becoming an object of curiosity to dock workers unloading cargos, Eva kept pressing her palms against each bollard hoping that Brendan might have paused here to touch one of these stones. But her silent vigil on the Barcelona docks brought no comfort, leaving her only plagued by uncertainty about whether, when he ascended a gangplank here, mistakenly believing he was being asked to repair a ship's radio, he had any inkling that he would be taken prisoner and transported back for interrogation in Moscow's Lubyanka Prison before being sentenced in a sham trial that probably lasted less than a minute.

Ever since Khrushchev's denunciation of Stalin's cult of personality to the Twentieth Congress of the Communist Party last spring, Eva kept hoping for more reliable news of Brendan's fate. While staying with Francis in London before she left for Spain, Eva even tried to deliver a hand-written appeal to Khrushchev when the Soviet leader held talks with Sir Anthony Eden. Eva had also hoped to persuade Art – who had moved to London after quarrelling with the small clique of fellow

Irish communists – to renew his inquiries. But she found that Khrushchev's condemnation of Stalin's murderous paranoia merely enraged Art. It took Khrushchev's suppression of the Hungarian Uprising to restore his credibility in Art's eyes: Art regarding the mass resignations from the British Communist Party in protest at Soviet brutality in Budapest as proof that Trotskyites were increasingly infiltrating every left-wing movement.

Eva's last meeting with Art was heart-rending because of the insurmountable distance between them as she sat on the solitary chair in his London flat and he hunched on the thin horsehair mattress on his small bed, inches from her and yet beyond reach. She had pleaded for him to inquire if – despite the official report of his death – Brendan might still be being held in some camp, like the Swedish diplomat Raoul Wallenberg was rumoured to be. Wallenberg had helped thousands of Jews in wartime Berlin before falling into Soviet hands. There were worldwide campaigns for Wallenberg's fate to be revealed, but Eva could not even persuade her brother to discuss Brendan. Instead Art obsessed about his latest self-published pamphlet, cheaply reproduced by Gestetner under his own imprint, The Proletariat Press. In this he argued that the Soviet tanks invading Budapest had actually liberated Hungary from a reactionary coup. Contacts in the Soviet Embassy in London had told him that his pamphlet could prove a decisive factor in him finally being rewarded with a visa to return to Moscow, ending what Art regarded as a twenty-one year exile from his real home.

He had now cut his final ties to Ireland by legally acknowledging ownership of his inherited acres in Donegal, after it was intimated to him by comrades in the Irish Workers League that it would greatly help the spread of communism in Ireland if he sold this property and donated all the proceeds to them so they could buy a party headquarters in Dublin. This still left Eva's childhood home, The Manor House in Dunkineely, which Art could not legally sell but only hold in trust for his eldest son.

His solution to this was simply to give away the house keys to the daughter of their former gardener, telling her that she was free to do whatever she wished with the house. These acts by Art had severed Eva's last links to her childhood village, increasing her growing feeling of being homeless in every sense.

After their conversation petered out, Eva had walked down the unlit stairs in that London tenement, with gangs of children stomping past her, knowing that – even if Art did not get his cherished visa to be reunited with his wife and child in Moscow – she had lost the heart to visit him again. Yet, unable to simply walk away, she had waited across the road until Art emerged into the twilight. Following at a distance, while he walked the streets in his ragged clothes and tried to entice hostile passers-by to buy his pamphlet, Eva had sensed that Art was in purgatory, haunted – like her – by the fate of the youngest brother who once hero-worshipped him.

But Eva hadn't come to Spain to uncover Brendan's fate. She picked Spain because it was cheap, although in Barcelona she realised how quickly her money would run out in big cities. Therefore after returning to the docks one last time to leave a bouquet of red roses on a mooring bollard, she left Barcelona and began to travel, unsure of where she was seeking, but trusting her instincts to recognise it when revealed to her. Plain-clothes police were everywhere, demanding her passport in railway carriages. Priests stared haughtily from café windows reading copies of *Fuerza Nueva*. But, once she ignored this strutting of triumphalist power, Eva felt comfortable among the ordinary rail travellers who offered her food and drink when they saw that she was a woman alone. Such passengers tried to teach her simple Spanish words, roaring with good-humoured laughter at her inability to pronounce them. She joined in the laughter, more intoxicated by their open-hearted companionship than by their proffered wine. Finding a cheap *pensión* in Zaragoza, she only realised that it was above a slaughterhouse when she woke to the terrified bellows of animals and saw the cobblestones beneath her window transformed into deltas of blood. She moved *pensión* and spent days exploring Zaragoza. But an instinct urged her on to seek a remote place where she could afford to live and work and think.

Eva had stumbled across this village by accident, after accepting a lift from a farmer who did not understand her simple Spanish words. He drove for so long and so high into these mountains – with Eva jolted about on the open back of his truck – that she had fears of being kidnapped. It was evening before he reached this village and stopped to help her down in the small square, lifting his hat respectfully before he vanished into the café. There were signs of recent festivity, elderly couples in their Sunday clothes, who seemed to be the remnants of a wedding party, lingering over a meal and raising their glasses in good natured toasts. Noticing how a faded sign above the café read *Posada* – she had inquired from the *posadero* about the possibility of renting a room. As the elderly couples clustered around – perplexed but not displeased by her arrival – Eva grasped from the *posadero's* broken English that one upstairs bedroom existed, but tonight it was *mucho* full, although from the following morning it would be *mucho* spacious if she wished to stay.

Initially she thought the *posadero* was turning her away, but his inherent sense of hospitality would not allow this. His explanations, accompanied by confusing hand gestures, made little sense until he brought her upstairs and Eva realised that the large front room overlooking the square was divided in two by heavy wooden partition doors that were closed. After the man left she listened at the partition but heard no sound from the other side. Indeed Eva might never have known that this other half of the room was occupied if she had not accidentally brushed against the partition when getting ready for bed. The doors opened at her touch to reveal two naked young newlyweds silently trying to make love on the moonlit small bed. The embarrassed boy tried to cover himself. But the girl

– immersed in her pleasure – simply gazed at Eva, woman to woman, and laughed unashamedly in the exhilaration of being alive and in love. Her laugh made Eva nod in silent affirmation before she swiftly closed the partition. But the glimpse of their intertwined bodies was as startling as the shock of bathing beneath a waterfall: the girl's unabashed laugh resonating with such joy that Eva felt revitalised. She knew that this was what she was seeking in Spain: unadorned life lived with gusto. Eva had crept downstairs to sit in the moonlit deserted square for hours, anxious not to disturb the lovers' privacy from that partitioned room. On the next morning she took a walk around the village and returned to find the partition doors folded back. The small bed where the young couple had slept was dismantled: a large writing desk occupying that space. Standing beside it, the *posadero* had anxiously inquired: '*Para tus necesidades*? It pleases? For your needs?'

For her needs? Eva stopped walking now in the evening light as the dirt track rounded a bend and a small mountain lake appeared before her. The mocking inner voice returned. The hillside was deserted, unless a shepherd was crouched among the stunted scrub where a sound of bells betrayed the presence of goats. On the first evening when she bathed here, naked and alone, Eva had worried about being spied on. This evening she was not here to bathe. She had chosen this spot so as to be alone when opening the long-anticipated replies that had finally arrived: the world's response to her dreams. These letters could only be from the editors to whom she submitted her first attempts at writing: nobody else – not even her children – knew her present whereabouts. Her dream of a new life was proclaimed in green fountain pen under the heading of '*Gairm/Profession*' in her passport. It was this description of her occupation which caused the border guard to look at her warily; *the posadero* to carry a writing table up to her room; the villagers – whom he surely alerted – to regard her with cautious respect. Now these letters would decide if she actually possessed any right to travel under her officially listed profession of '*schíbheoir/writer*'.

This title felt fraudulent with nothing yet published, but Eva had been unable to think of another occupation to list on the passport application which Freddie had agreed to sign. She refused to be classified as a 'housewife', but could not call herself a teacher since her studio closed. Some months after Hazel's marriage Francis had made his long-anticipated move to London. For three days after his departure Eva had sat in silence in her bedroom in Frankfurt Avenue, studying her half-completed in passport application form. Rain leaked through broken roof tiles, splashing into old jam-jars once filled with paint, but Eva had refused to panic, because she was not alone. She had the words of Meister Eckhart and Martin Buber and Rudolf Steiner for company, while the postman pushed bills through her letterbox. Only by meditating in silence could she hope to discern what purpose God intended for her. On the third night, when descending the stairs to empty jam-jars of rainwater, it occurred to her that great freedom must exist in being considered a writer. Such an occupation allowed you to move about like a blown leaf without attracting comment. Until then she had left the space for her occupation blank on the passport application, knowing that whatever she filled in must be a statement of intent. That night she entered her profession as 'writer' and slept more peacefully than in months. The next morning she visited an auctioneer to put her house up for sale.

The lake was silent now: the evening sky still except where a vulture circled high up, eyeing her with indifference. Eva weighed each envelope in her palm. Two contained more than one sheet of paper. This signified rejection and a manuscript's return, though perhaps editors sent stories back with suggested revisions before publication. Eva knew nothing about the writing business, except what could be gleamed from the *Writers and Artists Yearbook*. She felt too nervous to open the envelopes. If they contained rejections, she feared that the entire village would sense her disappointment when she returned. For just a moment longer she wanted to savour the possibility of acceptance, imagining what it must feel like to be a published author, like Max who had one poem published in *Envoy* before graduating from Trinity to return to Ohio last year.

The moment of truth could be delayed no longer. Eva had no choice but to open the first envelope. It contained a rejection from BBC's *Woman's Hour* of a travel piece entitled *Night Train in Spain*. '*Not for us,*' the letter read, '*but you have a gift for words and the ability to create atmosphere and character. Tidy this up and try Blackwoods Magazine or the Irish papers.*' The second envelope contained a rejection from a woman's magazine, with some words of encouragement scribbled on a pre-printed slip: '*far too sad for us, but full of local colour. Might be perfect for a novel.*'

Eva was half afraid to stare back down the dusty track in case a procession of jeering figures waited there: the Irish passport official, the border guard, the *posadero* ready to subdivide her room back in two. But there were no witnesses to her failure. Friends had always assured her that her stories would fascinate editors. But her inner voice – which bore a semblance of Freddie's mocking tone – reminded her that thousands of women of her age clung to this same illusion. How many rejection slips did BBC's *Woman's Hour* dispatch to them every day? Eva opened the third letter, from a literary agent picked at random from the *Writers and Artists Yearbook*.

'*Dear Mrs Fitzgerald,*

We have read your sample chapter for a book about teaching child art. We are prepared to submit this manuscript, when finished, to publishers on your behalf for our standard handling charge of one guinea per submission...'

Eva's hand shook. She had nothing published but if she had an agent surely she could call herself an author. If she worked hard she could finish the child art book within months in this village by writing short practical chapters. It surprised her that literary agents charged writers a fee, regardless of acceptance. She didn't know if this agent was a confidence trickster, but it felt like a star to steer towards. She would struggle to find a guinea, and several might be needed before the book was accepted. Maybe it would never be accepted and she would end up like her old Mayo neighbour, Dermot MacManus, who had been talking for so many years about producing a book on the supernatural that nobody took him seriously anymore. But life was full of risks. Before leaving Ireland she had posted some money from the sale of Frankfort Avenue to Freddie, knowing that Hazel's wedding had left him mired in debt. Her typewriter was purchased second-hand in London. As things stood, Eva existed mainly on bread and fruit. Now she would need to forfeit the occasional luxury of cigarettes or dark chocolate and put off buying new shoes, even though these roads had cut her old pair to pieces.

But this was the price of being a writer and at least in Spain she had no appearances to maintain. Eva didn't know what the old men who saluted her outside the village café really thought about her. But here she could observe life without becoming personally involved. She could eat simple food and sleep and rise when it suited her. It felt good to own nothing and finally have no responsibilities. Opening her bag, Eva took out the notebook intended for her own writings, although its pages were crammed with quotations to sustain her – like D. H. Lawrence explaining how true happiness only came after the experience of being goaded by life. She began to reread lines by Shelley. It brought back her mother's voice reciting her favourite poem:

'Life, like a dome of many coloured glass,
Stains the white radiance of Eternity
Until Death tramples it to fragments.'

Eva started to walk back down the mountain, closing her eyes to visualise this dome of many coloured glass. At times it felt like her life had been lived inside a prism where every experience merged into a spectrum of colours. If she had become a successful painter, life might have been different, with a reputation and a studio with windows open to sunlight and night stars. But would she have known this serenity only experienced by those who survive journeying alone through hurt and loneliness? She was lonely, but needed to ensure that her loneliness never became a burden on other people who might feel guilty. She longed to be in London because Francis was there, but he had a new life and she would be in the way, with Francis acutely sensitive to her moods and needs. This was one reason why she chose this remote village and had still not written to him from here. If Francis did not possess her address, how could he feel guilty about her loneliness when there was nothing he could do to relieve it? Eva had contacted Francis's friend Alan, asking him to let her know if any mishap or malaise afflicted her son. If she felt that Francis needed her she would move to London at once. But while a mother always had to be aware of her son's needs, it was vital to never let a son feel burdened by hers.

It was getting dark. Maria would be putting her children to bed above the post office. A friendship had sprung up between them, a form of mutual education whereby each night she taught Maria simple English words and Maria taught her Spanish nouns. Eva didn't want to learn verbs, knowing she could never grasp the proper tenses. She just wanted enough words to communicate about everyday life. Maria was one of the few young women left in the village. Eva never again saw the young couple who consummated their marriage in her partitioned bedroom. Next morning they had left, probably for a shantytown outside Madrid or Saragossa or to seek labouring work in France. Maria's husband was determined that his children be raised in his native village, but the price of this was his almost continual absence, as he chased seasonal work in French sugar beet fields or during the olive harvest in Jaén.

As Eva approached the village an elderly man passed her, carrying three hens strung upside down a long pole, legs tied together. They were still alive but too exhausted to flutter. The man hailed her cheerfully in Spanish, oblivious to the birds' suffering. Eva gazed after him, sickened not just by their anguish but by his casual indifference. Why could she not accept that cruelty was constantly intermingled with life? Why did she feel such affinity with every living creature, that she shared the pain of every tussled hen and starving alley cat? Eva walked on towards the village rooftops – those domes of many hidden colours – knowing that she had lied when filling in her passport application. Instead of the term *'writer'* she should have simply stated *'pilgrim'*.

The jangling bell above the post office door alerted Maria to her arrival. The young woman smiled, raising a finger to her lips to indicate how her youngest child had just fallen asleep. Yesterday Maria showed Eva her wedding photograph and – when Eva explained how her own daughter got married last year – she had asked Eva to see a photograph from Hazel's wedding. Sitting now in the back kitchen, where Maria could listen out for customers entering the shop, Eva produced the single wedding photograph she had brought on her travels, tucked with other mementoes inside the small bible her father had given her as a girl. Looking at Freddie's ashen face in the wedding photograph, Eva remembered a premonition outside the Dawson Street church that this might be the last time the four of them ever gathered together as a family. But Eva forget this sombre thought, caught up in Maria's excited curiosity in studying every detail of the photograph, asking a babble of questions in Spanish and broken English about Hazel's dress, the comical garb of Geoffrey's pals from the Trinity Boat Club who turned up with oars to provide a guard of honour, and about herself and Freddie standing awkwardly together on the church steps.

The two women's heads were bent over the photograph: both laughing as Eva tried to use a tattered English-Spanish dictionary to translate her replies. Then after a time Eva realised that Maria was no longer asking about Hazel's wedding, but inquiring about Eva's own wedding day. Eva had no photograph of this, but using a mixture of simple English and Spanish words, she began to describe her wedding in Donegal by drawing small comic sketches on white sheets of shop wrapping paper. The easy fluidity that Eva once enjoyed with a pencil came back in this relaxed atmosphere: Maria laughing in fascination and demanding more sketches to show her children in the morning. Eva's wedding was the last occasion when all five Goold-Verschoyle children gathered together. Eva sketched in the narrow main street of Dunkineely and the last glimpse she'd had, of all of her siblings standing together, from the back window of the car that took her away: all her family and neighbours waving and young Brendan running down the road after the car, both hands raised in joy. Maria pointed to this figure, amused by how Eva had captured his elation.

'*Que?*'

Eva had not cried during Hazel's wedding, but, without warning, this casually conjured sketch of Brendan proved too much. Maria held Eva's shoulders as unexpected tears came, then pointed again to the figure, trying to understand.

Tu amante?'

Eva shook her head.

'*Hermano?*' Maria guessed correctly. '*Se murio? Accidente?*'

'*Conflicto.*'

'*Conflicto? Donde?*'

'*España.*'

Maria crossed herself and walked out into the empty shop, glancing anxiously around as if it were filled with prying eyes. She removed Franco's framed portrait from behind the counter and returned, closing the kitchen door so that nobody entering the shop would see them.

'*De qué lado?*' she demanded. Which side? Eva dried her eyes, bewildered at how stupidly she had let her secret slip, despite Hazel's warning about never mentioning Brendan in

Spain. Maria's eyes blazed as she pointed at the portrait again. '*De qué lado?*' Eva had travelled here to escape her past, but the sanctuary of this village seemed about to be shattered. Yet even if she lost Maria's friendship and her room at the *posada*, it had not been in Brendan's character to lie and nor was it in hers. Eva picked up Franco's portrait and placed it face down on the table. Maria glanced over her shoulder as if expecting the door to burst open.

'My brother too. I too young to know him, but still I cry.' She turned over the portrait to spit vehemently on Franco's face, then wiped it clear with a rag and quickly re-hung it in its designated space in the shop. A child came in and Eva listened to Maria serving him. Brendan's story was too convoluted to explain by simply turning a dictator's portrait one way or the other, but this complexity was impossible to convey in pidgin Spanish. Maybe Maria's brother's story was equally complex, as were the tensions and fault lines existing beneath the seeming tranquility of this village, where Eva now sensed that, just like in Ireland, the Civil War would never truly be over. When Maria returned, Eva pleaded that it must be a *secreto*. The young woman nodded and mentioned the *posadero's* name, placing a finger to her lips to indicate that Eva should never confide in him. She pointed at the sketch and asked: '*Cúal era su nombre?*'

'Brendan Goold-Verschoyle.'

Maria produced a bottle of brandy and two glasses. She poured them drinks and raised her glass, making an effort to pronounce Brendan's name. This gesture touched Eva. Brendan had come to help the Spanish people and not just as Stalin's stooge. Songs would never be written about him, because no side wished to claim him. But this toast felt like an unblemished gesture in his honour. The brandy warmed her, going to Eva's head after having so little to eat. She was foolish to have imagined that cheques from editors would start arriving within weeks. Her stories had been rejected but the editors took her dream seriously. '*Too sad for a woman's magazine … perfect for a novel...*' It was a start to build on. Fifty-four was not too old to begin another chapter. She remembered the good-luck card Francis placed in her luggage before she left London, knowing how she would laugh when she discovered it. It depicted a naked middle-aged woman dancing with a rose between her teeth, under the heading: *Gather ye rosebuds while ye may*. This is what Eva would do in this village: writing her book each morning, walking in the hills each evening, listening out for faint whispers emanating from the unattainable.

The bell jangled over the shop door. Maria's father entered the kitchen with his limp, surprised to see the brandy bottle. Maria had sworn it would be a *secreto*, but Eva knew that she was about to tell him, because he had also been part of that war. Eva now realised where his limp came from and how difficult it must have been for his family to retain this post office amid Franco's reprisals. The old man fetched a third glass and sat down, refilling Eva's glass before offering a fresh toast. Eva touched her glass against his and drank, praying that somehow – whether alive or dead – Brendan's spirit might sense these glasses being secretively raised in his honour in a remote Pyrenean village.

Chapter Six

Who We Truly Are

The Isle of Wight, 1960

The schoolboy sitting opposite Eva was absorbed in reading Robert Louis Stevenson's *Treasure Island* all the way from London's Waterloo Station to Portsmouth Harbour. It was Francis's favourite novel as a boy of that same age, back when he was petrified of Freddie, yet still desperate to win his approval. The boy's mother smiled, catching Eva observing him. The boy reluctantly closed the book and took his mother's hand as they dismounted onto the crowded platform in Portsmouth. Eva longed to tell him her favourite quote from Stevenson: 'To miss the joy is to miss all'. But she remained silent because she was back in Britain, where – unlike Tangiers – strangers regarded you oddly if you addressed them.

As she walked along the wooden pier to catch the Isle of Wight ferry, the sea air brought back memories of her Donegal childhood. Eva was starting to feel more alive and like that untarnished child now, at fifty-seven years of age, than at any time during her trapped years of marriage. Or at least she had been until last week, when a letter arrived unexpectedly from Freddie's relations in Turlough Park. The Mayo postmark had induced a sense of foreboding, reducing Eva to being Freddie's wife once again – or at least the wife which he regarded her to be: impractical, perpetually in the ether with daft ideas, and unsuited to upholding the surname he had bestowed on her.

In fairness it was not Freddie who had contacted her with this news. He would have no wish to drag Eva away from her new life; indeed possibly no wish to ever see her again. So why was she about to join a queue of passengers for the Isle of Wight ferry? Out of duty? No. Eva freed herself from such shackles, even if freedom came at a high price. Freddie never understood her needs, which would make today's confrontation even harder. She was here because compassion was ingrained in her character – a trait which once attracted Freddie but he would now regard as weakness. Her instinct to feel other creatures' pain was one of what Freddie once mockingly called her imbecilic deficiencies. But Eva had earned the right not to care if she looked foolish, if this was how pragmatic people wished to see her. She had given up any safety net of domestic unhappiness to let her soul float free, at an age when men rarely bothered to glance at her. Indeed most people paid her so little heed that she felt invisible. Yet she felt a curious affinity among young people, even if some of them seemed unsure what to make of her. Among her own generation she often sensed an air of reproach, but in recent months she rarely cared what anyone thought of her. This new life she was creating in London – after selling her typewriter in Tangiers last autumn to pay for her passage home – was exhilarating. She felt immersed in the whirlwind of a world on the cusp of change. The 1960s were only four months old, but Eva sensed this decade would be different. Her role within this change would be infinitesimal, but at least she might have a chance to feel that she lived amid kindred souls.

She had never expected to regard London as home. But Francis lived there and her son rooted her to this earth. Eva would walk through fire for him. Therefore when she received his distraught letter last Halloween, her sole thought was to move to London to be near him. His natural radiance was absent in that letter and – reading between its lines – Eva had sensed he was close to a nervous breakdown after his traumatic encounter in Glanmire House. The start of a new decade seemed an apt time to start afresh and put another dream behind her, after three years of travelling through Spain and Tangiers, harbouring the fantasy of becoming a writer.

With her typewriter sold, all that remained of her aspirations was an envelope of rejection slips and receipts from the anonymous agent who had extracted eleven guineas from her from posting her manuscript about child art to random publishers. Sidgwick and Jackson had actually offered to publish the book if Eva dropped her financially prohibitive stipulation that it contain a colour section of the paintings referred to in the text. While Eva treasured their offer as a validation of the fact that she could write, her book would have felt hollow without the vibrant energy of those paintings and she was now reconciled to the fact that she would never become a published author.

She accepted this with the same stoicism as she had recognised, soon after arriving at the Slade School of Art, that her ability to express herself in exquisite line drawings was too ill-defined to survive as a commercially competent artist. What purpose she was put on this earth for still remained hidden to her conscious mind. If she had applied herself more methodically at the Slade School, her father might never have reluctantly agreed to her ill-matched marriage, although even now Eva clung to a hope that, at some stage of their courtship, Freddie possessed genuine feelings towards her and not just towards her dowry, which he had seen as the salvation of Glanmire House.

Eva hadn't dwelt on such questions for years, but last week's letter had brought her unresolved marriage back into focus. She had been too busy trying to make up for lost years of unhappiness. Her new life in London was financially difficult, but she felt a deep sense of wellbeing at being close to Francis and his dynamic new friends, although she worried about their closeted world in where danger could lurk everywhere. It thrilled her to see Francis recover from the horror of what happened the previous Halloween in Mayo. Once again he seemed held aloft inside a luminous, fragile bubble of happiness. His happiness connected her to a pulsating city. Young people were responsible for London's charged atmosphere. When Eva spent two hours last night selling the CND magazine *Peace News* outside Hyde Park, every copy she sold had been to someone young. Even passing gangs of Teddy Boys had winked at her, with Eva feeling no apprehension in their presence.

Why had she grown so passionate about the anti-nuclear cause? Certainly the planet was threatened, with de Gaulle exploding an atomic device, despite protests from America who wanted to keep such toys only for itself. Previously Eva had distrusted righteous public zeal, feeling that mass movements to improve humanity were like machines trying to sweep seaweed off a beach. No matter how hard they worked, the incoming tide invariably washed up more misery. But now she needed to believe that change could occur if enough individuals stood up to such evil men as the Mississippi police officers who shot ten black men on a segregated beach last month. As a token of this belief she kept a framed newspaper picture above her bed, showing Chief Luthuli of the banned ANC launching a passbook-burning campaign in a South African black township.

Gazing around now at the queue for the Isle of Wight ferry, Eva remembered the unsold copies of *Peace News* in her bag. Selecting an unoccupied pillar outside the terminal, she arranged copies at her feet and stood, patiently holding one aloft – glad to do something practical to take her mind off her confrontation with Freddie when the ferry docked in Ryde. Her practice was not to call out but let people approach if they wished. For ten minutes passers-by ignored her. Then a young African woman stopped to buy a copy, looking dynamic in a satin frock with a white nylon jacket, gold earrings, black gloves and a hat topped with a scarlet feather. Eva had barely finished talking to her when a peanut seller pushed his barrow up to where Eva stood and coarsely ordered her off his patch.

'Move along, wog-lover. Nobody wants that communist rubbish, you daft old bitch.'

The man dropped the barrow handles at Eva's feet in a territorial gesture. Shaken by his aggression, Eva joined the queue of passengers. It gave her a taste of the hostility Art had encountered in the early 1950s when he kept defiantly trying to sell the *Daily Worker* on Dublin's O'Connell Street. The ferry was so crowded when she boarded that she needed to stay on deck. Through a window she saw the mother and boy from the train seated in an inside lounge. *Treasure Island* was open again on his knee. Something about the boy's absorption was painful to watch, reminding her of Francis's vulnerability at that age. Eva found a space on a wooden bench on the exposed upper deck and a girl in her early twenties leaned across to touch her knee.

'The barrow-man shouldn't have addressed you like that,' she said. 'Joey was going to go have words with him, weren't you, Joey? But then the queue started moving.'

Her companion nodded, although he looked so slight that the peanut seller would have blown him away with one breath. The couple had a haversack and a rolled up tent. Their aura of love dispelled the miasma left by the barrow-man.

'It was nothing.' Eva smiled. 'I'm fine now.'

'What were you selling?' the girl asked.

'*Peace News.*'

'Joey will buy one, won't you, Joey?'

Joey looked less certain but carefully counted out coins to pay for the copy which the girl insisted that Eva take from her bag.

'Were you on the Aldermaston march?' she asked, oblivious to a look of disapproval from the middle-aged man nearby. 'My sister walked all the way and said it was fab.'

'That's because she met her new boyfriend there,' Joey interjected.

The girl pulled a face. 'Don't mind Joey. He can take nothing serious. She loved taunting the Yankee soldiers guarding the base. I bet you were there.'

'I wasn't,' Eva confessed. 'I was travelling at that time.'

'Where?'

'Morocco. Tangiers, Marrakesh.'

'What were you doing?' The girl almost bubbled with excitement.

Eva paused. She no longer told people of her attempts to become a writer. 'Just living my life. Gathering rosebuds is what my son called it.'

The girl laughed. 'I bet you're a beatnik and write poems. My name's Jade. Are you staying in Ryde? It's a dump but our friends say one café makes great cappuccinos. We're meeting them for coffee. Will you join us?' She spied Eva's hesitation. 'Joey will pay, our treat. Isn't that right, Joey?'

The young man nodded uneasily. With vivid clarity Eva could envisage him fifteen years from now, relieved to have entered the sanctuary of middle age when new ideas could be put away in favour of gardening. Jade might believe she could ignite Joey's potential, but if they ever married, Joey's growing waistline and cynicism would gradually extinguish Jade's sparkle unless she found enough courage to break free.

'You're kind,' Eva said. 'But I have to visit somebody and then I have these copies of *Peace News* to sell.'

'We'll help,' the girl persisted. 'Our friends would love to meet you. You dress so … well let's just say you don't dress like my mother. And they play music in this café.'

'I doubt if the lady likes skiffle, Jade.' Joey's affectionate exasperation was a carbon copy of Freddie's early in their marriage.

'I do,' Eva replied, partly to let Jade win the argument. In London she might have enjoyed going with them to one of the small Soho cafés where Francis took her. Eva loved the huge rubber plants and cane chairs there and the noise of Gaggia machines dispensing frothy coffee while young people listened to the jukebox or guitarists sang Lonnie Donegan numbers, accompanied by friends providing rhythm on washboards.

Francis preferred new-style British jazz and collected Acker Bilk EPs, although his special friend – as he liked to euphemistically refer to Jonathan – favoured old-style jazz and sometimes brought them to Humphrey Lyttleton's jazz club in Oxford Street. The innocence of skiffle appealed to Eva but she declined the girl's offer.

'I don't know how long I'll be staying in Ryde. It could be hours or weeks.'

Jade smiled. 'You sound like a nomad.'

Her father had used this word to describe the tinkers who camped each year behind the house in Dunkineely: the cook allowing them access to running water and the gardener told to turn a blind eye to any vegetables that disappeared from the garden, provided they stole no more than they needed. But such nomadic tinkers possessed a purpose, mending agricultural implements or making tin cans. What role had a separated, middle-aged woman?

'When do you return to London?' Eva asked.

'Tomorrow or even tonight if our friends don't turn up,' Joey said. 'It's too early in the year to camp but Jade has a daft wish to sleep out in a tent if we can find a remote beach.'

Jade poked him playfully. 'Are you saying you have the courage to knock at a boarding house and ask a landlady for a room?'

He shrugged, uncomfortably. 'It's not my fault if you wouldn't wear the wedding ring Sylvia offered to loan you.'

'I shouldn't need a fake ring,' Jade said hotly. 'This isn't the Middle Ages.'

'No,' Joey agreed glumly. 'But it is the Isle of Wight.'

'If you return to London tonight my son is hosting a barge party on the Thames,' Eva said. 'Francis's parties are always exciting. You'd love them. I'll write down the address just in case.'

Taking out a slip of paper Eva wrote down directions to the wharf where the hired barge was berthed. Joey suspiciously scrutinised the address when she handed it to him.

'But we don't know your son.'

'No, but Francis loves to meet new friends.'

'Hopefully we'll find a beach to camp on, but if we return to London this evening we'll definitely go,' Jade promised.

But Eva doubted if Jade would be able to overcome Joey's reluctance. Whatever Jade saw as an adventure, Joey would consider a threat. Eva suspected that he only felt secure when having Jade exclusively to himself. He would be happier if Eva moved away from them. Therefore she rose, complaining of feeling stiff if she sat for too long and walked towards the ferry's prow to watch Ryde come into view.

Eva had no idea how Francis found money for his twice yearly barge parties, inviting everyone he knew, rich or poor, to attend. He happily lived on bread and margarine for weeks in advance so that he could be an unstinting host. This afternoon he would start to cut up the full salmon kept in his bath for the past two days because it was too big for his fridge. By seven o'clock the salmon would be laid out with canapés and hors d'oeuvres on the barge, and borrowed wineglasses arrayed, with so many bottles waiting to be opened that Francis would be penniless for months. By eight p.m. conservative members of the Irish Genealogical Society – of which Francis was the London secretary – would be unwittingly mixing with homosexual cliques. There would be members of the Irish Club in Eton Square, fellow horticulturists and random strangers whom Francis invited, mingling together while 'All I Have to Do is Dream' played on a record player and coloured bulbs lent the barge a magical quality in the dark. On such nights it always seemed to Eva that this rented barge resembled an ark built by Francis to shelter everyone he loved. She had taken the morning train to Portsmouth to allow herself time to get to London and be part of tonight's magic if she wished. But Eva suspected that she might not be returning to London for some time, with Francis hurt and puzzled by her non-appearance, especially if she could not explain her absence to him.

Francis hurt easily. This was why she had felt so nervous when – before a dinner party eighteen months ago – Francis had confessed to having met someone truly special: a Welsh orthopaedic surgeon named Jonathan with his own practice in Harley Street. Eva had felt caught up in her son's excitement but also scared for him, begging him to be careful not to get hurt again. Francis had laughed off her concern, asking why Jonathan would possibly hurt him. Waving aside her mentions of previous romances, Francis had declared that love and hurt went together in a cocktail of risk.

Eva turned around on the deck to observe Jade and Joey lost in conversation. She doubted if Jade would care about Francis's sexuality, beyond the fascination girls often felt, but she knew that Joey would feel affronted and irrationally threatened by it. Jade sensed her gaze and waved. Eva waved back but kept her distance. If Jade were alone Eva would enjoy meeting her friends for coffee but she needed to be extra careful with her money now. Her poverty was more awkward in England than in Spain, because many of Francis's new friends – who were essentially Jonathan's friends – seemed as rich as Jonathan himself.

Francis urged her to teach child art again, but her attic flat was tiny and besides, when Eva closed any chapter in her life, she never wished to return to it. She survived because she ate little and was good at finding odd jobs. Two summers ago she worked as a hotel chambermaid on the island of Sark. The previous summer was spent in Tangiers, working as a child-minder for a rich English couple while using the British Council Library there to study the ancient Moroccan philosopher Sidi Ahmed abu al-Abbas al-Khazraji as-Sabti, whose simplicity she responded to. Eva needed to keep her poverty secret from Francis's wealthy friends or it would mar their relationship. They might try to loan her money or suspect her of wanting to borrow some. Worse of all, they would pity her. Men like Jonathan had no concept of how she juggled pennies because only big sums registered with them. Francis would gladly share every shilling he possessed with her. This was why she needed to engage in the subterfuge of keeping two pound notes in her purse which she could produce whenever her son pressed her for reassurance that was she not penniless. Occasionally if she felt that Francis was growing suspicious of seeing these same pound notes, she would exchange them for four ten-shillings notes, but she was careful never to dip into this float, even if sometimes it was virtually all the money she possessed. She would find it impossible to stay in London if she became a financial drain on Francis, who needed to juggle so many other worries to keep his garden-design business afloat. Eva could only be honest about money with her poorer friends. She loved to share her food with them or let them share with her, for the joy that people who understand hunger feel when helping each other. There was no charity or condescension in gestures between equals.

Eva dismounted the gangplank when the ferry docked. She would not mention the copies of *Peace News* in her bag to Freddie. She would say nothing to upset him, although her presence alone would do that. It was not easy to travel here, knowing she would receive no welcome. But she was still Freddie's wife and he had no other visitors. His soul belonged on a Mayo bog, not in an Isle of Wight hospital. She wondered if the Freemasons had got him this bed or if some ex-army chums from the British Legion pulled strings. She had not heard from Freddie since he lost his job in Wicklow. But she knew from Hazel that last year that he had secured a post as a maths teacher in a remote Devon school. Freddie remained on tolerable terms with Hazel. In contrast, he and Francis had spent years carefully avoiding each other, maintaining the semblance of a relationship by exchanging curt cards at Christmas. This uneasy truce had held until, unbeknownst to each other, both decided to spend last Halloween in Glanmire House.

Only last week, when reading the letter from Mayo, had Eva realised how much agony Freddie must have been enduring when he limped up the dark avenue to their crumbling house. But he had told nobody about his cancer, refusing to yield to pain or self-pity until he collapsed in that Devon school three months ago. By then – according to the letter – Freddie's cancer was so advanced that doctors could do little beyond amputating his leg to buy him more time.

Eva walked for fifteen minutes before she reached a small, nondescript hospital with neglected Victorian stonework down a Ryde side street. How typical of Freddie to choose to die in such a remote place without telling anyone. It reminded her of how animals instinctively move away from the herd when they sense their own death approaching. Freddie's preferred death would be to walk from a tent into the Antarctic, quietly saying 'I may be some time.' The Isle of Wight offered little room for such heroic gestures. The front-desk porter directed her up two flights of stairs and along a grey north-facing corridor. The ward nurse informed Eva that Freddie was mercifully asleep because they had managed to get sufficient morphine into him.

'He'll wake soon,' the nurse assured her. 'Not even the effects of morphine last forever. It's a bit early for visiting, but you're welcome to stay. You're the first visitor Mr Fitzgerald has ever received. Are you a relation?'

'I'm his wife.'

The nurse looked puzzled. 'Mr Fitzgerald gave a cousin in Mayo as his next of kin.'

'I'm Freddie's wife.' These grey walls were sapping Eva's will. She hated hospitals and never attended doctors, preferring to treat herself with homeopathic remedies.

'I don't mean to doubt you.' The nurse looked embarrassed. 'Why don't you return in half an hour? He'll be awake by then.'

But Eva didn't leave. She was glad of a chance to sit by Freddie's bedside without having to argue or explain. Freddie was in serious pain after the amputation. His rambling voice occasionally called out in unconscious delirium. There were other patients in the ward, but the nurse draw the screens for privacy. Eva held Freddie's hand and whispered 'It's Eva'; reluctant to wake him, yet trying to make him sense he was no longer alone. He seemed to respond because he muttered her name, but gradually she realised that, in this morphine-induced limbo, he was addressing a different Eva: the young woman with whom he once fell in love. Most of his words were unintelligible, but occasionally Eva found herself listening to snatches of conversations that might have occurred thirty years ago. Maybe these were the emotions he was never able to articulate. His voice alternated between whispers and shouts of pain that caused the nurse to check him.

Feeling she was in the way as the nurse adjusted the drips, Eva walked out into the corridor. One window had a view of the seafront. To keep her promise of attending Francis's party tonight she would need to get the late afternoon ferry across the Spithead. Her son – who had no idea his father was dying – wanted her in London and her husband needed her here. She had that familiar sense of being torn in two. Eva heard the nurse's footsteps approach.

'Mrs Fitzgerald?'

Eva turned. 'Yes?'

'Your husband is awake. I've made him as comfortable as I can.'

The nurse stayed at the window, allowing Eva to enter the ward alone. The screens remained drawn around the bed. Freddie had got the nurse to prop him up, although any movement surely caused him pain. She suspected that he had refused more morphine so as to be alert. There was no greeting, just a whispered question.

'How did you find me?'

'Your relations in Turlough Park.'

He sighed. 'I never took them for traitors.'

He had lost so much weight, he looked tiny in the bed. Wrapped in blankets he reminded her of one of the wounded birds who must have desperately tried to hide in the reeds after

Freddie shot them, knowing there was no escape as they heard his gun-dog sniff them out.

'They felt I should know,' Eva said. 'I'm still your wife.'

'Don't think you can butter me up by coming here dressed in rags.'

'I didn't come to butter you up and I like my clothes. They're comfortable.'

'You came because they must have told you that I've revised my will.'

'I know nothing about any will. I came because they said you are sick.'

'I'm not sick, I'm dying.' Freddie closed his eyes and breathed deeply as a wave of pain overcame him. Opening his eyes, he stared at her. 'You've been written out of my will for years. But now I've written out your son too. I've disinherited him.'

'Francis is also your son.'

'Hazel is ten times the man Francis ever was.'

'And Francis's soul is ten times deeper than Hazel's or yours or mine.'

'Soul?' Freddie almost spat the word. 'I've never seen a man's soul so I've no proof we possess them. But I know what I saw with my own eyes last Halloween.' Freddie's voice was low, fearful that other patients might overhear. 'Step out of the ether, Eva. See what you've raised, with your crack-pot ideas and mollycoddling. Francis is no Fitzgerald. When a Mayo mob put a noose around George Robert Fitzgerald's neck, he leapt to his death and showed that we're no sissies. Mayo people still remember him for that.'

'People remember a crazed brute who chained his father into a cave with a bear,' Eva chided. 'Is that the son you want?'

But Eva knew that it wasn't. Freddie had never needed Francis to be a genius or a statesman. He simply wanted a replica of himself: someone who understood the best cover for shooting woodcock and the measure of a good whiskey. She recalled Freddie buying Francis a gun for the boy's ninth birthday, helping to wedge it into his shoulder: one of the rare occasions when Freddie didn't seem awkward about having physical contact with his son. Francis's first lucky shot had killed a rabbit on the avenue, causing Freddie to rush off and boast about his son's prowess while Eva held the boy in her arms, letting him cry for the dead creature as they lay in Glanmire Wood like hunted creatures themselves.

'I have no son,' Freddie announced quietly.

'Don't say that.' His words hurt more than if Freddie had slapped her, more than the humiliation of him telling the hospital he had no wife.

'I've left Glanmire to my cousin's young son in Turlough Park. The boy is only thirteen, but they can hold it for him until he comes of age and he can add my land to Turlough Park when he succeeds to that in turn. The IRA failed to burn us out and Free State governments failed to wipe us out with their rates and inheritance taxes. I'll not betray my ancestors by letting Fitzgerald land pass to a degenerate. You've heard it from the horse's mouth, so now go away and let me die with whatever dignity I can muster in this place.'

'You could leave Francis one thing,' Eva said quietly. 'Your love.'

'Love?' Freddie looked so baffled that all anger drained from him. He gasped in sudden agony and closed his eyes. 'Forgive me, you shouldn't have to see this … phantom pain is sneaky, it catches you off guard. It's the queerest thing how part of you can be gone but its ghost won't go away. All my life this leg gave me grief: jeers of boys at school, even other army officers who saw my limp and felt cocksure I wasn't up to it. I showed them by being harder than them all, never letting anyone see my pain. So why does my leg hurt ten times worse since they amputated the damnable thing? Every blasted nerve end ambushing me. I'm shot through with morphine when I could really use a stiff whiskey, Eva.'

She noted how, almost accidentally, he uttered her name, perhaps without being aware of it. There was a time when

Freddie had a way of saying her name that was tender and affectionate.

Freddie opened his eyes to observe her. 'You've disappeared into the ether.'

'I'm here, Freddie. It's you who needs ether or laudanum.'

He grimaced. 'You might think this is the worst pain a man could endure, but you'd be wrong. All my life I've known physical pain. It's with me so constantly that you might call it my only true wife.'

'Don't say that, Freddie.'

'For the past year I've known there was something wrong that no doctor could fix. I have my flaws and don't deny them. My tutor in college once said that I had all the attributes to be a great mathematician – logic, mental exactitude. He said the one quality I lacked was imagination. I never understood why mathematicians needed imagination. Figures should just add up or condense to their square root: everything in its logical place, making sense. But great mathematicians see figures that aren't there; complex theorems that may never be proven; leaps in the dark that no club-footed student like me could make. Isn't it funny, Eva? This damnable foot even hobbled my imagination.'

'It was never your foot, Freddie. Who knows what you might have become if it wasn't for your weakness for drink.'

He shook his head. 'That's what everyone thought – poor drunk-as-a-skunk Freddie, in debt to every Mayo publican who hadn't barred him.'

'You were a prisoner to drink, Freddie. It's not your fault.'

'You're wrong,' he said. 'Drink didn't rule me; it set my imagination free without being burdened by logic. Some nights I ended up in low shebeens in Mayo, drinking in solitary confinement surrounded by ruffians who greeted me by respectfully touching their caps, but whose eyes warned me they'd never forgotten the evictions we Fitzgeralds carried out in bad times. You might think that drinking in such dens was as low as I could sink, but some nights when a space cleared around me at the counter and I'd take out a pencil and paper, under the pretext of adding up the game I'd bagged on the bogs that day, my mind felt free to solve the most abstract Algebraic equations.' Freddie looked up with pain in his eyes. 'Why couldn't the boy have at least been good at maths? If he hadn't the guts to grasp a rifle, was it too much to ask that he could grasp an equation? It would have given us something in common.'

'You have your love of Glanmire in common,' Eva said. 'Your son is intelligent: a qualified horticulturist.'

Freddie snorted. 'Can you really call that a profession?'

'He runs a successful garden-design business.'

'Garden design isn't a business.' Freddie shook his head weakly. 'It's a way to meet bored housewives when their hubbies are at work, though God knows the unfortunate hussies picked the wrong man with him.'

'You've never been fair to him. Mathematics isn't everything. In school he was brilliant at French.'

'But poor at Latin.'

'What's wrong with French?'

'Latin is the root of all language. French is just...' Freddie gasped slightly.

'Just what?' she asked.

He shook his head, struggling to speak. Eva saw how severe his pain was, but knew he would continue, fuelled by the dogged determination with which he faced every obstacle. He had lost his father at fifteen. Eva often longed to go back in time and place her arms around him when he must have sat alone in the kitchen of Glanmire House as a distraught boy, shoulders hunched in grief. Did Freddie possess a different personality before that childhood bereavement? After the loss of his father did he lock himself into this hard shell where nothing could touch him?

'French is a dalliance,' he said weakly. 'A coquettish trick they teach daughters in Swiss finishing schools to help them ensnare the right husband.'

Despite the grim surroundings, Eva laughed. 'Listen to yourself. You hadn't the money to send Hazel to Trinity, yet alone a Swiss finishing school.'

He shrugged. 'Hazel never needed continental airs or jiggery-pokery. I saw her leap ditches grown men baulked at, back when she was so young I needed to argue with the Master of the Galway Blazers before he'd let her ride with them. She used to be the talk of Dublin during Horse Show week – more men watching her jump than watched the Aga Khan's Nations Cup. No girl needs a Trinity degree to flag down a husband if she drives racing cars at daredevil speed. My only fear was that she'd have too much pluck for those anaemic young doctors and solicitors in Dublin rugby clubs. She was wise to bag an outdoor type with a Kenyan plantation. The police take no nonsense in Kenya. They deal with the Mau-Mau like the British should have dealt with the IRA.'

'You can't say such things, Freddie. An atrocity is an atrocity, whoever commits it.'

'Any atrocities in Kenya were against white farmers. Police reprisals were simply an eye for an eye. You always had too much time for the New Testament.'

Eva thought of Freddie's fury if he knew about the copies of *Peace News* in her bag. 'The New Testament is about love and forgiveness. Are they such terrible notions?'

'Were the IRA preaching love and forgiveness when they burnt the roof over Lord Mayo in 1923 or forced George Moore to watch his house and library burn to the ground, twenty miles from us in Mayo? That's another reason to leave Glanmire to a true Fitzgerald. We need to consolidate our land to stop us being driven from our rightful place.'

'You didn't change your will for that reason,' she said quietly. 'It's the last weapon you have to hurt your son.'

'What son?' Freddie summoned up such fierceness that Eva feared for him. 'What son disgraces his father? I have no son and if you think you can soft-soap me into changing my will, then get the hell away and let me die in peace.'

'I didn't come to make you change your will,' she said. 'Let's have no more talk about it.'

'Then why have you come?' Genuine bewilderment replaced his angry tone. 'Do you not think it's hard enough to die here without having an audience?'

'There's no good way to die,' Eva replied gently.

'There's a gentlemanly way.'

'What's that?'

'What I planned last Halloween. A shotgun can go off if a hunter is careless when cleaning it. There may be whispers of suicide, but nothing proven. If the Freemasons have a word in the right ear, life assurance companies generally cough up.'

Eva risked touching his hand. The skin felt like parchment, blue veins protruding. 'Would you have really done that, without telling any of us?'

'If a gentleman planned such a thing, do you think he would implicate anyone by burdening them with his secret?' He looked at her hand on his wrist and then at her face. 'You've aged.'

'I'm fifty-seven, Freddie.'

'But part of you is still young, whereas I'm an old man suddenly. The first time I saw you, you reminded me of an elfin creature. You still have that quality of not quite belonging to this world.'

His voice was more matter-of-fact than affectionate.

'I'd have found it heartbreaking if word reached me of you lying dead for months before somebody stumbled across your body in the basement of Glanmire House,' she said. 'You'd have only had the ghost of the butler who hanged himself for company. Glanmire is lonesome in winter.'

Freddie stared at her. 'I wouldn't have minded the lonesomeness. All my life I've dealt with lonesomeness. Last autumn I could barely walk, but I knew I only had two choices. To end it all with a shotgun in Mayo or end up dying in a godforsaken hospital like this. Maybe I'd have never pulled the trigger, sitting alone in Glanmire, but I wanted to give myself the choice. And more than anything, just one last time I wanted to feel the winter rain and wind in Mayo. I was in no fit state to travel but I said nothing to the headmaster of the penny-farthing school I was reduced to teaching in – just that I'd be gone for the mid-term break. The sea crossing was rough but I could always hold my drink, no matter how high the swell. I didn't care about the pain; I just wanted to see Glanmire one last time. Dublin could go to hell: I only dallied there long enough for one whiskey in the bar of Kingsbridge Station for old time's sake.'

He paused. Eva saw how chapped his lips were. She wanted to pour him water from the carafe on his locker, but sensed that it was wiser not to interrupt or give him cause to ask why she hadn't enough sense to smuggle in a half bottle of whiskey in her handbag.

'I've always loved that train journey across the length of Ireland: the lights of Athlone marking where you cross the Shannon into Connacht. Then the lights of every sleepy town bringing you closer to Mayo. Roscommon and Castlerea, Ballyhaunis and Claremorris and the halt at Manulla Junction for anyone changing for Foxford. I always get impatient at that isolated junction because the next stop is Castlebar. Sixty years I've been doing the journey, yet it still makes me feel like a boy. Last Halloween I cadged a lift from a motorist heading out through the dark from Castlebar to Turlough Village. Such a fuss the Durcan sisters made when I popped in my head into the Round Tower Bar for a drink and to purchase a bottle of Skylark whiskey. They insisted on me having a drink on the house, summoning old Mr Durcan from his fire in the parlour to shake my hand.

'I'd barely made my excuses to escape out the door before a customer ran out from Bridie's tiny grocery shop across the road. That Kate Dowling woman: the sister of our maid, Maureen, with whom you got far too friendly during the War. "You're so welcome home, Mr Fitzgerald," she gushed. I couldn't shut her up, rabbiting on about how well Maureen is doing since she hightailed it off to America in search of a man. But I didn't mind her delaying me because the woman made me feel ... I don't mind using the word ... respected. She understood the worth of the Fitzgerald name, unlike the dullards in the Devon school where I struggled along until the pain in my leg got so severe this January that I couldn't dress myself, let along beat trigonometry into yokel numbskulls. I'm not saying there was any badness in the teachers there, where the headmaster knew when to turn a blind eye to a man with the honest shakes on a Monday morning. But they had no spark or sense of breeding. So, to be honest, even though the wind and rain howled around me in Turlough, it did my soul good to see the respect in the villagers' eyes.'

Eva wondered if Kate Dowling knew that Francis was already staying in Glanmire House that night. The Durcan sisters always doted on Francis. It would be unlike him not to call into their pub and pop his head into Bridie's shop, even after travelling all day from London for the privacy of a romantic weekend away, afforded by the seclusion of Glanmire House. Francis probably introduced Jonathan to the Durcan sisters, who would have been awed by his patrician air, with Jonathan charmed by their Tilly lamps and local expressions, like all rich British visitors were. Francis would have mentioned Jonathan's interest in early nineteenth-century architecture, claiming that he was advising Francis on how to make parts of Glanmire House habitable again. Jonathan would have jested in the pub that, no matter how damp the house was, he had known worse billets when serving with the Army Medical Corps on the Mediterranean front during the war. Their age difference would have thrown Bridie and the Durcan sisters off the scent, although Eva doubted if women like Bridie ever guessed at Francis's secret or knew that such relationships even existed between men.

But all of Turlough knew about the unspoken estrangement between father and son. Had Kate's endless babbling been an attempt to delay the inevitable? The local women would have felt it no more their place to send a boy racing up to Glanmire House to warn Francis than they would think of disobeying their priests by entering a Protestant church. They would not wish to be seen to intervene in a family altercation, but Eva felt certain that, when Freddie extracted himself from Kate and began his journey through the dark, many locals had surely watched his progress from behind darkened windows.

'After you left Kate did you call into Turlough Park?' Eva asked. Freddie eyed her with suspicion.

'You know exactly what I did. Your blabbermouth boy always ran to his mother.'

'I only know what our son told me in a letter. He didn't say much, but enough for me to know he was hurting so badly that I sold my typewriter to pay my fare back to London from Tangiers.'

'You always came running at the first sign of tears,' Freddie said. 'You never let the boy fight his own wars.'

'Your son isn't at war with you.'

Freddie gasped as a spur of pain shot through him. 'He might have become my son if you hadn't always interfered. I knuckled down when I enlisted. Do you know how much hard work it takes to be promoted to be a Lieutenant Colonel? Finally by skimping and saving I could afford to enrol him in a good English public school that would give him backbone and contacts. Did you ever wonder what type of man he might have become if that school had time to toughen him up? But no: you had to whisk him away simply because he experienced a bit of character-building ragging for being Irish.'

'You didn't send Francis to that school for his sake,' Eva retorted, bitter now. 'You did it for your own ego, to ape your fellow officers. It didn't bother you that Francis was on the verge of a nervous breakdown at being bullied for being gentle.'

'Think of the trouble it might have saved if his classmates had knocked the gentleness out of him,' Freddie countered. 'Do you think I was not bullied at school for needing to drag one foot behind me? It toughened me up. Think of what damage you did by mollycoddling the boy in Glanmire House where he had no role model except a tutor who turned out to be decidedly queer.'

'You handpicked his tutor, Freddie, persuading a young officer the Mayo air would help him recuperate from his wounds.'

Freddie quivered with rage, but for Eva – who had seen him in full fury – there was something heartbreakingly pathetic in his inability to summon sufficient strength to properly rant at her. She sensed other patients in the ward eavesdropping on their every word.

'But if I'd known, I'd have had him dishonourably discharged.'

Eva had resolved not to slip back into the simmering rows that tore their marriage asunder – rows with Francis often at their core. Yet she couldn't stop her retort: 'Only one of you got discharged from the army: for drunkenly shouting your mouth off in the Officers' Mess. Francis's tutor earned his medals in France. You earned your MBE by shouting at recruits from the safety of a barracks in the Home Counties.'

Eva instantly regretted these words. She tried to reach her hand out, but Freddie tucked his skeletal fingers underneath the blanket.

'That remark was unworthy of us,' Eva said apologetically. 'As newlyweds we brought out the best in each other, but for years we've only brought out the worst. Nobody ever doubted your bravery, Freddie. You'd have been the first man up that beach on D-Day if God hadn't cursed you with your foot.'

'I wasn't aware you still believed in God.' Freddie's tone was mocking but her words had mollified him.

'I believe in a supreme being. I just don't believe he is an English-speaking Anglican who reads *Country Life* and agrees with the views expressed on the letters page of *The Times*.'

She was rewarded by the ghost of a smile. 'Trust you to believe that if heaven exists they speak Swahili there. A least you haven't gone native and started believing that God is an ignorant papist.'

'I don't know what God is,' Eva confessed. 'I don't believe that any religion represents the summit of wisdom. They're all stepping stones.'

'To what?' he asked, genuinely curious.

Eva's laugh was self-deprecating. 'The ridiculous thing, Freddie, is that even at my age I honestly don't know.'

Freddie's voice echoed the amused exasperation he once showed. 'That's my Eva. Leaping from stepping stone to stepping stone until you realise you're stranded in mid-stream with the tide rising and no way forward or back.'

'You're in no state to row out and rescue me,' she said in a consolatory tone.

Freddie looked away, as if frightened of betraying emotion. 'You're beyond saving. But at one time I'd have risked rowing through the widest river in flood for you.'

'But not now?'

His dry-eyed gaze was honest. 'Look at me: a fairground attraction to gawk at. I've a few weeks left at most. Intolerable pain when I'm awake and when I'm not the morphine makes me hallucinate and shout out.'

'Are you in pain now?' Eva asked.

Freddie gazed at the ceiling. 'Pain is determined to keep me company, whether I want company or not.'

'Will I call the nurse? Could you use a shot of morphine?'

'Not as much as I could use a bottle of Skylark and a revolver with a single bullet.'

'Poor Freddie,' she said softly.

His eyes were unable to disguise the pain. If Eva left he could succumb to whatever relief the stupor of morphine temporarily afforded him. She knew he was anxious for her to go.

'Tell me why the hell you came?' he asked.

'I'm still your wife.'

'I don't have a wife or a son either. I don't even have my good name left in Mayo anymore. Your son stole it.'

'Nobody in Turlough saw anything last Halloween.'

'Country people see everything. They've learnt the trick of acting deferential so we barely notice their presence, but they watch our every move to use any slip against us.'

'Mayo people are not like that. Think of how welcoming Kate Dowling was and even old Mr Durcan struggling up from his fire to shake your hand.'

'Old Durcan isn't the worst,' Freddie admitted grudgingly.

'I've never known him to be anything other than decent and considerate. I remember arriving back there in 1939. Petrol was rationed and the avenue to Glanmire House so overgrown it was barely passable. But he still insisted on driving Francis and Hazel up there that night.'

Freddie shrugged. 'Thank Christ he didn't offer me a lift last Halloween or he'd have had enough ammunition to destroy the Fitzgerald name in Mayo. I admire old Durcan. He built up his shop from nothing. But he's never forgotten how he was born by the roadside after my family had to level his father's cottage. During the war I always warned you to wipe provisions delivered from that shop because you'd never know if anyone spat on them.'

'That eviction was eighty years ago.'

'In Mayo eighty years is like yesterday. I took no lift from anyone last Halloween. Nor did I call into Turlough Park, although I knew my cousin's wife would set a place for me at dinner because she is the most decent and hospitable of women. I'd have found warmth and sympathy from her but I've never sought sympathy. It was late and I was in no mood for company because I found it hard to hide the pain, like someone twisting a blade in my leg. I set out through the rain at my snail's pace, passing the Protestant church and reaching the abandoned gate lodge at the entrance to Glanmire Wood. The feel of setting foot on my land. The avenue pitch dark, but I know every step of that uphill walk through the trees. I also knew how cold the house would be: pools of water where roof tiles were missing. But I didn't need creature comforts; I just needed the feel of reaching home. I'd bunk down in the kitchen: an army blanket to soften the stone flags. I'd get a fire going and feel a brighter flame inside me after I opened the Skylark whiskey. I didn't mind the rain or my aching leg as I limped up the avenue.

But when I came within sight of the house a light was already shining in the basement. I felt panic. I begged to God that it was tinkers or thieves; anyone except your son and some Peter-Puffer bum-bandit.'

'Don't call them that,' Eva said, hurt for Francis.

Freddie glanced sharply at her. 'Can you imagine the worse names they're called in any Officers' Mess? Do you think I never knew? That I'm blind as well as stupid?'

'I always thought you only knew whatever you wanted to know.'

'I know what's natural in a man.'

'Isn't it natural to want to be happy? Have you ever been happy, Freddie?'

He snorted. 'That's a stupid bloody question.'

'Why?'

'What has happiness got to do with anything?' Freddie's head lolled as if drained by this effort to talk. The nurse had not reappeared. Eva wondered if she was listening behind the screen. 'Come out of that ether, Eva,' he said weakly. 'Life isn't about being happy.'

'What's it about?'

'It's about a man knowing who he is and where he belongs. You belong nowhere – a misfit with your crazy causes. But at least try to understand. That was my father's home they were defiling, the kitchen I cried in as a boy after he died. For years I've avoided your son and he avoided me. I asked him no questions because the bloody fool is incapable of having the manly decency to tell a white lie. What filth he gets up to in London is one thing, but to do it in Mayo?' Freddie's voice was weak but his rage undiminished. 'I stood outside Glanmire House, too wet and cold to turn back. This was my home, yet I felt like the intruder, gazing down at the light pouring up from the basement kitchen. My son, my supposed heir, doing things with another man.' Freddie's voice rose. 'Can't you understand my shame, woman?'

'Freddie, lower your voice.' Eva glanced anxiously at the closed screens.

'I'll speak as damn loudly as I like. The Welsh cur was the first to grasp that they were caught. I didn't even realise I was making a sound, but every ounce of rage was coming out in one long scream. They were both half-dressed before I stormed down into the kitchen: the Welshman, calm as you like, offering me a cigarette from a silver case, trying to flatter me by using my military rank and casually mentioning how he had served as an army doctor. He had the audacity to mention my leg and how he specialised in treating such conditions. I don't have a condition, I told him. I have an affliction that never stopped me doing anything in life. But I'm sure your cry-baby boy has told you all this already.'

'Francis is no longer a boy. Thankfully his friendship with Jonathan has survived your vile remarks when turning them out of Glanmire House. But I know it was his worst nightmare come true.'

'And so you decided to track me down and plead for him.' Freddie's voice was so feeble he seemed only being kept alive by his anger. 'Where is that damned nurse? I don't know why she let you in.'

'I'm not here to plead for Francis. I came because I'm your wife. I can't bear to think of you dying alone.'

'You're not my wife,' Freddie protested weakly. 'You're a stranger to me.'

'Then let me visit you as a stranger.'

'I don't need your pity. I told the doctors to be frank. The cancer has spread everywhere. Every day I have left the pain will only get worse.'

Freddie's lips were dry. Eva picked up a sponge on the locker and moistened them. 'Maybe you don't need me, but I need to be here. It's hard to watch you suffer, but harder to know you were suffering and I did nothing to help.'

Freddie waved a hand feebly; his voice so faint that Eva knew he could not hold out any longer without morphine. 'So you want me to become your latest fad? It's too late for either of us to make up for everything that happened.'

'I know,' Eva said. 'But at least give me the chance to make your last days a tiny bit more bearable. I have a small bit of money. I can find cheap lodgings in Ryde. I know I won't be of much real use to you, although then again I never was. But your children need to know you're dying. If you won't let me tell Francis, at least let me wire Hazel.'

Freddie shook his head. 'I want no fuss and you know Hazel – she's so strong willed she'll fly home and drag Francis down here for a blazing row with me in a haze of morphine.' He paused. 'Does she know about the boy's peccadilloes?'

'Francis and Hazel have no secrets. She's known everything about Francis since she was fifteen years old.'

'I believe it.' Freddie nodded. 'The three of you – and the serving girl, Maureen – living secret lives in that wood during the war. Rushing down the front steps to greet me on the odd occasion I got leave, but I knew in my bones I wasn't welcome. I was paying for everything with my salary but in your hearts, you were all waiting for me to be gone.'

'It wasn't like that, Freddie.'

'It felt like that. I swear that my ghost will haunt you if you let your son near me. Don't even tell him I'm sick or I'll have the nurses bar you and, I swear to God, I'll get a boat to Ireland. To hell with morphine. I never feared pain. I'll stock up on whiskey in Glanmire House. Once I've wood for a fire, I'll manage fine on my own with none of you to torment me.'

'Freddie, you're raving,' Eva replied softly. 'You can't even get out of bed.'

'Swear you'll say nothing to him or Hazel. Swear and I'll let you visit when you like. But I reserve the right to die with no other spectators present.'

Eva nodded, reluctantly.

'And it won't matter how often you come,' Freddie added with weak defiance. 'I'm leaving you nothing because you'd only leave it to him.'

'You're leaving me two wonderful children and deliberately breaking one of their hearts.'

Freddie closed his eyes, making no attempt to reply. Eva reached across to take his fingers. It was so long since she'd held any man's hand. She suspected that it was equally long since any woman, except for a nurse, touched his.

'Your will is written,' she said. 'Let's never discuss it again.'

Freddie opened his eyes and she saw tears in them.

'I don't want to die,' he said quietly.

'I know.'

'Your final days should be precious but they're damnably slow. Company would be nice. But please call the nurse. I'm in such pain it's like the devil is inside me. You'll find some odds and ends in a shoebox in my bedside locker: the remnants of a life. It's taking up space so take it away. There's something in it for you. Keep or discard whatever you like.'

Eva pulled back the screen to find the nurse already waiting with an injection, as if astonished that he had lasted so long.

'Now, Mr Fitzgerald, let's attend to your needs.' Something in the woman's conspiratorial tone made Eva feel in the way. She removed the shoebox Freddie wanted taken from his locker but had no time to examine it. Freddie's eyes were so fixated on the injection that he seemed to forget that Eva was present. His expression changed once the nurse began to tend to him: all defiance gone, including the mask of haughtiness which for so long was all he possessed to protect himself against diminishing circumstances. He looked like a wizen old man but also a scared schoolboy no longer able to hold out against the pain. At any moment he might begin to shout, barely conscious of anything except his torment.

Freddie's pride meant that he would not wish her to hear him scream. But Eva knew she would witness terrible suffering during the coming weeks as his body caved in. For now all she could do was find cheap lodgings and hope she would be able to survive on her meagre savings. Freddie would grow more argumentative and bitter as he felt death approach. A sense of the horror to come left Eva shaken as she made her way out from the hospital into the midday sunshine. It was still not too late, if she hurried, to catch the late afternoon ferry to Portsmouth. She could be in London in a few hours' time, trying to lose herself amid the lights and gaiety of Francis's barge party.

Francis would already be on board by now, wearing his favourite wide-brimmed hat and dressed in overalls as he helped Peter – the young labourer he employed – with the final preparations. When Peter's wife, Pauline, recently gave birth to twins, Francis presented them with all his good bed linen, claiming he was throwing it out, when in fact this meant that he needed to sleep in old army blankets. But, like Freddie, Francis had little interest in his own physical comfort. Maybe if father and son had both travelled alone to Glanmire House last Halloween, they might have finally bonded, each content to sleep on the kitchen flagstones. Unfortunately life rarely worked out like that. Eva was not surprised that Freddie was leaving her out of his will. In truth, Glanmire House and its few areas were almost worthless. Even if left to Francis, it was beyond his means to make it habitable again. But this was always Francis's dream: he saw Glanmire as his refuge, the only true home he possessed.

For years Francis had lived in a succession of rented flats. Even now that he was in a sufficiently serious relationship to share Jonathan's bed almost every night, he still kept his own flat for fear of scandal. Assault and arrest were hovering spectres requiring him to guard against public displays of affection. When Freddie's will was revealed by the family solicitor in Castlebar, Francis would be scarred, not only by losing his childhood home, but by his father's public rejection that would have all of Turlough talking, the final spiteful act of an embittered man. Just thinking about this forthcoming public humiliation of her son made the spiteful virago side of her character want to damn Freddie to hell and leave him to die alone on this island. But Eva would never bring herself to board the next ferry and leave Freddie here because she could not change who she was. She was coming to a realisation that she possessed no special gift or talent in life beyond this sense of empathy, which was so engrained within her as to be both a burden and a benediction.

Reaching a small park near the seafront, Eva sat on a bench. She could no more return to London tonight than she had been able to stop herself, as a young mother in Mayo, entering the cold larder at night to sit in silence beside the plucked carcasses of the wild birds left there to hang. Her presence in that larder made no different to those dead creatures, but Eva had still needed to be with them to bear witness. Likewise she would remain by Freddie's bedside until his final suffering ended. This evening she would send Francis a telegram that would cause her son bewilderment by announcing that she needed to leave London for a while. Eva would keep Freddie's secret and remain with him, no matter how hard an ordeal it was for them both, because she could not change who she was and could only live her life on her own terms. She was coming to realise that she possessed no special talent beyond a sense of empathy so engrained as to be both a burden and a benediction.

She looked across and saw the schoolboy from the train on the next bench, still engrossed in *Treasure Island*. His mother smiled curtly at Eva – anxious to be friendly but not over-familiar. Eva leaned forward to address him.

'Do you like Robert Louis Stevenson?'

'Oh yes.'

'My son loved *Treasure Island* as a boy.'

'Are you visiting on holidays?' the boy's mother asked.

'My husband is dying in hospital here.'

'I'm most dreadfully sorry.'

Eva sensed the woman's attitude change. The context of grief made it acceptable to talk to boys in parks. And Eva's grief was intense, despite them not having lived as man and wife for years. Remembering the shoebox that Freddie had asked her to take away, she discreetly opened it. It contained his army records, his teaching notes, his MBE medal, an itemised list of his expenditure in the months leading up his hospitalisation and a notebook from the 1930s in which he recorded his daily 'bag' of birds killed on shooting expeditions. Underneath this were four five-pound banknotes neatly folded together with a paper clip. Perhaps this was what he wished to give her, money to help find lodgings. Then Eva noticed a tattered envelope at the bottom of the shoebox. Inside it she discovered a small picture of herself, taken in the year Hazel was born. Freddie had obviously asked the photographer to print it in an oval shape that bled away into whiteness. The words on the back of the picture were undated, but his handwriting was unmistakable: 'My treasure is in here safe forever.'

These words – and their proof that he had once loved her – affected Eva so deeply that she left the park, keeping her head lowered in case anyone noticed her tears. She felt weary as if she had let her life slip by without truly understanding it. She walked quietly along the seafront for ten minutes until she heard her name being called. Turning, Eva saw Jade, the girl from the ferry, run towards her. Joey followed more slowly. Now that Jade could not see his expression, Eva noticed his look of disapproval, as if no middle-aged woman had a right to dress like she did.

Jade was laughing, unaware of Joey's expression. The girl held out a small bunch of wildflowers. Her excitement was so palpable that it brought back Eva's earliest memory of being a toddler, intoxicated by the scent of daisies she had just plucked as she ran unsteady towards her nurse's lap, holding out the daisies to show her. Jade could not disguise her similar pleasure at being able to present the flowers to Eva.

'They're nothing special,' she explained, 'but I saw them growing on a beach when we were still thinking about pitching a tent. I picked them, hoping we might meet you again.'

'Did you find somewhere to camp?' Eva asked.

Jade shook her head. 'Our friends never showed up and Joey changed his mind.' She lowered her voice. 'He gets grumpy: I think he's scared of new experiences. We're taking the last train back to London.'

'Go to my son's barge party,' Eva said. 'You'll enjoy it. Just tell Francis I've been delayed but that I sent you.'

Joey had almost reached them. Jade's voice went even quieter.

'I'll never persuade Joey.'

Eva's voice was equally quiet. 'Then go yourself. Be yourself.'

Joey was upon them; his tone possessive. 'We'll miss this ferry,' he told Jade and turned to Eva. 'We decided Ryde wasn't for us. It's more for folk your age. Still it was nice to meet you, Mrs...?'

'Fitzgerald,' Eva replied. 'But please, call me Eva.'

'Lovely to meet you, Mrs Fitzgerald. Have a nice stay here.'

Eva knew that his copy of *Peace News* was already in some bin. He placed his arm around Jade's waist in a firm embrace. Jade looked embarrassed but also cowed, like a flower that had faded after being plucked and placed in a jar with no water.

'I hope you find the berth,' Eva said to her quietly.

Jade nodded before being steered into the ruck of passengers heading towards the ferry terminal. Eva watched the young couple being swallowed up. It was getting late. Soon she would need to start knocking on boarding-house doors to find a cheap room simple enough for her needs. Eva walked along by the Victorian railings that separated the wooden pier from the sea. Taking one wildflower from the small bouquet, she tossed it out onto the waves for her husband soon to depart this earth. *My treasure is in here safe forever.* She tossed a second flower onto the water as a prayer that her son might not get hurt in his relationship with Jonathan and a third as a prayer for Hazel in her new life in Africa, parts of which she suspected Hazel of shielding her from. She cast out another flower as a prayer that Joey, or any other man, would never extinguish the inner radiance which she glimpsed within Jade. Then she let another flower float aimlessly down onto the waves to represent how she seemed to drift through life with no true purpose revealed to her.

She raised the remaining flowers to her lips to breathe in their scent. Again they reminded her of being a child in Donegal, taking her first steps to let her nurse share the wondrous scent of plucked daisies. Those first steps on the beginning of the adventure she was still on. Tomorrow she would return to that hospital to play the role of Freddie's wife one last time. But this evening belonged to her. Tossing the remaining flowers into the waters, she rooted in her bag for the unsold copies of *Peace News*, smiling at the thought of Freddie's apoplexy if he could see her. Eva held them aloft on the pier to let anyone who wished to approach her do so. She strode proudly among the crowds hurrying for the ferry in her bright clothes that would look unsuitable on anyone of her age, except for someone with a pilgrim soul.

Chapter Seven

The Mayo Letter

August 1962

Glanmire House,
Turlough
Castlebar
Mayo   *17th August, 1962*

Dear Mummy,

How extraordinarily wonderful it feels to once more place this address at the start of a letter. After Daddy died I never imagined I would ever again write to you from here or spend another afternoon like I spent today, stripped to the waist as I laboured with a billhook, a slightly rusty bowsaw and a broad-axe in these woods. It's so late at night that I should be exhausted. My shoulders will ache tomorrow but I'm too exhilarated to sleep, although I have my sleeping bag rolled out and ready on the flagstones, beyond range of the occasional blazing sparks that shoot out from the grate like dancing fireflies. I should probably not have added more logs to the fire this late, but I love the warmth, the shapes which the flames cast on the cracked ceiling plaster and, yes, I love having for company the fizzing sound of exploding embers punctuating the silence, just like whenever I was ill here as a boy and you'd light a fire in my tiny bedroom grate as a treat. Not that I am lonely for company here, beyond the fact that I'd love to have you here just now, savouring this silence as only you can savour a silence, luxuriating in it as if it were the richest symphony ever composed. Maybe the thought of how you would enjoy this serenity has me sitting up by the light of a paraffin lamp to write this letter at our old kitchen table. It has miraculously survived, being too battered for anyone to bother bidding on it at the auction or perhaps because Mr Devlin's workmen considered it too cumbersome to bother manoeuvring out the doorway to be displayed on the daffodil lawn.

That is where so many of our old possessions wound up displayed for auction, that the lawn must have resembled a particularly eclectic bric-à-brac stall at the Portobello Road Market. Though I rather doubt if Mr Devlin – the Castlebar builder who bought this house for a song – used a Cockney barrow boy's accent to shout out: 'Get the last of the Fitzgeralds here' when trying to entice bidders for our old delph and china and cutlery; our pictures and books stacked in tea chests; the forty-gallon copper cylinder he took out, alongside two toilets and washbasins; the beautiful writing bureau where I can still see Hazel drawing sketches of ponies whenever twilight or rain forced her indoors; the mahogany walnut sideboard that Maureen always took such care to polish when Daddy was due home from the war; the six-piece oak dining room suite that seemed as old as this house itself; for miscellaneous chests of drawers and basins and probably even chamber pots that once bore the weight of the great and good; for that mahogany oval table you once loved to write at; for the deck chairs we sat out on during long summer afternoons; for the lino off the floor, which has probably been cut up into strips to let patrons of pubs in Ballavary tramp across it in their wellington boots; and for the ancient fireside chairs – priceless to us and surely worthless to anyone else – on which you and Harry Bennett would sit up reading French poetry aloud late at night during the war, while I lay awake, waiting for Harry to come to bed.

Presumably Daddy, as a proud Fitzgerald, never dreamt that such a public free-for-all would occur. He would have been mortified at our old furniture being gawked at, pawed and bid on – or sometimes not even bid on despite Devlin setting no reserve – by half of Turlough and curious onlookers coming from Breaffy to Bohola, with some families crossing the mountains from as far away as Pontoon for a chance to traipse up our avenue as if attending a circus or a county hurling final. But perhaps Daddy should have considered what his will would entail before allowing spite to rule him. I'm told that old Mister Durcan rose from his sickbed to drive his old car up here, dressed in his best as if attending Sunday Mass. He was too crippled with rheumatism to get out of the driver's seat, but they say he was the first to arrive and the last to leave, disconcerting Devlin by watching the sell-off with what someone called a judgemental expression: although Bridie in her little shop was caustic as ever when breaking her usual reticent silence to observe that this is how old Mister Durcan always looks when he forgets to put in his false teeth.

I laughed at Bridie's remark because this is what you must do in local shops – not that I go into too many here because the people in them think they know too much about me, although thankfully I don't think that they know anything at all about my real life. They just know that I'm the Fitzgerald whose father disinherited me and – as a proud Fitzgerald myself – this is a shadow I carry in Mayo. As our Turlough Park relations wisely declined to turn up to witness Devlin's hodgepodge fire-sale of the sweepings of Daddy's life, then – in so much as we were represented there – I like to think it was by that elderly, decent shopkeeper who drove us up here on the freezing winter night in 1939 when you brought Hazel and I back home at the outbreak of war. Bridie – if you could get her to express an opinion – might grumpily claim that old Mister Durcan only drove up to witness the auction because it warmed his old bones to see Fitzgerald possessions piled up, just like his own parents' possessions were once piled after their eviction from their cabin. But I like to think he drove up to bear witness not out of revenge but from a fundamental neighbourly sense of decency. Certainly his daughters in the pub were one of the few local families not to buy some keepsake. Our old table and chairs are scattered across a dozen local farmhouses now. On my first night home when I called into Bridie's shop and she insisted on bringing me into the little kitchen beyond the counter to drink tea, I found myself seated on one of our most comfortable armchairs, without Bridie making any reference as to how it came to be there. Even your old friend, Dermot MacManus, late of Killeaden House, who was back home in Mayo for a visit, turned up and bought one of our old oak bookcases – to be shipped to his new home in Harrogate, presumably to hold the research for the book of ghost stories he's been promising to publish since I was a child.

We could be bitter about what happened, but bitterness would only play into Daddy's hands so that he would still be manipulating us; we'd still be playing by his rules, even when he is not alive to impose them. As I write, the rooms overhead are denuded of furniture and while there is a curious echo throughout our old home with everything gone, there is also so much new space and light. That's what I've realised on this visit home, sitting in the quietude of this kitchen by night or working by day to reclaim the woods. In the strange way in which life evens itself out, while Daddy thought he had won by playing his ace card of spite, he lost everything, including people's respect. But he hadn't bargained on Hazel's stubborn bloody-mindedness and her Kenyan riches, thanks to which she was able to buy back whatever remains of this ark that you tried to build for me here against the world. Not that I wasn't bitter and wounded after his will was made public, but eighteen months later I refuse to feel bitterness now. My problem is that I always hurt too easily. A part of me still hurts from Daddy's *actions because rejection is worse than any physical assault. But during these past few days here every blow of my axe through the dense undergrowth besieging this house has felt like healing. I keep discovering so many trees slowly dying of strangulation from a lack of light and space in the undergrowth. Today, as I cleared space around one of them, I realised that this is what you and I both need to do with our lives: clear enough space to allow us to breathe and live simply as ourselves.*

If there is no point in feeling bitterness towards Daddy, then there is less point in even feeling the slightest animosity towards the Turlough Park folk who are just about managing to keep that house afloat by supplying Castlebar shops with fruit and vegetables from their gardens and tomatoes from their greenhouse. There is a good and practical woman there trying her best to raise a family in those big rooms. The last thing they needed was for Daddy to burden them by leaving Glanmire to be maintained – County Council rates and all – until my cousin comes of age to inherit. But I suppose Daddy's dream was always to have young Fitzgeralds playing in these woods and he knew I would never produce an heir, long before he discovered me with Jonathan here. I could never tell you the hurtful names he called me that Halloween night when he burst in half-drunk, so grey and ill that it seemed as if only rage was keeping him alive. Maybe his will was the survival instinct of a dying creature, his desperate wish to keep the Fitzgerald name strong in Mayo for another generation. But between the rates and death duties, Glanmire was a burden and not a blessing to our relations and they did the only practical thing by auctioning off the house and wood to pay the numerous expenses.

At one time the sale of Glanmire House would have been the talk of Connacht, but reports of the auction only crept into the Mayo News as a small item in the local parish notes section that Bridie kept for me. Obviously no local farmer cared to go to the trouble of felling these woods to create more pasture land because Devlin the builder bought the whole kit and caboodle for the knock-down price of two hundred pounds. I know it might have been better if our relations had told us about their plans in advance, because the parish notes in the Mayo News rarely gets passed around the Whites Only club in Kenya where Hazel drinks most evenings. Though I confess that in London I occasionally see copies of that newspaper being avidly read on the Tube by Irish navvies, dog tired from their day's labour on building sites, and I feel so overcome by homesickness that I often long to ask them if I can peruse the deaths and marriages and reports of court cases over claims of trespass, boundaries and after hours drinking.

I made a point of calling to Turlough Park on my first day back here. What is the sense in holding a grudge, when the family there was just as much an unwitting victim of Daddy's will: knowing that – as his executor – they would have reneged on their legal duty by simply giving Glanmire back to me, and possibly feeling too embarrassed to offer to sell it to me. Not that I could have afforded the two hundred pounds that Devlin paid and presumably they had no reason to expect that Hazel – with her new life in Africa – would have any use for a tumbledown house with its twenty acres of woodland.

The only person to emerge from the debacle richer is Devlin, who extracted five hundred pounds from Hazel's solicitor who had to negotiate a price to buy Glanmire back from him. Nobody says it to my face, but this caused great mirth in Turlough – the local builder outsmarting the fallen gentry. The grass along the avenue is still scarred by tyre track marks caused by Devlin during the two months he owned this land. The Durcan sisters say that, following the auction of our furniture, Devlin had planned to level everything, selling the felled wood for timber and scavenging any stonework he could when demolishing the house and then reselling the whole site as farmland.

But thanks to Hazel's money and also to her love for me, our home – in so much as you and I have a home – has been saved from his bulldozers. My only wish is that you were with me instead of being off on your travels again, gathering even more rosebuds in Morocco. Local people shake their heads when I tell them how you work at odd jobs in Tangiers, living on fruit and water and a weekly bar of the darkest dark chocolate. The villagers probably wonder when you will start to act your age, but I hope you never do. Bingo is the new craze in Castlebar for women who act their age, but I can't imagine you in any bingo hall, shouting 'Full House' and coming home thrilled to win a new-fangled electric toaster. I suspect you would drive the bingo caller to distraction, patiently insisting that no house can ever be truly 'full', that it is always possible to create more space for another few lost creatures to shelter, like the family of earwigs you refused to disturb after you found them living in an envelope on top of your wardrobe in Frankfort Avenue.

Looking back, I confess to being hurt that you never shared the burden of Daddy's final illness almost until the very end in that dreary Isle of Wight hospital. But you were wise enough to let me be part of the vigil after he slipped into that last coma, so I could at least sit by his bed and hold his hand, like he may possibly have held mine when I was a sleeping child in this house, who had not yet disappointed his expectations. In truth Daddy and I were probably only ever comfortable together when one of us was unconscious. You knew the details of his will when you helped nurse him right up to the end, but I remember how hurt you were to later discover that he had already drawn up his will to deny you or Hazel or I one single perch of land long before the Halloween night when he encountered Jonathan and I here. Daddy wrote us out of his life two weeks after doing what he obviously saw as his final public duty by walking Hazel up the aisle. I saw you try to suppress your hurt at this revelation before you left to go travelling again in Morocco. But anger is part of your Scorpio side and while no good ever comes from anger, no good can come from trying to suppress it. It's rare that I ask you to do something, but please do one thing for me: be angry with him just once for publicly humiliating us. Go to one of those remote places your soul always yearns for and shout his name in anger. Damn him aloud and it will be done and dusted and you will feel cleansed of bitterness, like I feel cleansed by working in these woods, because if we retain any bitterness in our hearts, Daddy will have won by tainting our spirit.

Devlin came round today to apologise for any damage caused. I chatted to him on the steps: the front door open into the hallway to reveal the gaping hole where his men removed the old fireplace before Hazel's offer reached him. I saw him glance up at the cracked window panes and slates missing from the roof. He was curious to know why a woman in Kenya would want to buy back such a ruin and kept asking whether Hazel wished to have the house repaired, presumably hoping to turn an even greater profit from his brief stewardship. I couldn't tell him how Hazel bought Glanmire primarily out of a refusal to be bested by Daddy and to publicly thwart his wishes.

The young lad in Turlough Park wanders across to help me in the woods some afternoons. He is wonderful company, clearing grass with a scythe. His people often ask when will you be coming back, but my instincts tell me you don't want to visit Turlough Park again: you always say that walking through those ornate gates made you feel like the poor relation. I no longer care about such things because I feel like Adam here in the garden, where I work each evening until the light fades, then play Handel's 'Water Music' on our old wind-up gramophone, which somehow survived in a cupboard that Devlin missed when rifling through the house. I sleep in old army blankets on our kitchen floor and always wake refreshed. I wish that Jonathan were here but he will be waiting for me in London when I return next week. He has persuaded me to give up my old flat and move in with him. But for appearances sake, if nothing else, I have asked Peter, who works for me, to convert Jonathan's basement into a self-contained apartment where I can have my own kitchen and be able to keep my books and files and sleep down there whenever Jonathan has family or important *guests staying over. It's so important to keep an independent address, even if only a notional one. So when you next write to me just add the letter A to the house number on the first line of Jonathan's address and the postman will drop your letter into the letterbox that Peter promises to have cut into the basement door by the time I return to London.*

While I miss Jonathan, the person I really miss is you. I keep remembering the miniature Eden you made here during the war years; Maureen watching over all of us, coming and going on her bicycle, laughing about all the young Turlough men in love with her. Maybe it's a fantasy to imagine that one day I'll create a nursery here, harvesting timber and commercially growing shrubs. But at the very least I'm getting Glanmire ready for your return. One day soon I'll lure you back to Mayo with me. There are so many wonderful old trees here and new trees I long to plant. I'm enough of a romantic to believe that our true home is not beyond repair. Hazel tells me to consider Glanmire as my home for as long as I live. This is where I plan to die: an old man surrounded by my own trees. These woods can become an Eden for us both again, Mummy, our sanctuary against the world. But this time will be different because it never belonged to us when Daddy was alive. From now on there is no more looking over our shoulders in case he comes back to catch us living our lives. He lost all his power by writing that will. If Daddy had left me this house it would never fully belong to us because we'd still owe his ghost a debt. We owe him nothing now because when Devlin briefly owned this house it broke the chain, allowing us to buy it back on our own terms and we're finally free to be ourselves here.

So write to me at my new London address and tell me you'll return to Mayo soon. Promise me this and it will be a promise I'll ensure that you and I keep together.

Your loving, sunburnt son,

Francis.

Chapter Eight

African Skies

Kenya, 1963

Throughout the night Eva's dreams were saturated in vibrant colours as she slept in a guest bedroom in Hazel's single-storey stone house, overlooking the paved courtyard besieged by intensely blue blossoms of the jacaranda tree and the unadulterated whiteness of agapanthus lilies. Not even the loud rhythmic chirping of the cicadas had disturbed her. Waking now to a blue sky where kites and kestrels circled, Eva felt as if she were opening her eyes in a new Garden of Eden. The metaphor seemed apt because Hazel had warned her to shake out her shoes – left airing on the wooden veranda – before putting them back on in case mamba snakes were tempted to creep into them during the night. Eva walked out on this veranda to gaze out at a dawn so fresh that it seemed to have materialised instantaneously from the darkness to reveal a distant vista of Mount Elgon, which a heat-haze would soon set in to obscure. Everything about Kenya felt exotic, with whale-headed storks and crested cranes wading along the nearby river's edge. Yet as she gazed around at Hazel's spacious home, besieged on all sides by lush vegetation, Eva felt a curious *déjà vu*; an uneasy sense of standing in a place that should be familiar and yet was so inexplicably altered that she could not immediately identify the memory it stirred.

A furious downfall of rain had beat against the slate roof last night and Eva could smell the parched earth greedily absorbing this rainwater before the sun could evaporate it. Deep underground the roots of the purple bougainvillaea would be competing for each drop of moisture, just like its vines fought for every inch of space and light above ground. The smell of the steaming red soil brought back a memory of how her father had loved the scent of the sweet pea plants beneath his window in Donegal after a downpour of summer rain. She closed her eyes momentarily, the better to remember this man who died while cradling a cat inside his coat in a bomb shelter during the Blitz, so serene in dying that the Londoners huddled around him never even noticed him suffering a heart attack. Father had been her great friend and confidant: her soulmate in ways which Eva knew she had never managed to be for Hazel.

But perhaps today some sense of closeness might occur, when Hazel drove Eva and three-year-old Alex into the mountains to Mount Elgon National Park to stay overnight at a safari lodge. Hazel was promising spectacular scenery that Eva would never forget, as if determined to provide her mother with a mental scrapbook of colour to sustain her through the long London winter ahead. This African trip was already proving to be the most extraordinary month in Eva's life. With typical generosity, Hazel had paid for Eva's ticket from Southampton to Cape Town on *The Oranjefontaine*, the lower decks of which retained the odour of onions after its cargo was unloaded in England. This route allowed Eva to visit her middle brother, Thomas, in South Africa, even though she felt uneasy at visiting a country whose apartheid system she frequently protested about during her stays in London. But Eva put politics aside because she longed to spend time with Thomas, who had moved to Cape Town in the late 1930s, primarily for health reasons after his doctor advised that his respiratory condition, following a bout of TB, needed a drier climate. Like many men of his background, Thomas had struggled to find work in this new Ireland after graduating from

Trinity College: his sense of disillusion before he moved abroad deepened by a bitter quarrel with their oldest brother about how Art's politics had torn their family apart.

Thomas shared her grave misgivings about apartheid, but little of her time in Cape Town was spent discussing politics. Instead she and Thomas had reminisced about their Donegal childhood: day-long picnics by horse-and-cart and evenings when all five siblings joyously bathed on a nearby jetty that they nicknamed Paradise Pier. Back then they seemed to possess an unbreakable closeness with no thoughts of future family schisms or tragedies. After a week in Cape Town, Thomas and his wonderful family waved Eva off on the final leg of her voyage, which brought her ever closer to her true reason for visiting Africa: to finally meet her granddaughter, Alex. Eva had travelled from Cape Town on *The MV Europa*, a small Italian ship filled with good-humoured passengers enjoying a long cruise from Venice. It moved slowly up the African coast, with afternoon string concerts featuring Strauss and Ferraris and dance music each night – or *musica da ballo* as the Italian captain called it. He made the band play 'Never on Sunday', after discovering that Eva liked this tune. After this, the Italian men gathered on the promenade deck would hum a few bars for her if she paused to watch their clay pigeon shooting contests in the Mozambique Channel. Eva spent hours up on deck chatting to everyone as she made pencil drawings and noted down material for possible magazine articles, even though in her years of trying to be a writer she had only sold three such pieces. But the important thing was to keep learning. The ship had docked at Beira, the gateway to Rhodesia, before sailing on past the Comoros Islands and the Seychelles before dropping anchor at Dar es Salaam, the principal port of Tanganyika, where the Captain advised her to stay on board unless inoculated against Yellow Fever.

Over dinner that evening the female passengers at her table described the coconut-lined avenues interspersed with mango trees and how, despite its intense heat, Dar es Salaam had a sizeable population – just under four thousand Europeans. This way in which her fellow passengers regarded all black Africans as invisible, except as nuisance hawkers or curios to photograph, marred her voyage. But she ceased arguing this point when the ship entered the Zanzibar Channel because the coast of Kenya lay ahead, where Hazel promised to be waiting at Mombasa. Watching the Kenyan coastline emerge on the horizon, Eva felt like a pilgrim: a Magi too poor to bear myrrh or frankincense but coming to kneel in wonder before her beautiful granddaughter. Hazel had seemed bemused by Eva's indifference to the landscape when driving along the highway beyond Nairobi, past the Chyulu Hills and skirting the Nyiri Desert. But by then Eva had eyes for nothing except the car's milometer: its slowly revolving digits bringing her ever closer to meeting Alex.

Hazel's houseboy, Juma, stepped onto the veranda now, carrying water for Eva to wash with. He bowed and left the jug in her room, before slipping quietly back out. The red soil on Geoffrey's plantation was ideal for growing coffee but it found its way into everything, including the tap water that needed filtering. Hazel was already up at this early hour, working with inexhaustible energy as she pruned shrubs that grew to twice her height. From the veranda Eva gazed at her daughter's bronzed legs beneath red shorts and her blonde hair tied into a ponytail. Alex ran out from the nursery bedroom, still in her nightgown, to chase her pet mongoose across the courtyard, laughing at the racket that this most unlikely and rather dangerous pet made. The child was chased in turn by Lillian, her latest young English nanny. Hazel stopped working to laugh at Alex's giddiness and then, when she caught Eva's eye, she stared across at Eva as if subconsciously trying to convey something that perhaps not even Hazel fully understood. Eva's sense of *déjà vu* deepened; the more unsettling for being inexplicable. But during those few seconds it seemed as if Alex had become Hazel at three years old and this lush Kenyan plantation was transformed into Glanmire Wood – not as Glanmire had actually been but as it should have been in an idealised world where the Fitzgerald family had not lost their wealth and status. Then the moment was gone as Lillian scooped Alex up to get her dressed and Hazel turned back to her shrubs, leaving Eva uncertain if her daughter had also experienced this *déjà vu* which made Eva catch her breath.

Because it now seemed obvious what Hazel was trying to create in this forest of coffee trees, subdivided by dirt tracks and shaded by silver oaks laden with golden orange blossoms. In Hazel's mind this was the woodland home that the Fitzgeralds should have possessed, but with Glanmire's flaws airbrushed out in this reinvention. Here Hazel would never need to cradle Alex's bare soles to make them warm at night. Here the plentiful servants knew their place. Here bedrooms were not damp and the stables were stocked with good horseflesh. The cordite of political change might hang in the air, like in Ireland during Eva's childhood, but, even with Jomo Kenyatta transformed from political prisoner into budding statesman, there was no sense that the looming threat of independence could infiltrate these coffee groves where obedient workers sang. Eva wondered if perhaps this was why all settlers made the trek to Africa: to try and mould their childhood illusions about how life should be into an eggshell reality.

It felt strange being her daughter's guest. Their relationship had subtly changed during the crises over Freddie's will. Eva and Francis now deferred to Hazel as if *de facto* head of the family. On the surface Kenya seemed to suit Hazel: her hair looked more golden, her body oozing vitality. Here she finally possessed the money that was scarce during her childhood; a large home and servants and the confident gloss bestowed by affluence. Outwardly she seemed blissfully fulfilled, but occasionally Eva wondered if Hazel's resolute show of happiness was a weapon to keep questions about her marriage at bay. Behind Hazel's zest for life, signs lurked that Eva could not decode. She was disturbed by changes in Hazel's personality, like how Hazel not only shouted at servants for making trivial mistakes, but regarded such behaviour as normal. Because her husband was away on business, Eva had no idea how Geoffrey addressed his workers. But several of Hazel's friends – in the awful but aptly named Colonial Club, to which she brought Eva on most nights – did nothing except drink and complain about their servants' stupidity. They claimed that the local inhabitants had spent centuries living in idleness, never doing more than what was absolutely necessary, until white people came to create jobs and put structure on what they said was previously a wilderness.

Last night two club members suggested that Eva photograph the village schoolmaster and his pupils outside the hut that served as a school. But they mentioned the pupils in the same way that they mentioned exotic creatures which Eva should look out for on today's safari in the National Park, as if the villagers were curios to photograph rather than people to befriend. Hazel ridiculed her friends during the drive home, claiming that both women had spent too long in Africa. But Hazel was relieved that Eva hadn't told them how she had already visited the bar attendant and his family in their hut in the compound behind the club. This would seem like fraternising, although in truth – while the attendant was welcoming – she had felt an uncomfortable social barrier that was absent during her travels in Morocco, where her obvious poverty eroded any chasm of class. At times Kenya felt like the Ireland of her childhood, with people mindful of their place and anxious to maintain a respectful distance.

Hazel finished sawing the shrubs and stepped back to inspect her work, leaving severed branches on the lawn for the gardener to clear away. She shouted across to ask Eva if she was ready for breakfast. As if awaiting her summons, Juma appeared and set down a huge tray on the veranda. The nursery door opened and Alex ran out to jump into Hazel's arms to peer shyly at Eva. Hazel claimed that Alex had been talking for weeks in advance about her grandmother's visit. But the child remained reticent around Eva, shyly answering questions but never initiating contact. This was another reason why Hazel was arranging for the three of them to venture alone into the mountains, hoping that Alex might overcome her shyness in the excitement of the trip. Hazel's version of going alone, however, did not preclude Juma and another servant being sent ahead to prepare the hired lodge.

Eva could see that Hazel was a superb mother, spending hours every day with the child despite the presence of a governess. She was vigilant about what Alex ate and careful not to spoil her, although her toys were all imported from Hamley's in London. Hazel was also planning ahead, telling Eva that she was in touch with her former headmistress at Park House School in Dublin to ensure that a place was kept open if they decided to send Alex to Ireland to complete her education. She was also a good hostess, convinced that Eva needed pampering after years of relative poverty. The cook had been told to practice vegetarian recipes, despite his bewilderment that anyone rich enough to afford to eat meat would not do so. Hazel's comments were hilarious about the charred vegetarian dishes the cook served up, but Hazel could be droll about most things. Pouring Earl Grey tea for Eva now, Hazel made Alex giggle by impersonating the sounds of the animals who might prowl around their lodge tonight: snarling hyenas, baying jackals and the menacing cough of a leopard waiting to pounce. Hazel's cigarette darted across the table to accompany this last impersonation, but Alex only laughed louder, imbued with the same pluckiness Hazel possessed at that age. Eva tried to join in by making the noise of a cheetah but, instead of laughing, Alex stared back at her grandmother with a shy gaze which Eva longed to break through.

The child finished eating and sat on the step to examine the book of children's bible stories that Eva had brought her from London, lingering over an illustration of Noah leading a line of animals into his ark. When Eva read this story aloud last night, it was the first time she had felt the child tentatively respond to her. Juma crossed the veranda, carrying several pairs of Eva's shoes dosed in paraffin to kill any jiggers who might crawl in and lie in wait to bite a tiny hole in her toe and lay their eggs under her skin. Jiggers were one reason why Alex was not allowed to walk around barefoot. She had been bitten once, though Hazel said the child was intensely brave when they had needed to peel back the skin to cautiously remove the bag of eggs without it bursting open and infecting her entire toe. Juma began filling her plastic bathing pool and Alex ran inside to get changed, delighted with the prospect of splashing about.

'It will get her nice and cool,' Hazel remarked. 'It will be hot in the hills later. I've packed some gin to compensate for you missing your new friends at the club tonight.' This was said with a dry laugh. 'You don't much fancy the club, do you?'

'Some members are nice.'

'What you really mean, Mummy, is that some others are dreadful snobs, so pretentious that they'd make a stuffed bird laugh. But beggars can't be choosers, we're not spoiled for choice. I'd go insane if I stayed at home every night. You need to be able to talk and hear other people's voices, even if they bang on like church bells and only talk tommyrot. One problem over here is that it can be hard to know who is talking rubbish and who isn't.' Hazel reached for the imported English marmalade. 'Like the drunken Londoner who washed up at the club one evening last summer, with a desperate craving for Pimm's Iced Tea with liberal quantities of gin, and an even more desperate craving for white company.'

'Who was he?' Eva asked.

Hazel shrugged dismissively as she sipped her tea. 'I can't rightly say, except that he appeared to live in squalid digs in a backstreet hotel in Homa Bay on Lake Victoria. Like everything else about him, his name sounded fishy. He called himself Smythe, though if that was his real name then I'd say he definitely started life as a Smith in some East End terrace. The man sweated far too much to be trustworthy. I can't rightly remember how he wormed his way into our company, although out here you tolerate any newcomer for a while, just to hear a different voice. But once he bagged a seat at our table, he clung to us all evening like a drowning rat. Claimed to be a former Foreign Office official, all hush-hush, dispatched here by MI5 to keep an eye on the communist agitators who were secretly behind Jomo Kenyatta's election victory. Everyone present could see that Smythe or Smith had simply been pensioned off as an unreliable drunk – and, God knows, you need to be a seriously unreliable drunk to be let go by the British Foreign Office. I told him there are no communists behind Kenyatta, despite his dalliance with Moscow before he got the sniff of power. Kenyatta knows that Washington has a fatter cheque book, even if he doesn't bell it aloud in his inflammatory speeches. Besides, I assured him that Kenyatta didn't sound like a communist and I should know as my uncle was Ireland's most notorious communist before he disappeared to Moscow two years ago.'

'Let's hope that's where Art actually still is,' Eva said. 'He fell out with so many people that he left no forwarding address and cut his ties with all of us.'

'That's what I told the other drinkers,' Hazel said. 'I said that everyone else who flees abroad is running away from having to cope with debt, but Art is the only person who ever fled because he was terrified of dealing with wealth. This got a laugh but Smythe or Smith was all ears, demanding to know my uncle's surname. Then he said the most extraordinary thing.' Hazel looked around, ensuring that Juma or Alex's nanny were not within earshot, then leaned forward towards Eva. 'He claimed to recognise the Goold-Verschoyle surname. He maintained that in the 1930s your brother acted as a secret courier for the Soviets and was controlled in London by a Dutch communist named Peick. Peick used him as a mule to smuggle dispatches into Moscow from a Foreign Office cipher clerk named King who worked for the Soviets. Apparently King confessed to spying when the Soviet defector Walter Krivitsky fingered him.'

'Don't be silly.' Eva put down her cup and laughed. 'Art always stood out too much; he was unable to stop himself delivering a speech in praise of Stalin if he found three people gathered at a bus stop. They wouldn't have trusted him to courier anything in secret, because he was the most obvious candidate to be searched boarding any ship. Besides Art lived in Moscow throughout the 1930s.'

'I'm not referring to Art,' Hazel said. 'Smythe or Smith had never heard of Art. The Goold-Verschoyle whom the Foreign Office kept files on was Brendan. Smythe claimed that Brendan's Foreign Office file described him as a naïve enthusiast on a guilt trip. Communism was quite a fashionable craze for young men in the 1930s, a bit like the Charleston was for flappers in the 1920s. His Foreign Office file showed that Brendan was recruited by the Soviets as a sub-agent, travelling to Moscow by circuitous routes in the guise of paying innocuous visits to see his older brother there, but in reality he was transporting undeveloped rolls of film containing photographed top-secret government documents. They think he underwent wireless training on each trip to Moscow, not for use in Spain but in case his services were needed as a wireless operator in London. When not being used to courier documents, the Soviets ordered Brendan to have no contact with communist sympathisers in London. They wanted him anonymously holed up in some Battersea flat: a sleeper whose services they could activate when needed. But like you once said about Brendan's character, it wasn't in him to be duplicitous and hide away, leading a double life. He so much fell in love with whatever version of Moscow his handlers let him see on his visits to Art that he disobeyed orders and turned up in Moscow uninvited, demanding the chance to be given something practical to do to fight fascism. That's why the Soviets sent him to Spain, to keep him under their thumb and wait for him to betray the first sight of thinking for himself, after which they snuffed him out like he never existed. It explains why the British Foreign Office didn't lift a finger to assist your mother after he was abducted in Spain. Even if only a naïve enthusiast, if you live by the sword you generally die by it. I'm sorry to say that Smythe claimed there is no chance of Brendan still being alive.'

The only name familiar to Eva was Walter Krivitsky. Her mother had sent numerous unanswered letters to this former Soviet intelligence officer who defected to the West in 1937 after learning of Stalin's intention to purge him.

'So did Smythe think Brendan really was killed by a Nazi warplane attacking the prison train he was on?'

Hazel shook her head. 'He laughed and claimed that this is the classic Soviet response to inquiries about foreigners who vanished during the war – to deftly blame their deaths on the Nazis. Smythe says the Soviets rarely bother wasting a bullet on foreigners: they simply work them in camps till they die from starvation, malaria, typhus, frostbite or exhaustion. The only merciful thing is that the conditions are so brutal that most poor souls rarely suffer for long. He said that not only was Brendan most certainly dead, but that everyone who volunteered to travel from Moscow to Spain – even the most loyal of party members – were executed within months of returning home as heroes to receive medals. You see, anyone who volunteered for Spain was contaminated by having fraternised with foreigners, and Stalin was too paranoid to allow the possibility of any cross-contamination being caused by ordinary Muscovites encountering anyone with direct knowledge about the outside world and life in the West.'

'Maybe Smythe was telling lies.' Eva felt chilled despite the warm African sun. In her heart she knew Brendan was almost certainly dead, but didn't want to let go of the last trace of hope. 'You say he was a drunk and a fantasist.'

Hazel gave a shudder of distaste. 'He was pathetic, slimy and lonely: unable to stop talking now that he'd finally latched onto white voices willing to listen. He puffed up his self-importance as he switched from gin to whiskey. His voice got so slurred it was hard to know or care what he was saying. They keep a bedroom at the club for whites like that; let them sleep it off, then sober them up and make them aware that they've overstayed their welcome. Ordinarily I wouldn't believe a lost stray like him, but if he hadn't seen a file on Brendan how else could he possibly have heard of Brendan's surname?'

Eva closed her eyes. She tried to summon up Brendan's face – idealistic, good-natured and sincere in believing that he was helping to build a New Jerusalem. But it was Art's features that came to her, his furtive gaze whenever she probed too deeply into what he knew about his brother's fate. Could Art have inadvertently lured Brendan into danger simply by encouraging – or being encouraged to encourage – Brendan to apply for a visa to visit him in Moscow?

'Maybe I'll never know the truth about any of my family,' Eva said. 'Perhaps that's true of all families, but our white lies are bigger than most. I nursed your father to his death, yet I still never knew for sure what was going on in his mind. No more than I really know what's happening in your life.'

Hazel laughed, unsettled by the remark. 'Look around you. What is there to know?'

'Where's Geoffrey, for example? And are you truly happy?'

'Geoffrey is away on business. And why wouldn't I be happy? For the first time in my life I have everything I want. It may be remote here but it's close to paradise. Besides, I would categorically refuse to allow myself to be unhappy.' She paused to take a final sip of tea. 'I wanted to write to you about this Smythe man, but it's so unverifiable, like everything in the Soviet Union, that I thought it best to wait until we had a chance to talk. I hope it didn't upset you.'

Eva shook her head. 'The unsettling thing has been not knowing how to make sense of his fate.'

Hazel patted her hand. 'Nothing about your brothers ever made sense. Still, wouldn't it be funny if Art was an unimportant sideshow all along, despite a life spent making grandiose gestures. I mean he gave away every penny he inherited and lived like a monk on a vow of poverty, being jailed for preaching revolution to bemused turf cutters or organising tenant rent strikes in Dublin, all to prove his devotion to Stalin. Yet maybe the Soviets never cared a fig about him. Maybe they just let Art stay in Moscow in the 1930s to lure his kid brother into their net as the big catch: an unobtrusive, presentable young man able to courier documents, never drawing attention to himself.'

'Art must have meant something to them,' Eva said. 'Otherwise they wouldn't have finally granted his request to be allowed return to Moscow.'

Hazel shrugged non-committedly. 'Maybe they felt sorry for him, in the same way as you'd let an unfortunate farm dog whose day is gone back into the kitchen on a rainy night to lie near the fire. Or maybe he was doing more harm than good in London, getting in the way of a new generation of British communists who got sick of hearing Art praise Stalin at a time when Khrushchev wants everyone to forget the past.'

'I don't even have an address to reach him,' Eva said. 'It feels like I've lost two brothers in my shrinking family.'

'Your family isn't shrinking, it's growing.' Hazel watched her daughter run out from the nursery in her bathing suit to clamber into the plastic pool. 'Alex is really excited that you're here, but just too shy to show it.' Hazel rose, dabbing her mouth with a napkin. 'I wouldn't treat anything Smythe said as gospel. The trouble with Kenya is that it attracts misfits who reinvent their lives as they go along. He may have been a drunk ready to seize on any name that got him attention and another shot of whiskey. Trying to fathom Brendan's fate is like walking through a hall of trick mirrors and seeing a different reflection in each one. A time comes when you must put the past behind you and get on with the opportunities presented in the here and now.'

Eva nodded. 'Spit out a bit of life a little further on.'

Hazel looked at her, amused. 'You say the most peculiar things, Mummy.'

'When your father died, I fell into a deep malaise,' Eva confessed. 'I wasn't just mourning his passing but the life we might have had. For weeks I cried every night in my London flat, then one morning as I woke I was convinced I heard a voice say those words in my head: spit out a bit of life a little further on.'

Hazel smiled. Eva knew that she was humouring her. 'Whose voice?'

'I don't know. You're the practical one in the family. You tell me.'

Hazel laughed as Juma came to clear away the breakfast dishes. 'It was probably caused by indigestion, but there are worse mottos to live by. Let's get packed, Mummy, we have a bit of life to spit out a good bit further on today.'

Eva returned to her room but for a long time all she could do was sit silently on her bed, going over every word this Smythe stranger had said. But it was too enormous to take in: she would have to let it filter through her subconscious to the bedrock of her being before one day, months from now, its implications would be clear. By the time she re-emerged with her small suitcase, Juma and the cook had left to travel ahead in the jeep. Alex sat on the veranda examining the pictures in Eva's huge *Birdwatchers Guide to Africa*. Eva sat quietly beside her, deliberately not getting too close, knowing it was important to wait for the child to initiate a conversation. Finally her granddaughter looked up, after skimming the pages.

'Were all these birds in Noah's Ark?' the child asked.

'Yes,' Eva replied. She tried to show Alex how to stare through her binoculars, but once Hazel appeared the intimacy was broken and the girl ran possessively to her mother. As Alex climbed into the car, Eva deliberately placed the book beside the child on the back seat. The governess waved them off and the gardener raised a hand among the vegetable rows. They bumped down a dirt track through trees, then out onto the open road and past a cluster of round huts where Eva could hear children chant their lessons through the open schoolhouse door. The heat haze had settled in. After twenty minutes they drove along the town's main street: an ugly row of flat-roofed shops.

The flagpole above the main store was bereft of any standard: the white owner prudent enough not to fly the Union Jack but too stubborn to replace it with the incoming national flag. A black workman set down a wheelbarrow to greet a cyclist whose carrier was so overladen that the cardboard boxes tied up with rope rose up behind him higher than his head. Their loud voices contrasted with the silent white women who remained seated in dust-streaked vehicles outside the shops while their houseboys packed groceries into their car boots.

The town petered out into countryside. Hazel stared ahead, her foot on the accelerator as they picked up speed. Even in Ireland Hazel always drove too fast. Here the roads were straight, the distances greater and there was nobody to stop her. They sped past a child herding two long-horned cows, his bare feet reminding Eva of boys herding sheep in Donegal half a century ago. The miles quickly passed as they climbed towards the soaring bulk of Mount Elgon, its brown stone face rising out of the green uplands. The road narrowed to become a red murram track of loosely packed dirt. It was hot in the car but unwise to open any windows, due to swirling dust being thrown up. A roadblock marked the entrance to the National Park. The black man at the barrier shouted through the open doorway of a wooden hut and a white man emerged in shorts and an official hat. Hazel lowered her window.

'Mrs Llewellyn: a thing of beauty and a joy forever.' The man smiled, leaning forward so much into the car that his head and shoulders were almost pressed against Hazel.

'Major, behave.' Hazel's tone was amused, like a school mistress mildly reproaching an impish child.

'Your boy came through earlier. You have a visitor, I see?'

'My mother, Mrs Fitzgerald. An artist from Ireland.'

'Pleased to make your acquaintance, Mrs Fitzgerald.' The man reached across to shake Eva's hand, gaining an even closer proximity to Hazel's breasts while she eyed him with wry disdain. 'You do know the rules about guns in the National Park?'

As animals were protected, dogs and firearms were completely banned. Eva knew that Hazel kept a pistol for protection in the glove compartment.

'Of course.' Hazel smiled at him. 'I trust you don't intend on frisking me.'

The man chuckled. 'I wouldn't dare try.' His index finger tapped lightly on the glove compartment. 'We understand each other perfectly.' He glanced at Eva. 'Enjoy our game reserve, Mrs Fitzgerald. Her beauty will seduce you but like all beautiful females, there are hidden dangers if approached too close. Our native beasts, once roused, can kill with one swipe of a claw.'

Hazel released the handbrake so that the car jolted forward a few inches, causing the major to bang his head as he hastily withdrew. Hazel began winding up her window. 'You're incorrigible, Major.'

Alex spoke from the back seat as they sped away. 'I do like the Major.'

'We all do,' Hazel replied. 'Loneliness lures him down to the Colonial Club once a month. He gets sozzled drunk for three days, rather like those Irish priests who spend their holidays locked away in the residents' bar of the North Star Hotel opposite Amiens Street Station. The Major flirts unsuccessfully with every woman and is put to bed in the guest room when he passes out. Then when the shakes get so bad that he can barely hold a glass without spilling it in the mornings, the bar attendants sober him up with black coffee and drive him back to this hut. He was born in Bradford, I believe, very redbrick. I doubt if he was more than a sergeant in the army, but we indulge his white lie. Kenya attracts men who were disappointed by life or want to reinvent themselves in a new life.'

'What about you? Are you happy here?'

'What exactly is so wonderful about whatever you call happiness?' Hazel seemed more perplexed than annoyed by the question. 'It's the second time you've asked me today. I have everything I need. Do you think I could ever have been happy as a barrister's wife in "Dun Leary" or whatever they now call Kingstown, with the highlight of my year being the January sales in Pim's Department Store? You're always caught up in a battle to be happy, like it's the be-all and end-all of life. Have you ever thought that there are more important things in life than being happy?'

'Like what?'

'Respect, social mobility, knowing people look up to you. Our old maid Maureen could have stayed a serving girl in Mayo all her life or married a farm labourer with a damp cabin. Instead she took the chance to make a new life for herself in Boston. Her life is ten times better than that of the tuppence ha'penny snobs who looked down on her in Mayo because they owned a few boggy acres and had a priest a distant relative in the family. Ask anyone in Turlough about Maureen and they won't say she's happy – because who knows who is happy – but they'll say she made a good life for herself in America. But what can they say about you? You clean kitchens for people with only half your breeding. Last summer you went back to being a chambermaid on some dreary Channel island. What sort of life is that?'

Hazel drummed her fingers on the wheel, her tell-tale sign of agitation, which had been absent so far on Eva's visit.

'I met the most interesting people when working on Sark.'

'Old dowagers saying "You may make up my room now"? Hotel guests barely notice chambermaids let alone talk to them.'

'I wasn't referring to the guests. I'm referring to the young people I worked with: girls who could quote whole pages from Kahlil Gibran's *The Prophet*, long-haired boys who wrote poetry...'

'You always had a thing for young poets,' Hazel snapped. 'You never did get over Max, did you?'

'That's unfair,' Eva replied, hurt. 'There was nothing between Max and me to get over.'

Both went silent as they drove on, conscious of a familiar gulf between them. There was a deep love in their relationship, but, as Hazel once said, they rubbed each other up the wrong way. In recent years their letters had seemed to bring them closer, allowing them to rediscover some common ground – not least a sense of humour. Hazel's letters always made Eva laugh, but perhaps this was because she had heard Hazel's old voice when reading them, not this new accent which seemed modulated to blend in among the English accents at the club.

It was Hazel who broke the silence. 'That remark was unfair of me. Poor Max. Who'd have thought that he would enlist in the marines and get himself killed in Korea?'

I think he was trying to please his parents or prove something to them,' Eva said quietly. 'He could never have expected life to work out the way it did, but my own life hasn't worked out like I might have wanted either. Still, maybe that's what I find exciting: how – unlike poor Max – my life is still finding its own pattern. I'm almost sixty and have virtually no income. But I'm happy to take any job I can find if it allows me to continue to live my life on my own terms.'

'I know.' Hazel slowed to allow Eva view a herd of wildebeest who began to run at the sight of the dust cloud around the car. 'You can only be yourself. That's why I want you to stay here in Kenya and live with us and have enough space to be just that.'

'Live with you and Geoffrey?'

'Live as our neighbour, on our land. In a few years' time you'll be an old age pensioner. Ever since you left Daddy it's like you've been needing to make up for lost time, with your teaching and writing and bits and bobs. Maybe it's time to simply enjoy the years you have left. Why not live them in comfort in Kenya? I know the natives are declaring independence, but even if they run amuck outside our gates, inside our plantation we'll still have a good life because if the whites don't stay then who else will employ them? You need your own space but we can build you that space. A small house among the trees near the lake. Big windows to let in light if you want to try your hand at painting again. You keep saying that in the London winters your arthritis gets so bad you are barely able to hold a pencil. The sun would be good for you. You'd feel ten years younger. We'd build the house close enough that it would only be a ten-minute walk to dine with us whenever you like. And you would finally be somebody.'

'Who?'

'My mother. Alex's grandmother. Geoffrey's mother-in-law. People would treat you with respect. That's the thing with Africa, you can reinvent yourself as the person you always wanted to be. Francis can have your books shipped over from London. You'd be free to write your stories and meditate and study any half-baked philosopher you like. We have enough servants to look after you and the people at the club like you. They say you add a touch of spice. You'd shake us all up with your daft ideas. Evenings at the Colonial Club can be a laugh when you get to know people and you always loved a good laugh.' Hazel glanced back at Alex absorbed in examining the birdwatching book. 'And Alex would get to know you properly. If you leave in two weeks like planned, God knows what age Alex will be when you next see her. If you stay you would be good for her and Alex would be good for you.'

Eva stared out the windscreen at the lush grasslands, nourished by waters from the vast lake near the crest of Wagagai. She had come on today's trip to see dome-shaped nests of hamerkops and African jacanas. Hazel had promised a glimpse of orange-breasted sunbirds and, if they climbed high enough, the African fish eagle, whose piercing scream terrified the small creatures it hunted. Eva had hoped to find reedbuck and fleet-footed hartebeest and maybe warthogs and grivet monkeys, or even tortoises who were unlike their slow-witted Irish cousins because the sun gave them such ravenous sexual appetites that males could be heard grunting in the throes of passion a hundred yards away. In this sanctuary the animals were protected, but what Eva had not expected was an offer of sanctuary for herself, the chance to start a new life in daily contact with her granddaughter.

Had Hazel discussed this possibility with Geoffrey or was it a spur-of-the-moment suggestion? Perhaps Geoffrey's absence was causing the malaise Eva felt she occasionally glimpsed behind Hazel's resolute pluckiness, or did his absence reflect problems in their marriage? Eva liked Geoffrey, who seemed rooted in this red soil in a way that Hazel perhaps never could be. Geoffrey saw Kenya for what it was and not a chance to recreate a better version of a flawed childhood. But perhaps Hazel wasn't trying to compensate for the early years of penury in Glanmire Wood; perhaps Eva's *déjà vu* this morning stemmed from an old guilt at being unable to properly provide for her children back then.

'What would Geoffrey say if I stayed?' she asked.

'Geoffrey likes you and he likes me to be happy. If it made me happy, he would be pleased.'

Eva glanced into the rear seat. Alex caught her eye and smiled. Slowly Eva stretched out a finger, hoping the child might clasp it, but Alex looked away shyly. How wonderful it would be to watch this child discover more of life every day. Eva's renunciation of her class never contained the grandiose gestures of Art who had actually possessed wealth to turn his back on. Instead her life had been a gradual slippage into ever less gentile poverty. If she settled in Kenya the sun would slow the grip of arthritis that seemed to permanently distort her fingers. The only home awaiting her in London was a cramped attic flat which the landlord had promised to hold vacant for the two months she was away. If she returned it would be to counting pennies into gas metres, to smog in winter, frozen mornings when she would wake to see her breath turn to condensation in a freezing attic and nights when she would go to bed at seven o'clock to skimp on the need to heat the room. But amid that London greyness there was Francis and her instincts told her that one day soon Francis would need her. Her heart skipped a guilty beat at the thought of her son. Hazel swung down a dirt track hacked out through bushes and entered a small compound where Juma and the cook emerged from a wooden lodge to greet them. Juma smiled heartily as he held open the door for Eva.

'Welcome, Mrs Fitzgerald.'

Eva smiled and thanked him. Of all the Kenyans she had met so far, Juma was her favourite. She loved the proud way he had held his son when Eva visited the hut where his family lived. His wooden house was the type of home she would like if she stayed here, circular and low roofed without any foundations so that it seemed to be part of the earth. But it could not be among the villagers who would feel inhibited by her presence. She would need to be alone in the woods, midway between the villagers and Hazel's stone house. Eva watched the cook carry their cases into the lodge as Juma swung Alex around in circles, happily laughing along with the child's excited cries.

The sight of this black man and white child moving as one made Eva feel good, but then a memory returned of taking part in a tiny demonstration in Hyde Park to protest at the capture of the Black Pimpernel, the military commander of the *Umkhonto we Sizwe*, Nelson Mandela. It had rained hard that evening, the loudhailer so crackly that Eva could barely hear the speeches as some passers-by shouted that Mandela deserved all he was going to get for being a saboteur. She had closely followed his trial and the trial of other ANC leaders seized in Rivonia. But the Rivonia trial was one of numerous topics not discussed at the Colonial Club, with Hazel keen that Eva never mention her protest activities in London because she claimed that the drinkers would mock her lack of understanding of Africa.

In her heart Eva knew she did not belong among the privileged caste in that club and yet could never blend in among the black locals, who were courteous but perturbed by her attempts at solidarity. Perhaps she was destined to forever remain an outsider, no matter what class she mixed with. But at least amid London's poverty and smog, fellow misfits existed who had slipped free of definitions. Francis had never visited Hazel, possibly because Kenya was too dangerous a place in which to be a homosexual. This was why Eva loved the melting pot of Tangiers: lonely old Englishmen openly falling in love with youths who indulged them while subtly bleeding them dry. It wasn't always nice to see but at least what happened in Tangiers occurred in the open. Kenya was no such melting pot. People drank here to excess, gossiping about rumoured scandals to ward off boredom. But they clung to a rigid social order, an exaggerated version of the Britain they had left. If she stayed, Eva would want for nothing and grow to know her granddaughter, but she could never be happy. The cry of a wild beast startled her. Juma noticed this and laughed.

'Wait till dark,' he said. 'The whole park is alive then. The big beasts even drown out the cicada.'

Hazel called her into the lodge where tea was being poured, laced with gin. Hazel took a sip, then added more alcohol.

'What was that recipe for a balanced life you sent me in a letter last year?'

Eva tried to recall the exact words that had come to her upon waking one morning:

'*A little bit of kindness,*
A little bit of gin,
A little bit of tolerance,
A little bit of sin.'

Hazel laughed. 'The little bit of gin was what Esther O'Mahony's tea up in the Wicklow Mountains always lacked.'

They drank in silence for a moment, watching Alex through the open doorway as she happily raced around in the dust. Then Eva spoke quietly.

'I can't stay here, Hazel. I'd never fit in.'

'And you fit in in London, do you?'

'London is different.'

'Because Francis is there.'

'It's not like that.'

'Don't hide it, Mummy. He was always your favourite.' Hazel's unperturbed tone was matter of fact.

'Maybe Francis needs me in ways you never will. And maybe something in me needs to be needed. I worry for the boy.'

'Francis is no longer a boy, Mummy. He has his own life.'

'Francis laughs a lot,' Eva said. 'But he hurts too easily and he's so honest that he leaves himself open to being hurt. There's no guile in him, no badness, no cynical protective coating.'

'And where's your protective coating?' Hazel asked. 'I worry for you, Mummy. What protection do you have from being hurt or going hungry or getting sick? Your situation is ten times more vulnerable than his.'

Eva nodded, unable to deny Hazel's logic. 'That's true. I'm naïve and foolish in some ways and that means at times I get hurt. But it's easier to be the one getting hurt than to see someone you love being hurt. Living hand to mouth these past few years has not been easy, but I only truly suffer when I watch Francis suffer. I need to give him space to make his own mistakes, but to also be there to pick the pieces up when it inevitably falls apart. Francis is wondrously happy, but he doesn't always realise how he has such a thin grip on happiness that he's only clinging to it by his fingertips.'

Hazel topped up their tea with more gin, then reached across to touch her mother's hand.

'You always worry too much about him, Mummy. His landscaping business is thriving and his lover is rich. Take it from me, there are no poor orthopaedic surgeons in Harley Street. If I'm honest I always found Francis's special friends rather drippy, but Jonathan is quite the Bobby Dazzler. Francis and he are perfect together and they're happy.'

Eva took a sip from her cup, feeling the additional alcohol go to her head. 'Happiness is fragile when disgrace is always just a phone call to the police away. His friend Alan tells me things that Francis would never admit to. Francis's workman Peter also drops hints. There are cracks in his relationship with Jonathan. Francis isn't as young looking as he once was and patrician men like Jonathan go for youth. I didn't like it when Jonathan persuaded Francis to give up his flat and move in with him, although officially Francis is just renting Jonathan's basement, with Jonathan so frightened of scandal he even has a different number plate on the basement door. Jonathan shares the master bedroom with Francis, but I've slept over in that basement and heard them rowing at night.'

Hazel shrugged. 'Rows are part of marriage. You know that. I know it and so does Francis, even if what he has can hardly be called a marriage.'

'That's the problem,' Eva said. 'What security has he? If Jonathan was knocked down by a bus, would his family even welcome Francis to the funeral in Wales? With a married couple all the social pressure is on them to stay together. That's why your father and I stuck it out so long. But with two men living together the social pressure is the opposite, because if the relationship breaks up life becomes safer, with less risk of exposure. Francis should never have given up his own flat. He's left himself very vulnerable.'

Hazel studied her with a brutally frank gaze.

'Maybe everything isn't all sweetness and light between him and Jonathan,' she said. 'Few marriages stay sweetness and light forever. But be honest: if Francis weren't in London, would you stay here?'

Eva gazed back at her and said quietly. 'I've asked you before and I'll ask you again: are you happy here?'

'Don't I look happy? I have everything I ever wanted.'

'That's not the same thing.'

Hazel looked away for a moment. 'If you did stay, we'd fight all the time, wouldn't we? Little differences would grow into big ones. I love you, Mummy, and I know you love me, but maybe we love each other best at a distance. But I'd have loved for Alex to get to know you. You would be good for her.'

Eva reached across to rest her fingers lightly on Hazel's hand. 'And I promise you I'll be there for her if you ever decide to send her to boarding school in Dublin. I know it's years away but I'll move back to Ireland and find a flat near Park House School so that she'll have family to visit. And Francis will be a short boat trip away in London. We'll bring her down to camp out in Glanmire House and tell her ghost stories while baking potatoes in tinfoil in the fire. If you do decide to send her at any age then I promise I'll be there.'

Hazel gripped her fingers momentarily. 'I know you will. Tiny undauntable you. Last year Valerie O'Mahony wrote to say that she was visiting London when she met you by chance making your way home from a Ban the Bomb march. A counter protestor must have struck you with a flour bomb because you were coated in white from head to toe, leaving a trail of flour behind you as you walked. Valerie wrote that you were so excited to meet her and hear her news that you never once mentioned how you had obviously been flour bombed half an hour earlier, as if your appearance wasn't worth commenting on because you were too caught up in being alive in that moment. Since then it's how I see you in my mind: a tiny woman covered in flour who'd walk through flames for what you believe in.'

Eva smiled at the memory. 'He was such a funny little man who threw it. Very respectable: a dentist or accountant by the look of his suit. I saw him step from the crowd watching the march and I badly wanted to shout a warning, but there wasn't time. Not a warning to the marchers beside me but to the man himself, because I could tell he'd obviously never made a flour bomb before and hadn't sealed the top of the package. The flour began to spill out as soon as he raised his hand over his head and by the time he threw it he'd poured more flour over himself than landed on me. I wasn't hurt and all I could do was laugh at the abject terror on his face. He wasn't scared of the marchers or the police, but he'd every tell-tale sign of being henpecked. I knew he was terrified of having to go home and face his wife in his ruined suit.'

Hazel laughed. 'That's you in a nutshell, more concerned for him than yourself. It would make a perfect story for BBC's

Woman's Hour. I've kept all your letters, especially the ones from Morocco. You have a knack with words. Keep writing, Mummy, and success is bound to come.'

'I doubt it somehow. All I have is a folder of rejection slips under my bed in London.'

'Never say never. I have a little present, just to show you that it's never too late to publish your first book.' Hazel rose and called in Alex from outside. A delicious smell came from the kitchen, where Eva knew that the cook – convinced Eva would starve without meat – had gone to great lengths to find unusual fruits for her. Hazel whispered an instruction and the child rummaged in a suitcase to produce a small gift-wrapped present.

'Seeing as you're sixty next month,' Hazel said, 'here's a gift from Alex to start the celebrations. Go on, Alex, give it to Grandmamma.'

Shyly the child placed the gift in Eva's hands and stepped back, wanting to share in the delight of opening it.

'It's to show that dreams are worth pursuing and that you must never give up on your dream of writing a book,' Hazel said. 'This is just published. I remember Mr MacManus talking non-stop about plans to write it when I was barely older than Alex and he used to bring his aunt over for dinner. It's hardly my cup of tea, but I ordered a copy from London. I daresay it barely made a dent there but it's probably the talk of Mayo.'

Eva asked Alex to open it and the child tore at the paper as excitedly as if the gift were for her. Inside was a book entitled *The Middle Kingdom*: a study of supernatural occurrences in Mayo, which Eva's old neighbour from Killeaden House, Dermot MacManus, had indeed talked about writing for decades. Eva had a vivid recollection of Dermot and his aunt Lottie coming to dinner in Glanmire House and Freddie cautioning Dermot with a laugh against putting the story of the ghost in the basement at Glanmire into it. Who could have imagined that this gentle old man, gassed in the First World War and regarded by some neighbours as slightly touched, would finally produce his small magnum opus? Eva scanned the two sections of black-and-white photographs sewn into the book. Here was Killeaden House, with the fairy thorn outside it that Dermot's grandfather had risked moving a hundred years ago. And here was the demon bush that Dermot once showed her in a low-lying field beyond Kiltimagh – two thorn trees and a bourtree mixed inextricably together, which he had claimed was guarded by malevolent spirits who waylaid travellers at night on that desolate road. Here too was a photo of his Aunt Lottie, exactly as Eva remembered her, looking Victorian and stern in her donkey cart. Dermot had surely risked ridicule by putting his name to these stories about ghostly black dogs and hostile spirits, but Eva admired him for having the courage to stand by his beliefs.

'He loaned me a horse when I was young, after my own horse went lame and I was desperate to ride in a show,' Hazel said, as if this equine gesture outweighed any eccentricity. 'I've never forgotten that. Or the midsummer eves when he'd light fires to appease the spirits in the woods. Everything in his book is tommyrot of course, but I'm delighted he finally has it in print. So you see, Mummy: you're never too late or too old.'

'Isn't it exciting?' Eva exclaimed. 'I'm so happy to have a copy.'

'Happiness is a rare gift,' Hazel replied quietly. 'Grasp it when you can.' Eva glanced up, but her daughter's cryptic smile was as close an answer as she was going to get to her earlier question. The cook called Hazel into the kitchen and Eva momentarily forgot about Alex as she turned the pages, absorbed in an account of the malignant spirit rumoured to haunt the stables at Killeaden House. After a few moments she was surprised to feel tiny fingers tentatively touching her hand. Eva looked down.

'Show me the pictures,' Alex said. 'Show me Ireland.'

The child clambered carefully onto Eva's knee and settled down, eager to glimpse her mother's childhood country. If Kenya was exotic for Eva, then these black-and-white photographs of roads winding across bogs were equally mysterious to the child. Alex asked questions but Eva barely heard her own replies. Because of all the sights and sensations Eva had experienced on this trip, none could compare with the balm of feeling her granddaughter nestle on her lap, the fragrance of Alex's hair as Eva's face brushed against it and Alex's excited breath when she laughed. In two weeks' time Eva would return to London, but for now simply cradling Alex in her lap felt like being made complete again, as if Eva were being cured of an ache she had borne for so long that she had ceased to notice it. Outside in the sudden darkness that descended there were bird cries she recognised and others she had never heard before. But they came from a faraway different world. Nothing else existed beyond this wicker chair where Eva cradled this gift who had come unbidden to her. The kitchen door opened and she sensed Hazel watching them. A moment later Eva felt her daughter's hand touch her shoulder, leaning over as if to glance at the pictures, but really just wanting to be part of this moment: three generations finally at ease with each other, all so utterly still that they seemed transfixed into precious stone.

Chapter Nine

A View from the Rooftops

London, 1st September 1966

There were times afterwards when, in her most bitter thoughts, Eva suspected that Jonathan might have initially phoned the police himself that night. Of course this was inconceivable: no Harley Street orthopaedic surgeon wanted to draw attention to his secret life, led away from the gaze of respectable patients. Jonathan's practice could be destroyed if his name was dragged through the newspapers. The British upper classes never could abide fuss and therefore he would have wanted no kerfuffle. Unfortunately it was becoming increasingly clear that Jonathan also no longer wanted her son.

Before the phone call to her came that night, Eva had kept trying to persuade herself to attempt to get some sleep or at least drape a coat over her shoulders for warmth if she intended to keep agitatedly pacing about in her tiny attic flat in Notting Hill. September in London felt cold after Morocco, where she had survived for most of the past year by finding occasional work in her old haunts and living in cheap hostels – a sixty-two-year-old curio happily mixing with hordes of young Westerners obsessed with travelling to Marrakech, as if enlightenment was a parcel they could collect poste restante if they finally arrived at the right post office queue in a crowded bazaar there.

But two months ago, she spent almost all her savings on returning home to London because she sensed – from words left unsaid in Francis's letters – that her son was in distress. Not that London actually was her home: Eva had no sense of having any particular home anymore. But London was where she belonged because someone here whom she loved needed her help.

Eva paused beside the attic window to peer down at the street where a young couple passed in the dark, indistinguishable from each other in their Afghan coats and long hair. Music came from the partitioned rooms beneath her: a jarring racket of zithers, Indian bells, harmonicas and mindless percussion. London throbbed with youthful anthems. At two a.m. this musical din was invariably replaced by faint sounds of slightly drugged young voices teasing and cajoling each other and then intimate whispers as bodies conjoined. Eva felt no envy towards the young neighbours in the flats below her, but their carefree vitality increased her sense of dread: not because their sexual freedom made Eva feel old, but because they made Francis – at thirty-eight – appear old in comparison.

More importantly she also knew that Francis appeared old to his rich older lover. Jonathan had recently celebrated his fiftieth birthday and the new fad being discussed in magazines – the midlife crisis – was not solely confined to heterosexual men. Not that Jonathan went out of his way to look young – what had first attracted Francis to him was his distinguished air. While the young people in these bedsits exuded youthfulness, Jonathan had looked older than his years from the first night Eva glimpsed him, eight years ago, at a small dinner party thrown by Francis in his flat during one of Eva's returns from her travels.

Eva still remembered the joy Francis had taken in preparing that elaborate, unstinting meal, growing ever more animated when he confided in her how someone posh and special was coming to dinner; someone whom, Francis hoped, also regarded him as special. Eight years ago she had felt joy for her son, but also anxiety lest he got hurt again. When Eva kissed him for luck, saying that she hoped he had finally found the right man, Francis only laughed, claiming that she made him sound like a scarlet woman.

These days perhaps it was the young occupants of the flats beneath her who thought that Eva was a scarlet woman, because just now she was roused from her thoughts by another late-night knock on her door. The Liverpool girl who lived in a ground-floor flat stood there, saying that once again a man wanted her on the phone. Eva followed this girl, dressed in hipster pants and low-heeled shoes, down the long flights of stairs, trying not to run. This was why she hadn't gone to bed. Subconsciously she'd been waiting for the communal pay phone in the hall to ring, await-ing yet another summons – she never visited Jonathan's house uninvited anymore. The tension between Francis and Jonathan had reached such a pitch that Eva was terrified in case one night soon the call to rescue her son might come too late.

'It's simply impossible,' Jonathan said as soon as Eva picked up the receiver. 'Your son is acting impossible; this whole situation is impossible. It's half eleven at night and he's up on my rooftop, threatening to throw himself off. I live in a respectable district. He listens to you, Eva. You simply must talk sense into him.'

The phone went dead at the same moment as the timer-switch on the light plopped out, leaving Eva standing alone in the dark hallway. She suspected that the Liverpool girl was listening behind her door. All the young tenants were curious about what someone old enough to be their grandmother was doing dwelling among them. What she was doing was trying to live her life and give Francis enough space to live his without him feeling abandoned. What she was doing now was running down the front steps, unsure if she had even remembered to lock her attic flat. Eva frantically ran towards the Tube station, not caring what passers-by thought. She was too anxious to wait for the slow lift when the train reached the old-fashioned small station near Jonathan's house, but climbed the steep emergency stairs instead, where an icy wind blew around every bend. She had to lean against the postbox at the corner of Jonathan's street to catch her breath, not wanting to look panicked when she arrived.

This became especially important when she saw a panda car pull up outside Jonathan's house. For a moment she thought that Jonathan had risked his cover by calling the police. This would have been so out of character that Eva quickly guessed that a neighbour must have witnessed a confrontation or heard voices raised. Jonathan's flat roof was overlooked by several houses. The prying resident who had summoned the police was probably watching this scene unfold as two police officers climbed the steep steps to knock at Jonathan's imposing oak door.

Taking a deep breath Eva approached the house. Part of her wondered if it might be prudent to hold back for fear of creating a further scene. But her overriding instinct was to rush forward, knowing that her son was in danger. Since returning from Morocco to witness this growing estrangement, she had been waiting for such a crisis to occur. Jonathan opened his front door as she reached the house. He looked so flustered by the presence of the policemen that initially he didn't notice her loitering at the base of the steps.

'We've had a complaint, sir.' The older policeman carefully placed one foot in the doorway. 'A public order disturbance. Reports of a gentleman threatening to throw himself off a roof.'

'My elderly neighbours have a propensity for exaggeration. I assure you, Constable, there is nothing to be concerned about.'

Jonathan possessed the clipped accent of someone who might be related to a figure high up in the police force, or maybe even a government minister. The older officer withdrew his foot, with the servility many English people of his generation displayed when confronted by an accent oozing authority. However, having knocked at the door, he would need to log a report back at the station and so a token investigation was required. The policeman glanced down at Eva, convinced she was merely an inquisitive passer-by: nobody in threadbare clothes could possibly have business in such a house. 'Still and all, sir,' he said politely, 'it might be wiser if we stepped inside, away from prying eyes.'

Jonathan had sufficiently composed himself to adopt an air of weary nonchalance. 'Like I say, there's no need, but if you insist.' He glanced at Eva, possibly regretting having phoned her. 'It would be better if you come inside so. All three of you.'

The younger policeman had not yet uttered a word. At first Eva thought he was cowed by such obvious wealth and was taking his cue from his older colleague. But when they entered the hallway and he coldly surveyed the modernist paintings and exotic vases on display, she sensed there was nothing servile about him.

'Now what exactly do you wish to see?' Jonathan inquired.

'There is, I believe, another gentleman in the house,' the older policeman said.

'That is correct.' Jonathan nodded. 'An Irish gentleman.'

'Might we speak to him, sir?'

'If you insist. But listen here, the poor chap is on medication. I'm a doctor. I know about these things. The chap has mood swings, a history of depression. It's such a long story that I wouldn't know where to start.'

The younger policeman finally spoke. 'If this poor geezer is so unhinged, governor, you might start by taking us up onto the roof to ensure that he hasn't topped himself already.'

His deliberately insolent tone reminded Eva of friends of Art whom she had met years ago: dogmatists who analytically categorized everyone they met in ideological terms. Art's comrades had never engaged in class warfare from behind a police uniform but – unlike his older colleague – this policeman came from an England with no intention of ever again being told to know its place.

'I hardly consider that necessary,' Jonathan protested, but the dismissive use of the term 'governor' obviously rattled him. One single word had changed the dynamic in the hallway.

'The shortest way up is the stairs, I suppose.'

The older policeman went to speak but his colleague was already ascending the staircase. Jonathan followed, still protesting against the intrusion on his privacy. The older policeman made way for Eva, confused by her presence. Eva prayed that the master bedroom door was closed. If this door was ajar, revealing the vast double bed and explicit homoerotic prints on the wall, a court appearance and scandal might be one step closer. It was a room she never liked to enter. Thankfully this door was closed and the décor on the landing merely suggested the discreet respectability of old money. Eva kept hoping that Francis would appear from another room, convinced that Jonathan would not leave him alone on the roof. However, not only was there no sign of Francis, but no sense of his existence in this house. She was perturbed to spy two empty picture hooks where Mayo landscapes owned by Francis previously hung.

Eva hurried on after the three men who were climbing the remaining steps up to a French door that opened out onto the small roof garden. At first she thought Francis was gone: there seemed to be no sign of anyone. But then she saw him hunched up near the chimney stacks. His gaze reminded Eva of a hare hunted by hounds who had found a last den to crouch in but knew it offered no protection from the baying dogs closing in. She wanted to run to him, but for his sake she need to remain calm.

'You see, Constable,' Jonathan said, 'the gentleman is safe and sound. Mr Fitzgerald, can you assure my callers that there is no problem here.'

'Are you the geezer disturbing the peace by threatening to jump?' the younger officer asked.

'Listen here, Constable, I'm not sure I like your tone,' Jonathan intervened.

'I wasn't addressing you, governor.' The officer glanced back at Jonathan. 'Then again, I'm not sure who I'm addressing. What exactly is your relationship to this man and what is he doing here?'

'That strikes me as a deeply impertinent question.'

'It strikes me as deeply pertinent.'

'Look here, this is a private house.'

'And I'm investigating a public disturbance. Two telephone callers claimed they heard a man threatening to jump. Telling us that this man is mentally deranged doesn't explain who he is and exactly what's going on.'

'Tell him who I am, Jonathan.' Francis's voice was so faint that Eva could barely hear him. 'I bet he was a schoolyard bully and his uniform has given him an excuse to never stop being one. I'm sick of being scared of bullies and hiding behind lies. I've crossed paths with this policeman a hundred times before.'

'I hardly think so.' The young officer bristled. 'I'm particular about the company I keep.'

'Then how come I know your eyes so well?'

'Because you've been drinking, sir. I can smell it from here.'

Eva noticed how he now addressed Francis as 'sir'. Like most bullies, he felt disconcerted when challenged.

'All bullies share the same eyes,' Francis said. 'You want me to be scared of you, but I'm not scared anymore. I've nothing left to lose. I know who I am and I'm not ashamed of it.'

'Be careful what you say, sir.' This time the older policeman addressed Francis in a gentle, almost conspiratorial tone. He turned to his companion. 'What's happening here isn't really our concern, Fred. We came to investigate a disturbance and any disturbance is obviously over.'

The younger man ignored his colleague and Eva sensed the animosity between the two policemen. 'You still haven't explained what a drunken Paddy is doing in your house,' he told Jonathan coldly, 'or your relationship with him.'

Jonathan glanced at Francis, whose eyes contained a defiant plea. Eva wanted to hold Francis in her arms, but the time had passed when she could shield him from the world. Jonathan stared at the ground. When he looked up, Eva saw how fearful and tired he was. The newspapers were full of speculation about homosexuality being decriminalised soon and in discreet but influential circles Jonathan was actively campaigning for this. But until the legal change happened, Jonathan was scared of losing his status, of no longer being able to exist in two distinct worlds and fearful too of tabloid newspapers spitefully creating a scandal out of just such a public row as this, which might set back the campaign for decriminalisation. However it wasn't the fear in his eyes that perturbed Eva, it was the tiredness: what he had grown most tired of was her son.

'Mr Fitzgerald happens to be my lodger,' Jonathan said. 'For some time he has been renting my basement flat, from where he runs a garden-design business. Unfortunately his clients seem slow to settle their bills. I have been patient about unpaid rent for months because I know he is presently unwell and addicted to pills for his nerves. But tonight his behaviour became deranged after I gave him notice of eviction. I mean, it is an impossible situation.' He looked at Eva. 'Anyone can see it. From now on the matter is in the hands of my solicitor, who will initiate legal proceedings unless he is gone within a fortnight. My patience is exhausted. I'm exhausted. I need to start again.'

There was silence after Jonathan finished speaking. Even the distant late night traffic seemed to have stopped moving. Everything was utterly still, as if the whole world was weighing up the enormity of this lie.

'Your lodger?' the young policeman asked finally. 'Are you not a bit rich to take in lodgers?'

'The sad fact, Constable, is one can never be too rich.' Jonathan glanced at Francis. 'Or too young.'

'And who is this woman who followed us in from outside?'

'My cleaner. She does the kitchen and reception rooms at night. You gentlemen are delaying her. If you would take your leave she could begin her work.'

'Why not do it with a kiss?' Francis's voice was barely above a whisper, yet everyone heard it. Eva felt that disapproving neighbours who had waited their moment to summon the police heard this whisper; surely all of London heard her son's words.

'We're just leaving, sir.' The older policeman glared at his young colleague, warning him not to intervene. Eva knew that he intended taking no further action, not out of awe at Jonathan's accent but out of pity for her son. 'I'm sure I didn't hear what you just said.'

Francis's eyes held no guile, merely the rawest hurt. 'I said if someone plays Judas they should betray their lover properly with a Judas kiss.'

Jonathan shook his head, addressing the policemen. 'You see? The situation is impossible, my tenant must go.' He turned to face Eva, unable to meet Francis's gaze. Jonathan, who loved being in control, had been set a test of love and courage which he had failed. 'I will show these gentlemen out, Eva. You might escort Mr Fitzgerald down to the basement flat that he has a fortnight to vacate.'

Jonathan led the policemen through the French door, the younger officer glancing back at Francis with contempt, disappointed that his older colleague had thwarted his questioning. Only when the door closed did Eva walk towards her son. Francis was so downcast that she needed to take his face in her hands and tilt it upward to stare into his eyes.

'What do I do now, Mummy?' he asked quietly.

'Start again.'

'What if I'm simply too old to start again?'

'You're never too old. Look at me. All I've really done for the past twenty years is to restart my life over and over. Let's get you downstairs.'

Francis looked so weary that he needed to lean on her. Eva was shocked at how thin he had grown, at how she was able to bear his weight despite being so hallowed out by exhaustion that her body felt as if sculpted from brittle glass.

Chapter Ten

The Basement

London, 1st to 14th September 1966

Eva wanted to stay with Francis after the policemen left, bedding down on his small Italian mohair sofa. But she knew that, for now at least, the crisis was passed and, as much as he needed her, Francis also needed space to be alone. He urged his mother to take a taxi home because the Tube had stopped running by now, begging her to take the price of the taxi fare from the small pile of money on his bedside table. To appease him she said that she had more than enough money for a taxi, although in truth she barely had money for food – a fact that, as always, she was careful to shield from him. Before leaving she persuaded Francis to lie down on his bed, though he swore he would never be able to sleep. But having nursed him through so many heartaches, at times Eva knew him better than he knew himself. He was so emotionally and physically shattered that he would fall asleep, despite himself, before she reached the corner of the street.

Tonight it was Eva who wouldn't sleep, even after completing her long walk home. In Morocco she learnt techniques of transcendental meditation from placid elderly men in shabby sunlit rooms. But such serenity was easy in Morocco when she felt liberated from the burden of being a mother. No mental training could quell her anxieties tonight. These anxieties fitted around her like a second skin. She had suffered through every breakup in Francis's life, going back to when he was a boy who had felt every emotion with absolute intensity; radiantly happy at the simplest things and devastated whenever life snatched such happiness away. These heartaches stretched back to his first relationship with his wartime tutor, Harry Bennett. Harry never rejected Francis but their parting was no less difficult when the young officer was ordered to end his convalescence and re-join his regiment, with Francis's newfound confidence crushed and Eva being left to try and pick up the pieces of his shattered happiness

Twenty-two years later, she was still trying to do the same thing. She finally reached her attic flat in Notting Hill at four a.m. The house was silent, save for the timer light switch on each floor going out with a soft plop seconds after she reached the next flight of stairs. Her flat was cold but she hadn't money to waste on the small gas heater, so she got into bed fully clothed with two blankets and an old coat over her.

Looking around her tiny flat Eva remembered how, in 1950 when she helped Francis to clear out his possessions from Colville's love nest, all he owned had fitted into a suitcase and two boxes, easily shifted to Frankfort Avenue by taxi. Eva no longer possessed a home beyond this attic and it would take a removal van to shift everything Francis now owned. Where would he go now when forced to leave Jonathan's basement? Francis was not short of friends, but a dozen tea chests and a broken heart could strain any friendship.

There was Peter – the labourer whom Francis employed. Francis was close to Peter and his wife Pauline, but they barely had room in their tiny house, especially with their twins now attending school. Francis was also too proud to let Pauline see him in this state. After fretting over this problem for an hour, Eva decided that Francis would almost definitely have to stay for a time with Alan, his old Dublin school friend who lived alone in a large basement flat. Francis and Alan had never been in a romantic relationship together and this was one thing that Eva noticed about the homosexual world: the men whom you turned to in times of most need were those with whom you had no unresolved history of physical intimacy. Resolving this problem defused some of Eva's anxiety because she remembered nothing else until she woke in late morning, dog-tired, but surprised and relieved that she had actually slept.

Francis was still asleep when she rushed over to check on him. He was groggy from sleeping tablets but looked less distressed than the previous night on the roof, when he'd been drinking on top of whatever medication he was taking.

She knew that her daily task for the next fortnight would be to visit this basement to wake Francis, being careful to try and avoid meeting Jonathan leaving by the front steps. She would need to get Francis sufficiently motivated to shave and face the complex financial problems afflicting his floundering business. Eva didn't care if the business collapsed, but hoped that his sense of responsibility towards Peter would give Francis something to focus on. He might have lost the will to be concerned for himself, but Eva urged him to stay strong for Peter's young family.

As the fortnight went on, rousing him became increasingly difficult. Francis needed such a cocktail of sleeping tablets and tranquillisers to fall asleep that he found it impossible to wake at any normal hour. His despondency increased when a severely worded letter arrived from Jonathan's solicitor threatening legal action if Francis had not vacated the basement within the stipulated two weeks. Eva did not know how to rouse his spirits, but midway through the second week – with that deadline looming – Francis's mood seemed to lift or at least his actions gained a renewed sense of purpose. Each morning when she arrived she saw further evidence of him at least starting to sort through clothes, books and numerous other possessions. One morning she saw he had unlocked the cupboard where he stored his Irish Genealogical Research Society files and was sorting these papers into piles neatly bound up with twine. Eva wasn't sure how much of this furniture he owned, but with nowhere to store it beyond the small yard used for his gardening business, he would be forced to leave most of it behind. Certainly there was no room for it in Alan's basement flat. She decided to broach the subject.

'It is Alan you're thinking of staying with?'

'He has offered to take me in. He's a good man, Alan.'

'He was always my favourite of your friends. There's something very genuine about Alan.'

Francis nodded. 'That's the irony of love, isn't it? Only opposites attract.'

Eva smiled and took his hand. 'Then there's no fear of you and Alan ever falling in love: you're both as gentle as each other.'

He squeezed her hand softly. 'Falling in love just now isn't part of the plan.'

He said no more and she didn't ask. Nor did she ask if he had spoken to Jonathan, who seemed to be avoiding his own house: no sign of lights on upstairs on any evening when Eva visited. Francis was making slow progress in moving out but at least he was making a start. Even if it took a few days longer than the solicitor's letter stipulated, she could not believe that Jonathan would change the locks. Despite the vehemence of their breakup, the surgeon surely still felt something for her son and besides, Jonathan would want to avoid risking a second public scene by calling in bailiffs when the fortnight's notice expired. She was shocked, therefore, when after ten days, a second and even more severely worded registered letter arrived from the solicitor, warning of the legal consequences of remaining on the premises after the date stated. Francis tried to shrug it off, joking grimly that strong-arm tactics would not make him work any faster, although Eva saw how shaken he was by the impersonal nature of these bullying threats.

She would get him through this because she was well practised in the politics of heartache. But this did not prevent her from constantly fretting throughout the fortnight. On no night did she sleep for more than half an hour at a time on the bed or the single armchair in her flat. Eva should have been exhausted, but her body had entered a state beyond exhaustion where sleep or food no longer seemed necessary. On the day before Francis's two weeks' notice expired, she washed and dressed at dawn. It was six Tube stops to Jonathan's house, but Eva automatically walked, not just because she needed to save every penny, but because her legs seemed to move of their own accord, propelled forward by the adrenaline of agitation and by her all-consuming love. She longed to be with her son but also wanted to let him sleep: sleep being the only time when he seemed to be at peace.

At eight forty-five she let herself into the basement with her spare key. The air was stale as she entered the kitchenette to boil the kettle. She discreetly glanced into Francis's bedroom, hoping against hope to glimpse a body entwined with his. Not Jonathan: she knew a reconciliation was impossible, but she would have welcomed the sight of any man there, even that rough type who always wanted to fleece men for money afterwards. At least it would mark the start of renewed human contact and surely nothing that a stranger might do could hurt worse than Jonathan's rejection? But Francis lay alone in bed, his clothes strewn amid an untidy pile of books and correspondence on the floor. Eva pulled the curtains and observed her son for some moments before he stirred. He looked so wretched that she was tempted to close the curtains again to let him at least enjoy his drugged sleep. Then Francis called her name and groggily reached out his hand. Eva grasped it, remembering holding him as a child when he would wake with night terrors.

'I've grown so used to you being here every morning,' he murmured, 'that if I wake and you're not here I'm scared.'

'Hush,' she whispered. 'What have you to be scared of? Sit up and I'll make us some coffee.'

Francis tried to smile, his eyes struggling to adjust to the daylight. When she brought in the coffee, he was sitting up in bed, smoking. Eva knew from his breath that he had been drinking heavily last night, but not in the carefree way she remembered from his barge parties. This was binge drinking, the brooding in unlit pubs that rots your soul. The sort of drinking that was Freddie's refuge in troubled times. It was a bitter irony that here at last was one trait which his son had inherited, his father's only true legacy. If Freddie were alive they might even have achieved a momentary reconciliation if they encountered one another by chance, both ruminating darkly in some pub. Though Eva doubted this. Freddie's public humiliation with his will marked the moment when Francis's fragile confidence started to disintegrate: a disintegration which culminated in another public denial of him by Jonathan to the police.

'Where did you go last night?' Eva asked.

'Some pub on the Isle of Dogs. I met a strange, dishevelled little man there: a poet, or so I was told. By the name of Paul Potts. Impossible to tell his age because those grey beards make all poets look ancient. Have you heard of him?'

'No.'

'Nor I. Oddly enough, the two men I was with knew him, though I doubt if either opened a book in their lives.'

'What men were you with?'

'Two conmen who sold me old railway sleepers for a rustic garden feature. Rough and ready chaps. We agreed a price, with a drink thrown in. But one drink leads to another with people like me whose behaviour is deranged.'

'Don't say that,' Eva pleaded, although she knew that this was an insult Francis could not stop picking over.

'Those were Jonathan's words to the police.'

'It was wrong and hurtful but he was scared you would let the cat out of the bag.'

'Just once I wanted Jonathan to stand up for love. But he is too busy canvassing his contacts in the House of Lords for law reform to bother with me. He's been cruel for months; that's why I climbed up on that chimney out of despair. I'm tired of being hurt. Why is it that the people who matter the most are the ones who always hurt you the most? After eight years he just orders me out of his life by solicitor's letter? Am I that old and unattractive?'

'Don't say that about yourself,' Eva pleaded. 'You have so many friends. Everyone loves you.'

'But no one is in love with me,' Francis replied quietly. 'I only feel whole when somebody loves me body and soul. We all want to feel we belong somewhere, Mummy. After Jonathan begged me to give up my old flat and move in with him, it felt like all we needed to do was close over his front door and the entire world was kept at bay. He used to plead he couldn't sleep unless I was in his bed beside him. This house felt like a sanctuary where nothing could hurt me. That was an illusion because I possessed no rights. When I was in such despair that I threatened to jump from the roof, I felt certain he'd take me in his arms and say I could stay.'

'He might have if the police hadn't arrived,' Eva said.

'I don't think so, Mummy. I'd have gone to jail rather than deny my love for him before them, but he's changed. People always change.'

A stack of untipped ash collapsed from his cigarette and scattered over the blankets. Eva brushed it away. 'He has so much to lose that he's scared of scandal. When it came to it he was a coward, but most people are. His lies were just to get rid of the police.'

Francis shook his head. 'They were to get rid of me. He had already dumped every trace of me down here. It upsets me that I acted crazy up on that rooftop. I no longer mind that I embarrassed Jonathan, but I'm still a proud Fitzgerald, ashamed to have embarrassed you and embarrassed myself.'

'You could never embarrass me, Francis. I could see the pain you were in. But you've been through pain before. You have your whole life ahead of you.'

'Jonathan was my whole life, Mummy. I accept that I've lost him, but I feel so weary that I don't know how to start all over again.'

The way Francis sat slumped in the bed filled Eva with despair. Yet she could not afford to show her emotions. She needed to stay strong.

'We've come through worse nightmares with other men and we will again.'

'But why start again if it will only lead to more hurt? More lovers tiring of me until there's no lovers left. I can't help what I like, Mummy, and I like older men. The problem is that older men want me to look boyish and I can't stay a boy forever.'

Eva took the remnants of his untouched cigarette before he burnt himself and squeezed his hand gently. 'You're a man, Francis. You have to be strong.'

'That's what I told myself last night, trying to prove my worth and show I was no weakling, like Daddy always called me, by drinking these two conmen under the table. But I only grew broody and sunk deeper into myself while they kept ordering drinks until this Paul Potts poet chap arrived with his entourage. Amazing how grey-bearded poets attract a coterie of bright-eyed young acolytes eager to sit at their feet? One of them – a lanky Irish youngster named Paul, with an untidy mop of hair, seemed to be drinking as much as I was. And do you know funny thing, Mummy? His father came from Turlough. I flee to the Isle of Dogs to be anonymous and wind up drinking with the grandson of old Mr Durcan who owned the Round Tower Bar.'

'His daughters still run that pub,' Eva said. 'Lovely women.'

'It is their brother who has gone on to greater things. A circuit court judge now in Galway. We didn't speak for long but he just stared at me and nodded when I said that I had been a monumental disappointment to my father.'

Eva remembered a small Durcan boy being brought to her art classes by his mother in the 1950s, eagerly applying vivid layers of colour at his easel and inventing extraordinary titles for paintings that stunned her.

'How long did you stay in the bar?'

'I can't remember. Maybe I ordered a taxi or else the men loaded me up onto their truck and dumped me back here. I'm afraid I have the most atrocious hangover.'

'Are you going into work?'

Francis grimaced slightly. 'Not today. We're finishing a small job and Peter can handle it. The garden is so small that we'd be in each other's way. These days the big gardens seem to slip us by.'

'You must keep going.'

'Can't you see I'm trying? Hustling for business, even quoting below the breakeven point just to let the bank see some cashflow. Most evenings I sit here trying to grasp the figures but they simply slide across the page.' Francis lit another cigarette, holding the tobacco deep in his lungs for a moment. 'Nothing feels real, Mummy, everything feels second hand.'

'I'm real. You're real.'

Francis smiled. 'That's true. I'd be lost without you. Remember the terrible English boarding school where Daddy enrolled me? I never told you but I was caught with a chap. Just one fleeting kiss but the other boys were like baying hounds sensing blood; teachers turning a blind eye, figuring I deserved whatever beatings I got – being queer and Irish too. I couldn't sleep or eat out of pure blind terror. Then out of the blue you came to rescue me, instinctively knowing I was in danger. Daddy would have left me there to toughen me up. But you arrived, all five foot two of you, like a tiny general leading an invisible cavalry. I swore then that if you were ever trapped I'd come and rescue you.'

'I know you would.'

'I often think about the daffodil lawn in Glanmire Wood. It's my favourite place on earth. My first memory is of waddling across that lawn with daffodils up to my waist.' Francis closed his eyes to quote: "*And then my heart with pleasure fills and dances with the daffodils.*" He opened his eyes. 'Wordsworth lived too long and became a bore. Maybe Keats had the right idea, his name writ in water.' Francis reached for the coffee beside the bed. 'I've made a decision, Mummy: it's time to get ship-shape and focused.'

'What do you mean?'

'Today I'm taking back control of my life.' He took a sip of coffee and looked at her solemnly. 'I'm wide awake, Mummy: your mission is accomplished. You should go home and get on with your life. You've spent too long looking out for me.'

'I'll make you some breakfast first.'

'Just some more coffee, strong and black and hot.'

'You need more than coffee.'

'I need two of those blue pills on the table.'

'What do they do?'

'They keep the pain away. Regrettably they can also make the figures blur on any balance sheet. Just give me one. I've so much to do and these blue pills stop me doing it.'

'Then stop taking them,' Eva pleaded. 'Let me stay today and mind you.'

Francis smiled. 'I'd love that but you'd only distract me, Mummy. We'd waste the whole day talking, because you love to talk, you can't help yourself. It's better if you go. I've so much to sort out. Just leave some coffee by the bed.'

Eva entered the kitchenette to re-boil the kettle. At least Francis sounded more like himself and yet Eva felt a gnawing unease she could not articulate, a sense that she was missing something. When she returned with the coffee, he had his trousers on and was examining the letters and files strewn on the floor. He looked so thin that she could see his ribcage. He was wearing a creased white shirt that needed washing, something he would never have done before. She placed the coffee cup next to the ashtray beside his bed.

'I'll call back tonight,' she said.

'Do that. And bring someone with you.'

'Who?' she asked, surprised.

'Alan.' Francis waved a hand distractedly, as if the effects of the pill were kicking in. 'He's a good sort, Alan. He's always felt like a sort of brother to me. Bring Alan. I'd like some company and I need to discuss how to move my stuff to his flat tomorrow. But leave it until after ten because I've so much to sort out today.' Tenderly he took her hand. 'I was a frightful disappointment to Daddy, but have I been a disappointment to you?'

'The moment you were born a light entered my life,' Eva replied. 'You give me purpose on this earth.'

'Do you believe in heaven, Mummy?'

'Maybe we all carry our private heaven inside us.'

'My heaven would be the lawn at Glanmire. One part of me will always be twelve years old, lying bare-chested in the sun there with our dog beside me.' He put his arms around her in a particularly effusive show of affection. 'Do you know your most special quality?'

Eva laughed, suddenly as shy as a young girl. 'What?'

'You have no notion just how special you are. Now away with you: you have your own life to lead.'

'Are you sure you'll be okay?' she asked, still perturbed by a foreboding.

'Remember when I was small and Daddy made me shoot a rabbit. You and I hid in the woods afterwards, hoping the world would never find us. But in the end we all need to come out from the wood and confront the hunters who are only happy when hurting someone. Do you know my biggest regret in life, the one thing I'd go back and change if I could? It was shooting that wild rabbit now that I know the pain he must have endured.'

'I love you dearly,' Eva said. 'I hope I've never caused you pain.'

'It would only pain me if you could never forgive any hurt I cause you.'

Eva looked up at his suddenly solemn face. 'You could never hurt me, Francis.'

'Never is a big word.' He kissed her forehead softly. 'Go now, Mummy. I love you so much.'

Eva climbed the steps from the basement and, glancing at Jonathan's house, which seemed utterly bereft of life, tried not to feel spiteful towards that man who was paying a solicitor to do his dirty work. Francis was right about her need to attend to her own life. Her meagre savings were gone and she'd had no time to try and find a small job to keep her going. Thankfully her rent was paid until the end of the month and she ate so little that she could scrape by on almost nothing. Hazel would gladly send money from Kenya, but it did not feel right for a mother to ask her child for money. If Eva wanted to be of help to Francis, she needed to find part-time work serving in a café. It was vital to focus on her own finances, but as she walked through the streets Eva found it impossible to think of anything except her desire to be back with Francis. Nothing else mattered: her inability to pay next month's rent, her patched-up clothes, the fact of not having eaten in twenty-four hours.

She recognised how necessary it was to give Francis the space to focus on saving his business, yet she just wanted to speed up the hours until ten o'clock tonight when she could return to that basement to be with him. The fact that Francis had asked her to bring Alan was a good sign: it meant he was ready to discuss the practicalities of temporarily moving his possessions to Alan's flat until he found a new home. That bearded science teacher who perpetually dressed in woollen jumpers was a true friend to them both: the calmest man she knew. She could phone him later, but for now she bought a ticket for the Circle Line because it was starting to rain and at least the Tube was warm. If you sat quietly as the Circle Line went on its loop people left you in peace, too preoccupied with their own concerns to notice your presence.

For hours London spun past her in an endless circle: South Kensington, Westminster, Embankment, Blackfriars. The carriage perpetually filled up and emptied out: busy people preoccupied with jobs and tasks. But eventually even Eva could no longer stand the constant swaying through dark tunnels. She realised that a man sitting across from her was also only there to avail of the free warmth and fill out his vacant hours. It was just a matter of time before he tried to talk to her and just now she wanted to speak to nobody. Emerging out into the air at Great Portland Street, she spent her daily food allowance on a bar of black chocolate and a coffee at a café in the station forecourt. She hoped that some customer would leave behind an *Evening Standard*, which would allow her to circle any small ads for flats of interest to Francis. After sitting in the café for so long that the waitress began staring at her, Eva decided to walk to Regent's Park.

But this was simply a ploy to allow her to pass by the chambers at Harley Street where Jonathan conducted his private practice. She paused outside but knew that if she entered he would refuse to see her. The notion of a separate basement flat had always only been a convenient cover, a token address from which Francis could entertain clients or fellow members of the Irish Genealogical Research Society: people with no clue to his other life which started after they left and he stepped through the baize door to join Jonathan upstairs. But now that door was kept locked: the break-up all the more harrowing for having to occur in secret. Yet everything in Francis's world was secretive. His friends' gaiety was the gaiety of desperation: their world built around invisible bars and secret fears – the fear of losing your liberty, losing your reputation or losing your looks.

Therefore Eva walked on past Jonathan's chambers and entered Regent's park. She sat alone there for several hours, allowing exhaustion to finally catch up with her. At sixty-two years of age her possessions fitted into two suitcases under her bed. Her most precious possession was a watercolour of an old woman sitting alone on a park bench, entitled 'Lonely Soul', which Francis had painted as a schoolboy in Aravon. This was who she had now become. When dusk came she left the park to phone Alan but got no reply. She walked for a while longer, but it was only on the second occasion when she entered a phone box to call Alan and listen to his unanswered phone ring, that she grasped the significance of why Francis did not want her returning to the basement alone. Why was she always so slow-witted, too caught up in the ether to grasp the obvious? The subconscious anxiety gnawing at her all day crystallised. There could only be one reason why Francis wished Eva to have someone with her when she re-entered that basement.

She left the phone booth without even replacing the receiver and started to run. It was seven o'clock. The worst of the rush hour was over. Light had drained from the sky. Francis had said to not return before ten o'clock. Did this mean that he planned to do nothing until close to that time? Panic drove her forward, passers-by surprised at how she elbowed her way onto a crowded Tube just as the doors closed. All day she had been longing for time to pass but now she yearned for the seconds to slow down.

She ran from the Tube station to Jonathan's basement, not caring if anyone thought that she looked like a crazed woman. She just needed to reach him, her first-born, her wounded fawn. The first thing she noticed upon opening the door was the cleanliness and order of the basement. Files, which had been untidy this morning, were meticulously arranged. An entire table of overdue correspondence was answered and stacked for posting. The figures had stopped sliding across the page. Francis had grasped them in his palm: every bill paid and a four week advance in wages totalled up for Peter in an envelope. Alongside it was a letter with detailed instructions concerning what to do with his genealogical research files. He must have spent the whole day finalising every detail with absolute calmness, even parcelling up all his books with string and attaching labels to denote which friend should receive each parcel. The only untidy thing was the two letters from Jonathan's solicitor, torn into tiny pieces.

Eva knew there would be no reply when she called out his name. She ran frantically towards his bedroom: each step seeming to take an inordinate time. The door was ajar. His death was the only untidy aspect in his plan. Francis lay on the carpet and there was no question but that he was dead because his face was discoloured by several blue blotches on the skin. His shoulder was hunched up and she knew that he had been trying to rise and get even more pills in case he had not taken enough. The door was open to the bathroom where several empty pill bottles lay on the floor, while the bottle beside his bed – filled with blue capsules this morning – was also empty.

Eva knelt to cradle his body in her arms. For a moment she prayed that by some miracle the touch of her tears trickling down onto his cold check might bring him back to life. But then she realised that she was being selfish. If Francis woke up again, it would be to endure more suffering and rejection that he could simply no longer bear. Here was the baby she had cradled with such hope; the child so compassionate that he used to make burial mounds for dead birds they found in the woods; the boy who had never grown hardened enough to accept life's perpetual betrayals; the man who had desperately needed his lover to stand up for a love whose name could not be spoken. Francis's nightmare was over, but Eva knew that her nightmare was only beginning. She had no idea how long she knelt there, stroking his cold face and listening to herself repeat the same words over and over: 'My precious, precious darling, I'm just so glad that they can't hurt you anymore.'

Chapter Eleven
The Moonlight Sonata
London, 15th September 1966

Without Alan she would never have got through that night after the police and ambulancemen arrived, with Jonathan's basement flat sealed off like a crime scene. The detective in charge insisted on her phoning someone. Alan knew what had happened from the tone of Eva's voice before she even told him. It was Alan who collected her from the hospital to which Francis's body was finally taken in the early hours and then drove her back to his own basement flat. He was calm and quiet, instinctively sensing that she would wish to sit out in the moonlight on the wrought-iron patio chairs, near the herbaceous border that Francis planted last year when painstakingly remodelling Alan's lawn. Eva could imagine her son carefully planting each bulb, conscious of their need for light and space. His personality seemed to radiate from the arrangement of shrubs, his handiwork even more beautiful now that the clouds had cleared to reveal the constellations of stars.

Alan urged Eva to have a stiff gin but she declined and requested instead that he simply take her hand. He sat beside her on the patio, never complaining even though Eva knew she was gripping his hand so fiercely that his fingers must be crushed. But she could not let go. As a fellow Scorpio, Alan understood that what she needed most was silent support. She made him promise not to call his two young nieces who lived nearby. They were wonderful girls, full blooming roses, but they would want to wrap their arms around Eva and kiss and console her when just now she wanted nothing like that. Her grief was too real for physical intrusion. It felt as if her life before finding Francis's body had belonged to someone else. She found it impossible to imagine ever rising from this patio to resume living. But she could not allow herself to think selfishly like this because Francis had left her detailed instructions. She had urgent telegrams to send, although she didn't know how she would find the strength. Closing her eyes, she tried to relax her grip on Alan's hand, but pain had locked her fingers into a tighter vice than arthritis ever could. The French doors were open, lamplight spilling out. Alan winced silently, trying not to complain. Eva finally managed to relax her grip. She saw how discoloured his palm was where her nails had dug in and apologised for hurting him.

'That's okay,' he said. 'You could dig your nails into me all night and I still wouldn't feel a fraction of the pain you're surely in. Do you want me to try again to see if I can put a call through to Kenya?'

Eva shook her head. He had already tried to contact Hazel twice without success. Just now she could not bear another wait while a London telephone operator contacted other operators in a line stretching to whatever remote telephone exchange was closest to Hazel's plantation, only for the chain to break down or Hazel's phone to ring unanswered. There was a new darkness hidden within Hazel's life in Africa that Eva felt she was being shielded from, an unspoken unhappiness lurking behind the brisk tone in Hazel's letters. But Eva longed to have Hazel with her in spirit at least, because Hazel and Alex were all that Eva had left now to root her to this earth. A memory returned of rocking Hazel to sleep on her knee in Glanmire House when Hazel was a child, after placing Hazel's favourite record, Beethoven's 'Moonlight Sonata', on the gramophone as a bedtime treat. Eva glanced at Alan.

'Do you have the 'Moonlight Sonata'?' she asked

'Yes.'

'I wonder could you possibly play it for me?'

Alan rose and after a moment she heard the record start in the room behind her. The music seemed to draw Hazel's essence closer and Eva wanted to believe that, whatever Hazel was doing now, her daughter would intuitively hear those notes inexplicably surface in her consciousness. Eva rocked slowly in the chair but this time her arms were empty; her arms that had held Francis moments after his birth and sensed her true purpose in life. She tormented herself with guilt for not having done more. There were enough signs if she had only allowed herself to read them. But, even amidst her grief, she took a curious comfort in the fact that his suicide had been no hasty decision. Francis had taken back control of his life. During his final hours he was methodical and calm in how he arranged everything. This was how he would wish her to behave in the terrible days ahead. She closed her eyes until the sonata's first movement ended.

'That's my favourite part,' Alan said softly. 'I love the quietude, barely ever a whisper above *pianissimo*. Would you like me to play the start again?'

Eva opened her eyes to see Alan crying softly without making a sound.

'No,' she said. 'We have too much to do for Francis. Maybe you could try the operator one more time to see if we can get through to Kenya? Hazel will want to travel to London. She will know exactly what we should do.'

Chapter Twelve

The Jacket and the Hat

London, Late September 1966

When Eva woke in Francis's bed on the morning of his cremation, she tried to convince herself that, after today's ceremony, the worst would be over. Yet she knew that her real grief would only start to seep out when the fuss died down and people drifted back to their own concerns. Every night since his death she had placed night-lights in front of a framed picture of him before going to sleep. Her mother once told her that candlelight was important if you wanted to contact the dead. Although she tried to keep her body busy with practical things during the day, her spirit was constantly with Francis and it felt as if he were always with her. But his presence never troubled her sleep. Francis must have wanted her to rest, because she had never slept so soundly as she had since temporarily moving into this basement to allow Hazel and Alex to use her attic flat.

She had not seen Jonathan since Francis's death. He had slipped away to the country, but his secretary sent a message that Eva was free to use the basement for as long as she wished. However Eva knew that he wanted every trace of Francis gone from his life. She would leave here soon and never return, but for now she cherished this chance to sleep among Francis's things. She felt a serenity in this basement, which she filled with the types of flowers Francis loved, so that she was surrounded by their scent as she busied herself arranging his possessions, parcelling up clothes to donate to charity and trying to second guess his wishes for any possessions unaccounted for in the list of instructions he left. Every night she ticked off items with the same pen he had used, arranging for his friends to collect the books and paintings he had wanted them to have. All that Eva wished to keep for herself was his bible, some photographs and papers and a pencil sketch someone had done of him.

There were so many tasks to do this past week that there was little time to mourn. Eva had not yet managed to cry, even when Hazel flew in from Kenya five days ago. She remained calm, knowing she needed to be calm and because Hazel deliberately had provided her with a purpose by bringing Eva the gift of her six-year-old granddaughter. While Hazel arranged to have Francis's body released for cremation – deflecting police inquiries and ensuring no publicity – Eva was allotted the task of minding Alex. Eva hired a boat to row the child on the Serpentine and brought her to London Zoo. Alex's needs were immediate and as Eva was responsible for her she was forced to focus solely on Alex.

Hazel, meanwhile, was determinedly tackling every loose end, meeting creditors, haranguing Jonathan's cowed solicitor and refusing to be fobbed off by anyone. Eva had never felt so close to her daughter as during these past few days. Hazel was devastated by her brother's loss, but determined to ease Eva through her pain by making her concentrate on practical matters, like writing a discreetly coded *Irish Times* death notice. This morning she had allotted Eva the task of selecting readings for today's cremation and deciding what hymns Francis would have wanted.

Eva rose from bed now to sit at the table where Francis wrote his final instructions and tried to focus on this task. Unzipping the leather-bound Cambridge Bible she had given him on his twenty-first birthday, she reread her inscription on the flyleaf – the same inscription her own father once inscribed for her – *'Prayer is the soul's sincere desire, uttered or unexpressed.'* She didn't know how often Francis prayed, but she saw how he had underlined a passage in Matthew, chapter twenty-five, verse thirty-five: *'For I was hungered and ye gave me meat: I was a stranger and ye took me in.'* She understood why he loved these words, but was perturbed to see how, at a darker moment in his life, he had highlighted a passage from The Book of the Prophet Isaiah: *'None calleth for justice, nor pleadeth for truth: they trust in vanity and speak lies.'*

These underlined verses brought her closer to Francis: revealing hidden aspects of him. But only when she turned over the bible did she unearth her most treasured discovery – a studio photograph of Francis glued inside the back cover. She had never seen it before and wondered if he had deliberately left it there for her to find. He was smiling in it and his face possessed a rare beauty, but a flaw in the exposure meant that the print was faded, almost as if he were mid-way between two places. She wanted to sit and contemplate the photograph but time was against her, so she made herself put it away and focus on selecting appropriate readings.

After she was finished she forced herself to eat something and get dressed for the crematorium. Francis's spirit was definitely still watching over her in this basement. But his presence seemed weaker than before and she sensed how, while she was sleeping last night, he had started to slip away. When Eva was dressed she sat in silence on a chair, cold in herself despite her buttoned-up coat, wondering how she could find the strength to endure the ordeal of watching her son's coffin enter the flames. But when Hazel arrived by taxi to bring her to Golders Green Crematorium, Eva felt that Francis's presence had grown strong again, anxious to help steer her through the crowd that would be waiting at Golders Green and ensure she did not say the wrong things in public.

The number of mourners present at the crematorium surprised Eva. Many were strangers whose lives were linked to Francis in ways she could not fathom. She had feared being unable to get through the service, but she had Hazel at one shoulder and an indisputable sense of Francis at her other shoulder to guide her. His presence seemed strongest when she stood up beside Hazel to sing his favourite hymn:

> *'Blest are the pure in heart,*
> *For they shall see our God;*
> *The secret of the Lord is theirs,*
> *Their soul is Christ's abode.'*

It gave her the strength to shake hands with everyone, even with Jonathan who turned up – camouflaged by being accompanied by a female friend – to hand Eva an expensive bunch of hothouse roses tied up with pink lace: the sort of flowers Francis always hated. For a moment her virago side – which longed to appropriate blame – wanted to hurl the bouquet back at him. But Francis' spirit seemed to say: *Look at him, poor man: he is grieving also.* Eva had ensured that the police report on Francis's suicide contained no reference to Jonathan except as a landlord, but she still sensed his fear as she forced herself to smile and even thank him for the ugly flowers. Then, as if fate wished to reward her, she turned around to discover Valerie O'Mahony standing there.

'I saw the death notice in *The Irish Times*,' Valerie explained. 'I just had time to drive into the Wicklow Mountains and gather these before catching a flight from Dublin. I think he would have liked them.'

It was a beautiful bunch of wild purple heather, tied with plain string: exactly what Francis would wish on his coffin. Eva ensured that this wild heather covered his breastplate when the coffin jerked along the conveyer belt to enter the flames. Jonathan and some others in his circle whom she blamed for

Francis's death left immediately after the service ended. For a few moments outside the crematorium it felt like being back at one of Francis's barge parties: Peter and his wife Pauline urging her to visit them soon and so many people telling interesting stories about Francis that it felt like he was merely delayed and would join them at any moment.

A small knot of friends brought her back to the basement. All remarked on how marvellously brave she was. Afterwards, when Hazel took Alex away, Eva undressed and realised she had not cried once during the service. There had simply been no time. Even now as she lay exhausted in bed she did not cry but allowed sleep to claim her. Just before she slept the vengeful side of her nature resurfaced and she thought, 'Why didn't I throw those horrible expensive flowers back in Jonathan's face?' But it was as if Francis were beside her, because she heard his voice in her head, lacking any vindictiveness as he said, 'Mummy, you couldn't do that; it wouldn't be right.' Eva had not let him down today, but she sensed that his presence would continue to diminish as he began his voyage away from her.

Daylight already filled the basement when she woke the next morning. It was late by her standards, time to get washed and dressed. But Eva realised that she had nothing to get up for. Having spent weeks urging Francis to rise from this bed, she now needed to coax herself. She was not due to meet Hazel until eight o'clock this evening so that Hazel could spend time alone with Alex. But Francis wouldn't want her to succumb to despair. Painfully and gingerly, she needed to start living again, though the thought of joining Francis was a constant temptation. Two bottles of pills remained in his bathroom. It would be so easy to lie down where he had lain, close her eyes and wait for him to beckon from a tunnel of light. But her soul knew that her time was not yet come and Francis's soul – or whatever part of his aura still lingered there – insisted that she must live on.

Today she needed to restart her life. Jonathan wanted her gone, but she could not bear to return to her attic flat after Hazel left. It had too many bad memories. A fresh start was needed. Fresh starts and new chapters were the only things she was good at. The first thing she needed to deal with among Francis's last remaining possessions in this basement were the files he kept for the Irish Genealogical Research Society. Even amidst personal turmoil, he always maintained these impeccably, keeping them locked in their cupboard. Two society members were due to collect them at six p.m. Eva checked that this cupboard was locked, then walked up the steps into the autumn sunshine, happy to be among strangers who would treat her with indifference.

She needed to discuss the fate of Glanmire House with Hazel. Hazel had bought it partly so as not to be bested by her father, but mainly as a retreat for Francis. With Francis gone, there was no practical reason for Hazel to hold onto the few remaining acres of her childhood home, but Eva hoped that Hazel might keep the wood as an Irish retreat for Alex. Hazel had once talked about one day enrolling Alex in the Park House Boarding School in Dublin and Alex might like the idea of owning a wood where she could camp with school friends in a ruined house. But since arriving in London, Hazel was being uncharacteristically vague about any future plans and Eva knew not to question her about her marriage, sensing that Hazel's Kenyan paradise was gradually turning sour.

She bought a newspaper from the old soldier outside the Tube station and tried to lose herself in the headlines. In South Africa a bible-quoting parliamentary messenger had knifed Dr Hendrik Verwoerd, the father of apartheid, to death: the government outlawing all interracial parties in response. In Rhodesia Ian Smith was denouncing as repugnant Harold Wilson's proposal that he appoint two black cabinet members. America was aflame with race riots: the University of Mississippi's first black student was wounded as he protested, carrying only a bible. It seemed clear that Eva's campaigning for social change had achieved nothing. Mankind remained locked in permanent war with itself. Opening her handbag, Eva discovered a petition for a posthumous pardon for Tim Evans, an innocent man wrongly hung for the murder of his wife and daughter. She was about to throw it away when she saw that the last signature she had collected belonged to Francis, who had felt a sense of injustice at Evan's fate. If she could even collect one more signature it might give some purpose to her day.

Eva decided to visit Peter's wife, Pauline, and ask her to sign. At yesterday's cremation she was relieved to learn that Peter had already found a new job. The twins, whom she adored, were home on their lunch break when Eva finally reached the house. They hugged her with a mixture of sympathy and delight. Pauline only managed to shoo them back to school after Eva promised to still be there when they returned home. After the twins left, the two women sat down to tea in the kitchen and Eva was glad that she had come. Pauline was a gentle Scorpio who understood her nature. They were so engrossed in talk that Eva didn't hear Peter arrive home until the man appeared in the doorway.

'Hello, Eva,' he said.

She rose to greet him but as Peter held out his hand, Eva realised he was wearing an old tweed jacket which had once belonged to Francis. Her fingers brushed against the familiar tweed and this slightest touch of Francis's jacket was enough to shatter the dam inside her. Eva began to cry and could not stop. The grief she had kept suppressed all week overwhelmed her and she needed to escape from the house. Distraught and embarrassed, she pushed past Peter to stumble down the hall and reach the front door. Eva began to run, terrified that Peter would follow her in Francis's jacket, trying to offer comfort. But she knew that Pauline would have the sense to stop him. These emotions were utterly private and she needed a quiet place where she could cry like never before in her life.

Eva didn't know how long she spent sobbing in the local park. Whenever people stopped she begged them to leave her alone. Eventually she felt strong enough to board a bus, which crawled through evening traffic towards Francis's flat. She just wanted to sleep now and realised she had never even got Pauline to sign the petition. Eva descended the basement steps, opened the door and then stopped, afraid to enter for a moment because the doors to the cupboard where Francis stored his genealogical research files were wide open. She had double-checked that the cupboard was locked before leaving and was sure that nobody had been here in her absence. Cautiously she approached the cupboard, relieved to see that the files were untouched.

Eva sat down on a chair, unable to stop trembling. She heard footsteps descend the basement steps. It did not sound like Hazel's confident tread. Eva gazed towards the open doorway, half terrified and half hopeful. It was probably just the men from the Genealogical Society, but what if it was Francis's ghost? Maybe she would see him walk over to those files, like she had often done in the past, anxious to check some fact, oblivious to her presence or to his own death, doomed to constantly relive this moment, caught in an air pocket of time. The footsteps hesitantly slowed and a young woman whose face was vaguely familiar appeared in the doorway.

'I'm disturbing you,' she apologised shyly.

'If you are looking for Francis then I'm afraid ...'

'I know,' the girl said. 'I was at the crematorium but was too shy to approach you. There were so many people and ... to be honest ... I didn't know what to say.'

'I know your face, don't I?' Eva asked.

'You have a good memory so. We only met once, six years ago on a ferry to the Isle of Wight. You were selling copies of *Peace News*. You couldn't get back to London because you had some business in Ryde, but you urged me to attend a barge party your son was hosting that night.'

'I remember now,' Eva recalled with some difficulty. 'Is your name Jade? You were with a boy. Rather possessive if I remember right.'

'Far too possessive,' Jade replied. 'Joey had our whole future mapped out. I might have gone along with his plans if I hadn't attended your son's party that night. Meeting people there opened my eyes in so many ways. Francis always remembered to drop me a card after that, inviting me to his parties. He didn't need to invite me: I mean we rarely spoke for more than a few minutes at any of them. But he knew I enjoyed meeting people and that was enough for him. I'd hoped to meet you at one of them but you were always away travelling.'

'Please. Come in,' Eva said, touched.

'I won't stay,' Jade replied. 'But I came because I don't think you'll laugh at what I have to say, like some people would.'

'Why would I laugh at you?' Eva asked.

'I had a dream about Francis. It was after he died but before I heard about it. I never dreamt about him before, but it was ever so clear. He was working in a cornfield with his hair blowing in the breeze. He looked different from how I'd ever seen him, but he looked happy. I'm not just saying this for your sake. He looked happier than I'd ever seen him and I have a sense that he wanted you to claim back this right to be happy. This was the message I think he wanted me to give you. There was more in the dream, but you know how details slip away. I think he was trying to give me an address, but I can't remember anything about it except that I think it was near Kensington Gardens or Bayswater Road. Do you know anybody he'd want you to visit near there?'

'I don't think so.'

'I feel stupid coming here and not even able to fully remember the dream. But he was happy, except for his concern for you.'

'Tell me again about the cornfield.'

Jade shrugged. 'It was in the middle of nowhere. A small wood beyond it and a ruined house with an open space in front of it, overgrown with long grass and wild flowers. And at the end of the dream a young boy stood up who must have been lying in that grass. He was stripped to the waist and a dog jumped up beside him. That's all I remember.'

'Thank you for telling me this, Jade.'

'It was just a dream,' Jade replied, embarrassed. 'But it was so vivid that I never had a dream like it before.' She paused. 'Jade isn't actually my real name. It's Janice, but I've always hated the name Janice.'

'Then be Jade,' Eva said. 'Be whoever you want to be. Do one thing for me, Jade. Please, take something here belonging to Francis.'

'What do you mean?'

'There's almost nothing left, but I want everyone to have something to remember him by.'

Footsteps began to descend the steps. Eva and Jade waited in silence until two soberly dressed men entered. Southern Irish Protestants in exile. Instinctively she recognised the class she had left behind and instinctively they recognised her as a lapsed member.

'Mrs Fitzgerald, we're sorry for your troubles,' one man said. 'Is this a bad time to collect the files?'

Genealogy was an interest of Francis's that Eva had never understood. An obsession with roots tangled in the past instead of branches soaring into the future. People needing to cling to family trees to define who they were.

'Take everything in that unlocked cupboard,' Eva replied. 'Take the cupboard too if you want.'

The men seemed perturbed by her remark. 'Just the files are fine,' one replied awkwardly. 'Your son did tremendous research. He'll be missed but he will live on through his research.'

'No, he won't,' Jade said, fiercely. 'He'll live on in people's memories and in all the lives he touched.' She pointed to a wide-brimmed summer hat hanging beside the door. 'I'll take this hat. I remember Francis wearing it at a party. I'm saving up for a journey next spring. To see the world at last or at least to see how far I can get. I'll bring this hat. Whenever I wear it I'll think of Francis and think of you.'

Jade put on Francis's hat. It suited her. She leaned forward to kiss Eva and this time when Francis's hat touched her skin Eva did not cry. The men were self-consciously packing the files into a suitcase. But Eva ignored them as she held Jade's hand and smiled.

'Good luck on your travels, Jade.'

'And good luck on yours.'

Chapter Thirteen

The Daffodil Lawn

London, Winter 1966 & Co. Mayo, Spring 1967

Three days after Francis's cremation Eva accompanied Hazel and Alex to Heathrow Airport as they commenced their journey back to Kenya. In the terminal bar, with Alex distracted by gazing out through the huge plate-glass windows, Hazel confirmed Eva's suspicions that her marriage to Geoffrey was over. She was evasive about the reasons or about her future plans, beyond affirming that Kenya would remain her home. 'Francis wasn't the only one receiving ultimatums from solicitors. Jonathan probably thinks his legal eagle is a Rottweiler, but he became a pussycat when I called into his office yesterday to give him a flea in his ear about those bullying letters he sent to Francis. If he gives you any trouble just let me know. I'll enjoy venting my spleen on the weak coward. I'm becoming well practiced in legal affairs. For months I've been dealing with big cats in the Kenyan courts; hyenas dressed in decorous wigs.' Hazel glanced protectively at Alex who was mesmerised by the size of the planes outside. 'We keep any animosity hidden from Alex. To be fair, Geoffrey is good like that. Alex brings out the best in him. Maybe in us both. They'll be calling us to board soon.' Hazel rose. 'Mind yourself. You might think you're doing all right, but that doesn't mean you are all right. I'll send you my next address when I have it. Who knows: I might even be sending you a new married name.'

Eva remained at the tall window in the viewing section long after Hazel's plane took off, her palms pressed to the glass as if this would somehow allow her to retain the warmth in Alex's final hug before she followed her mother through the departure gates. But eventually Eva felt foolish standing there. She needed to confront the loneliness of the Tube journey back into London, knowing that she would be unable to do anything except sit in silence for the next few days in the emptiness of Francis's old flat. But Jonathan had other plans. When she returned to the basement flat, she discovered that three painters had arrived in her absence to start redecorating it. It was the Welsh surgeon's unsubtle hint that he wanted her gone. The workmen were embarrassed by her arrival, obviously not having been told about the circumstances of her stay. They offered to cease work and return the next morning if they could leave their ladders and paint cans there. But, with Hazel gone, Eva felt overcome by such sudden, deep exhaustion that she was too bone-tired to even converse with the men. She smiled apologetically, conscious of being in their way as she motioned for them to carry on.

Gathering up the few remaining possessions belonging to her or Francis, she stuffed them into any bags she could find. It took three trips to bring everything up onto the pavement. She stood outside Jonathan's house, bewildered by what to do next and unsure if she had enough money for a taxi. Footsteps ascended the basement steps. It was the oldest of the workmen. She was immensely thankful that he asked no questions and said nothing beyond a single sentence, 'I could use a break; get a bit of air.' He stood beside her and lit two cigarettes. Only when Eva reached for the proffered cigarette did she realise how her hands were shaking. The man didn't comment on this as he opened the white van that the painters had arrived in and made space for her belongings to fit into it. Courteously he opened the passenger door to allow her to climb up into the seat. Eva did so, too weary to argue. He didn't speak again until he started the engine.

'If you had an address…?'

He nodded when she gave him directions to her attic flat, being wise and kind enough to say nothing else on their journey there. Only when they reached Notting Hill and he was taking out her possessions to stack them on the front step did he speak again.

'That basement you left has an odd atmosphere. Peaceful but I sometimes get a feeling working in places. When we came back from lunch every door we had left closed was wide open, even the little cupboard doors. It gave us all a bit of a turn.' He paused. 'Will you be all right from here?'

'I'll be fine.'

'It was nice to meet you, ma'am.'

Eva was relieved that he didn't try to shake her hand. Just then she was not able for physical contact. She was similarly relieved that the other tenants in the house seemed to be out when she needed to make several trips up all the flights of stairs before she had everything crammed away in her tiny room. She felt she had held onto too much but it seemed wrong to leave any part of Francis behind in that basement. She was not sure what time it was but she only had sufficient strength left to lie down on the bed and cover herself with as many blankets and coats as she possessed. When she finally woke, she thought she had only slept for a few moments because the same evening light filtered in through the cheap curtains, but then realised that she was so exhausted she had slept for almost twenty-four hours.

The days that followed were primarily about survival. Eva was desperate to find a small room where she could lick her wounds because she could not bear to stay in that flat any longer. She didn't know if Francis's spirit guided her or if it was by pure chance that she spotted a tiny notice in a shop window advertising a vacancy for a caretaker at the Quaker International Youth Hostel near Portobello market. Eva was taken on, two days before her rent ran out in Notting Hill. This hostel became her new home. Every morning she needed to rise before dawn to scrub down the long kitchen table where two cats always slept; gently swooshing them away so that she could lay the table for breakfast before the guests started to come down.

Her wages were tiny but the hostel provided a large room, rent free, where she could live and store the last of Francis's possessions, which she had now placed in a trunk. She knew he had wanted her to give away everything but Eva couldn't bring herself to destroy his letters, even old business ones written to clients outlining plans for gardens. Every night she added to the weight of the trunk by writing another letter to her son, knowing that she would trade all the remaining years of her life just to know that one of these sentences might actually reach Francis.

Over that winter and the following spring, the Quaker hostel became her sanctuary. She found herself drawn into deep conversations and friendships with many long-stay guests, especially the young American men who, refusing to fight in Vietnam, had fled to London when called up by the draft board. Often their fathers had disowned them, like Freddie disowned Francis. Watching these young men cope with being ostracized was like watching Francis's pain again, but Eva – who told nobody in the hostel about her son – found herself watching for signs of Francis everywhere. On freezing nights, she wandered through the parts of London he most loved or through unfamiliar streets around Bayswater and Kensington. Perhaps Jade was mistaken in her dream, but Eva yearned for one glimpse of his ghost there. At night she prayed for his younger, carefree ghost to appear in her dreams, but his will-o'-the-wisp spirit only populated other people's sleep. Two other friends of his sent her cards that described dreams which echoed Jade's image of him, radiant with joy as he worked in a cornfield. It was only in Eva's dreams that he never smiled. In these dreams all she ever saw was his distress, the blue blotches on his face and how his body had been slumped after trying to rise one last time to swallow more pills.

Dermot Bolger

Perhaps Francis smiled in strangers' dreams because his pain was over, but Eva's pain only deepened with each passing night.

This was why the routine of the hostel was good for her. It forced her to rise early and scrub down the table, to shoo away the cats and make porridge, to take bread from the oven and converse with guests. At Christmas, one of the American conscientious objectors – or draft dodgers, as she sometimes overheard Londoners unkindly refer to them – gave her a copy of *Meetings with Remarkable Men* by the Armenian philosopher G.I. Gurdjieff. She spent Christmas Day alone reading it – ignoring entreaties from Alan to join him. Gurdjieff was more than simply a distraction from her grief: she saw his book as a sign that it was time for her soul to resume its journey. Eva memorised passages about him voyaging into remote corners of Asia to seek the lost wisdom of antiquity. While engrossed in its pages, his Himalayan journeys seemed more real than the Portobello market stalls near the hostel. The first hints of spring were appearing when Eva finished the book for the third time and reached the realisation that she needed to bring Francis's ashes back to the Mayo wood that he loved.

Alan offered to accompany her on this journey, but it was something she needed to do alone. When the train from Dublin pulled into Castlebar station, Eva politely deflected all questions from the solitary taxi driver waiting there in hopes of a fare, and asked him to take the back road out by Brafey to avoid her being spotted in Turlough village. Hoping to buy his silence she gave a more generous tip than she could afford when he dropped her near the roofless, overgrown gate lodge at the entrance to Glanmire Wood. But Eva knew that he had recognised her and would probably spend his tip by stopping for a drink in The Round Tower bar to inform all of Turlough that the Widow Fitzgerald had returned alone, carrying an urn with her son's ashes.

But as soon as she began walking up the overgrown avenue that snaked through trees for a quarter of a mile before reaching

Glanmire House, Eva knew that she was not alone. The ghost of a twelve-year-old boy silently stalked her from among those trees. Eva had waited months to scatter these ashes, until certain that the overgrown lawn would be a blaze of daffodils. But she had also been waiting until she felt capable of letting go of these ashes she had kept beside her bed in the Quaker hostel.

Clouds hung low overhead, the day alternating between showers and sudden bursts of sunlight, which seemed to intensify the colour of every drenched leaf and wildflower and tuft of grass. The sky darkened again as she caught her first glimpse of the house, framed by the old chestnut tree whose branches spanned the width of the avenue. Rain began to fall and Eva sought shelter among a cluster of tress that allowed her to survey the house without approaching any nearer. She could almost hear Francis's voice in her head, softly scolding her for sitting alone, cold and hungry among these trees when so many old neighbours would welcome her into their homes. But Eva had not written to tell anyone in Turlough that she was coming. The village was surely awash with rumours about Francis's death. Over the previous six months sympathetic and circumspectly written letters had been forwarded to her by circuitous routes. Each letter was heartfelt, but left so much unsaid between the awkward clichés that Eva could not tell which details of Francis's death were common gossip here. Probably not the fact that he was homosexual – Eva suspected that many Mayo people knew little about such a world. But suicide was something everyone in Mayo understood and whispered about, with bodies recovered from lakes and causes of death fabricated to prevent the shame of a loved one being banished to an unconsecrated grave.

More messages of condolence probably awaited her at Turlough Park, if Eva could ever bring herself to visit her in-laws who were now trying to transform the family seat into a guesthouse to keep it afloat, like she had done with Freddie in the 1930s. They were undoubtedly being forced to field all kinds of questions about Francis's death. But in recent months,

Eva was too preoccupied with surviving to contact the Turlough Fitzgeralds. If she was honest, the Scorpio side of her nature still resented how Freddie had favoured his in-laws over Francis in his will, even if Devlin the Castlebar builder was the only person to make a real profit. Francis never bore any resentment towards her in-laws, who were placed in an impossible situation by having to execute Freddie's will. But to visit Turlough Park would make Eva feel poor in a way that no amount of living abroad in reduced circumstances ever did. In Tangiers or London she could slip free from her caste but here in Mayo she would feel imprisoned by everything left unsaid in the way that locals stared at her.

The rain had eased up and there was no excuse for Eva to remain hunched down under this great chestnut tree which marked the point where the front lawn began. She could hear Francis's voice in her head, urging her to find enough strength to step forward and set them both free. Eva slowly rose and approached the boarded-up house. There were more daffodils in bloom around her feet than she had ever seen on this overgrown lawn, intermingled with a proliferation of wildflowers. Francis's hand-painted sign still hung above the locked front door: *Please do not enter, this is my home.* It was the message he had first written on a piece of wood before leaving for England as a boy before the war, and a message he carefully repainted every time he came home. Eva feared that the sight of this sign would reduce her to tears, but she refused to cry here on the lawn where the ghost of his younger self might see.

Threading her way carefully among the wildflowers, Eva reached the spot where she could still remember Francis lying, bare-chested, many summers ago, joyously content like in Jade's dream. She did not kneel or speak and felt curiously numb as she turned in slow motion to let Francis's ashes spill from the urn until they lay in a perfect circle around her, dusting the long grass and stems of flowers. This wood was truly her son's home once more. Nobody could ever again disinherit him. The sun went in behind the clouds and she knew that rain would soon fall, gradually helping his ashes to seep into the soil and nurture these daffodil bulbs.

Eva had no idea how long she stood there, never wanting to leave the circle of precious ash. But because Francis's ghost was watching she needed to pretend to be strong. Unsure where she would sleep tonight, Eva finally managed to step outside the circle and not look back. Scrambling up the grassy incline into the woods, briers scratched her hands and tore at her clothes. She was afraid that, if she looked back, she would see a bare-chested boy standing on the lawn watching her. If she saw him she would not be able to go on living, such was her longing to be with Francis. She climbed through the trees at a frantic pace, hoping to fool his ghost into thinking that she was leaving him behind so that he could pass on unencumbered into the next life, but she would still have traded her soul for one touch of Francis's hand. Eva only stopped climbing when she reached the secluded spot where three old oaks clung to the crest of the hill: her secret haven to which she would run for solace as a young mother, whenever despair threatened to overwhelm her.

Eva leaned against these oak trees in the rain to catch her breath and try to regain her composure. This long journey was meant to be about attempting to let go of grief, but for now all that Eva possessed to hold onto was grief: it was only the ache of grief which made her feel alive. She had found the strength to come here, but even after scattering his ashes she knew that in her heart she hadn't the strength to let Francis go. She wrapped her arms slowly around one of the oak trees and pressed her face against it. Only then, in that most private of spaces, did she allow herself to cry.

Chapter Fourteen

The White Eagle Lodge

London & Morocco, 1967/1968

Eva worked as a caretaker at the Quaker International Youth Hostel in Portobello throughout the spring and summer of 1967. In June, *Sgt. Pepper's Lonely Hearts Club Band* began to be continually played in the common room. The young residents seemed amused at how much Eva liked the album and even more amused by her occasional references to the communal record player as a gramophone. Animated discussions occurred over the lyrics of each song but they never descended into arguments: the guests open to even the most outlandish interpretation or hidden meaning conjured from the songs. Their excited debates about this album and The Beach Boys' *Pet Sounds* reminded Eva of boisterous debates among her family during childhood meals in Donegal: her parents happily presiding over the mayhem of opinionated voices clamouring to be heard. Freddie always claimed that this unorthodox upbringing had left her out of synch with time, but maybe it was a case that she was simply born before her true time.

By the start of July, Eva found herself unable to listen to that Beatles album any longer. This was partly because she kept wondering what her father – who never went anywhere without a volume of Walt Whitman – would have made of it. But she especially wondered if Francis would have liked it. Eva kept trying to live in the here and now but all thoughts led back to Francis, even when joyously momentous events occurred. In July, Alan held a discreet party to celebrate homosexuality being finally decriminalised in England and Wales. Even though Eva tried to enter into the spirit of the occasion, inwardly she was plagued all evening by unanswered questions. If homosexuality had been legalised one year earlier, would Jonathan have been so panicked on the night the policemen called, convinced that any public scandal would set the cause back? Would Francis and he have drifted so far apart without the constant pressure to conceal their love? Decriminalisation was an issue Francis had passionately cared about, while knowing it would be no panacea because no law could banish prejudice. But at least if you were assaulted by gangs of thugs who proudly proclaimed themselves to be queer-bashers, you would no longer be afraid to report your injuries to the police. At Alan's party, she raised her gin and tonic at every toast and tried to feel happy for Francis's friends who had spent decades living in the shadows, but the evening was soured by her growing bitterness that Francis was not there to share in this victory.

This bitterness grew as September approached. It congealed into such a surge of renewed anger towards Jonathan that Eva could not bear to be in London on the first anniversary of Francis's death. This left the problem of what to do with Francis's trunk, but the Quakers assured her it would be safe in the hostel and they would hold open her job and room if at all possible. She suspected that she had just about enough money to live cheaply for the winter in Morocco and told anyone who asked that she was travelling somewhere warm due to the arthritis afflicting her hands.

But on her first night in a Moroccan youth hostel, she realised how she was using her acrimony towards Jonathan as a way to cloak the weight of unresolved grief suddenly overwhelming her again. A parting gift from yet another American conscientious objector stranded in Portobello had helped her through this wave of pain: *The Glass Bead Game* by Herman Hesse. When she started reading it by torchlight on her first night in Morocco, Eva sensed that the novel contained an inexplicable key to her survival. For three days Eva lay in her hostel bunk until she finished the book, surviving on fruit which the young girls sharing her dormitory brought her. She read it in a trance-like state until her eyes ached, then fell asleep and resumed reading immediately after she woke. The Moroccan hostel manager considered it strange for any woman her age to wish to stay in such a place. But the young girls who came and went – many reminding her of Jade – understood her instinctively. Eva knew that many people her own age regarded her as daft but this new generation were on her wavelength. Not that she believed in everything they did. Hallucinogenic drugs held no appeal and nor did she believe in free love in the sense of indiscriminate, mechanical sex. But an era seemed to be dawning when her ideals finally made sense, with the cruel irony being that it was only occurring when she was sixty-five.

Morocco in winter was cheap. When word spread about 'the Irish grandmother', she earned some money by teaching English to the sons of ambitious shop owners. The climate and pace of life suited her but after surviving the emotional ordeal of Christmas she longed to return to London, even though nothing awaited her there. She returned in March, touched to discover that the Quakers were true to their word and had kept open the position of caretaker for her. Her room had not even been slept in during her absence: Francis's trunk full of old diaries and papers still under the bed, waiting to be dealt with.

Two weeks after returning, she glimpsed Jonathan by chance on Kensington Park Road, although the Welshman didn't see her. Francis's death had aged him. His back was now stooped like an old man's. Eva stared at him so intently that for a second it suddenly felt as if she were inside his body, experiencing his grief. In that moment her bitterness abated. Eva recognised that she had allowed anger to grow inside her like a cancer, using Jonathan as a scapegoat for everything that occurred, as a way of whitewashing Francis's other difficulties with life. Silent and unobserved in a shop doorway, she watched Jonathan climb into a taxi: the orthopaedic surgeon unaware of how in this moment Eva was forgiving him for any unkindness towards her son, knowing that it was what Francis would have wanted.

That evening she was on her way to wander through the streets around Bayswater. This was where she had found herself walking every night since her return, regardless of rain or cold. There was no logic to this search but she was seeking any sign that might release her from the limbo of grief where, when she returned to the Quaker hostel, she could sit up until midnight re-reading every old letter in Francis's trunk. Eva began to develop different routes for these nightly walks, always feeling that she had only started her true search when she walked along by the wall of Kensington Park and turned up towards Queensway to disappear into the network of smaller streets: Moscow Road and St Petersburg Mews, Chapel Side and the synagogue near Orme Lane. She loved to pause and watch the light spill out from the ancient stained-glass windows of the Mitre Pub on the corner of Craven Terrace, knowing that she could linger across the street from it, utterly anonymous because nobody bothered to notice a woman of her age.

But somebody did notice her on those streets. Late one afternoon, Alan turned up at the Quaker hostel. They sat in the deserted kitchen at the long wooden table where two cats dozed in the twilight. It felt strange to have a visitor at the hostel, but everything about London felt strange after the sounds and rhythm of life in Morocco. Initially she did not know how Alan had discovered she was back, but she was touched by his concern when he mentioned being worried about her.

'But I'm fine,' Eva insisted. 'Can't you see that I'm coping well?'

'That's the problem,' Alan said. 'You're so desperate to show the world how well you're coping, that you're letting your pain fester inside you. You're still blaming yourself and blaming others.'

'I may blame myself,' Eva admitted, 'but I've forgiven anyone else involved.'

'Have you considered going to live with Hazel in Kenya?'

Eva shook her head. She didn't really know what was happening in her daughter's life since her divorce from Geoffrey: Hazel having never even confided as to why the relationship had floundered. It was better that Hazel and Geoffrey had parted rather than chugged along unhappily like Eva and Freddie had done. Hazel was never half-hearted in anything she did. But Eva worried about how quickly Hazel had remarried, to another farmer in Kenya whom she claimed that Eva once met in the Colonial Club, although Eva had no recollection of the man.

'How could I live in Kenya?' she said. 'I know nothing about Hazel's new husband beyond his name. The one time I visited her I hated how the white people drank in their club every night and shouted at servants. Kenyan independence hasn't changed them. Can you honestly imagine me over there, driving Hazel demented by handing out leaflets against the Vietnam War?'

Alan smiled. 'No. You get into enough trouble attending marches here. I'm just saying that while I'll always be here for you along with Francis's other close friends, there's nothing else for you in London.'

'There's Francis,' Eva said shyly.

'Francis is eighteen months dead, Eva. He's not coming back.'

'But his trunk is upstairs, all his papers. I loved the Moroccan sun, but London has memories that make him feel close. Maybe all I feel here is his absence but even that is something to hold onto.'

'Or to let go of,' Alan said quietly. He paused before continuing cautiously. 'The reason I knew you were back is that I saw you a few nights ago walking like a lost soul near Kensington Gardens. I was across the street. I said nothing because I didn't know where you were going, but after a while I realised you didn't know either.'

'Where were you going that night?' Eva asked.

'You might think it strange but I was going for healing.'

The remark surprised her. Alan was an atheist who always expressed a wry scepticism at her various beliefs. He seemed utterly self-contained. She had never even known him to have a serious lover, claiming to have reached an age where the only man worth taking to bed was Thomas Mann in hardback. Alan studied her face, as if trying to decide how to frame his next question.

'Have you ever heard of the White Eagle Lodge?'

Eva shook her head.

'That's where I thought you were going when I saw you, because it was where I was going myself. The lodge holds a healing service, a laying on of hands. It's a discreet, tiny church, easy to miss. A casual passer-by would mistake it for just another house on St Mary Abbots Place, a cul-de-sac off Kensington High Street. Its only difference from the other houses is a sign of a white eagle carved in plaster above the door of a small annex to one side.' He paused. 'A Mrs Cooke – Mother Cooke some people call her – is holding a service tonight. Would you like me to bring you?'

'I don't think so,' Eva said. 'I can't imagine liking such a place.'

'That's what I thought before I went,' Alan replied. 'You know me: normally I don't set foot inside kirk, meeting house or chapel.'

'Then what made you go there?' Eva asked.

He shrugged, an embarrassed sheepishness lending him a boyish look. 'I think Francis did. Or at least that story you told me about a girl having a dream in which Francis mentioned an address near Kensington Gardens. Dreams are pure nonsense, yet I couldn't get it out of my head, because what if her dream was meant to convey a real message but she got the details jumbled up? I know it's ridiculous and maybe even blowing my own trumpet, but I began to wonder if his message might be meant for me as well as you. Our friendship goes back to our school days. In Aravon I told Francis things that I've never told another living soul ... bad things that happened. Maybe it was curiosity that led me to stumble upon that small lodge, or the loneliness that sometimes eats into me so that I need to be out walking among other people. Don't ask me why, but this winter just passed was a damned lonesome winter after you took off for Morocco.'

He looked around the kitchen, uncomfortable at talking about himself. One cat on the table was studying him with unblinking eyes. Alan reached out a hand. Eva sensed that he wanted to shoo the cat away, but his gentleness would only allow him to stroke the cat's fur softly.

'If the girl's dream was real then she got the location wrong. While the place that I think Francis meant is near Kensington, it's on the Holland Park side, nearer Edwardes Square. As an atheist I find it pretty damned uncomfortable to countenance the thought that possibly Francis led me there, but for some reason, when walking one evening I turned down a small cul-de-sac off Kensington High Street which I have passed a hundred times before and never paid it any heed. I was admiring a few of the old houses there and fully expected to turn around at the end and walk back. I probably wouldn't even have spied the sign of the eagle if two women walking in front of me hadn't each separately entered the small doorway. I noticed a man coming behind me – very ordinary and conservatively dressed – about to follow suit. I apologised for disturbing him but asked what was in there. He replied, very matter of fact, "healing", and went through the door. I wanted to scoff, like I scoff at most things. Scoffing is my defence mechanism against life. But just then it was as if I could hear Francis's voice in my head ... you know his really gentle laugh, not mocking but chiding me like he often did, encouraging me to live a bit and take a chance. I followed the man into that tiny lodge on impulse, not sure what to expect, indeed not expecting anything. To my deep surprise I found that this healing service fitted my needs in ways I'd never expected, because it was addressing a need deep inside me that I never even knew I had.'

He paused and Eva realised that this was the longest, most revealing speech she had ever heard Alan make.

'I never thought of you as someone who needs healing,' Eva said. 'That was thoughtless of me, too wrapped up in my own pain.'

'I never knew it myself, Eva, but we all need healing. Maybe someone like me more than most. I know Francis could get over-emotional and fly off the handle and this had dangerous, tragic consequences, but at least Francis was able to express his emotions. I've also been let down and hurt so many times, but all my life I needed to suppress my emotions. It's how I was raised. It wasn't the done thing for Glenageary Protestants engaged in trade to show hurt or show anything except a brave face to the world. I kept telling myself I was fine, like you now keep saying you're fine. But I've not been fine for years. On my first night in that small lodge I realised that I was a clenched fist, my fingers scrunched so tight that I didn't know how to let go of all the pain I've been holding inside them.'

Eva reached across to lightly touch his hand. 'Poor Alan. And I never knew.'

'How could you have known when I didn't know myself? But say nothing to anyone, please, especially my nieces.'

'You know I won't.'

He was silent for a moment. 'Maybe you'd feel nothing at that lodge. It's not exactly overwhelming. No Indian gurus or Hare Krishna chants. It feels rather English, for all its mysticism. You might want to run out the door the minute you get there. But if you ever wish to go there, tonight or any night, I'll happily bring you.'

'Maybe we'll go,' Eva half promised, 'but not tonight.'

The noise of the kitchen door opening disturbed them. It was one of the Americans who was refusing to fight in Vietnam; a young man who had begun to pay Eva such attention that at first she suspected him of being romantically attracted to her. Then she remembered her age and realised he was seeking a surrogate mother in his exile. The young American hesitated, sensing he had interrupted a private conversation. He looked slightly jealous at seeing Eva with a visitor. He went to back out the doorway, but Eva beckoned him in to let him prepare his evening meal. His presence broke the intimate mood and Eva suspected that Alan might never again speak so openly about his emotions to her or anyone.

After Alan left, she slipped up to her room so as not to be disturbed by those troubled young conscientious objectors who found solace in telling her their woes. She needed space to think. The last thing she wanted was to find herself among throngs of Evangelists or Pentecostalists or Charismatics, swaying and speaking in tongues or embracing each other. Eva was wary of overt displays of emotion at public gatherings, where it was often difficult to distinguish between genuine feelings and the collective euphoria of whipped-up hysteria. Her pain was too real and too private for anything like that. She had vowed to avoid any place where her emotions might be manipulated. But that evening, when it came time to leave the hostel for her nightly walk, she knew that no matter what route she initially took, curiosity would lead her to seek out that tiny lodge she had missed on previous expeditions, having been searching the wrong streets.

In a self-protective way to quell her mounting hopes, Eva took the longest possible route to reach Kensington High Street to ensure that it was already late by the time she found the small turning for St Mary Abbots Place. The lodge or church was so inconspicuous that if Alan hadn't told her about the sign of the eagle above a side door, she would have walked down that cul-de-sac without noticing it. The tall house attached to it was in darkness and the doorway beneath the sign looked so dark and forlorn that Eva suspected that any service held was surely over by now.

Her intention had been to merely locate this building so that she would know where to come if she ever decided to attend a service. But now that she was here she felt so intrigued that she crossed the street to check if the door was locked. To her surprise the wooden door opened. Without giving herself time to think, Eva entered the building and stood at the back unobserved in the narrow space behind the last pew. The small congregation who quietly listened in that small room looked so ordinary that Alan would easily blend in among them; a mix of respectable, middle-aged West Enders and more casually dressed young people. Eva wondered how many admitted to their workday colleagues or perhaps even their families that they attended this healing service. But everyone present must have suffered in some hidden way. This leant them a quiet unity as they stood at the healer's prompting to sing a hymn while a young girl played the harmonium. When the singing stopped, the healer began to speak. Eva suspected that she was a medium, just from her weight. Mediums needed to eat heavily and be physically strong because they sacrificed so much psychic energy in allowing messages to be delivered through them. Eva instantly liked this white-robed, down-to-earth old woman who reminded her of a plump, gentle pussycat, sincere and unassuming. Tonight she seemed to have no personal messages to pass on to anyone. Instead she delivered a simple meditation on the words: '*Yea, though I walk through the valley of the shadow of death, I will fear no evil; for Thou art with me.*'

Despite her previous misgivings, Eva found herself enjoying this unassuming service. The healer finished speaking and placed her hands on several people who came forward to kneel before her. Eva suspected that people mostly only came here in times of crisis, then moved on with their lives. The woman reminded everyone present that they could write down the names of anyone whom they felt to be in need of absent healing. The image of a white eagle hung over the altar. Alan had explained that this symbolised the apex of spiritual development a person could attain if they allowed their inner light to radiate. But as the woman began to speak again, her sermon was not abstract: it contained sensible advice about coping with life's problems. Nothing felt phoney to Eva – unlike the two séances she had attended in desperation after Francis's death.

As Eva closed her eyes, it was Hazel's face which drifted into her mind. She could imagine her daughter's amused exasperation at the thought of Eva attending this tiny lodge which seemed to claim to be an invisible bridge between the living and dead. But Eva decided that if she wanted anything from tonight, it was to request absent healing for Hazel's troubled soul. Hazel never shared her problems and nothing in her brief letters from her new Kenyan address suggested unhappiness. But nothing indicated great happiness either. The healer finished preaching and nodded for the girl at the harmonium to play the first notes of the closing hymn. Eva found herself joining in, knowing how the streets outside would seem colder after the sense of companionship here. When the hymn ended, people drifted towards the exit, depositing contributions in a small iron box. Eva did likewise and paused in the vestibule to watch the healer shake hands with those leaving. Older men addressed her as Mrs Cooke, while some younger people simply called her Grace. When Eva reached her she smiled and accepted the proffered slip of paper with Hazel's name scribbled on it.

'For absent healing,' Eva explained, 'for my daughter.'

The woman studied the name on the paper and then scrutinised Eva's face. 'I don't think you're really here for your daughter, are you?'

'No,' Eva admitted.

The woman nodded. 'For months I've had dreams about a tiny little woman. At first you seemed a long way away but recently you have felt nearer. Have you been abroad?'

'Morocco.'

The woman nodded again. 'I must see these people out. Please wait here.'

Eva watched her bid farewell to the others, then bolt the door. She beckoned Eva through a doorway into a smaller chapel, furnished with just two plain wooden chairs. The healer sat on one chair and motioned for Eva to sit facing her.

'What is your name?'

'Mrs Fitzgerald.'

The woman leaned forward and smiled, with fat knees and a peaceful pussycat face. Eva found that she trusted her absolutely.

'Do you know something, Mrs Fitzgerald? I've become a great grandmother. I hope you live long enough to experience how marvellous that feels. I think you have lost someone dear to you. Is it your son?'

'Yes.'

'And you would like to know of him?'

Without expecting a reply the woman sat back: arms folded and eyes closed. Eva watched her for a long time, not nervous but enjoying the silence broken only by her peaceful breathing. Then the woman began to speak so quietly that Eva needed to lean forward to hear, not realising for a moment that the words seemed to belong to Francis.

'Mummy, I'm happy.'

The elderly woman began to unselfconsciously make shapes with her hands in the air. Ever since he was a boy this was one of Francis's mannerisms whenever he talked animatedly. Eva didn't make a sound, but at the word 'Mummy' tears of happiness entered her eyes. She felt convinced that this was Francis talking, though Mrs Cooke's voice had not changed. If she had tried to impersonate a male voice, Eva would have felt suspicious, but this message seemed utterly natural.

'I tried so hard to leave everything in order.' The woman's eyes remained closed, her breathing so peaceful that she might be asleep. Eva remembered how Francis's desk had been perfectly tidied, the only untidy thing in Jonathan's basement being the empty pill jar and the torn-up solicitor's letter. 'But move on now. Keep nothing of mine out of sentiment. Only keep what is useful and beautiful.'

Mrs Cooke opened her eyes and blinked twice. 'He seems to have gone,' she said in the same tone of voice, only slightly louder. 'I think there was more but it's late and I find it hard to keep focused. I'm not as young as I was. Did any of that make sense?'

Eva leaned forward to touch the woman's ringed hand. 'Yes,' she said. 'Thank you.'

'There's nothing to thank me for. He has obviously been hoping to reach you.'

'I've kept too many of his possessions. Possessions are a dangerous trap and burden.'

'It's never easy to let go, Mrs Fitzgerald. I feel tired now so I may just sit here for a while. Can you see yourself out?'

Eva left the motionless woman and walked into the main chapel, her footsteps loud as she entered the vestibule. Undoing the bolt, she closed the door softly behind her, knowing that she would never have any need to return. 'Mummy, I'm happy.' Eva knew that she had a duty to her son to find happiness again, to ensure that her sorrow never dragged Francis back. Last spring she had scattered his ashes, but only now did she feel able to let go of the infinite fragments of his soul. Holding out her hands, Eva imagined them swirling upwards, breaking into smaller and smaller particles until there was nothing left and Francis finally slipped free of her loneliness. Emerging onto Kensington High Street, she walked among the passers-by, unnoticed and unimportant. She was planning a bonfire of everything in Francis's trunk, so that – for his sake – she could commence a new life without him.

Chapter Fifteen

Eight Drafts of a Letter

Lundy Island, Bristol Channel, July 1970

This was Hazel's clear, precise handwriting. There was no doubt about it and it made each page precious. Every crinkle on the notepaper was also precious because, even though an unknown hand had flattened out the sheets to make them legible, surely it was Hazel who caused these creases by furiously scrunching up each unfinished letter to be discarded in her wastepaper bin. Though maybe she had not hurled them away in fury but in despair: despair at feeling unable to find the right words to express her frustrations at how life was panning out at thirty-seven years of age. The only problem with this notion was that Hazel didn't do despair: despair was a weakness and Hazel never succumbed to weakness. She did fury all right. She did anger as readily as she did generosity or spontaneity or radiated her unquenchable zest for life. Hazel had been angry with Eva or angry with life on the last occasion they spoke, six months ago: a crackling long-distance call routed through a dozen operators, any of whom could have been listening in as the minutes clocked up at an extortionate cost to be added to Hazel's telephone bill – or to the bill of whoever Hazel's new husband was.

Despite some distortion on the line that night, Eva had been able to recognise how alcohol was making Hazel slur and recognise also the unmentioned and surely unendurable stress that must have caused this anger to spill out as Hazel forensically dissected Eva's failings as a mother; detailing every poor choice made. The complaints had delved right back to when Eva uprooted Hazel from Winchester to drag her and Francis back to Mayo to avoid Hitler's blitzkrieg that all of her Winchester classmates had lived through, with friendships so strengthened by sharing this ordeal that if they remembered Hazel at all, it was as an Irish coward who ran away – the phrase someone in the Colonial Club used after Hazel described her wartime childhood. Collecting wild berries in the woods was all well and good but did nothing to prepare them for the real world. Nor did hauling Francis away from being bullied in that English boarding school equip him to deal with Jonathan's solicitor in London four years ago. Hazel had kept asking how could Francis have developed any backbone when Eva never allowed him the space to stand on his own feet, like Hazel now needed to stand on her own feet – alone or as good as alone – being blanked by former friends at the club since the divorce from Geoffry, leaving Hazel barely able to show her face in the one establishment within fifty miles where she was once able to at least enjoy a bit of company.

Eva could remember how at intervals a disembodied foreign voice interrupted the tirade, informing Hazel she had thirty seconds left, with Hazel demanding that another five minutes be added to the call, no matter what the cost. Eva had felt increasingly devastated, not at Hazel's accusations but at how her daughter seemed so isolated in her new marriage, that the only person left to vent her spleen on was the mother in London from whom she was growing increasingly estranged. At intervals when the phone line improved, Eva had heard the plonk of a crystal whiskey tumbler being placed down on a wooden surface as Hazel moved on to ridicule Eva's devotion to half-baked charlatan mystics and other ridiculous notions, which had always embarrassed Hazel when she brought home friends during her years at Park House School. By this stage Eva remembered realising how the phone call had ceased to be a conversation but a diatribe rehearsed in Hazel's mind on numerous nights lying awake in her new life, about which Eva knew nothing. Hazel had droned on about the Sunday when Eva shocked two of her school friends by suggesting that, because it was gloriously sunny, they would all feel closer to God and more truly celebrate His Sabbath by traipsing out into the countryside to rejoice in its beauty rather than listen to a stuffy sermon in church: another social faux pas which ended two more friendships when her friends told their indignant mothers. This was before she even started on Eva's weakness for idealistic young men like Harry Bennett during the war and Max in Dublin, back when Eva believed that letting children smear paint across whitewashed pages of *The Irish Times* stolen from neighbour's bins could prepare them life, by which stage Hazel had needed to seek refuge from her lunacy by living in at the Meath stables.

Eva could still vividly recall every word of Hazel's stored-up anger during that phone call: an anger being used to cloak ongoing tribulations about which she knew nothing. It made her scared now to pick up the first creased letter in case it contained another diatribe of bitter home truths. Yet she had no other option if she was to begin to make sense of what these two policemen who had arrived from London were trying to tell her. Eva didn't care what barbed comments these letters might hold, provided they revealed something about what had occurred in Kenya. Yet no words written here could explain the inexplicable. Alan and the policemen were cautiously watching, waiting for her to do something. All she could think to do was run her palm across the first sheet of crumpled notepaper embossed with Hazel's address and begin to read, trying to rationalise each word, to let what was being said and unsaid filter into her consciousness so she could make sense of it.

Dermot Bolger

The Argyllshire Farmstead
Kitale
Trans-Nzoia County
Kenya

7th July, 1970

Dear Mummy,

Thank you for your last three letters and apologies for my slow reply. I see your spirit of wanderings has taken you on yet another journey. Lundy Island sounds remote and peaceful and easier to reach than Tangiers. It may also have the advantage of possessing such a rudimentary telephone exchange, that your chances of being harangued some night from Kenya are slim. If truth be told I was slightly sozzled when last we spoke – and perhaps I spoke a trifle too frankly and unfairly. I can't really recall because my abiding memory of our chat is the frightful phone bill that arrived soon after and caused yet another kerfuffle with my less-than-better other half.

But I am glad you are off somewhere that suits your temperament and glad too that you are currently with Alan, who was always a brick and good friend to Francis and is that rarest of creatures: a fundamentally decent man. I rather suspect that Lundy is full of dreary people heartily tramping about in wet clothes and excitedly comparing what birds they spotted as they drink warm English bitter or whatever the local brew is out in the Bristol Channel. Being stuck on an English nature reserve would not be my cup of tea: though looking back over the past month, my life would have been better if I had stuck to tea. Abstinence is not an easy virtue in Kenya, but nothing feels easy just now, even just remembering to avoid looking at my face in a mirror. It's been a bit chaotic, Mummy, which is the main reason why I have not replied to your lett...

Hazel's handwriting spluttered out, midway through the word. Eva turned over the page in case anything was written there, but it was blank. She tentatively picked up the next crumpled sheet but this abortive letter was even briefer and less informative:

The Argyllshire Farmstead
Kitale
Trans-Nzoia County
Kenya

7th July, 1970

Dear Mummy,

As you well know it is not in my character to beat about the bush, so I have some bad news for you and you may as well hear it straight…

Eva looked up at the two policemen, not sure how they expected her to respond. She counted the exact number of words of this second unfinished letter as if this might yield some clue, before carefully placing it face down on top of the first one. There were six more letters in the pile that the policemen had carefully removed from a folder after arriving on the island. They watched her with solicitude and concern, as if the letters were a code that only she might be able to decipher. She felt pressurised to speak but had no idea what to think or feel. In so much as she could feel anything it was a numbness, as if the outside world was suddenly very distant and she could never fit back inside the life she was leading an hour ago.

'How difficult was I to track down?' she asked.

'You should not have been hard to find,' the first policeman replied. 'These letters explicitly state that you're currently residing on this island, but the Kenyan police forwarded them to the Met in London because London was your last known official address. Maybe nobody thought to read such personal letters addressed to you. The focus was on locating you so you could be officially notified. It has taken us ten days to track you down. There are procedures we follow, calling to the known address and then checking with the Gas Board or various banks to try and locate a more recent address if we draw a blank there. People would be surprised at the footprint they leave in their dealings with utility companies, but you didn't leave much trace, Mrs Fitzgerald. No forwarding address after you left London. Almost like you wished to make yourself invisible.'

Eva had not bothered to leave a forwarding address at her last flat because she had already written to Hazel about her plans to spend the summer on Lundy. Her family had shrunk so much that it only took one letter to Kenya to inform any next-of-kin about her whereabouts. All her possessions remained stored in one trunk, which the Quakers still allowed her to stow in their Portobello hostel when she went on her travels. Eva looked down, oddly shocked to observe that her hands, toying with the next crumpled page, were not shaking. Perhaps the truth had not yet sunk in. Perhaps she would never know the truth because, despite Kenyan independence, the white settlers there lived in a world within a world which dealt with uncomfortable truths in its own way. The one truth she was sure of was that she had not needed to travel to Lundy to render herself invisible: a sixty-seven-year-old widow was invisible, no matter what city she lived in.

Lundy was only three miles long and half a mile wide, yet every time Eva explored a new part of this island it yielded further surprises. The island off the Devon coast was uncluttered by roads or cars. Its sole pub was set amid a tiny cluster of houses called the village. These houses, and some other properties scattered across the island, had been restored by the Landmark Trust to be rented out to birdwatchers. Three months ago Eva had secured work with the Trust, thanks to a white lie about her age. If they knew she was an old age pensioner they might think her incapable of performing her duties, which involved cleaning cottages between lettings. For this she received a modest stipend and the free use of a cottage.

For the past month she had been helped by Alan, who was spending his summer with her. Eva loved the companionship of Francis's homosexual friends who looked out for her, knowing that they could confide in Eva in ways they could not talk to their own mothers, and who found in her a safe harbour from an intricate maze of affairs that still generally needed to be conducted in secrecy for safety's sake because no change in a law could simply eradicate hatred or random assaults. Eva suspected that Alan's usual summers in Tangiers were more romantically engaging than this summer on Lundy. But Alan lacked the hedonistic qualities she witnessed in some men who travelled to Morocco: their frantic quest for pleasure feeling like a cloak against loneliness. With Alan's prematurely greying beard and Eva's still youthful features, day-trippers who made the two-hour crossing from Ilfracombe on the *M.V. Lundy Gannet* sometimes mistook them for a contented married couple.

They had been content here, even when laughing at visitors' misconceptions of them. Alan passionately enjoyed teaching science in his London polytechnic. It was a secure job, and while he feigned poverty in his tattered jumpers and old tweed jacket she knew that this was just part the prudent camouflage that he had employed throughout his life to deflect attention away from himself. Like many gay men of his age who worked in the professions, he was finally secure without the usual economic strains of family life. Money was often their sole consolation amid the inconsolable loneliness of old age – a consolation Eva accepted that she would never know. Alan never argued about any of her beliefs but always agreed to disagree. Occasionally they discussed their experience of the White Eagle Lodge, but neither ever felt any need to return there. They possessed enough common interests, notably a shared love of birds, which made them often venture out each dawn to cliffs called The Devil's Chimney to watch for auks. Sometimes Eva saw birds of prey circle over Ackland's Moor, but otherwise this island would have felt cut off from any sense of danger had it not been for her growing concern about Hazel. Every day Eva had been anxiously waiting for a letter to arrive. She had never imagined eight of them – unfinished and unexplained – being delivered in this way. Picking up the third sheet, she steeled herself to read Hazel's words.

The Argyllshire Farmstead
Kitale
Trans-Nzoia County
Kenya

7th July, 1970

Dear Mummy,

Would you believe this is the third time I have tried to write to you this afternoon? I get exasperated after just a few lines because you really can be a fusspot in some of your letters. Was it really necessary to send three epistles in the past two months, filled with concern for me? Mummy, look at yourself, surviving on a rock in the Bristol Channel by cleaning toilets for redbrick birdwatchers who idolise Harold Wilson. I have a house and servants – even if I need to shout to get the simplest thing done. I can't pretend that life just now is easy. One might say that breaking up with Geoffrey was a terrible mistake, but at least I had the courage to make it. I did it because I have never been afraid to take risks. Kenya is the sort of place where everyone takes risks, maybe just to pass the time when there is not much else to do except watch the natives prepare to swamp all over us. So you take a small risk or maybe a stupid risk, because someone at the club dares you to, or you dare yourself, or because at certain times of night in that club – back when I felt welcome there – your skin starts to crawl because you're

249

sick of looking at the same faces or you have hit the bottle too early in the evening and you start to look back over your life and wonder how you ended up here.

Or maybe it's because the night train to Nairobi is the only thing still moving across that landscape and one night, once upon a time in a fairy tale which turned sour, you offered to drive a man home from the club who was too incapacitated with whiskey to drive himself. This man whom you half-thought you might be in love with because he paid you such attention and seemed infatuated with you – this man dared you to race the night train. Of course back then he didn't think you would have enough courage to do so, not knowing what stuff you are made of. That moonlit night you were determined to show him how much you love a challenge, how as a girl on your horse you often raced the Castlebar train pulling out of Manulla Junction to reach the level crossing before it did. This man didn't know that when your blood is up, fear is just another drug and suddenly you feel alive again, like as a girl jumping the steepest bank. You love how you suddenly have his full attention; how his amusement turns to fear in the passenger seat as you speed along the red dirt road running parallel to the train tracks. So close to the speeding train that you sense the driver and stoker stare out at you, so bewildered by what is happening that they don't know whether to speed up or slow down as you swing sharply left across the level crossing seconds before the hooting train reaches it. Suddenly the train has flashed past into the distance; the car has stopped dead, having swung around in a whirl of dust and you and he both laugh at the sheer outrageousness of it all, so exhilarated that it only seems natural to kiss.

But why am I telling you this? I'm getting as distracted as you are. That night is not the night I want to tell you about...

Eva placed this third letter beside the first two and looked up at the men seated around the kitchen table in her cottage. Alan sat in silence to her left. A man less attuned to her needs might awkwardly try to comfort her by taking her hand. Perhaps Alan still remembered how she gripped his hand so tightly on the night she found Francis dead that her nails drew blood or he instinctively understood that she was just not ready to be touched by anyone. Francis's death had been real. In retrospect, it almost seemed foretold so that the only surprise was that Eva had been surprised. This news was different. The more she thought about it the less sense it made.

She glanced at the mugs and plates she had placed to dry by the sink after breakfast this morning. How long ago those simple actions seemed. Was it really only last night when she and Alan tidied Castle Cottage for new tenants due to arrive on today's sailing? A lighthouse beam had swept across the rocks to light up that small granite dwelling, built by the Post Office in the last century as a cable station. She remembered extinguishing the gas jet and walking out to stare beyond Lametry Bay at the lights of a ship entering the Bristol Channel, before they companionably strolled towards home along a narrow path and she asked Alan if he was pining for Tangiers.

Alan had paused to enjoy the silence before admitting that the part of him which secretly enjoyed the thrill of danger did miss that city. Young Moroccan men were lovely, but lethally heart-breaking. He never understood how they could bear to divide their lives in two – being financially kept all summer by infatuated older European men, while maintaining relationships with their girlfriends with whom they shared any money subtly bled from such foreign visitors. He had teased Eva about accompanying him there next summer, saying that Moroccan boys would flutter their eyelids as beautifully for her as for him. Eva had laughingly replied that the only company she wanted in bed was a hot water bottle. When they reached St John's Well, Alan had suggested visiting the pub but Eva didn't want to face the smoke and noise.

She had walked on alone by torchlight to this tiny cottage to light the gas jet. Beside her bed she kept the Buddhist mantra, the *Vajracchedika Prajna Paramita Sutra*, given to her once by a working-class Glaswegian bricklayer who stayed for months at the Quaker hostel. Despite many long walks and picnics together in the countryside outside London, the earnest young man never converted her to Buddhism, although Eva loved its philosophy. But it was no more the final answer to her quest than the White Eagle Lodge or the Quakers' contemplative silence. Each belief system was too complex to be true. The truth of the universe was so simple that Eva often thought she had only ever grasped it once: as a child immersed in the joy of running with plucked daisies to share their scent with her nurse sitting with open arms beside the tennis court in her childhood garden in Dunkineely.

She had put on her nightdress and filled out some Amnesty International clemency appeals for political prisoners in China and Latin America, leaving them by the door to be posted. In bed she had opened her diary – an old ledger intended for her own thoughts, but filled instead with quotations to illuminate the darkness. She had read a verse that she loved from the *Vajracchedika Prajna Paramita Sutra*, allowing her mind to lose itself in each image:

'*Thus, shall ye think of all this fleeting world:*
A star at dawn, a bubble in a stream;
A flash of lightning in a summer cloud;
A flickering lamp; a phantom and a dream.'

Extinguishing the gas jet, she had sat back to look out her window. To her left the Cornish coast stretched to Penzance. To her right the coast of Wales jutted out. She had lowered the wooden window to allow night sounds to enter, the distant waves, a beat of wings, nocturnal movements among the heather. This routine emptied her mind, letting it drift beyond her own concerns and fall into a sleep so peaceful that Alan had needed to knock loudly on her door this morning to wake her to go walking on the cliffs at Stutter Point. Before noon they set off to enjoy their daily ritual of watching the *M.V. Lundy Gannet* reach its anchorage out in the bay: Eva always amused by Alan's darkly humorous speculation as to why each new arrival was visiting this remote hideaway.

Eva looked up again at the men around her kitchen table. Could it really only be an hour ago that the serenity she had striven so hard to achieve was shattered when the two rowing boats set out to ferry the *M.V. Lundy Gannet*'s passengers to shore? The first three passengers to clamber into a rowing boat were such innocuous looking birdwatchers that not even Alan could invent a dark purpose for them. The next two passengers to board the rowing boat wore police uniforms, though they had removed their hats in the heat. The first boatman began to row for shore while the second rowing boat moved alongside the ship to collect more passengers. Alan had made no comment on the policemen, sensing Eva's inexplicable alarm as she began to walk quickly towards the beach: Alan struggling to keep up amid the panic seizing Eva. She had imagined herself so well concealed here that ill-fortune could never find her. But instinctively she knew who the police were seeking. As the boatman moored his rowing boat to the makeshift jetty, the policemen asked him a question. By way of replying he glanced towards Eva and nodded. By the time the policemen descended the wooden jetty, Alan stood at Eva's shoulder, uttering a reassuring remark. Then he went quiet as the officers walked towards her.

'Mrs Eva Fitzgerald?' the tallest policeman asked. 'Can we go somewhere private please?'

'Just tell me quickly,' she had replied. 'Tell me who's dead.'

Those same two policemen were now patiently waiting for her to finish reading these letters as if they expected her to be able to decrypt them. One of them discreetly checked his watch, aware that they had a boat to catch. The busy outside world had pulled Eva back into its nets, and it was a world that could not afford to move at her snail's pace. Eva picked up the fourth sheet of crumpled notepaper.

The Argyllshire Farmstead
Kitale
Trans-Nzoia County
Kenya

7th July, 1970

Dear Mummy,

Ask yourself, Mother Dear, what sort of fool races against a train, even in a Bentley. You always say I drive too fast, but even as a child I always noticed how you do everything too slow. There are some things I need to tell you. One is that I can't do anything too fast anymore, even reply to letters because my right hand is broken in two places. Not that I can use my injuries as an excuse, seeing as numerous attempts to write to you last week got crumpled up in the bin. At least I am alone now. Half an hour ago I heard the door slam, his car rev up with the fall of dusk. Why should a man stay home to count the stitches on his wife's face? The fact of the matter, Mummy, is that I am not quite looking myself at present…

Hazel kept trying to tell her something but the words kept spluttering out. Hazel who always cut to the chase, resolute and certain in herself. The policemen needed her to read on. Their eyes were sympathetic but these men had been in this situation numerous times. Eva felt lost, as much bewildered as in shock.

Alan coughed as a form of subtle interjection. 'Perhaps Mrs Fitzgerald needs some time … to come to terms. She might be better able to help with your investigations if she could lie down for a while.'

The second policeman spoke. 'I know this is a terrible shock, sir, but the thing is that this it's not our actual investigation, if there is any investigation going on. To be honest, from the curt telex messages I've seen from Kenya, I'm not sure if there is one. The problem now with the colonies is that … well … since independence they are not actually colonies anymore. Naturally our High Commissioner in Nairobi can raise any questions that Mrs Fitzgerald has, but our hands are rather tied in that this has nothing to do with Scotland Yard. The Kenyan police would very quickly tell us to mind our own business, so in this matter we're only...'

He looked at his colleague for help in finishing the sentence.

'Messenger boys, unfortunately.'

'Why do you say, unfortunately?' Alan asked.

The first policeman shrugged, uncomfortable. 'I suppose it's a cultural thing, sir. Different police forces act in different ways, especially in the heat of hot countries. If this occurred in England I am not sure the funeral would have been a mere forty-eight hours later. Obviously they consider it to be an open-and-shut case, but for such a remote location they didn't leave too much time for an autopsy by a forensic pathologist. Still, I am sure that every procedure was followed and, like I say, we are only messenger boys here, notifying Mrs Fitzgerald on behalf of the Kenyan police. Indeed, normally speaking, we would not be involved at all, but Mrs Fitzgerald's son-in-law has been unable to contact her directly. The only address he had was the flat in London that we first visited. He also provided an address in some house in Eire which the Garda Síochána assure us is now an uninhabited ruin.' He looked at Eva. 'You have a million questions, and I wish we could answer them. But I think it best if you place a long distance call to your son-in-law. He is the person who can properly tell you what happened and I am sure he is desperately trying to reach you.'

'He is not my son-in-law.' Eva saw the policemen exchange a confused look. 'I mean he technically is, but I don't know him. The only person I know in Kenya is my first son-in-law. A good man. They seemed so well matched. Their breakup was acrimonious, like breakups are, but they have a daughter they both love.'

The first policeman nodded, his work making him undoubtedly familiar with the complex aftermath of fragmented marriages. 'The

Kenyan police took these letters away from your new son-in-law and forwarded them to us in London because they are addressed to you and therefore your property. If they cause you too much distress, please don't feel obliged to read right now. We merely wanted to give you a chance to ask us any questions about them that might help. However our governor expects us back in London, so we are rather dependent on the tides to get off this island.'

Eva saw Alan studying her. 'If you wish to go to Kenya, I'll fly there with you,' he said softly. 'I have some savings. Tomorrow we should probably return to London. All of this is too much for you to take in, Eva.'

Eva stared at him, baffled. It felt as if her brain had frozen, unable to conceive of any day beyond this one, of having the strength to ever again rise on another morning. It went against the natural order for a mother to endure being present at the funeral of one child, but to have to endure two? But what was she thinking? She had not even been present when – as these policemen kept insisting – Hazel was buried in Kenya two weeks ago. She could not even remember what she was doing on the night of Hazel's death. The dead needed three days to fully depart this world. During that time their souls were still confused and torn in two, hovering close to those they loved most, desperate to find ways to say goodbye. Had Hazel's spirit accompanied Alan and her on twilit expeditions to explore remote inlets and listen out for the Manx shearwater's unearthly cry? Had her daughter's ghost sat by her bed two weeks ago, invisibly stroking her hair in the moonlight, wanting to say so much but incapable of being heard? If so she must have been like the Hazel who wrote these discarded letters, struggling to find words that refused to come. Eva wanted to ration out each letter, pretending that for so long as she had new words to read it felt as if Hazel were somehow still alive, sitting at a writing desk in Kenya. But Eva's duty to Hazel was to not only read these words but to read between them. She ran her hand over the next crumpled letter.

The Argyllshire Farmstead
Kitale
Trans-Nzoia County
Kenya

7th July, 1970

Dear Mummy,

Thank you for yet another letter last week, although really I could do without your rather alarmist concerns. I mean, you don't need to constantly worry if I take a few months to reply to your latest communiqué from whatever far flung place you have currently decamped to. I mean, why this constant travelling, Mother Dear? What do you expect to find? Or maybe you're not trying to find something, but running away from the grief you still feel at losing Francis? I know you still feel it acutely because I feel it too. I miss my big brother. I miss everything about him. One thing I wouldn't miss is your annoying concern. Is it not about time you settled down and stopped pestering me with your anxiety about my welfare? Please don't add me to all your other causes…

Eva knew that Hazel only lashed out with such waspish words when trying to cope with stress. Their tone didn't hurt Eva. The only pain she felt was at sensing the pain her daughter must have been in to write them. If Hazel had played chess, this letter would be the perfect opening defence, deflecting all attention away from Kenya and onto Eva. But this was a tactic Hazel had mastered early. Whenever Francis or Eva were in trouble, Hazel was immediately there for them, the perfect confidant and friend, dispensing advice with such copious generosity that only afterwards did you realise that she had told you nothing about her world, her anxieties and problems locked away from public view, a proud Fitzgerald shielding you for her pain, until – if these policemen were correct – her pain became impossible to bear.

This letter was too truncated to reveal anything. Each draft felt like a clue in a crossword puzzle that nobody could ever finish, a labyrinth where all you could do was lose yourself. Alan reached across the kitchen table. This time he did touch her hand, for the briefest second, to remind her that she was not alone, although in truth she was. She passed him the incomplete letters she had already read, hoping that perhaps his logical mind could decode them. Taking a breath she picked up the next crumpled sheet.

The Argyllshire Farmstead
Kitale
Trans-Nzoia County
Kenya

7th July, 1970

Dear Mummy,

It's late at night here, with no sound except the hum of the generator. Alex was meant to be staying but she is with friends, which is no bad thing because of what I need to tell you. Before I do I just want to say that I flew off the handle when we last spoke by phone and said hurtful things. But never take those words to mean I don't love you even when I get so exasperated that I tell you I don't love you. I was thinking this last night when I woke up, alone as always, and I remembered how you would silently appear in my doorway if I woke as a small child in Glanmire House. Remember how ghastly cold those old rooms always were? The soles of my bare feet were always cold in bed at night there, no matter how many blankets you tucked me in with to try and keep me warm. One miracle of my childhood is that by some sixth sense you always knew when I was awake and needed you. It seemed like I had only to open my eyes and my bedroom door would silently open a moment later: you appearing in the moonlight to sit on the edge of my bed. No need for any words as you lifted my feet out from under the bedclothes to blow on my soles and rub them to make the cold go away and any fears or bad dreams disappear.

I'm a grown woman now – indeed at fourteen I was more grown up than you'll ever be. But that doesn't mean there aren't nights when I wish that someone like you was here to instinctively know when I wake up, scared and alone. I won't pretend that in actuality I wish you were here because you'd drive me demented with your crackpot notions. You're so immersed in compassion for the smallest creature crawling up a stalk of grass that often you're incapable of seeing the bigger picture of what's happening before your eyes. So I don't wish you were here, but I sometimes wish I were a small girl like Alex again, with my whole life before me and with my face as beautiful as her face that it will stop men dead in their tracks in time. Alex has part of your soul inside her – she comforts people. She would comfort me if she were here, she would curl in beside me in the bed and rub my feet if they were cold. But this house is not a happy house and no child should be forced to eavesdrop on rows. I know what rows do to a child because there were nights when I was young that I woke to raised voices and this damaged me, though it took me years to recognise the damage. I don't want Alex damaged, no matter what happens to me. Bad things have happened. They came to a head, Mummy, some weeks ago: an accident involving my trying to outdrive the night train to Nairobi. The doctor called my attempt to reach the level crossing before the train a suicidal manoeuvre, but I'd been successful before, doing it once to impress a man who seemed infatuated with me. On this occasion, however, I was alone and ready to show the world – or at least to show that same man – that I was still up to any challenge, still in control, still a fighting Fitzgerald, even if I'm now trapped with a new surname that no longer fits me. I am trapped because what exactly have I got to do back to in Ireland if I leave the red dust of Kenya? Perhaps my latest attempt to outrun the night train was crazy because as I sped along the road which borders

the track I could see the driver picking up speed too. He'd been
outrun by me several times before and didn't intend being outrun
again by any white woman. It felt like a challenge and I've never
backed down from any challenge. The doctor was wrong. It was
no suicidal gesture, but one of desperation. Suicide is not a word
in any lexicon of mine. I'm a fighter, Mummy. You know well that
I will never lie down, no matter who that might suit…

Eva only realised how slow she was in taking every word in
when she looked up and realised that Alan had already finished
reading the previous five drafts and was awaiting this next one. She
sensed that the policemen had read each draft on their way here.

'Tell me again what you know,' she pleaded. 'Please, from
the start.'

The policemen glanced at one another. Perhaps they were
weary, having already told her twice. They could tell her twenty
times and still Eva would be unable make sense of their words.

'The only facts we have, Mrs Fitzgerald, are those our Kenyan
counterparts passed on,' the first policeman said. 'All we have
been told is that your daughter was found in a parked car with
the engine running inside her garage. The windows were closed
except one rear window open wide enough to fit a hose leading
from the exhaust pipe. Presumably a coroner's inquest report is
being prepared but, like I say, the Kenyan police seem keen to
stress that the case is clear-cut.'

'That my daughter committed suicide?'

The policeman looked at his colleague for support. 'Sadly
this is what the evidence points to. We can't investigate this
matter, ma'am. The Colonies are not within our jurisdiction. We
can only report what we are told.'

'Then you've been told wrong.' Eva was surprised by the
momentary anger in her tone because she felt almost detached
from the scene, as if the chill in her bones was her body's way
of masking grief, its anaesthetic against an anguish making her
want to howl. 'I know my daughter. Hazel would never commit
suicide. She simply wasn't a quitter.'

The policemen's gaze was apologetic but firm. 'The truth, ma'am, is that we often know people but we don't know their circumstances or state of mind. That is why we were anxious to personally deliver these letters to you … in case they shed light. Lundy is a long way from Kenya. The letters – or drafts, because all appear to be written in one night – suggest that your daughter was enduring considerable personal anguish. They are dated three days before her death. They must still have been in her wastepaper bin because the police took them away as potential evidence. I think the Kenyan police initially thought the final draft was a suicide note. It was the only letter not crumpled up. It was neatly sealed in an envelope on her dressing table, with your name on it. Your son-in-law didn't want to open it as it was addressed to you. He claims that he and your daughter had a row that night over some jewellery which straitened financial circumstances compelled him to sell. I sense that a considerable quantity of drink was consumed. He went to bed and woke next morning to find your daughter dead in the back seat of the car, her head on a pillow, her body clad in a nightdress but wrapped tight in a thick woollen blanket as if she felt cold and wanted to stay warm. You have a million questions and I wish we could answer them. But I think it best if you phone your son-in-law. He may be able to put your mind to rest about the details of this tragedy. In the meantime, your granddaughter is being cared for by her father, a Mr Llewellyn, I believe.'

Eva nodded. In her mind she could picture Geoffrey consoling Alex, allowing the child to talk when she wished to and sitting with her in silence in other moments when what she needed most was a reassuring presence. She could picture the blue blossoms of the jacaranda tree overlooking the veranda in the courtyard of Geoffrey's house: Juma, the houseboy, and the cook and gardener all being there for Alex – like Eva desperately wished she could be – wrapping the child up in unspoken love. What she could not picture was the man whom Hazel wed after her first marriage collapsed. Hazel used to grow irritated on the phone when Eva claimed not to remember being introduced to him at the Colonial Club. But he had made no impression on Eva back then, being merely another white drinker. All Eva knew was that he was older than Hazel and his farm had been granted to him by the European Agricultural Settlement Board in the 1950s when what was then called the Colony and Protectorate of Kenya tried to bolster numbers of white settlers. Hazel had told Eva this in the phone conversation in which she announced her marriage: her voice sounding exultant when describing the new life she planned for herself, but Eva had sensed a brittleness behind her cheery tone. Her happiness in that phone call had lacked the unsoiled joyous expectation that Eva remembered in Hazel's voice on the morning she had wed Geoffrey in Dublin.

'Have you been to Kenya?' she asked both policemen who shook their heads.

'I did my National Service in Southern Rhodesia,' the first one said.

'You got lucky,' his colleague replied. 'I only got sent as far as Cyprus, which, to be honest, was hot enough for me.' He turned to Eva, apologetically. 'Sorry, ma'am, I'm straying from the point.'

'You're making my point,' she said. 'If you found Cypress warm, then imagine the heat of Kenya. I know July is the coldest month there and temperatures can plummet at night. But would you really wrap yourself up tight in a thick woollen blanket, no matter how distressed you are, especially when alcohol coursing through your bloodstream would already make you feel so hot?'

The policeman shrugged uncomfortably. 'Mrs Fitzgerald, as a policeman I can't really comment on another force's investigation. I came here out of compassion, with the sad duty of ensuring that you are officially informed of your daughter's death.'

'I didn't ask you as a policeman,' Eva said quietly. 'Are you a father?'

'I have a daughter, yes. She's seven.'

'Then I'm asking you as a father.'

He glanced at his compatriot. 'Well, the woollen blanket raised a few red flags for me. Not so much its heaviness as the description of how tightly wrapped up she was. I would have been keen to rule out any possibility of her having been rolled up inside it by persons unknown. But the Kenyan police report contains no suggestion of malefaction by any third party, no evidence of anything except death by misadventure.'

This time Alan spoke, framing words he knew that Eva barely dared to utter. 'Would evidence exist if Hazel passed out unconscious on a bed and someone wrapped her in a blanket to make it easier to carry her down to the garage?'

'That's speculation I can't engage in, sir. In Britain the garage would be sealed off, the hosepipe checked for fingerprints. I'm sure similar procedures were followed by the local police who seem to have found no grounds for suspicion.' He turned to Eva. 'Perhaps you might finish reading the letters, ma'am, in case they reveal anything of your daughter's state of mind.'

The man's voice seemed distant as Eva closed her eyes to recall Hazel as a child wrapping herself as tightly as possible in the blankets at Glanmire House after Eva finished cradling her soles to get them warm. Hazel, the plucky blend of mischief and courage; the blonde bombshell stock-car racing driver; the white butterfly fluttering down a Wicklow hillside with Max on their bicycles, freewheeling away from her. Eva could almost hear Hazel's resentful tone saying: '*You accepted Francis's decision to die. You cradled his body, relieved the world could no longer hurt him. Yet even now you treat me different, spending more time arguing with the police than mourning my death*'. But Eva knew their deaths were different. Francis's suicide was a methodically chosen last resort. If Hazel committed suicide, it must have been an impulsive lashing out at life. Maybe she simply intended to scare her new husband and had threatened to do this, expecting him to rush into the garage and find her in time? Eva would never know for sure because Kenya was a closed fist: a world that dealt with secrets in its own way. There was enough political upheaval without the authorities worrying about some white woman's fate. Eva picked up the penultimate letter, trying to visualise Hazel at her writing desk late at night, stubborn even in her determination to finish a letter in which she didn't know what to say, because how do you ask for help when it is not in your character, when all your life you have needed to be the strong one in the family whom everyone else leaned on?

The Argyllshire Farmstead
Kitale
Trans-Nzoia County
Kenya

7th July, 1970

Dear Mummy,

You have never set foot in my home, but remember how I described the train tracks running parallel to the road for a mile. The night train to Nairobi runs past after midnight. It is possibly the only thing still functioning on time since independence. A level crossing leads to the dirt track entrance to our lands. On certain nights it became a challenge for me to outdrive that train and swing across the level crossing before it reached there. A silly game really played on nights when I cannot bear to sit among the same faces in the damned club, half of them not talking to me since my first marriage failed but all of them knowing my business, the reasons why my second marriage is on the rocks; their smug judgmental sense that maybe I never belonged among them after all.

So on the few nights when I still go there, sometimes I finish drinking before anyone else is ready to head off for what passes for home here. I leave the lights of that club and suddenly I'm alone in the African night that is like no darkness in Mayo. I remember back to a night when the man whom I later had the misfortune to marry had a few Scotches too many and I thought it wise to drive him home to this farm, never suspecting that this farm would one day become my home. I remember how nothing was moving across the dark landscape that night except the shafts of light from railway carriages as the night train trundled past on its way to Nairobi. It was on that first night that he dared me to race the train, claiming nobody could beat it to the level crossing. He was wrong: I beat it, never able to resist a dare. Even as a child I needed to push myself to test the true horizons of my world. Or maybe to get your attention because you were always too wrapped up in Francis and while I loved Francis to bits that didn't mean I hadn't the right to feel jealous. Though even if I had to play second fiddle as a child, I fared better than Daddy, who always played third fiddle in your affections. It wouldn't have taken much to make Daddy content really, but to be fair I'm not sure anything you could have ever done would have made me truly content. For me there always had to be something extra. I don't mean more wealth or status or any of that silly stuff, but a new horizon, another test, more zest and zing and jizz and jazz, more to life than just this.

I've always wanted to live every minute of every day. Maybe that's a childish expectation now when I'm no child anymore. I'll soon not even be a young woman anymore. Thirty-seven last birthday. Forty lurking out there: an uninvited intruder. Thirty-seven probably doesn't seem old to you, but even at an impossibly young age, I always felt somehow older than you, somehow responsible because somebody in our family needed to be. I didn't have a great track record of predecessors, you must admit. Poor Francis, who tried so hard but was too easily wounded to handle life. Daddy, chronically unable to handle money or drink or show affection. Your two brothers unable to see the ugly truth behind their communist utopia. Your father hiding away behind his Walt Whitman poems or your mother keeping life at bay with beekeeping and séances. It's no wonder you never really grew up, Mummy, but out here I've had no choice.

I'm getting like you, rabbiting on to avoid the issue. It makes no odds I suppose because it's late and I know this letter will probably end up crumpled in the bin like all the others. So let me cut to the quick. It is not earth-shattering news – although definitely jaw-shattering. Foolish pride prevented me from writing before now – a last vestige of vanity. Lots of women my age are beaten up inside, I just happen to now also look beaten up on the outside. A map of my recent life is stitched across my left check. I remember people calling me a bombshell: now the expression would be a bombsite. I could always turn heads but I turn them now for the wrong reason. Because there comes a time when you can't outrun trains any longer, when your wits and reflexes and instincts let you down. There comes a night when no one is sitting beside you in that car daring you to take on the train, when the only person you are still trying to prove something to is yourself. When you think you will still make it to the level crossing in time; just like in the past when your car rattled across the wooden sleepers and reached the other side safely with seconds to spare. And by taking that risk you'll have proven your worth to yourself again and you will sit there, quietly pumped with adrenaline, not even bothering to look back at the startled faces of the passengers heading off on their long train journey, leaving you stranded on that red dirt road.

The reality, Mummy, is that I could have chickened out at any time, especially with nobody there to witness my test of courage. There was a second, or a lucid fragment of a second, when I knew I was not going to make it, that my reflexes and the battered engine of the Bentley had finally failed me, that I was beaten and the time had finally come to back down. But I could not back down because my character does not possesses a reverse gear. In that last second I knew the train would hit the back of the car, which would overturn. I also knew the train wouldn't stop and I'd be trapped there until men finally cut me out from the wreckage. Such pain, Mummy, bones broken, my face a mess of blood; my face that was once loved. It's a fickle thing, love. But I am not fickle. I am who I am and if I could start a car again and hold the wheel steady with my shattered wrist I'd go straight back to that crossing and race the train again. I refuse to be beaten. Even if I knew I no longer had the pace and was certain that train would hit me head on, I'd still put my foot to the floor rather than back down. Because that's who I am, because – to use the word you tried to instil in your art classes – that's my character and, despite your fears expressed years ago, let me tell you one thing: I've never lost my character…

A knock sounded on the kitchen door as Eva finished reading. The boatman was apologetic for disturbing them but anxious to know if anyone wished to be rowed out to the *M.V. Lundy Gannet* which could delay its departure no longer. Eva knew the policemen were keen to start their journey back to London. They had gone out of their way to find her when they could easily have let the local Devon police break this news. One reached across to softly touch her knuckles that were turning white from how tightly she gripped this letter – Hazel's words made more precious because Hazel had never wished her to glimpse this despair.

'If you'd like us to accompany you back to London, ma'am, your friend could help you to pack quickly. In London you can phone Kenya and have all your questions answered.'

'I think Mrs Fitzgerald needs some time on her own,' Alan said. 'We'll travel back very soon.'

The policeman nodded. 'I understand.' He turned to Eva. 'We'll give your friend the High Commissioner's contact details in Nairobi. You're in shock. You need time to absorb this news. But we can have someone call to see you in London if we receive any more information. Maybe you could give us your permanent address. Where is your actual home?'

'I don't know.' Eva felt too weak to rise from the table. 'My home rather got lost along the way. I don't seem to have one.'

'I will look after Mrs Fitzgerald and take care of matters from here,' Alan said. 'Please use my address as your point of contact if more information arises. I think she needs to be left alone now.'

'Thank you, sir. It's a terrible shock for the lady. This is one part of my job I hate.'

His colleague rose and picked up his hat. 'We're sorry for your trouble, ma'am. To be honest, I wasn't sure if giving you these letters would do more harm than good. But they may clarify some things for you so that in time all of this will make sense. If it's any consolation, in my line of work I've learnt that sometimes things never make sense, no matter how hard we try, and if we try too hard we end up inventing theories just to give ourselves an explanation because we find it so hard to live with the simple truth that human beings are complex and often do things for complex reasons that even they don't understand. I hope you find your answers, but maybe in time you'll just have to live with the harshest truth of all, which is that certain things are unknowable. My sincerest condolences, Mrs Fitzgerald.'

The two policemen shook her hand and walked out the open doorway with Alan. She saw the boatman signal out to sea and one policeman open his notebook to jot down Alan's address. Alan remained standing in the doorway, observing the three men hurry down the path. He seemed to be watching to check if the boatman could row them out in time, but Eva knew that he understood her well enough to give her this time alone. He understood loneliness: something she thought she understood before but now realised that she about to truly learn. Because until now her daughter was always a long-distance phone call away – no matter how strained those calls could be, how little she and Hazel agreed on and how far apart their worlds had grown. Now there was just a void. Eva tried to push through this pain by remembering how, even within this void, there was still Alex: a precious child who must surely be traumatised. Something of Hazel's spirit would live on inside Alex as she grew to become a young woman. Eva clung to this sliver of comfort, to the sense of purpose that somehow – even if penniless and on the other side of the world – she would do everything to be there for Alex if the child ever needed her.

With the policemen gone, her body trembled so much in shock that she barely had enough strength to pick up the final letter Hazel wrote: the one in pristine condition despite the numerous hands that surely held it over the past fortnight, scrutinising each word in search of a foretelling of what occurred three nights after it was written. But Eva knew her daughter well enough to sense that, if Hazel had placed this letter in an envelope to be posted, it would contain no chink to reveal the anguish hinted at in previous drafts. She knew this as surely as she knew that Alan would remain in that doorway, seemingly intent on watching the boat row out to the ship, but really allowing her the privacy to read these words and cry now that there was no one to see. He would not bother her with platitudinous comforts but wait patiently for the moment when she had absorbed these final words. Only then would he judge it right to turn and walk back into the kitchen to offer her the unadorned companionship of a lonely man.

The Argyllshire Farmstead
Kitale
Trans-Nzoia County
Kenya

7th July, 1970

Dear Mummy,

Thank you for your various letters and your concern. But I'm afraid you read too much into my silence. The fact is the last few months have been a bit chaotic and I was laid up. Well not exactly laid up, but I broke my wrist, a spot of bother with a motoring accident, but just a few cuts and bruises, nothing I won't get over. It made answering letters a bit difficult but my wrist is well on the mend. Nothing much to report from Kenya because nothing much happens here, but hubby number two and I knock along even when we rub each other up wrong. You'd think I would be used to the heat here by now, but what I would not give for one of those soft days of rain, as we called them in Mayo, when damp drops seemed to just hang in the air. Here it can be a case of monsoon or nothing. I suspect it is rather more temperate on Lundy Island, which sounds exactly your sort of place, full of people on your wavelength, as you like to say. I hope you are happy there, but you know that I would always find a place for you here, even if money is a bit tighter than it once was and life is just a trifle complex of late. But you know that I would never see you stuck and you are reaching an age when you need to properly look after yourself.

Still look at what I'm doing: worrying about you after scolding you for worrying about me. There's nothing to worry about. I'm fine. I always get through. I think it might be time to start planning for Alex to attend boarding school in Dublin, as some time away from Kenya might be good for her. But – like everything else when you're a divorced woman – this may need some subtle negotiation. My one great comfort is that Geoffrey loves her and wants what's best for her. Alex would love to scribble a few words of her own here or add one of her wonderful drawings, but she is staying with a school friend at present, although I know that she would wish me to pass on her best wishes and love to you. I must finish now because it really is frightfully late. It's astonishing how writing a short letter can take such a long time.

Yours as ever,
Hazel

Chapter Sixteen

The Ark

Curracloe Strand, Co. Wexford,
Early September 1972

This small caravan which Eva purchased last year cost every penny she had managed to save up. She was receiving a tiny English pension from her time working in different jobs over there. The Irish state took this sum into consideration before granting her an even smaller means-tested Irish old age pension. Between the two pensions there was barely enough money to survive on, but Eva was doing more than surviving: for the past week she had lived with such resolute energy and purpose that she barely found time to sleep. The caravan simply had to be made ready on time: the packed bookshelves tidied, the floor swept and all of Eva's papers and letters filed away into cardboard folders. Somebody precious was coming home today and homecomings always needed to be perfect.

Queensly, the mother puss whom Eva adopted as a stray, was curled up on top of two neatly folded blankets on the long window seat where Alex would be the first ever person to sleep. In the months since purchasing this caravan, Eva had started to mentally call this window seat 'Alex's bed'. Because, as she explained by letter to Alex, before her granddaughter left Kenya for Dublin, the caravan equally belonged to them both. Situated in the corner of a small field, a small distance away from other caravans in a makeshift caravan park, which a local farmer had created for Dublin-based holidaymakers, and near a tiny steep path that led down to the vast sand dunes of Curracloe Beach, it was not much of a home from home to offer to a child raised on a large coffee plantation. But it was only seventy miles from Park House Girls' School in Dublin, where Alex had arrived as a boarder ten days ago, and Eva would happily walk those seventy miles at any time, night or day, for the chance to spend ten minutes with her cherished granddaughter – the only family she had left.

In her letters from Kenya during the past year, twelve-year-old Alex always expressed delight at the idea of having a caravan as her private retreat on any weekends when she wished to escape from boarding school. Their correspondence started shortly after Hazel's death when Eva received a tender letter from Alex, in which the child desperately tried to comfort Eva at having lost a daughter. Her simply phrased words – and the thought of the young girl putting aside her own anguish to console her grandmother – had made Eva weep like she hadn't cried since being overcome by grief in a London park on the day after Francis's cremation. In the two years since Alex's first letter they had become weekly pen pals, sharing a similar childish delight in the everyday mystery of simple experiences while remaining acutely conscious of each other's unspoken loss.

The one thing they never discussed was the nature of Hazel's death. The Kenyan inquest had returned a verdict of suicide, but Eva still found it hard to countenance a fighter like Hazel leaving Alex without a mother. However, Eva was vigilant to ensure that she never even accidentally hinted in any letter at her doubts about the circumstances in which Hazel died; doubts that still ambushed her when she woke at night. That policeman on Lundy had been as wise in his own way as a Rudolf Steiner or Kahlil Gibran in forewarning her that she would have to accept the painful unknowability of certain truths. For months after Hazel's death, the only image of her daughter that Eva could summon up was an image she had never seen: her dead body discovered in a blanket. But over time, and especially through her correspondence with Alex, more joyous and vibrant memories returned that she stored up to share with her granddaughter when the moment was right.

Alex's growing intimacy with Eva, and the presence in Ireland of some of his own relations, may have persuaded Geoffrey to follow Hazel's wishes to see their daughter educated here. Eva was relieved that Alex was now away from Kenya until the school term ended next May. Uganda was only a day's drive from her father's land and Idi Amin's recent speeches in Kampala praising Hitler terrified Eva. Journalists, judges, politicians and anyone else who might potentially oppose Amin were being disappeared – their mutilated bodies sometimes found floating in the Nile. Recently Amin had announced the forced expulsion of fifty thousand Ugandan Asians to Britain, while his border war against Tanzania and Somalia threatened to further destabilise an unstable region. But from Alex's letters, the child seemed blithely unaware of such turbulence so close to Kenya's border, or else she had inherited her mother's pluckiness in facing down danger. Throughout the summer just ended, her letters to Eva had brimmed with excitement in counting down the days until she finally saw Ireland: her only anxieties ever expressed being about whether her new classmates would like her.

Such anxieties about making friends proved ill-founded. In the ten days since Eva had travelled to Dublin to be present when Alex first arrived at the school, she had eagerly awaited Alex's daily letters and rushed to the post office each afternoon to ensure that the child received replies by return of post. Alex had a gift for words, often enclosing small poems and drawings. Her letters were crammed with news about the other girls being fascinated by stories of Kenya, about how the winter clothing her father ordered from Cassidy's department store in Dublin was still not delivered to the school, and about how much she was looking forward to finally spending a Saturday night in Eva's caravan.

Eva's giddy sense of expectation reminded her of being a twelve-year-old herself, barely able to wait for a promised treat back in Donegal. All morning she had been cleaning and re-cleaning every surface in the caravan, finding this the only way to stop herself running out to the gate of the caravan park to peer down the small lane in the hope that Alex would arrive early. The child was being driven down by a Mrs Conyngham – the mother of a classmate who lived beyond Wexford town. Alex was spending tonight with Eva, who would accompany her by train back to the school on Sunday afternoon before rushing to catch the last train back to Wexford. Mrs Conyngham had offered to collect Alex tomorrow afternoon, saying that a train journey to Dublin and back in one day was too much for a pensioner. But Eva jealously guarded every second she could spend with Alex, who had expressed delight at a chance to see Wicklow by train. Besides, with her granddaughter now at the centre of her life, Eva no longer felt like a woman whose seventieth birthday was only a year away.

A car horn sounded at the gate and Eva needed to stop herself rushing out. She paused to check her hair in the mirror, then tried to walk calmly down the caravan steps and onto the grassy path. It was unusual enough for the grandmother of a pupil boarding in an exclusive Dublin school to live in a field, without the grandmother also acting like a madwoman. Eva's composure only lasted for the few seconds it took Alex to scramble from the car and run towards her. They hugged like schoolgirls, simultaneously talking and laughing until Eva broke away to thank Mrs Conyngham. Alex remembered her manners, shaking hands with the woman and wishing her classmate a nice night away. They calmly waved as the car drove out of sight down the overgrown lane, but were only just waiting to be alone before starting to hug each other again, laughing and swapping stories.

'Show me the two cats,' Alex said eagerly. 'I'm dying to pat them.'

When Alex entered the caravan, Eva saw how she had inherited Hazel's way with animals. Another child might have rushed over to Queensly, who had been joined on the blankets by Martin Buber – a stray old tomcat who found his way into Eva's life over the summer and whom she named after one of her favourite philosophers. Instead, Alex dropped onto her knees and gave the softest purr, patiently waiting until Queensly decided to approach. This allowed Eva the chance to study her granddaughter. Physically she would grow up to be as tall and beautiful as Hazel, but their personalities seemed different. Alex possessed her mother's inner toughness but seemed less highly strung. The fault-lines always waiting to surface in Eva's relationship with Hazel felt absent. Queensly eventually rose and cautiously padded over to brush against Alex's legs. The girl patted the cat's arched back, then examined all the food which Eva had prepared and laid out on the low table.

'You've gone to too much trouble,' Alex said, shy suddenly. 'There's no need to spoil me.'

'But I want to,' Eva replied. 'Let's spoil each other.'

The girl laughed. 'All right, Granny-Mum, you can spoil me if I can spoil you.' Alex glanced back out the open doorway at the empty caravans in the field. 'Have we the caravan park all to ourselves?'

'Yes,' Eva replied. 'They are mainly owned by Dublin families, but once the school term starts people rarely bother making the trip. I was alone here all last winter.'

The elderly farmer who owned this field was initially weary of Eva living here all year round, perplexed by what to make of Eva's accent. He feared taking in an eccentric who might become a charity case or create trouble. Although lured back to Ireland by the plans to have Alex educated here, Eva had no interest in ever again owning a house here, even if she could afford one. She had barely possessed the price of this caravan, but she liked the notion of a dwelling on wheels which could move as she moved. It gave her privacy, without anchoring her to one place.

Old friends from Dublin and London could stay a few nights as they wished, but after all her travels what she really wanted was the chance to be alone with two cats for companionship and enough space to finally unpack all her books stored in a trunk for years. When locking her door on her first night in this field, Eva had felt a deep serenity. Frankfurt Avenue was the last place where she possessed her own front door and could genuinely lock out the world. But Frankfurt Avenue was always too big once Hazel and Francis moved out, with constant worries about keeping up appearances. A different type of sanctuary existed in this field, a liberating sense of being safe and yet remaining outside the ambit of normal life.

'Show me the earwigs,' Alex said, examining the bookshelves built by a local carpenter who had been baffled by Eva's insistence on him using all the available wall space for shelving. 'I laughed so much when you described them in a letter.'

'I'm not sure they're still here,' Eva replied. 'The holidaymakers who own those caravans would call me slovenly if they saw this, but earwigs don't spread diseases or harm humans. I just think they have a right to live. They don't disturb me and I never disturb them.' From the top of the tall bookcase Eva carefully took down a brown envelope, inside which she had previously discovered a nest of earwigs. They now scurried around in panic at finding their small world jerked about. Alex peered into the envelope, fascinated.

'I also laughed when I found them,' Eva said. 'Your late uncle Francis used to be so amused when I left another family of earwigs undisturbed on top of my wardrobe in Frankfort Avenue, although back then, if I remember right, the envelope they took up residence in was white and considerably larger. So I suppose both the earwigs and I have needed to downsize. Maybe family isn't the right term for earwigs, but I see them as a family because earwigs are the only insects to harbour maternal feelings. The mother doesn't abandon her eggs after laying them, but watches over them even after they hatch.' Eva looked at Alex and smiled. 'Not many people know that, but not many people can stand the sight of earwigs. I'll put them in my bedroom if you're uneasy about having them so close to where you're sleeping.'

Alex smiled back. 'I grew up surrounded by snakes, so why would some harmless insects bother me? They belong here. If mice or wild dogs found their way to this caravan, I bet you'd let them come in too.'

Eva needed to stand on her tiptoes to carefully replace the envelope on top of the bookcase without dislodging its tiny occupants. She leaned down to stroke Queensly who, having brushed her tail one final time against Alex, lazily came over to her. Seizing his chance, Martin Buber now cautiously padded across the rush mats on the floor to make friends with Alex. 'Mice wouldn't last long with these two cats,' Eva said. 'I always leave the skylight slightly ajar to let Martin Buber venture out on nocturnal hunting trips and he likes nothing better than to be sitting on my bed when I wake, proud at having brought me an offering of a dead mouse. You can't expect cats not to be hunters when hunting is in their character. Animals are simple; they haven't lost their way. Give them warmth and food and they're content. Humans always feel that, no matter what they have, there's something else they need to chase after in case they miss out. Humans have forgotten the secret of how to be content. Friends in Tangiers and Dublin keep asking me to go and live with them, but I've reached an age when I'm happier living on my own with just cats and earwigs and the wind coming in off the beach at night for company.'

'Then I hope I'm not in your way,' Alex said, suddenly anxious. 'Do you mind me being here disturbing you?'

Eva laughed. 'How could you ever disturb me? Anyway, we're different when we're young, before we lose our inner radiance. Occasionally, if people get lucky they never lose this radiance and I think you're going to be one of those. You're not disturbing me at all. The very opposite: you root me to this earth. You are the very reason I'm here. I can't tell you how excited I've been, looking forward to this day: the most perfect I've known in years.'

Alex nodded deeply, looking carefully around as if trying to memorise every detail of the caravan. 'I love it here,' she announced. 'I feel at home already. The only thing it lacks is a name. I always feel strange just writing down your name and the location of this caravan site when addressing the envelopes. We should give this caravan a name. We don't need a name plaque at the door or anything. It can just be our secret.'

'You christen it,' Eva suggested. 'Then it will feel like it belongs to you as much as me.'

The child cradled the black tomcat to her breast and walked over to sit on the long window seat that would be her bed. She pondered this quandary seriously for several minutes while stroking the cat, who settled contently in her lap. Finally she looked up, face lit with excitement.

'The Ark,' Alex said, 'because that's what it is. It's the cats' ark and the earwigs' ark and my ark. Kenya is so far away and sometimes I get homesick when I wake in the dormitory at night. But if I can think of a light shining in the window of this caravan in this field I won't feel lonely knowing that you're here, just seventy miles away. Seventy miles is nothing where I come from.'

'The Ark.' Eva nodded as if a solemn decision had been reached. 'I'll never refer to it as anything else, even though it's not much of an ark. Barely space to swing a cat: not that Martin Buber would let you swing him.'

Alex laughed. 'The name suits it. Some girls at school rattle on about their fathers owning things, but we can ignore such talk and be ourselves here. Like living inside an adventure. This Ark has everything we need.' She hesitated. 'Except a television.'

Eva's heart sank. 'I've never felt a need to own one even if I could afford it,' she explained apologetically. 'I listen to the BBC World Service, but you'd probably find that dull. However, we can find the foreign station that plays pop music: Radio Luxembourg, isn't it? But I'm sorry if you're missing all kinds of television programmes by being here.'

'Most programmes I've seen in Ireland are silly and I prefer reading,' Alex explained. 'I devour books. But it's just that Kipchoge Keino is running in the steeplechase this afternoon at the Olympic Games. For months all of Kenya has been talking about him. After what happened last Tuesday the races probably don't seem important anymore, but as the Olympic Committee President said, the games must go on because no matter how dark life gets, we still need to go on living.'

The child went very quiet. Eva knew that Alex was not just speaking about how the Olympics in Munich had been overshadowed by the massacre of Israeli athletics by terrorists earlier this week. Alex's words bought the weight of their shared private tragedy into the sunlit space of this caravan. She imagined all the nights when Alex surely lay awake in Kenya, grieving Hazel's loss, at this age when more than ever the girl needed a mother to confide in. Eva had endured so many losses, but this was no time to be ambushed by grief; this was the time to be strong for her granddaughter and rejoice in the miracle of them being together here. Eva sat on the window seat beside Alex and took her hand.

'There's a pub called Furlong's in Curracloe that is my local grocery store. Mr Furlong always puts on the television on Saturday afternoons. Normally it's horse racing but I'm sure RTÉ will be showing the Olympics instead, especially after all that's happened in Munich. We'll walk down after lunch. Mrs Furlong would love to meet you. I told her you'd be visiting. You're all I've talked about for the past fortnight. Would you like that?'

Alex looked up and squeezed her hand. 'I'd love it. Can we go by the beach?'

'Yes, but let's eat first.'

Eva intended to make up a proper plate of lunch for her granddaughter, but instead they remained sitting on the window seat, chatting and snacking on whatever food was on the small table. It felt like a picnic indoors. Alex wanted to see every photograph that had survived Eva's numerous moves. Eva dug out dusty old albums of Hazel as a girl in Glanmire Wood, standing proudly beside her pony and even older photo albums from Eva's own girlhood: Eva and her brothers wearing such old-fashioned bathing costumes that they made Alex laugh. She stared at photos of her great uncle Brendan at the same age as she was now, smiling down from a hayrick in a comically wide-brimmed hat, and at a battered sketchbook in which Eva had recorded family gathering in delicate line drawings that had barely faded after more than half a century.

Although Alex admired these sketches, she continually went back to the albums featuring Hazel as a child, to scrapbooks of newspaper cuttings about Hazel winning prizes at horse shows and photos of her setting out from Frankfort Avenue with joyous optimism on her wedding morning. Alex didn't cry when examining these photos and neither did Eva. Instead they spoke simply about the woman they had both loved; sharing anecdotes which conjured up such a sense of the absence that bound them together, that Eva half-expected to feel Hazel's hand on her shoulder, like on the evening when Hazel had gazed down on them sitting together in a remote lodge in Mount Elgon National Park. The photographs that Alex studied most were those of Hazel at her own age, as if desperate to gain a sense of her mother as a child. Eva tried to convey Hazel's essence, but realised how she lacked the words to capture her effervescence and vivacity at that young age.

At two o'clock they put on their coats, collecting shells and coloured stones during their walk along the deserted beach to reach the small cluster of shops. Furlong's pub was empty, apart from two elderly farmers drinking slow half pints at the counter, who nodded to them with silent but hospitable reticence. The television was on, showing coverage from Munich. Eva had only previously been in the grocery section of this shop, partitioned off by a small door. But now she ordered two minerals from Mr Furlong and they sat on high stools at the counter to await the steeplechase. Alex was saying how her new friends at school envied her because the Kenyan athletes were so good. She found it strange that classmates regarded her as Kenyan, whereas people in Kenya always called her Irish. There was a delay before the steeplechase final and the coverage switched from the stadium over to the Olympic Sports Hall where a gymnastics competition was occurring. Mr Furlong called in his wife from the kitchen and even the two old farmers halted their muffled conversation to stare at the television. The tiny gymnast who walked onto the floor area looked younger than Alex, and barely old enough to be a spectator let alone an athletic. But a quality within her caused a ripple among the crowd, with an echo of that same anticipation pervading the pub. It was impossible not to watch this girl stand there, poised and awaiting the music, without fearing for her and wondering how such a waif-like imp could perform before a vast audience.

'Who is this?' Eva asked.

'Olga Korbut,' Alex said. 'All the girls say she was cheated out of a gold medal in the asymmetric bars. Even the crowd booed the result. Just watch her, she's marvellous.'

Olga Korbut was indeed marvellous. As the music started the tiny gymnast came to life with a leap that defied gravity. She turned and somersaulted, coiling her body into extraordinary postures that she lithely sprang out of to bound across the floor, performing an impossible succession of cartwheels and twists. She landed perfectly, within an inch of the white line, and fell backwards, subtle and languid, holding the crowd, this tiny pub and – Eva suspected – the watching world fixated in the palm of her hand, as she momentarily paused, prior to commencing the second half of her floor exercise. Eva was transfixed, not just by this sight but by a memory that came unbidden of another spellbinding figure thirty years ago. She urgently tapped Alex's shoulder.

'You asked me earlier what your mother was like as a girl. Well, that's Hazel up there on the television. Oh, I don't mean the same petite figure, but the same boundless joyous energy. I remember one afternoon during the war, Hazel began to blow bubbles from a jar on the daffodil lawn in front of Glanmire House, twisting her body this way and that, totally immersed in the magic of what she was doing. She knew she was magical in that moment and all of us watching – Francis, myself, Maureen the maid, even the barking dog dancing around her – knew she had turned the moment into magic too. Your mother radiated magic just like Olga Korbut.'

Alex made no reply but Eva sensed the renewed intensity with which she watched the television as the gymnast sprang into action once again. The bell over the door jangled as another customer entered and stopped, sensing the atmosphere. Nobody spoke in Furlong's pub until, with a final impetuous sequence of tumbles and falls, the young gymnast halted on the last note: her head tilted back, her figure utterly still except for an irrepressible smile that grew as the crowd applauded. Even the two black-coated farmers at the counter began to clap, shaking their heads in wonderment. Alex applauded so loudly that Eva feared she would fall off the stool. Mrs Furlong reached down to the shelves under the counter and presented Eva and Alex with two complimentary bottles of lukewarm lemonade.

'Seeing as this is a special occasion, Mrs Fitzgerald. This must be the granddaughter you were telling us about.'

'It is indeed,' Eva explained. 'I brought her in because she wants to see the men's steeplechase race. There's a Kenyan runner, you see…'

'Two Kenyan runners,' Alex said. 'Benjamin Jipcho is running as well.'

'And have you come all the way from Kenya?' the woman asked. 'What a journey for a girl of your age. I've a brother a priest over there in the missions, teaching at St Patrick's High School in a place named Iten in the Rift Valley Province. Father

O'Leary is his name. Would you have come across him at all? He's always saying how the young lads at his school are fierce runners, pounding out the miles on dusty roads, barefoot and all.'

By now Alex had everyone's attention: even the two old farmers who began to shyly ask questions and marvel at the scale of her father's plantation and the enormous size to which crops grew in Kenya. Eva felt inexpressibly proud at how well Alex answered each query. By the time the steeplechase began, the two farmers were shouting encouragement at the screen, as if Kipchoge Keino was a local lad, born and raised in Kilmuckridge, and Benjamin Jipcho had grown up playing hurling with their grandsons. More afternoon drinkers drifted in and got caught up in the race: a huge roar going up when the Kenyans sauntered home for gold and silver medals. After four hours in Curracloe, Alex was already famous. Everyone offered congratulations, insisting on shaking Alex's hand as they left the pub.

Grandmother and granddaughter dawdled for hours on their walk home. They encountered a stray dog on the strand holding a stick that Alex repeatedly threw into the water for him to fetch. The child screamed with delighted laughter, trying to dodge the seawater spray each time the dog vigorously shook himself when racing back to her with the stick. After the dog got tired and bounded off, they chatted to two fishermen digging for bait and spent twenty minutes patting a donkey tormented by flies, who was gazing out over a five-barred gate leading into a field that overlooked the strand. Sharing secrets never to be revealed to anyone else, they linked hands and walked along the darkening strand. Eva could not recall a more idyllic day since the mornings when she used to set off for day-long picnics as a girl in Donegal.

The cats were out hunting for prey when they returned to the caravan, or The Ark, as Alex reminded Eva. The field was deserted, with no light of any house within sight. They lit candles wedged into the two candlesticks, which were all that remained of the Fitzgerald family silver. The world outside felt hugely distant. Inside this tiny ark they needed for no one else and for nothing else as they made up Alex's bed, delighted when Queensly jumped down through the open skylight to settle herself at the end of the blankets so that she could curl up at Alex's feet while she slept.

Eva did not set an alarm clock. They would rise whenever they wished and have the whole of Sunday morning and afternoon to themselves before the train journey to Dublin. They would have all this and many more weekends to come. Eva would lose her granddaughter each summer when school ended and Alex re-joined her father in Kenya, but for the next five years the child would return to Park House School every September. Once again Eva felt part of the cycle of life, with a purpose to live for. To watch Alex grow into a beautiful, intelligent and confident young woman and to one day possibly even hold a great grandchild in her arms. Such hopes belonged to the distant future. For now it was enough that they were both safe in this Ark amid the fields, briefly lying awake to savour how the caravan gently rocked in the tides of the wind before they closed their eyes to succumb to dreams about all their tomorrows to come.

Chapter Seventeen

Winter

Turlough, Co. Mayo, 1974

The driver of the tow truck was unsure if he would make it up the overgrown woodland avenue to her former home. Luckily the day was so cold that last night's frost had not fully thawed. It was setting in hard again as dusk approached. So although the wheels churned up ugly tyre marks from the grassy avenue, the truck had not yet become stuck. A branch broke off an overhanging tree, leaving yet another long scratch mark along the side of the caravan the truck was towing. Walking behind it, in her seventy-second year, Eva threw the branch into the undergrowth. This second-hand caravan and these few acres of woodland were the last two things she owned. Glanmire Wood had grown neglected during the three decades since anyone last lived here. Fences were broken, damage caused by cattle wandering in and farmers freely helping themselves to fencing stakes. The woods were silent in this November twilight. This quietude, unbroken even by the cry of a solitary bird, made the engine sound even louder as the driver switched gear, preparing for a particularly steep bend ahead.

This was the third time in fifty years that Eva had arrived to make her home in Glanmire Wood. On the first occasion in 1927 she was a young bride, unwisely marrying into a family who still expected locals to lift their caps and step off the road whenever a Fitzgerald motor car passed. These woods were rarely silent back then, with Freddie loving to stalk through them clutching his Holland ejector twelve-bore gun. Drink took possession of him here in equal proportion to how loneliness took possession of her, with few paying guests, two small children and the county bailiffs drinking in Durcan's bar for Dutch courage before venturing cautiously up this avenue to serve writs on them. Their hesitancy had partly related to the four hundred years' residency of the Fitzgeralds and partly to the twelve-bore gauge of Freddie's Holland ejector. Those rooms had been freezing on the second occasion Eva came home here: a winter's night in 1939 as cold as this one, the war allowing her to run away from a faltering marriage to hide in these wood, with her children and their young maid, Maureen.

But tonight, thirty-five years later, as she returned for the third time, Eva was running away from nothing. She was only returning because this wood was the last place left from which nobody could evict her. When Freddie disinherited them all, he could never have expected his estranged wife to eventually inherit this wood, and certainly not in the way it had now come into her possession. Glanmire Wood finally belonged to her, but at an unbearable price. Eva doubted if she would ever feel warm again or experience hunger or any sensation except numbness. Since receiving the news from Kenya two months ago she rarely bothered to light the small stove in her caravan. Whenever she remembered to do so it was only for the sake of the three cats who had found their way into The Ark as strays. Her malaise had perturbed the two younger cats, who incessantly rubbed against her legs, wanting Eva to stroke them. But Eva had spent most of the past two months sitting motionless indoors in the small caravan park at Curracloe, only venturing forth to buy cat food. When news of the tragedy spread, local people started to bring her beef stews, possessing no understanding of what a vegan ate and imagining that she only abstained from meat because of poverty.

Old married couples like Mr and Mrs Furlong had shyly appeared in the muddy field when nobody else was around, pleading with her to take some nourishment. They talked about how isolated she must feel in that makeshift caravan park where she was the sole occupant in winter. These neighbours meant well, and, after they left, her cats feasted on the meat stews, while she broke up the proffered cakes to scatter as crumbs for the small birds who flocked around her home.

A caravan park was an odd place to call home, but Eva lost track of the places she had called home since the morning in 1949 when she left Freddie standing watching her from the doorway of Glanmire House. Home had been a succession of cheap pensions in Tangiers and rented rooms in Spanish villages, where her dream of becoming a writer faded. It had been an attic flat in London when forced to bear witness to her son's agony in the garden of Gethsemane; a Lundy Island cottage on the day she received news of Hazel's death. But Eva never had a proper home since the Frankfort Avenue house, until the morning when Alex christened this caravan The Ark. It was not just Alex's act of naming for it which transformed it into a true home, but her youth and love and vitality when it was a dwelling to be shared by her granddaughter on any weekend when the child wanted to escape from boarding school.

The only person who did not call to see her in Wexford in recent weeks was the farmer who owned the field where the caravans were parked, a man who wanted rid of Eva so he could rent her berth for more money to some rich Dublin family who would only bother to turn up on summer weekends. For over a year Eva had resisted his unsubtle hints for her to leave because it felt important to stay parked within reach of Alex's school. But that Wexford field held too many memories now. She was surprised by how the most unlikely neighbours called into her when news spread that she had hired this truck to transport her to Mayo: people with whom she had previously only exchanged a few words when proudly wandering with Alex along Curracloe

Beach, or when she spent last year walking around the small lanes in search of her tomcat, Martin Buber, after he ventured out on a night hunt and never returned.

The tow truck slowed to a halt now, blocking the avenue. Eva picked her way carefully around to the cab door, which opened.

'There's a chestnut tree overhanging the path,' the driver explained. 'I just might be able to swing around it.'

Eva walked past the truck and onto the daffodil lawn where she had scattered Francis's ashes eight years ago. The boarded-up house looked to be in the same condition as when she came here last spring on a day trip with Alex to show the child where her mother was born. However, the sun had been shining on that day, wildflowers in bloom. Eva sat on the front step to watch the man manoeuvre past the chestnut tree and park her caravan in front of the ivy-covered, boarded-up main door. He switched off his engine, climbed down and looked around, concerned.

'Is this really where you want it, Mrs Fitzgerald?'

'Yes.'

'I can swing it around to the side if that would make it easier for you to run a water pipe from the kitchen.' He paused. 'I mean you have a water supply, don't you?'

'There used to be one decades ago.'

'How will you survive without water?'

This man thinks I am demented, Eva thought, a lost old bird who should be kept in a cage. 'Survival is the one thing I'm good at. The poor cats will be terrified. You might lift down their baskets.'

The driver went to say something and then changed his mind. He released the three cats, who ran around the lawn in great circles after their confinement. The oldest, Queensly, glared reproachfully at Eva and refused to let the old woman come near. The driver put concrete blocks in place to stabilise the caravan and Eva climbed inside. Her books had been packed into boxes for the move, the crockery carefully wrapped up. The cats would be starving and she needed to feed them. The responsibility for their care was the only thing keeping her going. She called their names at the door but they refused to respond, still having not forgiven her. The noise of the spoon against their bowl brought them scurrying in, however, ill-tempered after their long confinement. They pushed each other greedily aside as they ate. Dusk had settled in. She went out to the driver who was putting down additional concrete blocks to serve as steps up to her door. He would be anxious to get his truck back down the avenue before all daylight was gone.

'You've a long journey ahead,' she said.

'Sure haven't I the radio for company,' He looked around him at the darkening trees. 'This is a lonely spot. Is there anything more I can do for you?'

'No. You've been really kind.'

'Does anyone know you're here? You're very isolated in this wood. In Wexford they said you were some class of artist or was it a writer? Nobody seemed quite sure.'

'I was never quite sure myself.'

The man opened the cab door and climbed up. 'Whatever you are, Mrs Fitzgerald, I wish you happiness.'

'Thank you.'

He switched on his headlights, slammed the door and drove off. The gathering dusk seemed more pronounced after he was gone. Eva re-entered the freezing caravan, suddenly nervous on her own. It felt ridiculous to feel anxious in this place that was once home. But she had always slept in the house, with paraffin lamps and log fires lighting up familiar rooms. It was too dangerous to enter any part of the old house now except the basement. Eva had lost count of the number of fallen trees that had smashed onto the roof over the years. Last spring when she explored the basement with her granddaughter, they had climbed halfway up the back stairs to peer towards the rooms where Hazel and Francis once played as children, unsure if the floorboards would still take their weight if they tried to enter. On that trip she discovered how intruders had torn out the last

Georgian fireplace with its black marble surround from the main bedroom. When dragging it across the hallway the floorboards had collapsed, plunging the heavy fireplace down into the haunted wine cellar below. Traces of blood had suggested that at least one intruder was injured, though since the Troubles started in the North, you were never sure what blood in a remote location signified.

Tonight as she stared out of her window at this ruined house, Eva questioned the wisdom of returning to a place with so many ghosts. An anonymous pension in Morocco might have been better, somewhere warm for her arthritis and her soul. But she lacked the will to start travelling again. Finding some candles in a packing case she struck a match. It spluttered out and she had to close the caravan door before a match would stay aflame long enough to light two candles. Placing them on the low table, she sat back on the window seat, which she still thought of as Alex's bed. It didn't feel like an ark now, but the walls would look better when Eva's pictures were re-hung and the shelves less bare after she unpacked her old books. Eva understood this routine of moving better than anyone, having spent much of her life doing it.

Tomorrow would be time enough to start unpacking. The clock had not been wound for days, but she knew it must be around half past five. There seemed nothing else to do except get into her bed fully dressed and hope not to wake until morning. Eva ate some carob chocolate, because she felt she ought to. Then she opened the skylight to allow the cats to come and go. They were disorientated but would enjoy exploring the crumbling house to the consternation of mice who had found refuge there. The caravan felt even icier with the skylight open, but – apart from her concern about what might happen to her cats – Eva hardly cared whether she was found frozen to death here.

This thought sounded self-pitying and therefore wrong. She remembered a D. H. Lawrence poem about how a bird could fall dead from hunger without having felt one moment of self-pity.

But such stoicism was easy in print. In the past two months Eva had found that the solace of books failed her. Even Martin Buber's great theological study, *I and Thou*, brought none of the comfort that one touch from his namesake, the missing tomcat, would have provided. But where philosophy failed, her body's instinct for survival took over. Tomorrow she would try to uncover the pipes from the ancient water tank mounted on masonry piers behind the house and use the rainwater collected there for boiling.

The two kittens scrambled up the empty bookshelves and jumped expertly through the gap in the skylight. But Queensly stayed behind, watching Eva with wise, compassionate eyes. The old cat climbed slowly onto Eva's lap and settled down, seeking not to be patted but to offer what warmth she could.

'Good mother puss,' Eva said softly. 'Wise old mother puss.'

Queensly lifted her head to listen, then sprang off Eva's lap to approach the door. Somebody was out there. Eva heard solitary footsteps crunch across the frozen grass. She remembered how Freddie had often returned alone to Glanmire during the last years of his life. Perhaps this was his ghost outside, about to enter that dark ruin with a bottle of Skylark whiskey in his pocket. But these footsteps lacked the peculiar sound which Freddie's club foot used to make. The footsteps stopped outside the caravan. The voice that called out belonged to another time. It had aged greatly but was still unmistakable.

'Mrs Fitzgerald? Are you in there?'

'Yes,' Eva replied, unsure if the voice was real.

The door opened and a figure stooped her head to enter, stamping her wellington boots to inject some warmth into her feet. 'Mother of God, Mrs Fitzgerald, you can't just sit here getting your death of cold. Have you not even got a stove?'

'I have,' Eva said. 'I just haven't lit it.'

'Well it's high time you did.' The young woman drew closer, only she wasn't a young woman anymore. Maureen's figure had become thickset, with glasses and permed hair that was tinted slightly blue. But her essence had not changed since the morning in 1939 when she stood before Eva as a girl in old clothes, ready to scrub down the flagstones on her first day as a maid here.

'Is that really you, Maureen?' Eva asked in wonder. 'You went to America years ago. I often think of you enjoying every mod con.'

'Ain't I the dumbest woman in Christendom not to be over there still enjoying them? Instead I'm back living in my sister's bungalow. My weekly highlight is bingo in Castlebar every Tuesday night. You remember my sister Kate, don't you, Mrs Fitzgerald? She married Jack Dowling from out Carrowkeel way.'

Eva nodded, recalling a barefoot child standing up proudly on her father's ass and cart whenever Maureen's father arrived with turf during the war. Freddie had always referred to Maureen as 'that maid', but during the war she had been like a younger sister to Eva and an older sister to Hazel.

'Now let's get a fire going before we turn into icicles.' Maureen opened the cast iron stove to peer inside. 'Mother of God, but you're an awful woman, Mrs Fitzgerald. The fire is set and all if you'd only toss a match in it.'

'I wasn't cold.'

'Are you codding me? A polar bear would need an electric blanket tonight. Will you not come up to Kate and Jack's bungalow and stay with us?'

'No.' Since receiving the news from Kenya, nothing was able to touch Eva. If she cut her own wrists she would not have been surprised to find her blood too frozen to seep out. But now in Maureen's presence she felt an infinitesimal stir within her, a foretaste of human warmth, like a hairline fissure in a sheet of ice.

'Well, pass me the box of matches and we'll make do here. We knew colder nights together in that old house during the war.'

Maureen closed the skylight despite Eva's protests, saying that if the cats wanted to come back in they could knock at the door like Christians. She rigged up a cylinder of gas and soon had a kettle boiling under a blue flame as she opened the stove again and added in larger sticks and some turf. Finding a fork among the cardboard boxes, Maureen knelt before the stove to toast a thick slice of stale bread.

'I had every mod con in the States, true enough,' she said. 'A dishwasher, air conditioning and more television stations than you could shake a stick at. But some nights I'd have swapped them all for the chance to make toast on a fork by an open fire.'

'When did you come back?'

'Six months after my Frankie died from cancer. They introduced protective masks in the chemical factory where he worked twenty years too late.'

'I'm sorry,' Eva replied.

'You would have liked Frankie. He was a laugh. Even with a name like Bergeson he claimed to be half-Irish. Bald as a coot by the age of forty and always smiling. He had a black man's teeth and a Cavan man's laugh.'

'You're still hurting over him,' Eva said softly.

'To tell you the truth, Mrs Fitzgerald, every week the loneliness hurts more. When I was a girl the nuns made it sound like I had only to hold a boy's hand to fall pregnant on the spot. Frankie and I were thirty years sharing a bed without a sign of a child stirring, and it wasn't for lack of trying. Oh, I had the best of neighbours in Boston, but neighbours are no substitute for kin when you find yourself alone. This toast is ready now. Where did you pack your butter?'

'I'm a vegan now. I don't eat butter.'

Maureen raised her eyes. 'Mother of God, won't the cows be thrilled? They can enjoy a lie-in on Sundays. What do you eat so?'

'A soya spread, when I can get it.'

Maureen brought over the toast and two cups of black tea. The caravan was starting to feel warm. Queensly deserted Eva to settle on Maureen's lap.

'This is the high life,' Maureen remarked. 'Here I am, dining with the gentry.'

Eva smiled. 'I'm hardly gentry. I doubt if there's a soul in the village who is poorer. Name anyone else living in a caravan.'

'Where you live doesn't change who you are. Folks around here still see you as a lady. That big fool of a truck pulling this yoke was spied coming through the village. The whole parish is wondering how you think you can survive up here. Now eat up your toast.'

Eva put down the cup she had been holding between her hands mainly for its warmth. 'I'm not hungry.'

'I know,' Maureen said. 'Food has lost any taste since my Frankie died. But I make myself eat. I can't believe poor Master Francis and Miss Hazel are dead. I can see them still as children, roaming about the woods here. After Frankie died I found myself talking about him to strangers on the subway in Boston, to anyone who would listen. I couldn't seem to stop blathering away. But a real lady like you wouldn't do that. She'd suffer in silence, bothering nobody, stuck alone in a wood. Kate and I cried our eyes out for you when news reached Mayo about your granddaughter. You and I never had secrets during the war, Mrs Fitzgerald. If you'd like, you could talk to me.'

Maureen's fingers stopped stroking the cat and slowly entwined themselves with Eva's gnarled fingers. Both widows sat in a silence broken only by the cat's peaceful breathing. Then Eva spoke.

'She was two months away from her fifteenth birthday and ever so beautiful. You never saw a child like her, Maureen, interested in everything, longing to embrace life. Every girl in her boarding school loved her. They envied her going back to spend the summer with her father in Kenya. It was such a simple thing to happen, to get an insect bite. But they had no antibiotics and she caught a virus out there in the bush, too far away to be rushed to any hospital. Everyone did everything they could, nobody was to blame. Everyone was heartbroken. I keep trying to be positive, Maureen. Alex will never face the problems you and I have, she'll never grow old and lonely or lose her radiance. She was perfect and died perfect. I tell myself her death was quick and she didn't suffer much. But my heart is broken beyond repair. Ten years ago I had a son, a daughter and a grandchild. I'd give my life gladly to have saved any of them. It makes no sense that I'm still here and all three are dead. Life is simply not fair.'

Eva's voice was quiet but she was crying. A kitten began to scratch at the door. Queensly stirred and stretched. Eva kept a tight hold of Maureen's fingers.

'But life isn't fair, is it?' Maureen said. 'It's not fair on those it takes or fair on those of us who get left behind. But what can we do?'

Eva relinquished her grip and rose to open the door and let in the kitten. The faintest trace of blood stained his paws. Out in the dark he had been on a killing mission. Eva gazed out at the darkness.

'We can live our lives,' Eva said, 'What other choice do we have? These mornings when I wake up – barely caring if I wake up – I feel oddly free. It's a terrible freedom, but the freedom that comes from knowing there is nothing else that life can do to me: fate can have no more tricks up its sleeve. I'm numb with grief, Maureen. I don't know if I'll ever feel warm again. But I'm afraid of nothing now. My sleepless nights are over because life has nothing left to steal from me.'

'Close over that door and keep out the cold,' Maureen replied. 'Remember the long nights during the war when we'd sit up talking, only leaving the house to fetch firewood? This time we can do it in reverse. We can sit out here on the lawn and only enter the house for firewood. There's enough timber in that ruin to keep this stove going forever.'

Eva laughed: a sound she had forgotten. 'Won't Kate be worried?'

'She'll think I'm off in Castlebar chasing after some bingo announcer with sideburns.' Maureen's smile could not prevent a glimpse into her own loneliness. 'Jack will have the telly blaring full-blast at home. They can have a good bicker like married folk do and I'll not be in their way. You tell me your story, Mrs Fitzgerald, and I'll tell you mine. We're two old ladies going nowhere fast. We've all the time in the world now.'

Chapter Eighteen

Company

Turlough, Co. Mayo, January 1976

For several days now the black-and-white stray collie had skulked fearfully about in the high meadow at the top of the small field behind the Round Tower Bar, into which local farmers had helped to transport Eva's caravan six months ago. The young dog disappeared into the bushes separating the field she was in from this meadow whenever anyone appeared along the isolated road where a five-bar gate marked the makeshift entrance to Eva's latest home. But several times each day, hunger forced the dog to make abortive forays down through a flooded ditch that passed close by her caravan. From here a gap in the hedge might allow him to slink out from the ditch and raid the open bins in the back yard of The Round Tower Bar – the front entrance of which faced onto the single street that Turlough village possessed. This street consisted of two pubs, Bridie's tiny shop that hadn't changed in half a century, a garage with a disused petrol pump, a two-roomed 1920s schoolhouse and a scattering of houses.

On every occasion when the dog made this excursion through the wet ditch, Eva sat quietly in her window, anxious not to frighten him. Once he even turned his head to bestow on her a timid, co-conspiratorial glance, before making himself small again in the ditch as he peered intently towards the bins that might contain scraps of food. Eva willed him on but inevitably his courage failed. The pub yard betrayed occasional signs of human life and the welts clearly visible on the dog's back showed that, for him, people represented sticks and beatings.

The collie was older than most puppies dumped on country roads in January by parents whose offspring had grown tired of their Christmas gifts. He looked like he had been systematically kicked and tormented by an owner who was probably a pillar of his community. It was possible that this dog had been wandering since New Year's Eve: he was so lean that his bones were visible whenever he limped into view. Realising that he belonged to nobody locally, Eva had left food for him outside her door on one particularly freezing morning. But though she kept the door closed, the dog knew that Eva was inside the caravan and, being a person, he could not be sure of trusting her.

Eva was aware of the danger of starting to feed him because she did not want to be burdened by the responsibility of another pet. Yet if he stayed living in the bushes, the local farmers would soon learn of this stray dog and consider him a menace to their sheep. But she could not bear to see him suffer, so on the next evening she carried food up to where her field joined the high meadow that had become his sanctuary. She placed it down, aware of him watching her from within the thick bushes. Only when dusk provided sufficient cover did he risk slinking out from the undergrowth. He approached the food cautiously, tail lowered as if convinced it was a trap that would result in another beating. After wolfing down every scrap, he stared at her caravan until Eva opened the door. Momentarily they scrutinised each other before he limped away.

In contrast to the dog, Eva had experienced nothing but kindness in the fourteen months since returning to this Mayo village. During the weeks after her caravan was towed up the overgrown avenue to be moored on the unkempt lawn outside Glanmire House, Eva simply wanted to hibernate in the depths of winter, unnoticed by the world. But while she may have wished to hide away in a cocoon, the innate decency of her old neighbours ensured that she came through this worst period of grieving. People tried not to be intrusive, but Eva noticed their protective attitude towards her within days of trying to settle back into Glanmire Wood. Maureen had just been the first and most frequent of numerous callers, returning the next day with her sister Kate and brother-in-law Jack: a ladder tied to his roof rack so that he could disappear into the foliage covering the side of Glanmire House to try and see if the ancient water tank was workable. Within weeks, all of Turlough had called to welcome her home. Middle-aged women who had last ventured up the avenue as barefoot girls were driven up it by farmer husbands, awkward in their Sunday suits. They brought small gifts and shyly mentioned their own sorrows to let Eva know how they understood her suffering. Every visitor insisted that she was too isolated up there without water or electricity. But she had not been ready to leave Glanmire Wood, even when conditions grew so harsh that she was snowed in and neighbours sent up their hardiest sons on tractors to check on her. It was hard living but the frozen whiteness of those woods had perfectly suited her sombre mood of mourning.

When spring came, the farmer who owned this field behind the Round Tower Bar offered her a small site within the field to park her caravan for a peppercorn rent. The other local farmers who towed her caravan here refused all offers of payment. The Durcan family no longer owned the pub, but the new owners remembered her from the 1940s. The gate into her field was only a hundred yards from the gable of their pub, with Bridie's small shop located on the other corner of this small junction. Eva's location was screened from the pub and the road by bushes. It was near the village and yet private: just one street light visible outside a farmhouse at the crest of the bend, where the farmer's wife told her to come with a jug for milk any time she wished.

A week after moving into the field, Eva made her first trip into Castlebar and got caught in the drizzle and the dark when beginning the six-mile walk back to Turlough. The narrowness of the winding road perturbed her, although she hoped that motorists would spot her bright yellow oilskin raincoat and matching hat. Three cars passed, too close for comfort, before the fourth car halted. The driver – a local man who worked for Telecom Éireann by day and was a St Vincent de Paul volunteer at night – insisted on driving her to her gate and shining a torch across the rough path in the field to ensure she got safely inside The Ark. She thought no more about him until he returned with three of his work colleagues on the following Saturday morning. Armed with shovels and spades, they spent the entire weekend digging two trenches from the road right up to her caravan, installing electric cables in one and a hosepipe in the other so that, by dusk on the Sunday, The Ark possessed not only running water but electricity and a telephone. She would still need to empty out an Elsan toilet but this was no hardship. The work being done that weekend created a carnival atmosphere in the village: the owner of the Round Tower Bar constantly appearing with trays of ham sandwiches for the men and Bridie providing over-sweetened tea, caustic advice and grudging praise. Passing local motorists even stopped their cars to remove their jackets and take a turn at the digging, loudly discussing local Gaelic football matches and politics. Eva had spent all the Sunday excitedly chatting to everyone present, praising their kindness, laughing at remarks and getting so caught up in the excitement that only later, after everyone had gone, did she realised how this was the first day when she had not been ambushed at some stage by such grief that she could do nothing beyond sit in silent despair.

That weekend of voluntary activity, with the St Vincent de Paul volunteer liaising with the utility providers and the social services, made her famous in the district. In the months afterwards, the five-bar gate into the field constantly creaked as elderly farmers shyly brought small housewarming gifts with an apologetic shrug, saying, 'It's the least we can do and you a lady.' Sometimes the gifts were household items from Glanmire House, purchased at the auction held by that Castlebar builder in 1962, but now being returned to their original owner.

The move into this field opened another chapter in her life, with Eva resisting the easy option to remain paralysed in perpetual mourning. Her mother's ghost seemed to haunt The Ark, reminding Eva of her promise to strive tooth and nail, no matter what blows life dealt her, for the right to be happy. She refused to become one of those elderly widows, permanently dressed in black, whom she often saw sitting alone in the window of cafés in Castlebar, like fossilised relics from a forgotten era. Despite all the grief her heart had endured, she was somehow still alive and did not possess the right to refuse this miraculous gift of life. One morning in April as she woke, she felt she heard an inner voice relaying a psychic message, insisting that she had no option but to embrace whatever possibility of happiness life might still hold, even at the age of seventy-two. Her anguish at losing Alex would never ease, no more than the pain of having lost a son and daughter. She was essentially alone. But on that April morning, Eva rose to write into her diary the words of the Indian poet and philosopher, Sri Aurobindo: '*Joy; yes, if we have the courage to want it! The laurel and not the cross should be the aim of our conquering soul ... but men are still in love with grief ... therefore Christ still hangs on the cross in Jerusalem.*'

In the eight months since then, these words had become Eva's mantra against any urge to suspend herself on a cross of sorrow. The grief of the living could imprison the souls of the dead, holding them back on their journey from this world. Alex once sang her a Joni Mitchell song about all human beings being stardust in search of a path back to the garden. As last summer bloomed, Eva kept seeing Alex's spirit in cherry blossom petals and spurs of dandelion clocks drifting across the fields. She refused to yield to any loneliness or self-pity that might entrap these infinitesimal remnants of her granddaughter's soul. Eva had kept herself busy by commencing a daily routine of long walks up into the mountains to seek out old friends and make new ones. She took an equal interest in everyone and felt no envy at what other people possessed. Being poor felt like a blessing, as she realised that the secret to serenity was to let go of every possession that might complicate the inner simplicity of life.

While she came to know everyone within a twenty mile radius, the truest friend she made last summer was an ungainly old ewe among the flock of sheep who grazed in Eva's field. The ewe's hind legs had once been hobbled, leaving her with the uneven gait that first elicited Eva's attention. Trust was slow to come, but eventually the ewe allowed Eva to feed her by hand in the field. By summer's end, she had taken to scrambling up to the concrete steps twice a day. Eva's cats always bolted for safety when the caravan shook as the ewe padded clumsily over to where Eva sat. These visits only lasted for a few moments as the ewe chewed on the proffered bread and allowed Eva to rub her uncut fleece. But the contact was important to them both: two old mothers who had seen their offspring taken away.

Their unusual friendship only became problematic last autumn when Eva caused a terrible scene, sobbing inconsolably after she returned from a walk to discover the ewe being herded onto a truck with the other sheep for slaughter. This loss was miniscule compared to the other losses Eva had endured, but even such a small loss could trigger the accumulated pain of previous bereavements. The farmer was embarrassed by her tears and over the following days Eva was careful to remain indoors when she felt swamped by unassailable grief: aware of just how tenuous her position was – her tenure in this field being dependant on his goodwill. Since September, the field remained empty and only in recent weeks had Eva started to truly feel that she was reaching home when opening the five-bar gate. This feeling took longer in some places than others. As a young bride, her soul had never felt it belonged in Glanmire House. Yet when travelling in her sixties, sometimes a shabby pension in Tangiers felt like home within hours, as if she had been born to the trapped heat and raised voices shouting in Arabic on the street.

Fewer visitors called to The Ark in winter, but Eva did not mind because January was when she got her proper reading done, perusing books with snail-like slowness, until each layer of meaning filtered down into her bedrock. By day she wrote letters to old friends like Alan and Valerie O'Mahony. But she always welcomed dusk creeping across the sky because it heralded the time when she could light a candle, add more turf to the stove, turn off the harsh electric light and commence her true inner life. Every evening since Christmas, Eva had allowed herself to digest a chapter of *The Bell* by Iris Murdoch, with Hermann Hesse's collected poems beside her bed for company. Often a sentence in Murdoch's book would stir a memory, making Eva close her eyes and meditate in that rich silence broken only by wind and rain.

Therefore January should have been an oasis of serenity: the first and quietest month of the year, when she wished for nothing more than silent contemplation. But Eva was unable to find any peace since she first noticed this stray dog in the high meadow. After another few days of watching him crawl through the ditch to halt within sight of the pub yard, famished but still unable to find the courage to raid the bins there, Eva began to leave more food for him near a gap in the bushes where he generally hid. But on the first three nights when she did this, she was unable to sleep, convinced that she could hear him whimpering above in the meadow. She had to remind herself that she was too old for more pets. It was too big a worry, having to fear that they might outlive her and be ill-treated after her death, and yet it caused too much pain in her life when they died before her. To take on the care of yet another animal would tie her down when she needed to be free. A passing car had killed one of her two young cats last October. The other one ventured out hunting a week later and never returned. This just left Queensly, who was already old when she had wandered into Eva's life. Queensly would surely die from old age soon. After that, Eva wanted to be ready for one last adventure. Mayo was too damp for her bones and too full of memories. But before she went anywhere else, it was her duty to find a suitable buyer for Glanmire Wood. Any local farmer would simply fell the trees to create more pastureland. She needed to find a buyer on her wavelength, who would retain it as a wildlife sanctuary. When she had accomplished this task, Eva now planned to emigrate to Costa Rica. She had heard that people in Costa Rica were so sufficiently unspoilt that they possessed a gift which Europeans had lost: the ability to genuinely be themselves. Life in Costa Rica would be cheap, the sunshine might help her arthritis and it would be a truly fresh start, an entirely blank chapter. But if she gave her love to this stray dog, she would never be able to leave him or Ireland behind.

It was vital to find him a home. Therefore she set out walking the next morning, calling on everyone in the locality to see if they might take him as a pet. She felt more accepted now into daily life of Turlough than during all her years in Glanmire House. Reduced circumstances eroded social barriers. People addressed her in a chatty way, so different from how they had always been careful when speaking to Freddie, who may have been impoverished but had retained the manner of a haughty Fitzgerald. The women in many new bungalows she called into that morning were curious about what they called her 'quack beliefs'. While pre-school toddlers lolled before televisions, young mothers asked if she really treated her aliments with herbal remedies and made soup from weeds plucked off the roadside. Often women conceded that there was possibly wisdom in her distrust of drug companies, but they would be too afraid to go against the local doctor by trying any herbal remedy she suggested. For all their friendliness, nobody would agree to give the stray collie a home, although one elderly woman who seemed oddly petrified that her niece might show Eva into the good front room, offered to phone the dog pound in Castlebar and have the dog taken away.

But the pound was merely a prison camp where listless animals padded, instinctively sensing the approach of death. Eva dejectedly returned home, passing the mobile butcher shop which parked twice a week outside Bridie's. Dismembered slabs of meat and sides of bacon hung on hooks behind the counter as the butcher served his customers. Unable to avoid glancing in, Eva momentarily envisaged a row of skinned dogs hanging there. Then she shuddered as this mental image was displaced by one of a row of skeletal carcasses of prisoners hanging upside-down, having succumbed to beatings, starvation and typhoid in a Soviet gulag, with Brendan's corpse among them.

This nightmarish image now only very infrequently recurred in her dreams, but Eva had never lost her sense of horror at what her youngest brother surely suffered. Eva found herself shaking on the footpath as she stared into the butcher's van. Her more recent bereavements preoccupied her so much that they left little time to contemplate her brother's fate, but even now she remained susceptible to being ambushed by unresolved grief for him. In this moment of epiphany outside the butcher's van, Eva realised that because she had been unable to protect so many people she loved, she could not bear to fail this stray dog and see him put down. She entered Bridie's shop for advice. The huge television blaring on the shop counter was the elderly shopkeeper's sole concession to the passing years, the only feature that was different from when Eva first stood there forty years ago. Bridie rarely said much during their daily chats, beyond passing acerbic comments about the world, though Eva generally talked enough for them both. But today when Eva mentioned the stray dog, the shopkeeper warned her that local farmers would take matters into their own hands before he started to worry their sheep, especially now that Eva had notified the whole neighbourhood about his existence by seeking a home for him.

Eva knew that Bridie was right. She had witnessed the kind side of country life, the fundamental decency which had resulted in neighbours banding together to supply her with electricity and water. But country life possessed a tougher, practical side: a necessary ruthlessness in dealing with any creature who might threaten their farming livelihoods. Shooting the stray collie would be seen as the only practical solution, because even the most placid dog could grow savage once he smelt blood. Eva felt certain that this collie was no killer, but by leaving food for him beside the bushes in recent nights perhaps she had inadvertently endangered his life, encouraging him to linger there where he would be a *dokhodyaga*, as they used to call a prisoner so wasted by exhaustion in the gulags that he was a goner, an easy target for his executioners when they came. After leaving Bridie's shop and opening her gate, she saw a stir in the bushes and knew that the dog was watching from the undergrowth that divided her field from the high meadow, hoping she might leave food up there again tonight. Eva felt like running towards the bushes with a stick to try and frighten him away, but she simply did not possess such violence within her.

But perhaps she should have scared him away, because dusk was setting in and it was starting to rain heavily when the slam of a car door alerted her to the arrival of two strangers. She saw them open the car boot to remove guns. They spread out – one at the top of her field and one in the high meadow – stalking their way down the length of the long bushes. The furthest man could have been Freddie's ghost: his gun held in the same way and even his cap pulled down at a similar angle. Opening her door, she hurried up towards the bushes. The nearest man saw her and called out.

'Go back inside now, like a good woman. This isn't something a lady like you should see, and if the beast makes a break for it you'd be putting yourself in danger from him. Those wild dogs can be savage.'

His eyes regarded her with pity. The whole neighbourhood knew about her hysterical response to the elderly ewe being taken to be butchered.

'The dog is doing no harm.'

'He's not doing any good either, the poor creature. He's wild entirely and a famished dog is dangerous.'

A gunshot from the far side of the bushes startled them. The man speaking to her called over the bushes to his companion.

'Did you get him, Joe?'

'I think I wounded the cur,' his companion called back. 'If I did, he won't get too far and even if he tries to hide he'll leave a trail of blood. Now please ask Mrs Fitzgerald to get back into her caravan for her own sake and you watch from your side of the bushes because I'm no sharp shooter like her husband was. If Mr Fitzgerald was still alive, he'd have killed this dog with one shot.'

'That's true.' The first man nodded. 'He'd have put a bullet clean through one eye and out the other. They say Mr Fitzgerald was an equally fine shot, whether he had a bad dose of the shakes or not.'

Both men went quiet, fearing that their attempted compliment to Freddie had strayed into dangerous familiarity. They began to move carefully down each side of the bushes, looking for any hint of blood while Eva fretted as she slowly walked backwards towards her caravan. She was dreading the sound of a second shot, but the man who fired the shot continued to curse as he tramped about in the high meadow, kicking the bushes. Something – not a movement because the dog was utterly still – made her glance towards the ditch that led down to her right towards the pub yard. The collie was there, immersed in freezing stagnant water, closer that he had ever been to her. For one awful second she feared that he would climb out and limp towards her, endangering his life by revealing his position to the man still searching the bushes a hundred yards away. But he just stared reproachfully and loped away to slink out of the ditch where it went behind The Ark, and silently hid behind the bins in the yard, unnoticed by the men who eventually gave up searching for him.

Lying awake in bed after the men left, Eva knew that she had only one day left before they returned the following evening to shoot her dog. Her dog? The phrase was unintentional, but Eva realised that this was how she now viewed him. Not as her possession, but as her equal: someone else who was alone and seeking sanctuary in these fields. She arose from bed in the middle of the night to open her door, letting an arc of light flood out like a beacon across the dark field, but she knew the watching dog lacked the courage to approach. Pulling a coat over her nightgown, Eva stood on the gravel, staring into the dark. Poor Alex had christened this caravan The Ark. Since her death, the name had seemed redundant but maybe this was what it could become for her and for Johnny. Eva did not know where the dog's name came from, just that Johnny suited his gentle nature. The rain had cleared and the stars looked huge. Frost would have formed in the wet bushes where he was lying. Taking a flashlight, she walked up towards those bushes, calling his new name softly, then turned off her flashlight and waited in the dark, hoping he might emerge.

When the freezing cold finally drove her back inside, Eva knelt by her bed – constructed from boxes of old books with a mattress on top – to stare at an ancient picture of a small child kneeling beside a bed. It was a childhood memento which she had managed to hold on to, ever since taking it down from her Donegal bedroom wall on the night before her wedding forty years ago. She tried to clear her mind to let the Infinite Being enter her thoughts and inspire her if he wished. The plan that came to her was childishly simple, but simplicity was the only thing which life had taught her to trust. She slept peacefully after that, underneath two blankets and an old coat. The field was white with frost when she woke: the water from the hosepipe almost frozen. A thin trickle emerged before an icy spray eventually splurged forth. After breakfast she walked to Bridie's to purchase two packets of Mikado Biscuits.

'Visitors in January?' Bridie asked in surprise.

'No.'

'I heard a gunshot yesterday evening. The poor wee dog.'

'They missed him.'

Bridie shrugged, unsurprised by the news. 'Those same two fellows couldn't hit a bucket if they were sitting on it.'

When Eva reached the five-bar gate, she saw that the dog had risked coming out into the open, frantically rooting on her side of the bushes for any trace of food. He turned his head to stare when he heard the clang of the gate, but quickly slunk back into the bushes as Eva climbed up through the scraggy field towards him. Reaching the bushes, Eva opened the first packet of biscuits and threw one towards where she had seen him disappear. She stepped back and broke a second biscuit in two, dropping one half on the grass there and the other half a few feet behind her. The collie never emerged from hiding as she worked her way along by the side of the ditch that led down past her caravan, leaving a trail of broken biscuits in her wake. Only time would tell if hunger might tempt him to scramble out and follow the trail. Eva opened the second packet, extending the long biscuit trail so that it led right up to her caravan. Relieved that Queensly was prowling elsewhere, Eva left a full biscuit on each of the three concrete steps up to her door and a trail of crumbs along the floor inside the caravan, right up to the window seat where she sat and waited.

It was ten minutes before the dog emerged into the open. He ate the first few biscuits ravenously, then seemed to lose the trail or distrust it. At times he stopped and stared anxiously around before his nose sought out the next one and he resumed eating his way down the length of her field. So far his route had not taken him far from the safety of the ditch, but it now reached a point where the trail of biscuits led across open ground towards her caravan. Timid and uncertain, the dog crawled back into the ditch and lay there, his eyes staring intently at Eva, who remained on display, seated in her window. Five minutes passed before he found the courage to crawl from the ditch. Ravenous now, he eat each biscuit with a desperate hunger, creeping closer until he passed underneath her window and out of sight. Eva sat in silence, knowing that the smallest sound would frighten him. It was now his decision whether to become part of her life or not. She heard him prowl hesitantly around the gravel beside the open door. Then came the sound of him climbing up the first concrete step. He stopped again, still out of sight. Eva could imagine him staring in at her caravan, crammed with books and paintings, and then gazing back at the wet fields that had been his home. An eternity seemed to pass before his paws touched the lino and he entered her world, eating his way along the line of broken biscuits.

Only once did he stop to look up at her. There was no fear in his gaze, just a bewildered hurt. She returned his gaze and shared that hurt. Tonight he would sleep on this window seat that had once served as Alex's bed. Eva understood the pain in his eyes and the dog recognised the pain in hers. He limped the final few steps without hesitation and climbed up onto the seat where she could properly see his welts and a cut festering on his face. If he allowed her to place a length of old twine around his neck, they could walk to the post office and purchase a dog licence. He would then officially be registered as her dog when the executioners returned and they would have to put away their guns. The sunlight of Costa Rica would have to wait. After all her decades of trying to fathom what purpose life intended her for – efforts to be an artist, a teacher, a writer, a wife, a mother and a grandmother – maybe all that life could offer was this one simple task: to give shelter to a beaten stray dog and spare him being shot? She would look after him because there was nobody else left who needed her now and because poor Alex would have wanted her to. Johnny gazed into her eyes, then laid his neck on her lap. Eva placed her arms gently on his neck. Neither moved for the longest time until Johnny lifted his head to lick away the tears on Eva's face.

Chapter Nineteen

The Hiker

Finglas, Dublin & Turlough, Co. Mayo, September 1977

The eighteen-year-old boy's journey began at dawn when Donal waited, as instructed, opposite St Canice's Church at the crest of the sloping main street of Finglas village: a working-class suburb three miles from Dublin. An open-backed truck was due to pass this spot after leaving the nearby Unidare industrial complex to deliver a cargo of spools of heavy-duty electric cable to a building site in Roscommon, one hundred miles away. Donal was familiar with these massive wooden spools, having previously had a temporary job hammering six-inch nails into the slats of wood that sealed each tightly wound coil into place before the spools were loaded by forklift onto lorries. The drivers were forbidden to carry passengers, but Donal's older brother, who worked in an adjoining office, had arranged this clandestine lift to take Donal across the Shannon and into Connacht. This would leave him with just sixty more miles to hitchhike to visit the seventy-three-year-old lady with whom he had been corresponding for months about his dreams of becoming a published writer. At times such an ambition seemed outlandish, but each of her replies – long handwritten pages crammed with encouraging comments about the typed poems he sent her – felt like beacons of hope, guiding him to take the first tentative steps to try and unearth imaginative worlds which seemed to lurk in his subconscious, if he could find the courage to delve deep enough. Her letters felt like a poultice against the only other post he received: the crushing disappointing rejection slips that punctured his fervent hope that some editor might like his work.

The Main Street was deserted apart from some Premier Dairies milk floats passing by. A former classmate shouted out a greeting as he sat amid crates of milk bottles for delivery. Donal nodded to the old age pensioners hurrying for half-seven Mass. He still could not enter that church without recalling his numb bewilderment at eight years of age, when its aisles overflowed with mourners after his mother had passed away four days before Christmas. This bereavement left him feeling as if his childhood and personality were severed in two. He could subdivide every experience into those that had occurred to the naïve, secure child he was before her death and the boy who had needed to grow up quickly afterwards. However his tough protective persona could not disguise how even an innocuous glimpse of anyone being buried in a television programme still left him ambushed by paralytic terror. As the Unidare lorry rounded the corner from Jamestown Road, he pulled up his collar and nodded almost imperceptibly in reply to the driver's nod – their exchange so discreet that no passer-by would notice the lorry momentarily halting as a passenger climbed illicitly up into the cab to commence a journey across Ireland.

8○

Little traffic drove along the narrow side road that wound past the tiny Protestant Church, but for safety's sake Eva always kept Johnny on his lead until they reached the entrance to Glanmire Wood: hidden from the road and marked by an old rusty iron gate. To this she had affixed a hand-painted sign that would have affronted Freddie: 'Nature Sanctuary. No hunting. No shooting.'

When leaving the caravan for their daily walk, Johnny had guessed, racing around in circles to show his delight, that the woods were today's destination. Yet even though his tail wagged with increasing vigour throughout their companionable stroll here, he never strained at his lead, because he knew how Eva could only go at a certain pace and his nature was too gentle to rush her. But once he saw this rusty gate he became so overcome by excitement that all restraint vanished. The woods allowed him the chance to chase rabbits and Eva knew it was cruel to detain him for more than the few seconds needed to slip off his lead and watch him bound in a paroxysm of trembling anticipation into the undergrowth. Perhaps it was contradictory to let a dog loose in a nature sanctuary, but it didn't seem so to Eva. It was in Johnny's nature to chase rabbits and if he managed to catch one, such a death would be part of a natural cycle, in a way that Freddie's shooting parties had never been, when they slaughtered everything that flew simply to prove their manhood. Besides, just as surely as Eva knew that she would not see Johnny again for twenty minutes until he re-emerged, panting loudly and rolling about on the daffodil lawn to shake off the twigs and brambles that would attach themselves to his coat, Eva also knew that Johnny possessed an singular inability to ever come close to catching a rabbit: a continual failure that never affected his enthusiasm to try again and fail again every time he accompanied her up here.

This morning's visit to Glanmire Wood needed to be shorter than their usual expeditions when she and Johnny often happily spent hours lost in their private world here. Today a young poet was hitchhiking from Dublin to stay with her. It was impossible to predict how long any journey which involved hitching lifts could take, and so it was important to return home early in case he arrived unexpectedly. Eva still wasn't sure what had compelled her to send this poet a postcard some months ago, after he was interviewed in *The Evening Press* about a tiny debut collection of poems he had just produced, which was being sold at 30p a copy by his friends and relations in local factories, pubs and offices. The interview made great play about Donal being an unemployed school-leaver who had found a back-lane printer to print four hundred letterpress copies of the collection, in between the printer's usual jobs of printing football pools coupons for amateur league soccer teams. Perhaps Eva had sent the postcard because the journalist's slightly mocking tone reminded her of feeling hurt, a quarter century ago, when an *Irish Times* journalist wrote a similarly patronizing piece about her dreams for her child art studio. Donal, likewise, seemed to be trying to start something new with an arts movement in Finglas, bringing together local poets and musicians to stage events in any makeshift space they could find.

Or maybe what caught her eye was Donal's mention of a book about the supernatural, written by her old Kiltimagh neighbour Dermot MacManus. Donal had expressed a desire to hear from anyone who had experienced supernatural occurrences because he wished to write a similar book about the paranormal. The boy's reference to MacManus's long-forgotten book brought back precious memories of the night in Mount Elgon National Park when Hazel surprised her with a first edition of that book: Alex climbing onto Eva's knee to study its photographs of Mayo. But maybe she wrote to this young poet because he was the age that Alex would be, if poor Alex had lived, and the mixture of vitality and vulnerability in his photograph in the newspaper so reminded Eva of her granddaughter that she had needed to close her eyes and sit still to let the buried ache in her subconscious settle back so that she could breathe again.

Or had her impulsive decision to drop him a card stemmed from Eva's memories of her own purgatory of waiting for post – any post – when trying to become a published author, sending off stories to editors from that *posada* in a Pyrenean village twenty years ago? Maybe she had sensed that – although no substitute for an acceptance letter from an editor – a postcard from a stranger to wish Donal success might serve as a quiet token of encouragement to a writer just starting out. But for whatever reason, she had written to tell Donal of her desire to buy a copy of his poetry collection, adding that she had known the late Dermot MacManus, and if Donal ever visited Mayo he was welcome to stay with her for a few nights as she possessed a wood where he might enjoy doing some writing. The boy's reply was floridly written, like an adolescent trying to sound grown-up. But Eva felt that his true essence came across in the unpublished poems he enclosed, reminding her of verses Francis wrote at eighteen, although Donal's words were more intense. In the letters exchanged since then, Eva had grown to admire his quiet resoluteness in being fixed on his own course.

Donal would not be the first poet to sleep on the window seat. Two months ago, a young Canadian poet named Teresina had spent three weeks in the caravan while travelling around Ireland. Valerie O'Mahony, who had moved to Canada, had put Eva in touch with Teresina who was wonderful company, joyously telling Eva how she loved to wake at night and savour the feel of The Ark swaying in the breeze. On most days she had taken a flask of coffee and some fruit up to Glanmire Wood, spending hours working in the fresh air on her first poetry collection. A local scandal even ensued when Maureen's brother-in-law, Jack, found Teresina sunbathing topless on the daffodil lawn when he came up in search of fencing posts.

As Eva reached the overgrown lawn now, she paused in her walk to turn in a slow circle, savouring the warmth of the morning sun. It seemed extraordinary to think that four decades had passed since she came here as a bride, knowing as little about men as she'd known about life. There had been times here when she'd felt isolated and overwhelmed by despair, but also sunbursts of great happiness, as if happiness were a comet whose elliptical orbit no astronomer could calculate. This past year felt like one such sunburst, because after all the anguish and soul-searching of recent decades, all the bereavements she had been convinced she would never recover from, who could have predicted that now, in her early seventies, she would be experiencing this plateau of equilibrium and tranquillity? Maybe it came from recognising that there were no stepping stones left: her sole task was to simply accept this benediction of sunlight and the companionship of Johnny who, at any moment, would come tearing out from the undergrowth as if returning from the most tremendous adventure. She would gladly have forfeited her life to give Francis or Hazel or Alex the chance to stand here, relishing this sunlight. But fate denied her any chance to make a heroic sacrifice. Eva needed to accept that, for some mysteriously unjust reason, she was the last one left standing and needed to live this moment on their behalf. Her final remaining duty was to treasure life to its last breath for their sake, because only she could keep alive the memory of how Hazel had loved certain pieces of music; only she could tend to these woods that were precious to Francis; only she remained to laugh freely, knowing that each time she did so she heard an echo of Alex's laughter somehow still living on within her.

Over the past eighteen months, her chief task when trying to maintain these woods was the endless chore of repairing its boundaries. Glanmire Wood had been deserted for so many years before her return that some local farmers grew accustomed to neglecting to mend gaps which appeared in bushes and barbed-wire fences. Until recently this meant that – despite Eva's painstaking efforts – cattle regularly pushed their way in through such openings to damage trees and graze on the daffodil lawn and overgrown avenue. It proved impossible for one elderly woman to herd these cows back through the gaps. Her only chance of removing stray cattle from her land had involved long walks to farmers' houses, where she was greeted with endless cups of tea and excuses, especially in poor weather if farmers were anxious to avoid the expense of bringing bales of silage up to the fields adjoining Glanmire to feed their cattle. For over a year Eva exhausted herself in this struggle to repair gaps in bushes, often returning a few days later to find her barriers of branches spirited away by unknown hands or physically kicked in. One dank winter afternoon, when physically drained from trying to shoo trespassing cattle off her daffodil lawn despoiled by cow pats and hoof marks, she decided to sit quietly on the steps of her former home and ponder how Mahatma Gandhi might have peacefully resolved this problem. The solution which came to her was so simple – like all true solutions – that it had never crossed her mind before. That evening in the winter dusk, she ceased trying to herd the cattle back into their field. Instead she summoned Johnny to her side and walked home, leaving open the gate at the end of her avenue, as if by accident. Within hours the cattle had meandered down the avenue. They grazed on grass verges along local roads, halting passing traffic until their owner was alerted and had to spend all night frantically tracking them down. After this, only once had a farmer tried to use Glanmire Wood for free grazing again, with Eva responding in the same way. Since then, Eva rarely discovered breaches in her boundary fences and knew – from a sly comment by Bridie – that Eva had risen in some farmers' estimation by outwitting them without any need for confrontation.

A burst of excited barking disturbed her thoughts now as Johnny emerged from the trees, defeated but not discouraged by his daily rabbit hunt. He rolled about in the long grass before bounding over to sit at her feet, as if reporting for duty in their regular boundary inspection. But Eva could tell that no cows had forced their way in during recent days, nor had any nocturnal intruders tried to enter the house and scavenge material to sell as scrap metal. She would be powerless if confronted by such men, but her fear was more for their own safety due to the weakness of the floors, rather than for any further damage they might do to the house. She knew that the countryside was never as deserted as it seemed, and news of Glanmire Wood having a custodian, even one as frail as herself, would discourage thieves. Not that she wished to discourage anyone else from enjoying her woods. On several occasions she caught glimpses through the trees of courting couples hastily rearranging their clothing when they heard her approach along the avenue. She never betrayed any sign of having seen them, but would call Johnny and turn back as if she had forgotten something, affording young love the privacy it needed. On other occasions she encountered foreign backpackers who wandered in out of curiosity and with whom she shared her flask of black coffee and squares of vegan chocolate made from coconut and cocoa butter. One afternoon, upon climbing to the most remote part of the wood, Eva startled a middle-aged local widow, initially too embarrassed to speak, but who then confessed to often visiting this clearing where three old oak trees grew when she could not bear to be alone in her house. The woman explained how she found it preferable to sit amid the trees, even on cold days, rather than sit alone on public view in coffee shops or pubs in Castlebar, where other customers eyed her with sympathetic glances or avoided acknowledging her presence and where men sometimes made unwanted and inappropriate approaches. Eva wanted to explain how this spot had been her own refuge decades ago, a place where she'd had the privacy to cry, but the woman's expression told Eva that she did not want commiseration or invitations to call into The Ark anytime she needed to speak to someone. She made it evident that she wanted no association with Eva, whom she regarded as a crank. Since then, Eva had seen this widow cross the street in Castlebar to avoid making eye contact with her. Eva did not feel offended because grief seized everyone differently, but she now rarely ventured near those oak trees lest she intrude on the widow's privacy, although she was unsure if the woman still visited.

Today Eva felt certain that nobody was about. Her main purpose in coming here was to give Johnny a run because after, she would be confined to the caravan until the hitchhiker showed up. Calling Johnny, she began to walk back, pausing occasionally to collect plants and herbs to use when cooking her food later on. She had told Donal in a letter that, although a vegan, she had no objection to guests cooking meat, provided they did not ask her to do it for them. Everyone had the right to live according to their own beliefs and she was no proselytiser. Indeed proselytising was the only thing she did not allow in her caravan, as she was forced to gently explain to two elderly Jehovah's Witnesses who often visited her, when she discovered them discreetly leaving behind copies of their *Watchtower* magazine for other visitors to find.

Numerous visitors were due over the next two months before The Ark grew quiet again with the onset of winter. Donal would stay for three nights before an American arrived: one of the Vietnam War conscientious objectors Eva had befriended in the Quaker hostel. A French woman whom Eva met on Lundy Island was due to follow him and then Francis's old friend Alan, recently returned to London after what Eva suspected was a lonely summer spent among other ageing gay men in Tangiers. At some stage, her old lodger from Frankfurt Ave, Camille, was promising to call by on route to Dublin from the cottage where she painted on Achill Island. Throughout this summer the most interesting people had slept on her window seat or camped out in the field. By some miracle her home had become an ark, just like Alex had christened it: a shelter where the most unlikely people felt drawn to come and talk – about their most precious dreams if young, and often about their most difficult personal problems if older. Perhaps they felt that nothing could shock Eva after all she had endured. These visitors included not only old friends and children of friends, but also hitchhikers passing down the mountainy road from Pontoon Bridge, with whom she fell into conversation. She sometimes invited them to pitch their tent in the small strip of field which the farmer had now fenced off around her caravan.

She had no idea who might be waiting outside The Ark when she got back today. With the tourist season slackening off, she was receiving fleeting visits from a handful of artists who had swapped conventional lives in Düsseldorf or Leipzig to eke out precarious livings trying to sell their work in remote cottages near Parke or Pidgeon Hill, painting or throwing ceramic vases on potters' wheels in byres where cattle were once milked. Some easily bonded with elderly neighbours who were happy to just see another light in a window on lonely stretches of road. Others struggled to adapt, unable to grasp that the tranquil pace of life here came at the cost of losing some of the social efficiency they were accustomed to. Last week she needed to soothe, with homemade dandelion and elderberry tea, a Dutch potter who had been baffled by the abusive phone call from a staff member of the *Connaught Telegraph* who called her 'an interfering mongrel fox blow-in' for posting them back a copy of their newspaper, imagining they would be grateful that she had taken the time to painstakingly correct every typographical error by hand. Eva had laughed, saying that some locals probably considered her a blow-in, despite having lived here on and off since 1927.

The main street of Turlough was empty now as she led Johnny back up it on his lead. Soon it would teem with life, when classes ended in the primary school across the road. The younger children who spilled out loved to chat unselfconsciously to Eva, but this changed after they entered secondary school and grew too self-conscious to be seen talking to her. But some local children never lost their inner radiance: teenagers who resisted the herd instinct to avoid standing out. One was the daughter of the generous Telecom Éireann workman who arranged for his workmates to voluntarily install electricity for her when she moved into the field. Some months ago Eva heard a timid knock and opened her door to find his daughter standing there, having cycled from the far side of Castlebar to shyly show Eva the most marvellous poem she had just written. Eva would never forget how the girl blushed with shy pride when Eva praised it as a true poem, shot through with vitality and insight. Nor would she forget her own astonishment after the girl confessed that it was the first poem she had ever written, explaining how, until Eva arrived in Turlough, it had never occurred to her to write anything because there was nobody with whom she could have thought of sharing it.

Turning up by the gable of the Round Tower Bar, Eva saw a boy's bicycle lying on the grass and a pair of knees belonging to someone sitting on the five-bar gate. It must be Marcus, a local boy who first turned up at her caravan on his fourteenth birthday to shyly ask if he could browse the bookshelves that he had glimpsed when passing the caravan. She had loaned him Kahlil Gibran's *The Prophet* on that visit, and when he returned it two weeks later he gave her a pirated cassette recording of an album called *In the City* by a new band called the Jam whom he urged her to listen to. Every time he visited her since then she left it up to him to select which books to borrow, while accepting his gifts of homemade cassettes of David Bowie and a Dublin band named The Radiators from Space. Once he overcame his initial shyness, she realised that Marcus had an intellectually curious mind, fascinated by ideas his classmates could never comprehend. Some locals found their friendship strange enough without pop music blaring from The Ark during his visits. But from the animated way in which he discussed each song he played for her, Eva recognised how this local boy was baring his soul. These songs were his code to emotions he did not yet possess the vocabulary to express. Marcus heard Johnny's bark and leaned forward on her gate to wave. Eva waved back and hurried to meet him, hoping that Donal would not arrive until Marcus was gone. She wanted to give them both the attention they needed.

ဆ

The journey of the Unidare lorry through Kinnegad and Mullingar passed uneventfully. Outside Ballymahon, a motorist alerted the driver that the wooden spools were coming loose by frantically beeping his horn. The driver pulled over on the narrow road and Donal climbed up onto the back to help retie the safety ropes: the heavy braided cords cutting in his palm as the driver urged him to knot them tighter. He dropped Donal a mile beyond Roscommon town, responding to his shouted thanks with the same inconspicuous nod with which he had greeted Donal at dawn. From here it should have been a short hitchhike through Castlerea and Claremorris and on to Castlebar, but because of Donal's long hair and beard, his flared jeans and faded army jacket, few motorists seemed inclined to stop. Those who did were often elderly farmers only going a few miles out the road but glad to have someone to talk to for the ten minutes it took before they left him at isolated bends where it was even more difficult to persuade speeding cars to halt. It was dusk before he reached Castlebar. He began to walk out towards Turlough as the darkness grew: cars refusing to stop and some passing so close to him on the twisting road that he feared being knocked down. He had little real idea of where he was going. The only address he had consisted of four words: 'The Ark, Turlough, Castlebar.' Exhausted from walking, he sought directions at a bungalow. The middle-aged woman who answered his knock regarded him with initial suspicion when he sought directions to The Ark.

'The what?'

'The Ark. Mrs Eva Fitzgerald lives there.'

'Do you mean the caravan behind the Round Tower Bar? Why didn't you just say so?'

Until then, Donal hadn't even known that The Ark was a caravan. The woman sized him up with circumspection.

'And what business have you with Mrs Fitzgerald?'

'She is my friend.'

This sounded like an exaggerated claim for someone Donal had not yet met, but something in his tone made the woman relax her guard and nod with a shy smile.

'My aunt inside mightn't think so, but if that's the case I hope you know how lucky you are. Walk on for another mile until you reach Turlough village. Swing left up at the small road just before the pub. You'll see a gate into the field where she lives.'

Footsteps sounded down the hallway and an elderly woman appeared dressed in black. 'What mightn't I think? What are you saying about me? Who is this fellow and what does he want at this hour?'

'He's seeking directions to Mrs Fitzgerald's caravan.'

'And when did I ever say a bad word about Mrs Fitzgerald? Apart from the time she arrived here looking for us to take some mongrel dog before she adopted him or he adopted her.'

The two women seemed so caught up in their private conversation that they almost forgot Donal standing there.

'You often say that, for the life of you, you can't understand head nor tail of her.'

'It's true. I don't understand the woman, but it doesn't mean I don't like her. I didn't even really mind her calling in here that time. I just got fussed in case you'd bring her into the front room because the two armchairs in there were bought by my poor Tommy at an auction that gombeen, Devlin, held at Glanmire House, the year when May McLoughlin's son was among the Irish troops sent off to keep the peace among them Balubas in The Congo.'

'None of us understand some of Mrs Fitzgerald's peculiar notions, but she's a lovely woman.'

The elderly aunt shook her head, even more infuriated. 'Did I ever say I had any problems with her notions? It's not her notions I don't understand.'

'Then what is it?'

'It's her.' She glanced suspiciously out at Donal. 'This is not your business, sonny, so don't go telling tales to nobody.'

'I won't,' Donal assured her, slightly alarmed.

The black-clad woman turned to her niece. 'All I ever said is that I don't understand how she can go about walking for miles every day, chatting and laughing with everyone she meets. Such laughter isn't natural.'

The niece threw her eyes to heaven. 'God forgive you, you'd provoke a row even if you were just trapped by yourself in a paper bag. What's wrong with Mrs Fitzgerald's laugh? She has a lovely laugh.'

'What's wrong is that she has no right to still be laughing. You wouldn't understand with your husband still alive and your children doing well across in London. You don't see me swanning about laughing since Tommy died, do you? Maybe your generation never heard of decorum but we did. She's lost far more than me and it's not natural for her to gad about so carefree. I'm not criticising her. I'm just saying it shows a lack of respect to those you've lost.'

'So you'd sooner she was an old misery guts sitting in the corner, would you?'

'I don't just sit in a corner. I do things too, but I do them with some decorum.'

'I never called you a misery guts.'

The elderly woman retreated down the hallway. 'You didn't need to. Give that boy a glass of milk for the road, bet you he's parched. Mrs Fitzgerald has daft notions about cows and probably won't have a drop in the caravan.'

The middle-aged woman looked at Donal and shrugged. 'Don't mind her. Every time she meets Mrs Fitzgerald she walks away beaming, looking ten years younger.'

She closed over the door and reopened it some moments later with a glass of milk. Donal drank appreciatively, then listened to her directions again and set off with a renewed sense of vigour. The last mile was less dangerous as the road straightened out. He came to a small cluster of street lights, a garage with a single petrol pump and a tiny corner shop where an old woman shifted her gaze from a blaring television on the counter to appraise him caustically as he passed the open doorway. Reaching the junction beside the pub gable, he walked up the dark side road and located the five-bar gate mainly by touch. He might never have found it without directions because the field looked empty in the dark: the main caravan window facing the other way. The gate creaked when he opened it. This must have alerted whoever was inside the caravan. He was halfway across the field when a door was thrown open to reveal a tiny woman standing in the arc of light which spilled out. Her face lit up with incredulous joy at him having succeeded in finding his way.

'You've found us,' she said, laughing. 'How marvellous you're here! Isn't life exciting?'

ℊ

When darkness fell, Eva had grown anxious about the young hitchhiker and was relieved when Johnny lifted his head, alerting her to the creaking gate. Donal looked shy and uncertain as she welcomed him. A poor attempt to grow a beard could not disguise his age. Johnny made friends with him while Eva opened the stove door to toast a thick wedge of bread on a long fork held close to the flames. She could smell the peat flavouring the toast, which she heaped with butter and served to Donal with tea, using the unpasteurised milk she always got in a jug from a nearby farmer when she had non-vegan visitors. The important thing with shy people was to give them enough space to finally feel comfortable talking. For a while the boy focused his attention on Johnny, using the dog as a conduit to find his way into the world of this caravan. But soon he was examining her bookshelves and her most precious paintings and photographs. Although he tried to affect a sense of being streetwise, she liked how his wonder and innocence came out when she lit two candles and they began to talk. Donal lost his shyness when excitedly describing the broadsheets of local poets he had produced using a Xerox copier: a far less complicated process than the Gestetner duplicator on which Art used to produce his homemade pamphlets.

Three hours later Donal was still talking on the window seat with Johnny beside him and Queensly curled up on Eva's knee. The table was covered with food she had bought in for him, old photo albums he asked to see and copies of new poems, which he read with great seriousness, his hand shaking as she sensed that this was the first time he had read them aloud and her response was vital, not in having to like everything he wrote, but in taking his dream of becoming a writer seriously.

His naïve determination came across as he talked of finding a factory job that would pay enough to feed him but not distract him from his real work as a poet. If a poet he admired, Francis Ledwidge, could labour as a road worker by day and cycle home to write poetry at night, then Donal felt sure he could combine poetry and factory work. But despite such animated talk, Eva worried about him surviving in factories. Art had coped on the Dublin docks because Art was physically strong and thrived on hard labour, regarding it as penance for his privileged upbringing. The tall willowy figure on her window seat didn't look strong. Donal looked more delicate, like Francis. But perhaps he reminded Eva most of herself at his age, a dreamer who had enrolled in the Slade School of Art, not realising how her small flame of talent would be extinguished when exposed to the competitive reality there.

As with all visitors who found their way here, she said nothing to disillusion Donal as he laid bare his dreams. His art movement was indirectly subsidised by a weekly allowance from his seafaring father: money which Donal more frequently spent on producing broadsheets of other poets than on food for himself. With his father mostly away at sea, Donal had lived alone since the age of fifteen: three older married siblings regularly calling to ensure he was okay. He told Eva about sitting up writing on most nights until dawn and how, when unable to afford a new typewriter ribbon, he would continue to type poems unseen onto a blank page, knowing that a copy of the words would appear on a second sheet underneath this blank one, thanks to the carbon paper stuck between them.

Their immediate affinity made Eva wonder if they had been close in a previous existence, although, when she asked him, Donal claimed to have never previously thought about reincarnation. Eva suspected that perhaps he had half expected to meet a conservative old woman who did not possess books about Andy Warhol's films. This was a reaction she sometimes encountered when shopping in Castlebar: some people shocked that an elderly widow would wear bright clothing or advocate radical causes. As Donal talked, his enthusiasm brought back Alex's bright-eyed look. But his face changed when Eva inquired about the book on the supernatural which he had mentioned wanting to write in his newspaper interview.

'I had to stop writing it,' he said. 'I hope you don't think I'm here under false pretences because you first wrote to me to say you knew Dermot MacManus. But I wanted to come to give you my book of poems anyway.'

'You're welcome for yourself, but why did you stop?'

He went quiet, searching for the right words. 'I received such bizarre letters after the newspaper interview that I got scared. Two men from Meath wanted me to visit an old ring fort at dusk, where they claimed they had a strange experience when shooting rabbits with their dogs. They wouldn't divulge what terrified their dogs, but said that they would only risk going back again if accompanied by someone like me who had studied the supernatural.'

'Please tell me you didn't go.' Eva remembered her fears when Francis was young that, in his good-natured way, he could be lured somewhere by men who might overpower him. Donal was not gay but she had seen enough of life to know that unscrupulous men sometimes preyed on young people's naivety.

'When I got their letter, I felt I should go with them, although I didn't want to,' Donal admitted. 'You see, in the newspaper interview I wasn't setting myself up as an expert on supernatural occurrences, but just someone who was curious. But the tone of the men's letter made it sound like they would expose me as a fraud if I declined. So I wrote a reply to say that I'd get a bus to Navan on the night they suggested. I placed it on the hall table to post next morning and headed upstairs to bed. What happened next sounds crazy because I was alone in the house, but seconds after I closed my bedroom door something or someone hurled themselves against the bedroom door, almost knocking it off its hinges. I was almost too scared to open the door. When I did, the landing was empty. I didn't know what had stuck my door with such force. But I sensed someone was trying to warn me. I went downstairs, tore up my reply to the men and abandoned any thought of such a book.'

'Who do you think was trying to warn you?' Eva asked gently, suspecting that he had never told another soul about this.

'I think it was my mother. For years I thought her death hadn't affected me because I was getting on with life, and on the outside, I didn't seem to be suffering, not like I see my father suffer when he comes home on shore leave to the bedroom they once shared and hits the bottle hard at times because that's what men do. He's a good provider and a good man, but I see him marooned in grief so deep it makes anything I feel seem inconsequential.'

Eva nodded. 'After my son died, I was so busy showing the world how well I was coping that I didn't realise I was blocking out my true feelings. I think we fool ourselves to protect others, so they won't feel guilty for not doing enough for us, when in truth there's nothing they can really do. Time is the only healer.'

'Do you think so?'

'I do.'

The boy nodded seriously. Eva studied him, aware of a strange symmetry: here was a son trying to come to terms with the loss of a mother, while Eva still struggled on certain nights to come to terms with the loss of her son.

'When I spoke in the interview about wanting to write a book on the supernatural, I think I was trying to make myself confront my fear about anything to do with death since my mother died. You can't stay trapped by childhood fears forever, so maybe I tried to tackle it head on. But I believe that I was firmly told from beyond the grave to avoid going near the ring fort with those men.'

'You think you were being protected?' Eva asked.

Donal nodded. 'Twice I've walked away from accidents where I should have died. One time the ambulance driver was shocked that I'd survived unscathed. Living on my own is lonely, sitting up typing half the night just to hear the keys break the silence. But when I'm truly in trouble, I sometimes sense I'm not alone. There's someone at my shoulder, not all the time or very often, but at crucial times when I'm in danger. That's probably stupid to say, because how can the dead look out for us?'

It was one a.m., the candles almost burnt out. Eva glanced at her photographs of Hazel and Alex and Francis above the window. 'I don't think the dead fully leave us. I don't understand what level they exist on, but I don't feel I've lost them. I think they're waiting for me.'

'Does death frighten you?' Donal asked.

'No. I love life but I'm prepared for death. I want to savour it, but not in a morbid way. My mother talked about death as second nature and as a child I was frightfully interested in her beliefs and allowed to read her books on the supernatural. I think I'll be curious to discover if the experience of death is anything like I've always imagined it would be.'

'What do you believe in?' the boy asked.

'I don't believe in any organised belief. Instead, I believe beyond all belief. I've never read the Bible much, except the Psalms which Mother taught me for their poetry. She would have liked your poems. You're lucky.'

'In what way?'

'You know what path to follow. Throughout my life I've searched for that, trying a dozen paths without success. But it is late now, time you slept.'

Eva blew out the candles and let the dog out into the field one last time. After ensuring that Donal had everything he needed, she retired to her small room. She needed to sleep because she did not know who might call unexpectedly to see her tomorrow. Eva noticed that the light was still on in the main room of the caravan. She had shown Donal the chapter in Colin Wilson's *The Occult*, entitled 'The Poet as Occultist' and could imagine him curled up in his sleeping bag, reading into the night like Alex used to love to read. All these new friendships were extraordinary, but none substituted for the absences that still haunted her subconscious. She suspected that some local women regarded Eva's refusal to live out her days in mourning as an affront to the dead. But her determination to embrace life was her homage to the spirit of those she had lost, it was her way of keeping their spirit alive. She had few possessions left. All she had to give was her time to people who knocked at her door, her window seat to strangers needing a bed, the breadcrumbs on her bird table to robins and finches who came at dawn, and her companionship to anyone who needed to tell their story or simply sit in silence. Yet even though she cherished her visitors, she was looking forward to winter when her battered ark would be quiet: just her and Johnny and the cats enjoying the peace. Savouring this promise of silence to come, Eva closed her eyes and allowed sleep to claim her.

⁊ↄ

Everything felt strange about being in this caravan when Donal turned out the light and tried to sleep. The way that the cat dropped down through the skylight to nestle at his feet, the dog's breathing in the dark and the silence of the fields. Something seemed to push against his brain, revealing a different way of seeing things. This old woman had stripped away everything that might burden her soul. Seventy-three sounded impossibly ancient, yet she radiated the sense of being young. The Ark had its own unique smell: a blend of incense and turf smoke. But what excited him most was the attention with which she listened to his poems, making him repeat certain verses, willing to engage with his imagination. The seriousness with which she took his dream erased the sting of jeering voices occasionally heard on the street, the rejection slips from *The Irish Press*, the two a.m. loneliness in his father's empty house as he repeatedly retyped the same lines of verse like a code he needed to crack. This old woman made him feel that he wasn't stupid to live by his dream. Donal knew that whenever he needed refuge or wrote a poem that particularly excited him, she would be waiting here to listen with two candles lit and the world locked out. The cat stirred, then settled back down in the crook of Donal's knees. He reached out to stroke her, then slept.

The darkness was so black – almost pressing down on him – that when he woke he felt scared before remembering where he was. A plaintive, weak cry had woken him. Was it the old woman, upset by all their talk about the past? Or – the thought unnerved him – the ghost of her granddaughter? The cat was alert, listening intently and Donal knew that Johnny could also hear the cry, close by and yet muffled. Putting on his trousers, Donal knocked softly on the woman's door and heard Eva say, 'Yes?' in a sleepy, puzzled voice.

'I think there's a child crying.'

He waited while she dressed in her tiny room. Johnny licked his hand, disturbed by this continuing crying. Eva emerged and listened.

'You're right,' she said, 'but I don't think it's a child.' She opened the caravan door and called out into the dark. 'Hello?'

Donal looked past her, across the field towards where one solitary streetlight illuminated an isolated gable. The stars seemed unnaturally bright. Taking a torch, Eva stepped down onto the grass. The crying became more urgent.

'It's under the caravan,' Donal said.

Both knelt to peer in past the cement blocks that propped up the structure. There was a hosepipe for water, some cables and rubble and nothing else. Then the cry came again and, as Eva swung the flashlight, they saw a young cat. A car must have run over her. Her fur was caked in blood and, from the angle at which she was lying, her hind legs seemed broken.

'Do you recognise her?' Donal asked.

'I've never seen this cat before.'

Donal reached in but the cat shrank back, hissing.

'Let me try.' Eva slowly stretched her hand under the van. The cat crawled towards her, inch by agonising inch, until Eva was able to gingerly lift her out. Carrying the injured animal into the caravan, Eva asked Donal to fetch an old white jumper in which she laid the cat.

'How did she know to crawl here for help?' Donal asked.

'I don't know,' Eva replied, 'but every inch must have been excruciatingly painful. Some motorist just left her for dead. How could anyone do that to such a beautiful creature?'

Eva's voice held no anger, just concern for the cat. Donal felt almost excluded from this scene, sensing an affinity between the cat and Eva that he could not fully comprehend. Murmuring softly, Eva stroked its fur. Now that she was inside The Ark the cat had ceased its crying, but her eyes never left Eva, who finally looked up at Donal.

'We can't save her,' she said. 'All we can do is put her out of her pain. Comfort her for me.'

Eva slipped into her room, leaving Donal holding the cat, who stared past him towards Eva's room. The boy didn't know what to do. He had never seen a creature die and the cat's eyes frightened him. Eva returned with a small bottle and a handkerchief. Johnny lay on the window seat with his tail down. Queensly had disappeared.

'What's that?' Donal asked.

'Chloroform.'

Eva let some poison soak into the handkerchief, then gently placed it against the cat's nose. There was no struggle. The cat breathed in, each breath growing more peaceful until her breathing faded away. Throughout this, Donal stroked the cat's fur and Eva brushed her neck softly. There was such a sense of repose in the caravan that gradually Donal sensed that – for all his fears since his mother's death – death was nothing to be scared of. Knowing that her time had come, this cat had instinctively sensed where to go for help. Eva covered the bruised body with the old jumper and laid it on a chair.

'Are you okay?' she asked, concerned.

'Yes.'

'Tomorrow you might dig a hole in the field so we can bury her. Isn't life strange? Good night, Donal.'

'Good night, Eva.'

Putting out the light, he undressed and got into his sleeping bag to lie again on the window seat. As a child, he was once present when three older youths had dug up a cat who was several weeks' dead and forced him to stare at the decomposing corpse. Did that brief glimpse into a plastic bag start his terror about death? In the months after his mother died, Donal secretly refused to accept the reality of her death, inventing an imaginary world in which he waited for her to return: a fantasy universe where he could pretend there had been a mix-up in the Richmond Hospital; another body had been placed by mistake in her coffin while she was still wandering the streets, suffering from amnesia. By concocting such fantasies he had started to live in his head and became a writer by accident. Tomorrow he would bury this cat, still wrapped in Eva's old white jumper. Now it felt almost as if he had been led to this caravan so that he could witness how death was a simple passing on from one state to the next.

The way in which Eva had listened to his poems made him feel like a true writer, even if for now she was his sole audience, beyond his sisters and some local factory hands who had parted with 30p but probably binned his book after barely flicking through it. In two days' time he would pack his haversack and hitch back across Ireland. There was so much to be done: poems to write, gigs to stage in local halls. But after this trip he would never feel foolish again when walking the streets at night to beat out lines of verse. This old woman had given his dream validity. Like her other friends whom she had talked about, Donal knew that he would always be welcome in this ark amid the fields. He would not even have to make the journey here to be warmed by this sense of belonging. He would need only to close his eyes to imagine the darkness being broken by a square of light as Eva opened her door and stood on the step, laughing as she exclaimed, 'How marvellous you're here! Isn't life exciting?'

Chapter Twenty

The Darkest Midnight in December

Kilmore, Co. Wexford, Christmas Eve 1990

It was late on Christmas Eve night by the time the young man from the small shop located a mile from Kilmore village drove his car across the muddy gravel to park as close as possible to Eva's caravan. The Ark was now situated in a small field behind the old schoolhouse which her friend, David Sumray – the young man whom Eva had now come to regard as being like a great-nephew – was restoring: transforming half of the classrooms into a studio for local artists and the rest into an independent hostel for backpackers. Eva opened her caravan door when the headlights lit up the tall piles of wooden rafters that were salvaged from a demolished local asylum. David had stacked these old beams between clusters of wild nettles in a far corner of the overgrown field. This weather-beaten timber was about to be given a new life by being recycled into elegant floorboards, when David found the time between the myriad other tasks he was always undertaking. Four months ago – after hiring a truck to drive to Mayo and carefully transport Eva and her Ark back to Wexford – David's first task had been to cut a path through the long grass to let Eva walk up to mix with the artists and guests who used the old schoolhouse and allow cautious visitors to gain access to this: the latest place for Eva to call home.

The young man from the shop raised a hand in friendly greeting: his way of acknowledging Eva, standing in the light spilling out from her doorway. She saw him open his car boot and lift out three bales of peat briquettes that would keep her warm over Christmas. Until recently she had kept her stove alight with a mixture of turf and small logs that she chopped slowly and methodically, using a small axe kept for this purpose. But arthritis made it much harder to grip the axe handle, and the young artists coming and going in the makeshift studios were so busy leading their own lives that she was anxious not to make them feel obliged to run down to help when they heard the soft blows of her axe interrupting the quietude of this field. Therefore she now only burnt peat briquettes. They were safer because they never sparked and Eva liked how the scent summoned up memories of the turf fires she used to light as a source of inspiration for wide-eyed children in her art classes.

Such memories made for good companionship at night when her eyes grew too tired to read and her fingers too stiff to hold a pen to write campaigning letters for animal and human rights causes. Eva had no idea how many handwritten notes she had written over the decades. Most had probably been shredded or filed away unread. Powerful leaders could ignore such letters, but they could not stop the annoying trickle of such letters which kept coming from people like her: unimportant and unnoticed but undeterred in their insistence to one day make their voices heard. Such a day occurred last February when Eva stood at the counter of Bridie's shop in Turlough, mesmerised by televised images of Nelson Mandela walking free from prison, twenty-seven years after she was verbally abused on the streets of London for campaigning against his detention. Perhaps her years of addressing postcards about Mandela's incarceration to Hendrik Verwoerd and P. W. Botha, to Johannes de Klerk during his chillingly repressive reign and, more recently, to his more conciliatory son F. W. de Klerk, had counted for nothing. But just maybe each one of her cards – like the thousands of other letters from thousands of other unknown people – had been like the ostensibly ineffectual weak blows of her axe against the logs she still kept trying to chop for kindling until a few months ago: no blow seeming to have the slightest impact until the first almost imperceptible fissure appeared and eventually, and only after infinite patience, did the log split asunder.

There would be no logs this Christmas, just the warmth of these briquettes, which the young man was now carrying with some difficultly across the flattened grass. Two months ago, she would have run forward to take one of the heavy bales from his hands and lighten his load. But a recent fall on the frosty concrete steps up to her caravan had shaken her confidence. She had not confided in anyone about the fall because no bones were broken, the bruising was on parts of her flesh that nobody else ever saw, and she knew the importance of not alarming people. But she also knew that she needed to resist her compulsion to help this young man. The important thing was to stand in her doorway and look sturdy as she called his name in greeting, knowing how blessed she was by his simple act of kindness and how vital it was not to cloud his Christmas by leaving him with the slightest worry about her. Johnny left the sanctuary of Alex's bed, where he now spent most of his time asleep, and padded over to stand protectively at her feet, gazing out across the moonless nightscape. The dog's arthritis was almost as bad as Eva's, but he wagged his tail, recognising a kindly soul who had come bearing gifts of briquettes and friendship that were as wondrous as myrrh and frankincense.

Now that the young man was almost at the steps, Eva realised why he was carrying the three bales of briquettes so awkwardly. He was dressed in his Sunday suit and was trying to hold the briquettes as far away as possible from his clean shirt and tie. He must be going directly from here to the Catholic church to rehearse the singing of the first Kilmore carol at Midnight Mass. Eva had never heard of the thirteen Kilmore carols until David Sumray rescued her from the prospect of being made homeless in Mayo by bringing her to this small village. When tourists sped past en route to visit the famous fishing village of Kilmore Quay, three miles further along this twisting road, all they saw of Kilmore itself was a small huddle of shops and pubs, a church and an old convent converted into a nursing home. But in this quiet village, two hundred and forty years ago, these unique carols – composed on his sickbed by a priest named Devereux – were introduced into the Christmas services in the local church. Since then an unbroken tradition existed where six local men, including one member of the Devereux family, sang eight of these unique carols over the Christmas period: the first one being sung at Midnight Mass and again at first Mass on Christmas morning.

'There you are now, Mrs Fitzgerald.' The young man smiled as he placed the briquettes beside the steps. He used a sheet of plastic to cover up two of the bales, then carried the third bale into the caravan, placing it down beside the stove. Aware of how stiff her fingers could get, he used a penknife to cut the stiff plastic strip holding the briquettes in two rows. 'We'll have you as snug as a bug for Christmas.' He knelt to affectionately rub Johnny's fur. 'And Sir Lancelot here can keep you safe from all harm.' He stood up. 'I've more stuff in the car for you, or at least tins of dog food for Johnny, food for the cats and a bag of nuts for the winter birds. But you ordered in very little for yourself. Are you sure you'll have everything you need? It's no trouble to go back and reopen the shop if there's anything you've forgotten.'

Eva smiled her appreciation. 'If you have most things on my list, I'll have more than enough, and even if you don't I'll have enough to make do. I'm just sorry that you're still working at this late hour. If I'd known I was putting you to this much trouble I'd have never phoned in my order.'

'Sure what trouble are you putting me to?' The young man laughed, anxious to minimise his efforts on her behalf. 'If I wasn't here I'd only be sitting at home in my vest, with the mother taking the shirt off my back to iron it for a third time. When I was small the nuns told me that God sees everything, but not even God has an eye for invisible creases in a shirt like a mother has.'

'You look very dashing,' Eva assured him. 'And isn't it exciting that you'll be one of the six singers this year? That's what I always find about life: it's just so exciting.'

'Exciting is one word, I suppose.' The young man's features took on a certain circumspection. 'But it will be an odd feeling. I remember, as a boy, hearing my late father sing these carols and him telling me how his own father sang them back before the war. I've no idea if my great-grandfather sang because he had a fierce weakness for drink and drank his way through two farms until cirrhosis of the liver saved his wife and children from total ruin. My great-grandfather doesn't get mentioned too often in family chats, but we wouldn't be a proper family without at least one black sheep in the shadows. If you think hard enough, there was probably even one in your own family too.'

Eva's peal of laughter sounded girlish as she thought back over the journey which had taken her to this field. 'To be honest, my problem would be trying to name a white sheep in my family. But they were all wonderfully true to their character and beliefs, no matter where those beliefs took them. Besides, nothing is ever black and white. Everything is a hotchpotch of dabs of this and that. The wonderful thing with colours is that they're just as muddled up as we are.'

'I'll tell you someone who is muddled up.' The young man laughed as he removed a cassette of The Smiths from his inside pocket. It had been a parting gift from Marcus when she was leaving Turlough. 'Mother of God, but that Morrissey chap could moan for Ireland – and him an Englishman. I stuck it in the cassette deck of the Massey Ferguson when I was bringing winter feed to the sheep, and the journey never seemed as long. I had to stick on Garth Brooks to lighten the journey back. Say what you want about Garth Brooks, but he definitely has the tractor factor.' The young man placed down the borrowed cassette, almost apologetically. 'The Smiths are just not my type of music, no more I suppose than the old carols I'll be singing over Christmas. But I'll still sing those carols, even though it will be a queer feeling knowing that my father stood in the same spot at my age singing them. Still, I suppose that's the thing with Christmas: it's hard not to remember those you've lost.' He paused, fearing he might have strayed into private emotional territory. 'And I know you've lost more than your fair share, Mrs Fitzgerald.'

'I have.' Eva glanced back at her arrangement of old photos on the one small strip of wall not lined by bookshelves. Francis and Hazel and Alex were there, and a photo of Freddie too, arms folded while wearing a military uniform so that he still managed to look like a countryman out in a field. 'The funny thing is how over time – an awfully long time – you realise how we never truly lose them. I don't mean that their ghosts are standing watching down over us, but I think that if you love someone they leave an essence, an infinitesimal radiance of who they truly are, and this shines on like the light from a dead star so you're never truly alone after they're gone.'

'Maybe you're right,' the young man agreed. 'I never much thought about it that way. I was only taught about heaven and hell and by the age of fourteen I wised up to how everything I'd been told was hocus pocus. I'm not saying religion is a bad fairy tale as fairy tales go, because it plays a big part in my mother's life and her friends, and I won't belittle them. But it's just not for me. Do you know what I mean, Mrs Fitzgerald?'

'I do.'

The young man looked embarrassed, as if he had revealed too much. 'I don't know what has me rabbiting on … maybe it being Christmas and all.' He hesitated. 'You'd never mention…?'

'I'd never discuss your business – or any friend's business – with anymore.' Eva assured him. 'Not that I'm presuming that you consider me a friend.'

'I'd consider myself lucky if you thought of me as one. Dropping in here for our little chats is better than going to confession and there's no three Hail Marys or three bags full at the end of it.' He laughed. 'That is except for the three full bags I still have for you in a cardboard box in my boot. And here's me after leaving your door open so the cold air is getting in. I won't be a tick.'

She returned to the doorway to watch the young man cross the grass. Last week his mother had called to The Ark, bringing a small box of Nestlé Black Magic chocolates as she urged Eva to join her family for Christmas dinner. It was one of four invitations Eva had received, the most recent being when David himself called in this afternoon to again ask her to spend Christmas with Jacquie and their small children in the old farmhouse they were restoring. Eva had assured David that – while deeply touched by their concern – she was looking forward to spending Christmas day alone in The Ark. Kilmore was not Costa Rica, but over the past four months it had proven to be the sanctuary that, at eighty-seven years of age, Eva needed most. Leaving Mayo after fifteen years was difficult, but now that the move was made she hoped to rebuild the peace of The Ark for Johnny and her two remaining cats. She was infinitely grateful to David for making her feel welcome here, while also understanding that she needed to retain her independence by possessing her private space in his field.

She missed the friends she had made in Mayo, but would not miss the bleak winters there, which played havoc with her bones. She now knew that she should have left Turlough after the sale of Glanmire Wood. That was when she had truly become a woman of no property, with no remaining link to that village. Over the years, she had no shortage of offers from local farmers wanting that land, but she had been patiently waiting until she found the perfect owner for Glanmire: a quiet-spoken organic farmer whom she encountered through an environmental campaigning group. Eva respected this man's integrity and knowledge of nature and knew that he would preserve the wood as a wildlife sanctuary. Eighteen months ago, when the deeds were signed over and Glanmire finally passed out of Fitzgerald hands, she had experienced a deep sense of relief, as if a millstone were removed from around her neck. Beyond a sadness in knowing that she would never again set foot on the lawn where Francis's ashes were scattered, Eva felt no nostalgia for a place that had intermittently been her home for over half a century. Nostalgia was a dangerous sentiment used by people as an excuse when afraid of change. Eighteen months ago, Eva had been ready for change, still possessing her dream of a move to the sunlight of Costa Rica. What had prevented her leaving Ireland was Johnny and the two more recent stray cats who decided to take up residence in The Ark: creatures whom she could not bear to see starve. These would be her last pets and when the final one died, she would eventually be released from all earthy responsibilities and free to once again be blown about like a sepal at her creator's will.

The young man was returning across the field with her provisions neatly arranged into different bags inside a cardboard box. She stepped back to let him enter The Ark and set it down on the low table. After he was gone Eva would slowly and painstakingly put every item away but it was important not to delay him now. Nor should she offer him any money beyond the price of the groceries, which he had told her in advance and she had carefully counted out into an envelope. He would be embarrassed by any suggestion of a tip. This would change their relationship and make it harder for him to speak with such candour whenever he stopped by The Ark. The young man looked around as if checking for any other task he could usefully perform.

'You're sure you'll be all right over the Christmas?' he asked. 'You do know if there is anything I can do...'

'There is just one thing,' Eva said. 'If I am not delaying you.'

'You're not delaying me at all,' he assured her, although she had seen him discreetly check his watch. 'What can I do?'

'Sing me for,' Eva said. 'I don't mean the whole carol, just the opening lines. I never found any organised religion that I felt I belonged to, although I liked sitting in silence among the Quakers in Dublin years ago. I'm a bit like my father, who went to church but only so he could sing. The joy in the singing is the only thing I miss about religion. Would you sing some of the carol for me?'

'You won't get much joy from a crow like me,' the young man said, so bashful now that Eva was convinced he would not sing. But after a moment, he closed his eyes and the same words that had been sung in this village for over two centuries filled up her caravan.

'The darkest midnight in December,
No snow, no hail, nor winter storm
Shall hinder us for to remember
The Babe that on this night was born.
With shepherds we are come to see
This lovely Infant's glorious charms,
Born of a maid as prophets said,
The God of love in Mary's arms.

No earthly gifts can we present Him,
No gold nor myrrh nor odours sweet.
But if with hearts we can content Him
We humbly lay them at his feet.
'Twas but pure love that from above
Brought Him to save us from all harms
So let us sing and welcome Him,
The God of Love in Mary's arms.'

The young man stopped and opened his eyes again. 'That's the gist of it anyways, although you can hear that I'm no Caruso, or Joe Dolan either.'

'The magic would be destroyed had Caruso sung them,' Eva said, her heart uplifted by the lyrics. 'Their magic is that they were written for ordinary men to sing. The mystery is in the ordinary – where all mystery lies in the end. You sing beautifully and you'll sing even better at the Mass. It's your turn to be the guardian of those words and they are safe in your hands. Now off you go and enjoy it. It will be exciting: I promise you.'

'I will enjoy it,' he said, enthused by her enthusiasm. 'I'll remember my late father when I sing and think of you also. Am I your last caller of the night?'

'You are. I have everything I need for the coming days, though I suspect David will pop his head in at some stage tomorrow evening, despite me telling him I'll be fine. Now go and enjoy it.'

'I will.' He leaned down awkwardly to lightly kiss her on the check, something totally out of character. 'You lock up tight and answer that door to nobody, do you hear me, Mrs Fitzgerald?'

The young man was gone then, racing across the grass as he became conscious of the time. From her doorway Eva watched his headlights swing around and his red tail lights disappear. She was alone then, gazing out into the darkness. Johnny was beside her, tail down, his nose sniffing the night air as if some instinct made him uneasy. Eva grew aware of how cold the night had become. A low moon beyond the hedgerow cast just enough light on the empty landscape for her to become conscious of just how isolated she was in this field a quarter of a mile away from the nearest house. In Turlough, the pub yard, just a hundred yards away, had always given her a sense that other people were close at hand. She shivered unexpectedly: Johnny's unease was somehow permeating her own mood, which had been upbeat until the car's tail lights disappeared. It made her uncharacteristically cautious as she locked the caravan door and checked it twice for reassurance, although she knew it was too flimsy to stop any determined intruders, who could make as much noise as they wished with a crowbar and not be overheard.

There was a soft thud behind her as one of the cats entered through the open skylight and jumped down onto the table where the box of groceries needed to be put away. Normally Eva attended to such chores at once. The caravan was untidy enough with her numerous cardboard files of letters to attend to, newspaper articles cut out from *The Observer*, if she felt they would interest particular callers, and lists of new books to ask for on trips to Wexford library. She could live with paper chaos because it was a trait of an active mind, but in such a small space it was vital to be punctilious about household chores. Despite this, she allowed herself to sit in silence on the window seat with Johnny beside her, panting slightly even in his sleep. The larger cat regarded the single armchair as her private fiefdom and would hiss at the smaller cat if she ever tried to stretch out there. Both cats observed her now, heads utterly still as if listening for sounds. Hazel used to scold Eva about what she had called Eva's stubborn refusal to allow herself to be unhappy, claiming that Eva used happiness as a way of blocking out the inevitable day when she would need to go back and confront the weight of the tragedies she had endured in her life. But just now she was forced to admit to an unexpected surge of loneliness on this, her first Christmas in Wexford since the days when Alex's presence used to light up The Ark in Curracloe.

She was not entirely cut off from all sounds of human life because occasionally she heard cars pass on the winding road into Kilmore as local people drove to the church to get an early seat for Midnight Mass. With most of the cars the sound faded away within seconds but one driver seemed hopelessly lost: Eva became conscious of the same noisy engine passing close by The Ark several times before speeding off again, almost as if it were a gang of robbers casing the area for soft, isolated targets. Curiosity made her want to open the door and listen, but prudence made Eva light a candle, turn off the electric blub and sit still, knowing that this one flickering candle would be impossible to glimpse from the road and would render her invisible to any driver prowling these unlit lanes. It took ten or fifteen minutes of total silence outside – although time was hard to measure without a watch or clock – before she felt reassured that this lost driver was gone. Even then she did not switch back on the electric bulb, preferring this candlelight to meditate in.

Last Christmas, she had no real thoughts about leaving Mayo, or at least not until Johnny's spirit passed on to wherever dogs go if they have known love in this life. Maybe she should have been listening more carefully to her intuitive inner voice: it was now clear that her purpose in Mayo had essentially ended when she signed over the deeds of Glanmire Wood. But mentally she had let herself grow complacent, forgetting that she possessed no legal claim to that site in Turlough where her caravan had been parked for the previous fifteen years. As well as her state pension she was still receiving her biannual annuity of one hundred and thirty pounds, purchased from Standard Life back in the 1950s when she had no idea of inflation and presumably Standard Life had no idea that she would live so long. But it would have been prudent to have held onto more of the money received from the sale of Glanmire Wood, rather than relish the chance to finally be able to donate to the antivivisection, vegan and animal welfare campaigns whose newsletters littered the table in The Ark. At least she had used some of the money to repair the leaking roof of The Ark and purchase strong ropes which local men had stretched over the caravan roof to firmly anchor it to the ground after it came close to being blown over in several winter storms.

Looking back, it felt as if that day, when workmen battened down her battered caravan with ropes as if staking her claim to that field, was an omen that marked the start of her irreversible uprooting from Turlough. In truth, the farmer who owned the field only ever treated Eva with courtesy and kindness, refusing to increase her peppercorn rent. But it was inevitable that, as a new generation grew up, his family would one day need to ask for that plot back. Being situated so close to the village, it was the perfect site for a new bungalow. This was the sole reason she was asked to leave, but in her mind it became tied up her starting to gain a reputation for interfering in animal welfare cases. Two farmers had stopped their cars while she was taking a walk to remonstrate with her after young people in Castlebar established a branch of the Irish Society for the Prevention of Cruelty to Animals. Perhaps she made a nuisance of herself when visiting another farmer on the road to Breaffy to plead with him to take better care of young calves crammed in a shed, whose bellows of distress went through her with equal pain as if someone had hammered a nail into her palm.

Or maybe people grew tired of her trying to interest them in the increasing local pollution, rumoured to be linked to a nearby American chemical factory. One teenage boy timidly called to her one morning, distressed by how the local river had turned the colour of red lemonade overnight, with dead fish floating on its surface. But people shrugged when Eva suggested organising a protest. Times were hard, with young local people having to emigrate again to Birmingham and Boston. Nobody wanted to initiate protests that might jeopardise local jobs. Therefore no one complained either about open-backed trucks driving through Turlough to dump chemical waste in a disused quarry behind Glanmire Wood. When that dump went on fire, a plume of carcinogenic smoke hung over Turlough, with many leaves on the trees in Glanmire Wood turning black, and parents urged to keep their windows closed until the wind changed direction. Afterwards, everyone angrily agreed that it had been a danger to their children's health. But once the fire burnt itself out, the trucks resumed their daily convoy through the village and Eva again made herself unpopular by continuing to raise awkward safety concerns that might endanger the jobs of young neighbours – already struggling to cope with crippling mortgages – if the plant closed down. Most locals who held opposing views still treated her with great civility, but something subtly changed after she ceased to own the last of the Fitzgerald land. It was Eva who always talked about one day moving to Costa Rica; Eva who had claimed to only want to stay for a short while in that field in Turlough. So why was her self-confidence utterly shaken when the kindly farmer, who eventually needed to apologetically call to say that, while nobody was rushing her, it would be greatly appreciated if she could seek an alternative location for The Ark because there were plans afoot to build a bungalow on the site where it was parked?

Eva had known good years in Turlough, although last spring she had wept following Maureen's death from cancer in Castlebar Hospital. Maureen's sister Kate was doubly distraught at the funeral. The only reason why her husband, Jack, looked well enough to stand by Maureen's graveside was due to the steroids that were just about keeping the more visible symptoms of his own cancer at bay. Jack's cancer claimed him two weeks before Eva left Turlough, with Kate occasionally turning up at Eva's caravan during his final illness – not to talk, but to escape from having to talk to daughters and daughters-in-law who fussed around her when what she really needed was the space to sit in silence. It was a space that she knew Eva would unquestioningly allow her. Kate wasn't the only elderly woman to discreetly visit The Ark. Often they had nothing in common with Eva, but they knew how she understood the loneliness of grief or the loneliness of being trapped inside the silence of a soured marriage. In her presence, they no longer needed to keep up the brave face they showed to the world. These women no longer saw her refusal to eat meat, take prescription medicine or attend doctors as quite so eccentric. She deliberately never handed out homeopathic remedies to any caller, but referred people to a Castlebar chemist who was being asked for so many remedies on Eva's recommendation that he had started to study alternative medicine.

Not all of her visitors were brow-beaten by life. Over the years, she made huge numbers of young friends in Mayo, like the social worker responsible for checking on Eva from the Health Board in Castlebar, who rarely turned up alone at The Ark, but invariably brought out some new girl just starting work at the Health Board. These exuberant young women often treated Eva as a surrogate grandmother, asking her intimate questions about relationships that they would never dare ask their own grandmothers. They formed a habit of popping in at unexpected times to seek Eva's opinion on a new outfit when setting out on an important date or to show off a new boyfriend, invariably phoning Eva afterwards to ask her what she thought of him. Some evenings the Health Board girls called in for no reason, beyond the chance to steal a moment away from their busy lives, when they could chat with her other random callers, their young voices filling up The Ark with laughter.

These were just the local callers. What truly astonished Eva was how the most unlikely faces from her past somehow found their way to that field in Turlough: pupils from her art classes decades ago or travellers whom she once befriended in Morocco or at the Quaker hostel in London. These visitors seemed to feel such a connection to Eva that she would have barely got over her joy at seeing them again before they picked up the threads of past conversions as if the intervening decades were no more than the blink of an eyelid. It was in Turlough that she saw Alan for the last time, when Francis's school friend turned up on a walking stick, clean-shaved for the first time in decades and so gaunt that his features seemed oddly boyish. He preferred to sleep in a hotel in Castlebar rather than on the window seat, as in past visits, because – as he wryly told Eva – his body was like a census form: broken down by age, sex and religion. Trying to hide her apprehension at his appearance, she teased him by saying that his remark implied there were all kinds of exciting new men in his life.

'One man only and only fleetingly,' Alan had replied with a sad smile. 'Indeed, I'm so out of practice that the whole sex act was rather perfunctory, like a sudden sneeze that came so quickly it caught me off guard. But the chap left such a lasting impression that I fear he will be the death of me. The doctors tell me I have it, Eva, the illness none of my friends want to talk about. It's so ironic. All my life I was a cautious mouse, but loneliness can make even a near hermit throw caution to the wind just once. I should have stuck to Thomas Mann in bed liked I planned. I wouldn't mind so much if the chap hadn't been such a plain Jane to look at. He really should have had drop-dead gorgeous eyes to die for. The doctors give me six months but death is a singularly inexact science. On the journey over here, I had it in my head to ask you whether you wouldn't mind – after the ghastly business is over and I've been cremated – if I could have my ashes posted over and you might consider scattering them in that wood where you scattered Francis's ashes. It would be nice to be with him: I always felt much better around Francis. But driving across the midlands I realised that Francis belongs here in the West and I don't. The fact is, cremation isn't something which Protestants involved in trade in Glenageary really do. Or maybe it's all the rage there now – like homebrew – but it wasn't a part of the Glenageary that I came from and the Glenageary I don't seem to have ever quite escaped from, despite getting out as soon as I possibly could. There is space in the family plot in Mount Jerome Cemetery. I don't expect you to attend the interment. It's too far a journey at your age. You'd also need to bring Johnny, having never been separated from him since the day you found him, and I suspect that dogs are not among the usual attendees at Glenageary funerals. There may be no attendees because I can't imagine anyone left in Dublin who knows me. But still, I shall be buried alongside my father who abused me when I was nine and my mother who caught him and warned me so severely to never tell a soul that I never did until this moment. I don't know why I'm telling you but maybe I just don't want to die with that old pain still festering inside me.'

By the end of this speech Alan seemed unaware that he was silently crying, with Eva so shocked that she was equally unaware of it until Johnny climbed onto the window seat and licked the tears off Alan's face. This had made Alan laugh, as if at the absurdity of the situation, as he gently brushed the dog away. They had sat in silence for an indefinite time: Eva holding his hand and Alan squeezing her gnarled fingers so tight that they remained bruised for days afterwards.

If Alan's final visit was the saddest occasion she had known during the time The Ark was parked in Mayo then perhaps the most exciting occasion was the arrival into her life of David Sumray, who turned up on her doorstep in Turlough three years ago, after returning to Ireland following a period spent in the Amazon rainforest. She had been friendly with David's parents when she lived on Frankfurt Avenue: people on her wavelength who had raised their son to follow his star as an adventurer and dreamer. Eva had been mesmerised to hear David's stories about his time in the Amazon rainforest: how he had cleared a space in a remote spot near a river and slowly proceeded to build a timber house, using techniques learnt from indigenous tribes, who could not speak a word of his language but shyly found ways to communicate with their visitor after realising what he was trying to do. When David ran out of money and needed to leave the rainforest to seek work, they never touched his unfinished dream house. He would return with provisions in a flat-bottomed boat and recommence his solitary task. Because he loved the feel and the mystery of timber, the construction of this house consumed him. When it was finally completed, David had travelled to the nearest town to send invitations to numerous friends across the globe, suggesting that they join him on a certain date for a house-warming. He could not believe how many people arrived by divergent routes, all somehow managing to follow his directions. The party lasted for days that merged together: the world beyond the rainforest temporarily forgotten by everyone present. When the party ended and the last guest left, David realised he had no reason to stay. His dream was to build a house, but not to be burdened by living in it. He had left the door ajar as he pushed his boat away, hoping that some future traveller might chance upon it.

On his first visit to Turlough, this young man, who was only a child when Eva last saw him, talked at great length about his next dream, which was to restore an abandoned schoolhouse in Wexford. On subsequent visits, he always assured her that there would be space for her caravan in the field adjoining his schoolhouse if she ever needed it. David was so much on her wavelength that when Eva was asked to leave Turlough, it was David to whom she turned for help. Unhesitatingly, he arrived within days to tow her caravan here to this overgrown field to allow her to continue to lead an independent life at her own snail-like pace. She missed the easy stroll to Bridie's shop but felt secure here, held tight in the care of this young couple. For now, Eva's dream of Costa Rica would have to remain a dream. But here she had time and space to sit and read and slowly write letters in thick black marker, to meditate and leave open the channels of her imagination to supersensory experiences.

Not that she didn't need to keep both feet firmly on the ground at eighty-seven. It was vital to concentrate fully when completing her daily chores, like emptying out buckets of hot ashes on the grass and taking Johnny for the daily walks that he still needed, even if they could both only walk a fraction of the distances they once traversed each evening. Eva was finding each winter increasingly difficult. Even when wearing her hernia belt, she needed to wheel her supplies purchased in the health food co-op in Wexford very slowly and carefully in a battered shopping trolley, finding it hard to cope with the extra weight of the library books she was constantly changing, as the library staff valiantly coped with trying to find the obscure books she requested from them. It was vital to remember to carry in only four peat briquettes at a time because if her hernia strangulated it would mean an immediate operation. In hospital she would be powerless to prevent doctors poisoning her body with antibiotics.

At least in The Ark she could still nurse herself through colds or flu with the natural remedies whose properties she had first learnt in the Culpeper's herbal store in Winchester. These remedies took far longer to work than the drugs manufactured by the multinational pharmaceutical companies, but contained no poisonous side effects. The old people on the bus that she took into Wexford each Wednesday laughed when she said this, but then questioned her about homeopathic treatments for their own aches. In her few months in Wexford she had grown to love the comedy on this bus journey: the passengers being almost exclusively pensioners with free travel who boarded the bus as much to gossip and joke with each other as to go shopping in Wexford. These pensioners immediately made Eva feel welcome in their midst because, even if she were a blow-in with what they considered to be odd ideas, she had lived through the same harsh decades they had known. But it wasn't just old people who afforded her this welcome. The young artists who used David's schoolhouse as their studio also adopted her. Most had little money and needed odd jobs to buy themselves the time to paint, but their enthusiasm for life made her feel young. When they invited Eva up to the schoolhouse for a party to welcome her, one of them – a poet and painter named Andi who produced beautiful hand-stitched books of poems about the sea – embarked on such a riotous dance that it culminated in him joyously somersaulting off the walls before landing at her feet with a bow.

Their openness and innate understanding of who she was contrasted with the young Health Board official sent to assess her when Eva arrived in Kilmore. Eva accepted that recently her caravan had grown shabby, but because she never measured wealth in terms of what she possessed but only in terms of what she needed – and because she needed very little beyond books and food and writing material – Eva had never considered herself destitute until this young official briskly began her interview, which felt like an infuriated interrogation. Eva realised that she had been spoiled by the interest taken in her by the Health Board girls in Castlebar, who treated her more like a friend than a client. This immaculately coiffured young woman with makeup as thick as body armour had prissily perched on the window seat as if fearful that her outfit might become stained by sitting there. It was such a shock because young people were normally so engaged with life and open to new ideas that welcoming them into The Ark was a pleasure. But the more that Eva tried to make her life fit into the neat boxes on the official's form, the more she was made to feel like a daft old woman burdening the local authorities by having the audacity to plant herself here. At the end, when the young official finished her inquisition of endless questions, Eva did not rise from her armchair to see the visitor out but sat alone and just for once succumbed to tears, remembering her parents' hopes for her. The young artist who once enrolled in the Slade School had become an arthritic old woman, humiliated by a slip of a thing from the Health Board. Johnny had rested his old head on her knee and whined at seeing her so upset.

Even now, three months later, the memory of that interview made her feel dirty. But Christmas Eve was a night for repose and not regret. How long had Eva allowed herself to sit here by the light of this single candle summoning up memories? She might have remained lost in thought if another sound had not permeated her thoughts, bringing with it a frisson of unease. Eva realised that she was listening to that same noisy car engine circling around these isolated roads again. But she refused to sit here in fear, turning herself into the pitiful creature the haughty Health Board official had categorised her as. Johnny needed to make his last trip outdoors to cock his leg. She opened the door and watched Johnny limp down the concrete steps. The noisy engine was still out there. Surely it must just be a visitor having trouble locating the church. Johnny limped slowly back up and Eva closed the door. But the dog had barely returned to his armchair before he raised his head to stare quizzically at her. Eva knew that the dog wasn't quite sure if he heard something, because, like her, his hearing was going. They made for a right arthritic pair, she thought, both straining to listen. Perhaps it was a ghost. She recalled lying in bed on a Christmas Eve eighty years ago, awaiting Mother's step up the staircase in Dunkineely, and the rich scent of the hand lotion she always used after gardening as she gently stroked Eva's hair on the pillow.

But this was no ghost because Eva could now hear the noisy engine again, drawing so close that it was hard not to be frightened. Through the window she saw headlights sweeping over the deserted schoolhouse. Then the engine and the lights died. Eva had reason to be scared. Recently there had been a succession of violent robberies on old people who lived alone: elderly bachelors beaten with sticks and hammers, their mattresses ripped asunder in pursuit of any mouldy banknotes hidden away for safe keeping. She took several deep breaths, steeling herself for whoever might be about to break in. Ever since discovering how isolated this field was, she had prepared herself for such an eventuality. She would need to stay calm and tell the intruders that she had no money but they were welcome to take anything else they found. It was important not to panic them into violence. If they did attack her then there were worse places to die than her own home, with at least the horror of having to one day enter a nursing home being avoided. But while the cats would flee out the skylight, Eva simply could not bear the notion that violence might be inflicted on poor Johnny, who would never abandon her. Maybe it would have been better if she and Johnny had been burnt alive last month when she had stumbled with a lit candle and accidentally set the curtains alight before she managed to put them out. Such an inferno would have at least have been brief and left behind no unfinished business except the two cats that surely Jacquie would take in.

Through the window, Eva watched as a torch traced its way along the rough path through the long grass. It could be a friend of David's checking on her, but she had asked him not to bother returning this evening. The torchlight stopped as if the holder were sizing up the situation. Then it shone slowly over the caravan: the beam blinding Eva so that she needed to look away to see Johnny's tail down, as it so often was recently. The seconds stretched out as the torch-holder made their way around by the side of the caravan, until a knock came on the door. There was no point in trying to keep it shut when it could so easily be prised open by a crowbar. Slowly Eva opened the door, blinded again by the torchlight until the beam was switched off. The darkness seemed magnified beyond the weak light emerging from the doorway. In the arc of light, looking awkward and embarrassed in a long winter coat, she recognised Kate, Maureen's sister from Turlough, standing there with a bag at her feet.

'Kate? Is that really you, Kate?'

'It's me all right, Mrs Fitzgerald. I'm after running away.'

'From what?'

'What do you think?' the widow replied. 'From Christmas. For weeks my daughters keep quarrelling about whose house I should go to on Christmas Day, but with Jack dead I just want to be left alone. Grandchildren don't want to see their grandmother in tears when they're sitting down to their big dinner. I asked myself what would Maureen do, and then it came to me. She'd have driven down to you to escape the whole circus. I remember you were always a great woman for the birdwatching.'

'I still am.'

'I've always liked birds myself, leaving out bread for them and watching out to see if any new bird flew into the garden. I never went birdwatching or anything like that because I didn't want people to think I was soft in the head, but I always envied you going off for the day with your big binoculars, the size of something that Rommel would have carried. Am I an awful woman to be intruding on you like this? Have you plans for Christmas Day?'

'I've no plans at all,' Eva said. 'Would you care to spend it here?'

'To tell you the truth, Mrs Fitzgerald, I'd love that. I've spent the past hour circling these roads trying to find you and I was scared I'd have to drive back to Mayo.'

Johnny came to the door, his tail up, recognising an old friend. He knew there would be talking, with tea made and biscuits for him. Kate bent to hug him, stiff from her long drive. 'My other bag is in the car. I didn't want to just presume, you know.'

'We'll walk up together later and fetch it,' Eva said.

'You're sure you don't mind?'

'It's absolutely wonderful. Isn't this exciting? How brave of you to run away.'

Kate laughed. 'There will be hell to pay. My name will be muck when I return. They all only mean good and would do anything for me except leave me alone. That's what I feel since poor Jack died, utterly alone. So if it's no trouble I'd sooner be all alone with you. We can have any class of Christmas we want, with no young fusspots trying to jolly us up.'

Eva smiled as she patted her hernia belt. 'Sure, we're young ourselves still.'

The stove was almost out, but a few more peat briquettes would soon have it ablaze. Eva lit the candles and put on the kettle. The two old women forgot about their tragedies and laughed at the idiosyncrasies of young love as they opened the stove door and held out thick slices of bread to make toast in the old way. Johnny dozed peacefully on the window seat between them. For all his arthritis, Eva knew that he would love a run tomorrow when they would have themselves a Christmas to remember, driving out on the Wexford slob lands where nobody would ever find them, to watch Greenland geese. She could almost hear Alex saying, with her beautiful young laugh: 'Look Granny-Mum, the roof may be nearly caving in, but I named it well. The wounded are still finding their way here. It's still an ark in the fields.'

Chapter Twenty-One

The Last Cat

Kilmore, Co. Wexford, Autumn 1995

Last night, the struggle to continue living in this caravan ended when the last of her cats finally died. He was in such pain that Eva had needed to use the dregs of her chloroform to put him down. She lay awake for most of the night: his small corpse against her breast, forced to accept that – with all the animals in her care now dead – this dilapidated dwelling could not be called an ark. Its roof leaked in two places: buckets placed to collect the drops of rainwater. Even in dry weather, the aluminium walls were now so damp that many books were succumbing to mould. For weeks she had been carefully selecting which unblemished ones to give away as gifts to visitors, being guided in this task by the memory of how thoughtful Francis was in making up parcels of his books to bequeath to friends. The empty bookcases gave The Ark a curious echo, but letting go of possessions was a necessary part of the process of preparing for her eventual death. Eva did not know how long more she had: she just knew that she finally needed to accept the advice of her friends and leave behind this sanctuary. In recent days, the majority of her possessions had already been moved to a small County Council bungalow in a nearby remote hamlet. Eva had resisted leaving The Ark until now because it was the only home her cat ever knew, and it was hard enough for him to be dying without also suffering from the anxiety of being disorientated. But when David came to check on her this morning, Eva had sent him off to fetch a spade. She now sat alone during these final moments in The Ark on the window seat that was once Alex's bed, awaiting his return, finally ready to acquiesce to the inevitability of time.

For a year now she had known in her soul that it was impossible to continue this struggle. Her legs were as thin and brittle as sticks. Last month, she tried to cut down some tall nettles growing near her caravan, not realising that they were screening a hole until she tumbled into it. It had happened just after dawn, when nobody was stirring in the independent hostel which David now ran in the old schoolhouse a few hundred yards away: the art studios needing to be closed because every old classroom was required for guests. Eva had resisted the urge to call out for help from those guests, knowing that if she managed to eventually wake someone, it would probably be some foreign backpackers with little English who would not know what to make of the situation. They would have only made it worse by phoning for an ambulance to whisk her away into the maelstrom of a crowded Accident and Emergency ward that would feel like a prison. Instead she had strained every shred of willpower to haul herself out of that hole, inch by agonising inch, her hand further stung by nettles as she somehow found the strength to mount the caravan steps: the sickly elderly cat circling around her, meowing in distress. Consulting her homeopathic books on how to keep the bruising down, Eva had declined to mention this latest fall to the various kind friends who checked in on her over the following days, because every time that people found her collapsed it only increased their concern for her to leave The Ark.

It was the quest to find Johnny after he went missing last year that drained the remaining strength from her legs. For six days, Eva walked every side road in search of him: her friends driving around at dusk to search for her and eventually persuade Eva to let them drive her home. The whole parish helped to look for her half-blind dog after he wandered off. Eva had babbled on fretfully to these kindly neighbours about fearing how someone working for a pharmaceutical company might have kidnapped him to use in some excruciating animal testing experiment in their torture chambers of diagnostic laboratories: Johnny ending up as trapped and friendless as Brendan, decades ago in that gulag. But this had only been her way of keeping her worst and most irrational fears at bay, by mentioning them aloud. In her soul she had known the truth was more prosaic: Johnny was simply following the instinct of all dying animals.

To ensure that the herd was not forced to leave the lair after one of them died and the body started to rot, animals who sensed their time had come often slipped away like this to await death on their own. It was for her sake that Johnny had limped back out to the wet, lonely ditches from which she once rescued him as a starved beaten pup. During his last week in The Ark, Johnny constantly whined at the door, wanting to be let outside to stand trembling on the wet grass, tail down, staring at the moon. Poor Johnny Joe-Joes, her truest friend. Initially, after his disappearance, Eva felt unable to stay in The Ark without him. Even when neighbours brought her home at nightfall, Eva would slip out again by the light of a handheld torch, stumbling and falling and picking herself back up as she called his name aloud along the tiny roads they both loved. When she eventually accepted that Johnny was not coming back, Eva was touched by how many local people called to sit with her while she wept like she had not wept since Alex died. Her loneliness without Johnny was intense, yet she had needed to embrace this isolation because her great fear had always been that she might die before the last of her pets, lest they suffered neglect in her absence. Today she could finally put that fear to rest: when Eva buried this dead cat after David returned with his spade, her last duty would be completed in The Ark.

At ninety-three years of age, the prospect of again living in a house frightened her after years of seclusion in the fields.

David and Jacquie had asked her to come and live with them, but her soul needed its independence. Over the past year, a local woman, Brenda, had become her great protector. Eva admired her strong stance against cruelty to animals locally, how she stood up to farmers and to Department of Agriculture officials if they showed reluctance in enforcing laws to protect livestock. It was Brenda who forced Wexford County Council to provide Eva with a tiny bungalow in the nearby hamlet, Brenda who raised funds to furnish it and Brenda who organised the clean-up after the previous tenants left. From now on, Eva would no longer need to fret about The Ark toppling over in winter gales. She would have a paid home-help calling in for one hour each day and dry shelving for those of her books for whom she had not yet found the right recipient. So why was Eva – who never feared change and had so often moved home in her life – dreading the moment when David transported her remaining books and papers and her solitary two suitcases of clothes to this small dwelling amid a dozen similar bungalows occupied by families she didn't know?

Not that she intended to stay long in that small Council bungalow. It would be a staging post, providing breathing space in which to regain her strength and plan her final move. What she really longed for was a chance to finish her life among young people who shared her beliefs. While physically unable to march in demonstrations anymore, she dreamed of being allowed to sit in the offices of an animal rights movement and slowly compose handwritten letters of protest in thick black marker, still able to fight at her snail's pace for what she believed in. If only she could be allowed to occupy even the smallest corner of such a campaign office, it would keep her in touch with young people, just like living here in this caravan had done for the past five years.

Eva had lost track of how many fascinating visitors from around the world had stayed in David's hostel: curiosity causing many to wander down the field to find out who lived in this caravan. Sometimes girls who had travelled alone across India had tapped at her door to ask if they could sketch her. Their sense of unencumbered joy reminded her of Jade, to whom she once gave Francis's hat as a gift when the young Londoner was setting off to explore the world. Or sometimes it was young men with barely any English, content to simply sit for a few moments, gazing around at her books and paintings as they stroked her cat, which had loved to curl up on visitors' laps. They were young seekers after truth, intrigued to discover an old woman who had read the same books they were now discovering and once enjoyed the nomadic life they now led. Visitors living out their dreams, who possessed little money and who occasionally baffled her with wild talk which made her suspect they might be high on some narcotic, and sometimes overstayed their welcome, or who sometimes betrayed how Eva's stories had started to bore them. But they were young people who had made her laugh with their zest for life and who filled up her caravan with their laughter. People to whom she never needed to explain her life, because this ark made her seem like a fellow traveller. Eva recognised that the caravan was now dilapidated: its insulation so poor that the cold crept into her arthritic bones, no matter how many layers of clothes she threw over her makeshift bed. But it had still always acted as a beacon, luring in exciting new visitors. Eva knew little about the isolated hamlet she was moving to, but she doubted if such unusual visitors would stumble across her in that bungalow where she would now live in far more comfort, but her life would lack any context.

Eva gazed out the window but there was still no sign of David returning with his spade. Sitting quietly, cradling the dead cat's body on the window seat, she scolded herself for yielding to pessimism. Life had taught her how impossible it was to know what adventures lay ahead. How could she have imagined the extraordinary miracles that had occurred in this field? Like the evening when her sister Maud's son turned up from Dublin, accompanied by a foreigner who embraced her, announcing that he was her Art's Russian son, free at last to visit his late father's homeland under *perestroika*. Or the miraculous letter which arrived after Eva told an Auckland backpacker about how a young New Zealand officer once wanted to marry her when Eva was only seventeen and he was recuperating from the Great War by staying with her family in Donegal. Eva never knew how the backpacker tracked Jack down in New Zealand, but one morning a letter arrived in handwriting that Eva still recognised three-quarters of a century later. Jack had married twice and known joy and tragedy in his life, but although he enclosed a recent photograph, Eva could not see him as this old man in his nineties. Holding his unexpected letter, she was able to conjure up his laughing face, aged twenty-two, his lips so close to hers that she could still recall her sense of being both thrilled and scared, on the cusp of womanhood.

Or the night when a friend collected her from this field to drive to the Garter Lane Art Centre in Waterford, where the poet Paul Durcan was giving a reading and how, before the reading started, he presented her with a collection of his poems, *Crazy About Women*, all composed in response to paintings in Ireland's National Gallery. From the stage, the poet spoke about how his lifelong obsession with painting had stemmed from magical childhood afternoons when his mother brought him to Eva's art classes in 1950s Dublin. Paul's reading gave her a sense, decades later, that perhaps she had not failed as a teacher after all, because just maybe the joyful chaos of her small studio had opened up a handful of children's minds to new ways of seeing the world. Indeed, in recent years she was continually surprised by how the most unlikely people – often strangers on the street – claimed to have somehow drawn solace and inspiration from her. Perhaps her years of struggle had some small effect after all, although Eva could think of nothing special about herself. So maybe it was a case that her increasingly shabby ark retained something of the aura which each wondrous visitor left behind after they had sat here with her over the years. Maybe this was the aura which new visitors felt when they climbed up these steps. If so, it meant that her way of life only made sense out here in the fields.

The prospect of a cul-de-sac of small houses filled her with dread. But she knew it would be selfish to remain here any longer, being a worry for all her friends by falling into bushes and nearly setting the caravan alight several times. She had lived in houses before. Brick walls would not feel strange once she got used to them. Her bird table was already erected in the back garden and she would leave extra nuts on the windowsill. For years now, wild birds had flocked around her caravan at dawn, some virtually alighting on her shoulders if she stood still for long enough after putting out the nuts and stale bread they feasted on. Perhaps in time these birds would eventually learn to seek her out in her small garden there. She would regain her strength by not having to endure the hardships of caravan life. She would have more time to read and think and campaign. She would try to blend in with new neighbours and make them understand her. But she would miss the open space where young friends could pitch their tents alongside The Ark. She would miss hearing Marcus from Turlough, who had grown into such a lovely young man, rise when it was still dark, on his visits to girlfriends, to walk to Kilmore Quay and watch the sun come up. Such friends would still visit her in this Council bungalow, but she knew that the psychic energy would feel different in an estate with blaring televisions and children aimlessly kicking football.

Still, such a wonderful group of friends had gone to such trouble to arrange this move for her that it would be selfish to feel sad. She had to embrace the future, always remembering George Orwell's words: '*no bomb that ever burst shatters the crystal spirit*'. Eva rose and walked to the door as David's car drove in through the small entrance at the hostel. Eva saw Jacquie in the passenger seat: a young child on her knee. It was typical of Jacquie's generosity of spirit to come and support her in this leave-taking. They emerged from the car and David took a spade from the boot. All that remained in The Ark were ghosts whose whispering voices she could no longer hear. Eva could imagine those ghosts sitting there, shimmering shapes merging into each other: her departed fellow travellers on this long voyage. A song entered her head that Alex used to love, written by an interesting young thin-as-a-rake Englishman, about an astronaut stepping from his capsule into the infinity of space. The sun emerged from behind clouds, making the wet grass glisten so that Eva felt almost blinded. Standing as tall as her stooped shoulders would allow, Eva declined to look back as she stepped forth from The Ark, cradling the corpse of the last cat tenderly in an old white jumper.

Chapter Twenty-Two
Beethoven's Ninth
Co. Wexford, Autumn 1998

Eva's hands were now so stiff that trying to write even one postcard exhausted her, but she could still manage to read books slowly with the aid of a magnifying glass. The important things were to try not to get frustrated by life or panic about not being able to achieve something in every remaining day. Her bedroom light would be put out soon, although she saw little chance of getting any sleep in this nursing home. Strangers kept her awake by walking in and out of her room all night. The night nurse denied this, claiming that Eva was always asleep whenever she checked on her. But the staff presumed that everyone slept soundly. Eva suspected that this was because they drugged every other patient at night except for her. She was the only patient still with her wits left, the only patient who seemed to somehow always create a fuss and yet the only patient who could truly make the staff laugh. Eva was not complaining, because everybody here was kind, especially the matron who – being an Aquarius – understood her. Adjusting to life here was proving difficult and Eva had no intention of staying for much longer before resuming her travels. But she knew she would not have survived another winter in that bungalow if her friends hadn't found her a bed in this small, remote Wexford nursing home.

Dermot Bolger

When she had first moved to that small estate, Eva used to occasionally wave from her window to the children kicking football on the green in front of her Council bungalow. At first the children ignored her, then some started waving back in exaggerated gestures of ridicule. The tightknit instinct of people born within that community was strong and Eva was an outsider – albeit one who could rarely venture outside. On the last occasion when she tried to leave food for the birds on the bird table in her garden, she fell and lay on her path for twenty minutes. Her suspicion that some neighbours, reluctant to get involved, might possibly have watched her sprawled there, hurt worse than the physical pain she remembered when lying in nettles in that isolated field in Kilmore. But two men had eventually emerged from a nearby bungalow and very kindly picked her up. After settling her into a chair and satisfying themselves that no bones were broken, Eva had seen them glance askance at the books on her kitchen table about the occult and animal rights. They left, with Eva sensing that they seemed anxious not to get trapped in conversation with her.

Nobody in that estate ever meant any unkindness: she just needed to accept that they thought differently to her. Some neighbours disliked her leaving out bread for the birds, claiming it attracted rats. People there watched television ceaselessly and gossiped about soap opera characters as if they were living people. But this did not make them peculiar: the longer that Eva lived there, the more she was made to feel that she was the peculiar one, living her life to the rhythm of an ancient unwound clock on the mantelpiece from which she had removed the hands and simply scrawled the word 'NOW' across its face. After decades of independent living, it had been perturbing to see herself being reflected back through the wary looks of people in this small community into whose midst she was parachuted. If ten years younger, she might have gradually been able to mix properly, slowly coming to understand her neighbours and make them understood her. But the increasing infirmity of old age hindered any such intimacy. When Eva once described a childhood tennis party to a neighbour and told the woman how she still respected her brother Art for giving away the family's land to support communist causes, Eva slowly realised that the woman did not believe her story, finding the childhood world which Eva described so bizarre that she obviously imagined herself to be listening to the ramblings of a senile old woman. But when Eva's once-privileged background became known, it increased her sense of feeling an outsider: people seemingly unable to grasp how Eva rejected her social caste. While some neighbours were baffled, others went out of their way to be truly considerate: none more so than one busy young mother whom Eva called 'her guardian angel', who found time to call in each evening to help sort out Eva's bills and problems.

But in the end, after two years of struggling to survive there, Eva had been simply unable to cope any longer. She deeply appreciated the efforts made by her friends to raise funds to get her into this nursing home, but nonetheless she had her own plans to escape and find a new sanctuary when the weather turned warm again next spring. Matron understood this and had promised to help Eva pack as soon as the forthcoming winter ended. Matron argued that spring would be the best time to move. Since Eva arrived here eighteen months ago, Matron was always encouraging Eva to stay on for just another three months, to gain enough strength for her next move. But next spring she would refuse to be fobbed off any longer in her determination to find a vegan nursing home somewhere, where only homeopathic doctors were allowed to attend patients, using acupuncture and herbal and Chinese medicine. Such a vegan nursing home would be a stubbornly independent institution and therefore not plagued by the curse of interfering health inspectors.

Eva tried to stay calm now, but the thought of these health inspectors made her long to rise and defiantly force open her window. She had been asked to keep this shut after Matron discovered Eva secretly leaving out bread for birds on her windowsill and grew alarmed that a Health Board inspection would close down the nursing home if the bread crumbs attracted mice.

From the outside, this nursing home, located on a bend on a remote country road, resembled two ordinary bungalows knocked into one. It was not luxurious but Eva liked its simple intimacy. Her fellow patients spent their time mostly dozing in the dayroom that Eva refused to enter. As Eva disliked communal activities such as bingo, she knew little about them. This caused her some guilt because she so deeply enjoyed meeting all of their visitors, who now knew Eva by name and always lingered in the hall to chat to her. Each afternoon, after being dressed in layers of old cardigans and a woollen hat, the nurses brought Eva out to lie on the sofa in the entrance hall. She had commandeered this sofa as her unofficial office, as it allowed her to greet everyone who arrived. Whenever Matron scolded her with gentle exasperation because of the voluminous quantity of documents which the nurses needed to bring out before Eva felt fully settled on her sofa, Eva always quoted in reply the Austrian Holocaust survivor and psychiatrist, Vicktor Frankl: '*Without a sense of meaning and purpose, a man will either be despairing or dangerous to himself and others.*' At ninety-six, Eva possessed so little time left that each day needed to be given a purpose. Today she managed to scrawl a protest card to the Irish Minister for Agriculture about the live export of cattle and to British Nuclear Fuels about their MOX facility in Sellafield. These two relatively simple tasks took hours because she got distracted talking to other people's visitors or regularly lost her thick black pen among the blankets covering her. But eventually she had succeeded in having the postcards ready for Matron to post and therefore earned the right to feel this exhausted now at nightfall.

Her longest chat today was with a new priest who came to say Mass in the common dayroom and initially seemed perturbed by

369

Eva's disinclination to join in. After the nurse whispered to him, he apologised and offered to bring his Church of Ireland counterpart next time to pray with Eva. She had declined, explaining how she preferred to reflect in silence on Socrates's belief that we must constantly strive for the virtues to perfect our souls. The priest seemed so genuinely nonplussed by her reply that Eva recited lines composed eight decades ago by her father in Donegal:

'You can abolish God,
You can crucify Christ
But you will never smother
The Holy Ghost.'

Eva's plans for her death did not include letting her body fall into the hands of any clergyman. She wanted no grandiose hearse or impersonal undertakers, just a plain unvarnished wooden box that David had promised to make for her when the time came. Last year she got David to measure her carefully from head to toe, allowing space for the curvature of her spine with age, and asked him to promise to transport her to Dublin in the back of his lorry for her cremation. When he explained that he had sold his lorry, she offered to pay for him to purchase a roof rack to strap her to the top of his car. David had laughed at this image, saying how perhaps it was not either legal or wise, but he would ensure that her body was quietly brought to Dublin with no false note of affectation or ostentation which might take away from the natural simplicity of her death. Jacquie had promised in turn to paint this box containing her body in the most joyous of swirling colours. Eva envisaged her cremation as being like a Quaker meeting with no formal religious service, but just the space for people to pray in silence or speak aloud in their own unadorned words if moved to do so. She only had two other wishes. The first was to have the finale of Beethoven's Ninth Symphony, *Ode to Joy,* played – those wonderful notes composed by Beethoven late in his life amid a deafness so acute that people needed to pluck at his sleeve before he turned to witness the crowd's rapturous ovation at the symphony's premiere. Her second wish was to have her friend Donal read her mother's favourite poem, Tennyson's 'Crossing the Bar':

'*Sunset and evening star,*
  And one clear call for me!
And may there be no moaning of the bar
  When I put out to sea,

But such a tide as moving seems asleep,
  Too full for sound and foam,
When that which drew from out the boundless deep
  Turns again home.

Twilight and evening bell,
  And after that the dark!
And may there be no sadness of farewell,
  When I embark.'

Eva planned to die exactly as she had tried to live: all artifice and veneer stripped away. Yet despite her calm preparations, on certain nights like this, death's looming closeness scared her because she had so much left still to do. Eva sighed now, frustrated at the night nurse's delay in coming into the room to turn out her light. Did the nurse not realise that Eva needed to get asleep before intruders started to sneak in and out of her room? They were probably health inspectors, seeking to hunt down and kill harmless spiders and other defenceless creatures. But there was no point in complaining when there was always something to look forward to. Tomorrow Jacquie or Brenda or one of her other friends had promised to take her out in her wheelchair. This expectation of being wheeled out into the fresh air was exhilarating. And even if it rained and no one came, then George Bernard Shaw's humour would sustain her as she used her magnifying glass to painstakingly reread the enormous volume of the *Collected Prefaces* to his plays, which she had once skimped on food for weeks to save up and purchase in Foyles Bookshop on Charing Cross Road decades ago.

But now her mind was becoming muddled as she tried to remember clearly if it was tomorrow when this friend was due to take her out. The days were growing more confusing and often she didn't know who was due to come. Last week a man came to visit, who – when she lived in Curracloe twenty years ago – borrowed a book from her as a boy, which he now wanted to return. His young wife had breast-fed the most beautiful baby while they sat in Eva's room and Eva laughed so much with joy at seeing him again that she felt like a girl. Then, when he mentioned his memories of watching her and Alex happily walk along Curracloe Beach, Eva had started to talk about the deaths of Francis and Hazel and Alex. There was nothing in her story she had not told other people a hundred times before, but when Eva caught sight of sudden tears in his wife's eyes at the details of Alex's death, Eva unexpectedly started to cry inconsolably as well. This was the strangest thing about living to be ninety-six. Her grieving should be long over, but recently her children's deaths were starting to hurt more with every passing day. For decades Eva had imagined that her grief was slowly dissipating, but instead it felt as if all that anguish and anger was secretly festering inside her, waiting to ambush her one final time. Perhaps Hazel had been right to complain that Eva buried each heartache behind her quest to be happy, as if the state of happiness itself could act as an opiate and panacea against every loss endured in life. But maybe happiness was just like one of the pharmaceutical concoctions that Eva had spent her life warning people against, claiming that such drugs never cured the illness but just suppressed the symptoms. For years, had she imagined that she was over the anguish of cradling Francis's dead body in that London basement or the ache of never truly understanding the circumstances of Hazel's death? But maybe all this time that grief had remained lodged inside the hidden, spiteful Scorpio aspect of her soul, which now desperately needed to expel all this torment before her body succumbed to death.

Could this explain the impulsive, uncontrollable rage that sometimes overtook her now, vanishing as quickly as it came: a pent-up fury at the unfairness of life? Her long years of philosophical study and reflection were rendered helpless before the unquenchable wrath she felt at such moments. Thankfully tonight she felt calm: beyond longing for the night nurse to come and allow Eva to escape into sleep before she started to have angry thoughts again about the hatred which health inspectors must feel for the small birds that Eva was no longer allowed to feed. Tonight she would not think about the tragedies of her life. Tonight 'the ship' – as Eva liked to refer to this nursing home – would sail nobly on: its staff doing their best to keep every passenger safe. Despite her complaints life here was good. Nobody tried to force-feed her milk or eggs. The cook puréed the vegetables she liked and, because she resisted all attempts to let a doctor near her, she still possessed her wits, unlike the other patients on their concoctions of drugs.

The noise of her bedroom door opening disturbed her thoughts. Eva felt a surge of relief as her great friend, the night nurse, appeared. This young mother – with two young children at home being minded by her husband – did not look as tired as on some nights. Eva was always the last patient she looked in on. With the other patients asleep, the nurse might even find time to talk.

'How was your day, Eva?' she asked, leaning down to pick up the various papers and books which had fallen from where they had been spread out on Eva's bed.

Eva reflected for a moment on the day's trials and frustrations, the tiny tasks accomplished and decisions taken. 'It was good,' she admitted. 'I met some lovely visitors out in the hallway. I like watching all the comings and goings. Isn't life here exciting?'

'It is, but I hear you're still planning to leave us.'

'I am. Once spring comes.'

'Off on your travels again. You've had a few travels, haven't you? I envy you. I was never outside Ireland, beyond two charter holidays to Tenerife where every second pub is Irish.' She paused. 'You had that poor priest perplexed today until he realised you are Anglo-Irish.'

'I'm not Anglo-anything,' Eva protested. 'My father once traced our ancestors back to Niall of the Nine Hostages. He raised us up to be Irish, but to also be true to ourselves and live according to our own conscience, recognising any act as being noble if inspired by love.'

'Lucky you.' The nurse laughed and sat down on Eva's bed. 'The only advice my father ever gave me was to be wary around fellows and twice as wary around flyboys who hail from Wexford town. Anyway, whatever you are, the new priest took off like a scalded cat.' She smiled at Eva and lightly brushed her hand. 'You do know that we'd all miss you if you took off on your travels.'

'Would you?' Eva felt humbled and touched.

'Truly. You're a wee dote except when you get into your moods.' She glanced at the wall behind Eva's bed. 'Where on earth did you get that odd poster?'

Eva looked up at a photograph of an impoverished young man seated at a bare wooden table: a pile of roughly cut sandwiches on one side and a heap of books on the other. He was ravenously eating while devouring a book at the same time.

'A friend saw it in a bookshop in Holland and sent it to me. I laughed when I saw it because it so reminds me of a young Glaswegian bricklayer I knew when I was caretaker of a Quaker hostel in 1960s London. He was a Buddhist.'

'I thought you said he was a bricklayer from Glasgow.'

Eva nodded. 'You can be a bricklayer and also a Buddhist, even in Glasgow. We used to catch a train and go hiking on Sunday afternoons. He'd bring me off to a cave in the hills.'

'Did he now?' the nurse teased. 'And what did your handsome Buddhist bricklayer do in this cave?'

'He'd light a fire to keep us warm while he read me Buddhist poetry and I would share a vegan picnic with him.'

'Merciful hour!' The nurse stood up. 'You've ruined my illusions about London in the swinging sixties, but I obviously haven't lived. Here, let me tuck you in for the night so that you're snug as a bug in a rug.'

Eva allowed her to adjust the bedclothes. 'You were gardening earlier.'

'How did you know?' The nurse checked her fingers. 'Are my nails still dirty?'

'Not in the least, but I can smell the hand lotion you used afterwards. My mother always used that exact same lotion after gardening.'

'You're surely cracking up now.' The nurse laughed. 'All I ever use is soap and water. Don't tell me you're going to start on again about people disturbing your sleep.'

'They come in at every hour, like they're checking on me,' Eva protested. 'I can't imagine why. I can hardly run off, can I? Inside I may still long to leap over the moon but I can barely walk. Do me one favour, open the window.'

The nurse tutted in mild reproach. 'Now you know well, Eva, you can't be leaving out bread for the birds.'

'I do know. But open it just for a minute. There's something I want to hear.'

The nurse shook her head with the same good-humoured, exasperated look she used to see on Freddie's face in the first years of their marriage, the look used by Hazel and by various other people whom Eva had tried to live among. But the nurse opened the window all the same, then stood back to listen before shaking her head.

'You see? There's nothing to hear.'

'Oh, there is.' Eva closed her eyes to listen to the night's luxuriant silence, to the infinite possibilities of the unheard – to the silence out of which the deaf Beethoven had plucked his marvellous *Ode to Joy*. 'There's an entire symphony playing out there.'

The night nurse listened also, then shivered and closed the window. 'Maybe you're right and the rest of us are daft. I don't know. Goodnight, Eva.'

Eva didn't reply or open her eyes even after the door closed. She wanted to lie still and hold on to the majestic chords of the earth at peace, on to a silence so vast that it took on the true voice of prayer.

Chapter Twenty-Three

The Cleaner's Daughter

Co. Wexford, 2000

Who but who was going to come and rescue her from this God-forsaken prison of a new nursing home, where staff could not be trusted and most patients were sexually frustrated widows who had sold their houses after losing their husbands and got their hair done before booking themselves in here in pursuit of men? These woman resented Eva for revealing this truth aloud to visitors but, at ninety-seven, Eva was beyond bothering with lies. Therefore her fellow patients – except for one kindly old man who sometimes sat and calmed her with his quiet fortitude – kept their distance.

It was too late tonight to place a long distance call that would need to go through numerous operators with headsets and switchboards before eventually getting through to someone in Dublin. But if she did not die tonight then Eva was determined to telephone her family's old firm of solicitors tomorrow and instruct them to sue everyone: the small group of friends who had made these arrangements for her care without understanding her needs; the architect who had converted this old convent into a nursing home gulag; the cook whom she accused of secretly adding meat stock to the special vegan dishes that Eva felt too suspicious about to eat, despite the fact that Eva always insisted on being wheeled down to the dining hall early to make sure that nobody tampered with her vegan food – because Brendan himself had come all this way back from the dead to tell her that, if you wanted to survive in the gulag, you must fight your way into the dining hall on time or there would be no vegan food left. And who would any sensible person believe: their own dead brother or the staff who told her that she didn't need to be wheeled downstairs at all if she was too tired and she was welcome to have her meals in her room? But Eva couldn't be sure if the staff were telling the truth – if anyone was telling the truth – and even if they were, it still left the biggest worry of all which was that, if she somehow managed to live through yet another of these indescribably long nights, then who but who would come here to rescue her?

Eva had felt utterly different about life this afternoon when she was calm and lucid, able to tell the two local women who came to visit her about the kindness of the staff in this new nursing home and her contentment here. This afternoon the sun had been shining as Eva sat in her wheelchair in the orchard behind the nursing home, shaded under the leaves of apple trees that magically dappled the warm summer sunlight. This afternoon she had laughed and chatted for two hours while the nursing home cat purred in her lap. Eva had known the names of her two visitors, unlike on some days when she grew confused, and was able to savour their local gossip. She even delighted in being able to add her own titbit to the conversation by revealing how one of the cleaners, who worked at night in the nursing home, was starting to occasionally smuggle her young daughter into her workplace because there must be nobody at home to mind the child.

Relaxing there in the sun with the cat in her lap, she was able to calmly discuss her move from the previous small nursing home which needed to close due to a shortage of staff to this renovated convent, not far away from the field where her ark last stood. David's hostel was now crammed with refugees:

people fleeing from strife in the Democratic Republic of Congo and Albania and Nigeria who had smuggled themselves onto container trucks bound for Rosslare Harbour to begin the long process of claiming asylum. The hostel was permanently block-booked by the Health Board to hold refuges and, while some locals were apprehensive about this influx of outsiders, David always described how harmonious the hostel was, with remarkable communal meals being cooked by the asylum seekers. How marvellously exciting that hostel sounded, filled with fascinating people ready to share their experiences. The great mixing together of humanity was happening at last, even if too late for Eva, who desperately longed to be back in her Ark, greeting any asylum seekers who wandered down the field to talk to her. But Eva was stuck here in this nursing home, and likely to remain grounded after her misbehaviour again last week.

In recent months, kindly local people would frequently take out Eva for drives to Kilmore Quay, where the ocean spray remind her of childhood in Donegal. But last week when an elderly couple had brought Eva out and then attempted to bring her back to this nursing home, Eva started to rant in their car, demanding to be driven instead to an old farmhouse which a young local artist and her husband were restoring. This young couple made her welcome as always, serving herbal tea on the lawn. The artist was such a dear and so kind and something about their tumbledown, bohemian house made Eva feel, if not actually at home, then at least in a place which held an echo of the sort of free-spirited haven she once tried to create for Francis and Hazel in Glanmire Wood during the war. The problem was that, even after the coldness of dusk settled around her, Eva kept resisting people's entreaties to return to this nursing home or to enter the farmhouse. She had insisted with sudden irrational fury on remaining out on the lawn in the growing darkness, shocked by her own vehemence because it was not in her character to be a nuisance, still stubbornly ignoring the pleas of those who kept anxiously coming out from the house to check on her. Eventually David was summoned and Eva reluctantly allowed him to drive her back to the nursing home. However she had not wanted to return here, she had wanted to be allowed remain out there on that lawn, shivering under the trees at dusk, because at times this nursing home felt like a prison and only out there in the cold fresh air had she felt sufficiently able to organise her thoughts and try to remember all the faces from her past to whom she felt an overwhelming duty to recall one final time.

That evening on the lawn she had wanted to be allowed to slink off and disappear into the deepest bushes like Johnny had done when he knew that his time had come. Death felt preferable to being here where this terrifying new rage engulfed her. A rage that, in lucid moments, she saw was causing hurt to the friends trying to mind her, but a rage that needed to pour out after being suppressed for years – a rage stoked by the kaleidoscope of faces that kept haunting her dreams. Dreams where she cradled Francis's dead body again and saw Hazel's corpse wrapped in a blanket and poor young Alex dying in the African bush and Brendan starved and beaten in a Soviet gulag and Freddie's face in that Isle of Wight hospital telling her that he would leave Francis out of his will; and the angle at which Francis's body lay when she found him, as if he had tried to rise and swallow more pills and the blue blotches on his skin; and Hazel wrapped in a blanket in the African night suffocated by exhaust fumes and Hazel as a girl in bed in Glanmire, the white soles of her feet needing to be warmed.

Her thoughts straightened out for a moment to allow her to wonder how many – if any – mourners from Glenageary had ever turned up when Alan's coffin was lowered to rest beside his parents in the neglected family plot in Mount Jerome; if any distant relation had ever thought to engrave the name of that most gentle of men on the tombstone there and how she cried alone in her caravan on the day of Alan's funeral, desperately wishing that her legs had possessed enough strength for her to travel to Dublin for that sparsely attended entombment, clutching the sort of glorious spray of Wicklow heather with which Valerie O'Mahony once lit up Golder's Green Crematorium.

Then her thoughts plummeted back into the maelstrom where she wondered how she could ever have brought herself to pluck the feathers from the innocent birds that Freddie and his guests used to blast to death with their blunderbusses; and how tragic it was that the smaller first nursing home she had been in had closed down when Eva only realised now in retrospect just how happy she had been there; and what she would like to say to those evil, unscrupulous scientists who conducted horrific laboratory experiments on defenceless animals, despite Jesus's words to them as he entered Jerusalem on a donkey on Palm Sunday and preached that *Thou Shalt Not Vivisect Thy Fellow Creatures.* Jesus was the great outlaw, which was the title of a book about Christ that Mother used to love, which Eva must ask some friend to buy for her – and what happened to all the letters poor Mother wrote to the British Foreign Office seeking news of her lost son; and the thought of poor Art going demented in old age and dying in Moscow and her middle brother and rock, Thomas, dead in South Africa, a proud ANC member in his final decades, and her sister Maud dying in the Molyneux Protestant Nursing Home in Leeson Park in Dublin, having insisted on booking herself in there, strong-willed to the end, bringing with her only the bare minimum of possessions; and Johnny's body lying undiscovered in some ditch and The Ark cats who seemed to still be alive at times because they crawled about in her mind; and the black tomcat who used to sit utterly still on the piano when Father was composing his never-to-be performed symphony in Donegal; and the warmth of the fur of her pet rabbit pressed against her skin as she watched Father at the piano through the window as a girl; and long before that, right back to her earliest memory of taking her first tentative steps, hardly daring to believe that she could walk, but intoxicated by the scent of daisies pressed against her face as she longed to reach her nurse's lap and share that moment with its magical smell of freshness; and her nurse's inviting wide-open arms sitting beside the tennis court in Dunkineely; and the suffering of cows penned in on factory farms like she was trapped here; and Father's lost symphony that would now surely never be performed; and how gentle Father always was, more like a best friend to her, and how Alex's smile had always reminded her of Father's tenderness; and the desolate beauty of St John's Point in Donegal and the feel of Art's fingers holding her hand when she tried to climb the One Man's Pass on Slieve League as a girl; and the smell of Mother's hand lotion when she would call in to say good-night to Eva and Maud in their beds; and how Francis as a teenage boy stole away the affections of that handsome tutor during the war; and how Hazel whisked away that young American painter from her in Esther O'Mahony's cottage in Wicklow; and the awful hothouse flowers that Jonathan brought to Frances's funeral and the beautiful Wicklow heather Valerie O'Mahony placed on his coffin; and Francis's ashes scattered on the daffodil lawn and Freddie's ashes scattered by some drinking buddy on a Mayo lake among the bogs where he loved to shoot; and how Eva used to love to sketch while sitting on the ditches amid banks of wild flowers as a girl and the night when she walked the road from Dunkineely to Bruckless to see the moon and stars and a drunk raiding party of British Black and Tans stopped her on a bend, menacingly dismounting from a Crossley tender with rifles cocked until the officer heard her accent and ordered them to let her go unmolested; and the jangle of the horse-drawn cart transporting all of her family and their guests off for picnics lasting from dawn to dusk; and how Francis lay dead with his skin turned blue amid the picnic hampers piled up on that cart; and how this could not be right and her mind was surely slipping because Francis had not even been born back then; and poor Francis crying among the trees as a child after Freddie made him shoot a rabbit in some woodland but where exactly was that wood again and when and why.

And was the ghost of the poor butler still trapped in the wine cellar in Glanmire House: the man falsely accused by Freddie's guests of stealing a five pound note simply because he ran across their line of fire to try and protect those poor birds they were intent on slaughtering? The innocent man driven by their lies to take his own life, with poor Hazel lying dead at his feet in that cellar, wrapped up tight in her African woollen blanket and Francis lying beside her, shoulders hunched from trying to rise to swallow more tablets. And no sound in that lonely cellar except the creak of the rope on which the butler's ghost swung for eternity and no smell there except for the exhaust fumes pouring from Hazel's car, while from some unlit room upstairs in the ruin of Glanmire House there came the distant crackle of the 'Moonlight Sonata' being played over and over by a child on an ancient wind-up gramophone.

Eva knew suddenly that none of this made the slightest sense but it was too much of a strain to try and comprehend the exact nature of this malaise which made her mind meander like this, unable to keep proper track of her thoughts anymore; and why had she not thanked dear Jacquie for the lovely wildflowers she brought into the nursing home yesterday, when she knew how hard all of her friends had worked to find this nursing home and organise the subventions and payments that Eva could no longer keep track of; and why was she putting down the names of those same friends on the long list of suspects that she intended to sue when the telephone operator put her through to her solicitors in Dublin on the black and silver candlestick-style telephone apparatus that Father kept in his study with its heavy nickel-plated brass mouthpiece? Was her lovely friend who regularly visited from the Wexford Freemasons on this list and, if so why, when he had taken the time to read her aloud the lovely letter that Thomas's children had written from South Africa last week – the day after some of Maud's children and grandchildren visited from Dublin, so full of kindness and concern; the day when she was able to think absolutely straight; and how one friend laughed last week when she asked him if he could fit an electric lawn-mower engine onto her wheelchair so that she could venture out again by herself into the fields, amid all the wild birds who would surely recognise her after decades of feeding them and flock down around her to perch on her shoulders; and where had she put that long list of people to sue anyway and how had she managed to write all the names down when she could barely hold a pen? And again and again and again the question of why she could not still feel as calm and happy as she had been feeling this afternoon? Why did she feel so agitated and confused tonight when she had been so at peace with the world in that orchard just a few hours ago?

Then it came to her: all this malaise was because of the nursing home cat. That was it. She could remember clearly now how the nurse frightened the cat away from her when putting Eva to bed this evening. All afternoon the cat had happily nestled down in Eva's lap while she chatted to her visitors and then, after the visitors left, Eva and the cat became fellow conspirators when the nurse wheeled Eva back to this bedroom. The cat never once purred or stirred from underneath the blanket on Eva's lap, knowing that he was safely concealed there. He would have happily spent all night curled up at her feet in this bedroom where Eva was generally left undisturbed except for when the night cleaners came in and insisted on sweeping away any cobwebs in the corners, despite Eva's protests to them that she loved the company of all living things, including spiders, because hadn't Pythagoras proclaimed the kinship of all of life. Eva's conspiracy with the cat had almost succeeded, with Eva trying to cling onto the bundled up blanket in her arms in which the cat was concealed when the nurse helped her to shift her shrivelled body into this bed. But her hands could no longer grasp hold of things properly and although Eva strained to cling on, she dropped the blanket, causing the cat to leap from its folds in alarm and race out the bedroom door before anyone could catch him.

The nurse had laughed about the incident, joking that Eva had her heart scalded. But was it so awful to want to have a warm and living creature in your bed at night? Her own hands and feet remained icy cold, no matter how many blankets or hot water bottles the nurses gave her. Indeed her hands felt colder now than any corpse she ever touched and had felt like this for weeks. Death was close at hand, but Eva still didn't know if she was ready. Her remaining books were gone to David for his hostel. She had told her poet friend Donal to take anything he wanted and was amused when he chose only her broken clock embossed with the word 'NOW'. When Marcus flew over from London to spend a day with her she had asked him to take away her letters and papers. All that remained were these inexplicable outbursts of anger simultaneously keeping her alive and killing her. But even this residue of all the hurt she had carried inside her felt nearly exhausted, which meant she would not need to carry it forward to whatever world she was going to. But where was she going and why would somebody not come and rescue her from this gulag, bringing her out into the fresh air amid the fields? This type of death seemed unfair because she had always anticipated being able to savour the moment of death when life's great questions would finally be answered. Her grip on life felt so slight that it would have been easy to just close her eyes and embark on this last journey by ceasing to take these laboured breaths. But Eva could not let herself die just yet because of her worries that the night cleaner's young daughter might wander into her room while she was dying and be forced to witness the death rattle that no child should have to hear.

Eva first noticed this child one afternoon last week when she woke to find Donal seated quietly by her bed. At first she was unsure if he was real but it was one of her serene days. It was while they were talking that she saw the girl several times shyly peering in at them through the open door. Eva knew that Donal only had two young sons and so the girl could not have come here with him. It took Eva several nights to realise that the child must be accompanying one of the cleaners who worked here at night, although – probably because they were anxious not to lose their jobs – every cleaner she questioned denied having smuggled in a child. The girl was not here every evening, only on nights when no babysitter could be found and it was safer for the mother to bring her into work than leave her alone at home. Eva understood the problems of raising a child but she resented the slyness of this cleaner who always waited until she thought Eva was asleep before allowing her daughter to slip into Eva's room and play imaginary games on the floor, having obviously been warned to stay quiet in case her mother was caught. Eva never made a sound lest she frighten this child who sometimes glanced shyly up at Eva's bed, but never approached. In fact Eva rather enjoyed having the girl there for company, but would have preferred to have been asked before being forced to play a part in this conspiracy.

Tonight it was proving to be an extra worry in case the child wandered in when Eva felt so weak. This was one more item that she needed to phone her solicitor about, if she was still alive in the morning. But would she be able to remember? Her brain was tired of all this remembering and all the mornings. The way dawn used to occur suddenly out of the darkness in Kenya, like a speeded up film. Kenya where Hazel was buried and Alex had died. Why did she have to upset herself by thinking about Kenya now? Why couldn't sleep or death claim her and switch off this torrent of thoughts and memories, this constant stream of words rattling around her head? Words that could never add up to the truth because the truth was beyond words; the truth flashed past too quickly for words to describe it: ninety-seven years being constantly relived in nine point seven seconds. What was the point in even trying to think straight anymore when she could hardly hear her own thoughts because of her breathing having become so loud and forced: each breath seeming to last an eternity of seconds. Eva opened her eyes and strained to identify the person who had just entered the room to lean over her bed and check on her. She recognised the patient night nurse whom she liked. Eva expected the nurse to turn away and close the door again, leaving her to this isolation, but instead she sat on the side of the bed to take Eva's cold hand in hers. Why was she doing this? Then Eva understood why – because the approach of death must be showing on her face like it once showed on Mother's features all those years ago, and Eva was relieved that someone was here, willing to hold the fort and hold her hand until the rescuers arrived.

Because surely there had to be rescuers, perhaps little people like in *The Borrowers*, the series of children's books that Alex once loved. Eva could see Alex in The Ark in her bare feet reading a book and looking up to ask '*Granny-Mum, should we check on the earwigs*' while the sun shone in through the caravan window onto the window seat where Johnny lay with his tummy upturned. Of course none of this could be real because it was night-time and this kindly nurse was leaning forward, straining to make sense of Eva's ceaseless low mumbling. Someone needed to keep the talk going because Eva loved to talk and was waiting for someone to rescue her. Surely that someone had to be Francis who once swore to rescue her if she was ever in trouble. Sure enough her door opened and in Francis waltzed, dressed up in Mother's silk scarves, like on the night he danced for them after Eva rescued him from that boarding school and he had promised to one day rescue her in turn if ever in trouble. Only it couldn't be Francis because Francis was dead and when Eva managed to focus her gaze she saw that her door was closed: the nurse still here keeping vigil.

Eva was glad of her company because this was the end and she was scared, now that she understood that nobody could come to rescue her. But the bedroom door did open again behind the nurse's back and at first Eva imagined that all her ghosts were going to crowd in, the ghosts she had kept alive by patiently remembering each one. But instead it was the young girl whom Eva now realised had never been with the cleaners after all but was surely the daughter of this nurse and had probably grown tired and scared of waiting alone out in the corridor while Eva delayed her mother by taking so long to die.

It was wrong to have a child here though and Eva would sooner die alone than see this toddler be forced to witness death. The child held out a cluster of fresh daisies in her two hands, although Eva could not smell them because, as the nurse leaned over, the scent of the hand lotion that Mother once used became so strong. The nurse did not touch her hair and yet Eva could feel someone's comforting fingers stroking it. This sensation frightened her, although she knew in her soul that she had no reason to be scared. The girl was standing beside the nurse now and Eva wanted to say, '*Please, for her own sake, take your daughter away from this*'. But the nurse seemed unaware of the child. Instead she began to recite a prayer for the dying. Eva knew that the nurse wanted to call someone, yet was afraid to move from the bed in case Eva died alone in her absence. The child held up the daisies, which Eva now realised were a gift for her, but Eva could not reach out to take them because her arms had no strength. Yet the child was so excited and proud of having managed to gather these wild daisies that Eva needed to try. But all she could so was stare at the child, silently beseeching her to bring the daisies closer until their vibrant colour and marvellous smell blocked out every other sensation and, as the child's tiny fingers touched her bony hands, Eva finally recognised who had come to rescue her.

She could no longer distinguish the child's fingers from her own or exactly be sure of where she was. But she felt calm at last, with her mind clear, having floated free from needless clutter to be allowed to simply be herself: that untainted essence of joy which she had been as this tiny child, before her life grew entangled with so many other intertwined lives. She knew that all she needed to do was trust in her ability to learn to walk further that she had ever walked unaided before; to stand upright and take those giant steps across the grass bank beside the tennis court in the garden in Dunkineely where her nurse was beckoning. She could see nothing because the fresh daisies were pressed right up against her face, but beyond them she knew that eternity or rebirth or oblivion beckoned. The answer was not to question but to simply *be* – to show the same trust as a sycamore sepal willing to be whirling in the wind to wherever its creator meant for it to fall. Intoxicated by this scent of daisies, Eva rose on her unsteady young legs and began to wobble blindly forward, scared and yet excited, certain that she was running across these tumultuous, immeasurable seconds towards the waiting clasp of widespread welcoming arms.

Postscript

Sheila Fitzgerald (née Sheila Dorothea Goold-Verschoyle) died in a nursing home in Kilmore, Co. Wexford in the early hours of August 3rd, 2000 – twenty-five days shy of her ninety-seventh birthday. David Sumray and Jacquie Kehoe, who along with so many other friends, worked so hard to allow her to lead as independent a life as possible, tried to honour the spirit of her last wishes. At her request, David Sumray had already taken her measurements to personally make the small wooden box that she wished for as a coffin. In honour of her radiance, Jacquie Kehoe helped to paint this box in such an array of bright colours that it matched the vibrancy of any painting produced in her child art studio amid the conservatism of 1950s Dublin. Sheila was anxious to avoid what she regarded as the ostentatiousness of being transported in a black hearse. While her body needed to legally be held in the care of a Wexford undertaker, they respected her wish by transporting her body to Dublin in an unassuming white van, to the surprise of staff at the Glasnevin Cemetery crematorium. No clergyman spoke in that crematorium but I recited her chosen poem, Tennyson's 'Crossing the Bar', before the body she had outgrown entered the flames to the sounds of the joyous final chorus of Beethoven's Ninth Symphony. Friends from across the decades were present, along with the gracious children and grandchildren of her older sister.

Some months later I travelled to Wexford with my late wife and our two young sons for another simple ceremony. Many of her Wexford friends and neighbours gathered to watch David Sumray plant a tree close to where her caravan, The Ark, had last stood. I was tasked with scattering her ashes into the hole which he had dug to let them nurture the roots. Having poured several handfuls of ash in the Wexford clay, I asked every child and adult present to scoop out one handful of Sheila's ashes from the urn so that everyone there could share in this task. Observance was then paid to her final request, which was that not only should her ashes be spread in a spirit of celebration, but this should culminate in everyone present joining in a joyous shout at the end. It seemed superfluous to ruin the simplicity by placing a plaque to mark this spot where the final remains of Sheila Fitzgerald have been absorbed back into the natural landscape she cherished, on a peaceful corner she would have so often passed in the final walks she took with her beloved dog, Johnny.

I hope this tree has flourished. Unobtrusively it marks the last resting place of Sheila Fitzgerald, who was among the most remarkable and inspiring people I ever met. The question of how much of Sheila lives on within my fictional creation of an alter ego for her in the character of Eva Fitzgerald, is one which I cannot honestly answer. While I felt that I possessed a unique relationship with her, her great gift for friendship and empathy meant that a hundred other people equally felt that they shared just as strong a bond. Each one of us would therefore recreate a different version of her, depending on what she told us about aspects of her life, and on what impact she had on ours. After shaping and reshaping the manuscript of this novel for well over a decade, retuning to it afresh every few years, I can only present this fictionalised account of the second half of her life, hoping that parts of it will ring true to those who knew her and that some part of her unique essence will comes through to readers who never had this privilege.

Our first meeting was similar to how the teenage poet, Donal, meets Eva in this novel. In 1977 Sheila read some small thing about me in a newspaper and wrote a postcard to say that, if ever in Mayo, I was welcome to sleep in the window seat of her caravan in a field in Turlough village. Darkness had fallen by the time I hitchhiked to Turlough on my first visit. I stopped at a bungalow to seek directions. The householder asked if I was a friend of Sheila's, adding that if I was, 'Then you are a very lucky young man'. When I turned up a side road by the Round Tower Bar there was only darkness. I located a gate and entered a field, not sure of where I was going, though I saw a faint glow: light emanating through the curtains on her windows which faced the opposite way. Putting out my hands blindly they made contact with the door of her caravan.

I knocked. Nothing happened for a few seconds. Then the door burst open in a luminous square of light. Standing radiant at its centre was a tiny little woman with a shock of white hair and a delighted smile. 'You're here,' she said. 'Isn't life exciting?' It felt like glimpsing a ball of energy or flame of life. I entered her small den crammed with books and paintings, heated by a wood-burning stove. Three cats lazily bestowed upon me their friendly hospitable gaze. I didn't know it then, but the caravan was truly an ark: a citadel of refuge and happiness. Yet even on that first night I discovered that its name – The Ark – was linked to one of the tragedies in Sheila's life. It was named by her granddaughter who died just two years previously and would have only been a year younger than me. Many events in this book are invented, by necessity or by discreet subterfuge. But the visitation by the dying cat, who instinctively knew where to come for help, happened exactly as described.

The tragedies that Sheila had endured during the decade before I first met her might have overwhelmed a lesser soul, but at her lowest ebb – when she seemed to have lost everything – Sheila made a deliberate choice in old age to resolutely embrace happiness. At eighteen I was too inexperienced to understand how difficult this choice was, when it would be easier to sink beneath the weight of grief. But in the years since, whenever bad things happened to me, as they invariably happen to us all – it is Sheila's example I try to emulate when picking myself up, feeling myself borne forward by the inner strength of this woman I first met in a Mayo field.

Sheila was a bohemian alternative thinker who would stand out in any generation. Her bookshelves were crammed with thinkers like Meister Eckhart and Martin Buber, but also with books about Andy Warhol and Nelson Mandela. There was only one clock in The Ark. Just like in this novel, Sheila had removed its hands and covered the clock face with a piece of blank paper on which was written one word: NOW. This clock – which now resides beside my writing desk – always told the right time, because Sheila lived in the present. This did not mean the past was buried away. Her walls were lined with pictures of family members she had loved and lost. I became a regular visitor in those first few years. If you have a dream – and my dream was to be a writer – you need one person to take you seriously. Sheila became that person. Unemployed in Dublin, I would hitchhike across Ireland to sit in her caravan with the candles lit and read aloud my latest poems, seeking her honest opinion. A poem only felt finished when Sheila heard it. We always talked long into the night and, while immersed in the present, she was unafraid to address the sorrows she had known in life, so that many of the stories recreated here in this book were tales that I heard on my first visit to her caravan and on many subsequent visits.

There was a fifty-five-year gap in our ages, but maybe because I had lost my mother at an early age and she had lost a son, there was an affinity between us. Sheila opened my eyes to new ways of seeing things. Although penniless, she was the richest person I knew because she wanted nothing. She had her beloved dog, Johnny, her books and the cats who shared her caravan, along with numerous callers of all ages, inspired by her positive attitude. I remember her walking for miles with Johnny, stopping to talk to everyone she passed as we approached the small woodland wildlife sanctuary on the site of her old house from the 1930s.

She took seriously the advice she felt she had received from her late son on that night in the White Eagle Lodge in London, and tried to keep only possessions that were precious and important. Amid all her moves, a sketchbook of exquisite drawings from her girlhood in Donegal somehow survived. But it needed to be snatched from a bonfire in the field in Mayo by a friend who chanced to call as Sheila was about to add it to the fire, convinced that nobody would be interested in her drawings, which capture everyday life for her family as the Irish Free State was awkwardly being born around them. I helped to edit them into a small book, entitled *A Donegal Summer*, published in a small edition by Raven Arts Press in 1985. I still remain moved at the vibrant joy they radiate and the carefree life they chronicle, with no forewarning of the tragedies awaiting her family.

Sheila was the second oldest of five Goold-Verschoyle children, growing up in Dunkineely: all headstrong and raised amid a babble of debate where no viewpoint was taboo. Sheila was closest to Neil, who is called Art in this novel, and who was her childhood confidant and minder. Neil was destined to inherit The Manor House in Dunkineely, as the eldest son of the eldest son, under a legal indenture. But Neil Goold (he dropped the Verschoyle part of his surname) rejected his inheritance and become a communist. He moved to Moscow but was forced to leave a wife and child behind there during Stalin's 1930s purges. He worked and proselytised in Dublin's worst slums and was jailed for communist agitation. Brendan Behan's mother – who considered Neil to be a saint – sheltered him in the Behan corporation home in Crumlin, as he continued to renounce his upbringing and isolate himself from the family he loved.

Neil seems an idyllic, happy figure in Sheila's sketches, as does her beloved youngest brother Brian. Nothing prepares you for the fate that Brian (named Brendan in this novel) later suffered after volunteering to fight with the Soviets in the Spanish Civil War. Growing disillusioned, he was tricked onto a Soviet ship in Barcelona and disappeared. His mother spent her final years desperately seeking news of his whereabouts; the family never knowing whether to believe the information they eventually received, claiming that he had died in an attack by a Nazi plane on a Soviet train transporting political prisoners between gulags. Indeed when I first knew Sheila she remained haunted by uncertainty as to whether Brian could somehow, against all the odds, still be alive as a political prisoner who might one day be released from that limbo.

Brian Goold-Verschoyle rarely gets mentioned in history books. The two other Irish victims of Stalin's gulags, Patrick Breslin and Sean McAteer, are only slightly better known. The enormity of the gulags is barely comprehensible: the lives of three random foreigners easily forgotten amid the millions who suffered there. But in recent years the Irish historian Barry McLoughlin has authored a fine book, *Left to the Wolves*, a factual account of those three young Irishman who died in Stalin's gulags. McLoughlin's carefully researched account of Brian Goold-Verschoyle's interrogation, captivity and death makes for stark reading. But much of the information it reveals – gleaned from MI5 files (describing him as 'a naïve enthusiast' recruited by the NKVD to be a 'sleeper' in Britain) and from Soviet transcripts of his interrogation – contain information which Sheila never knew during her lifetime.

This is one of the problems for any novelist trying to recreate, in a parallel fictional world, the life story of someone who, like many of us, may not always know the full facts about what happened to people they loved or what motivated people's actions. Whether when dealing with her daughter's fate in Kenya, which she always struggled to accept, or her brother's death in the gulags – the only way that I could tell Sheila's story was to remain as true as possible both to what she knew and also to the gaps in her knowledge and the subjective ambiguities contained in anyone's memories. This novel has tried to follow, where possible, her account of how she remembered certain aspects of her life: an account which she gave to me during long conversations in her caravan, which I tape-recorded in 1992. However, insomuch as the characters that I have invented here reflect her interpretation of certain real-life people, about whom she talked at length, I must insert the caveat that, while I have tried to remain true to how she remembered them, any real-life people upon whom these characters were originally based are portrayed only through the prism of how she recalled them. I have changed all their names and certain details to emphasise this subjective fictional quality. I am cognisant that, from their own perspective, their stories and roles may be undoubtedly more complex and that, if alive today, they might recollect certain of these events from differing viewpoints. So I have tried to show this version of them solely in the moments when their lives intersected with Sheila's life, rather than to try and present the far wider lives that they undoubtedly led and which I have tried, insomuch as possible, not to unnecessarily intrude upon.

Although Sheila never became as entangled in politics as her brothers, she campaigned tirelessly for causes she believed in. The artist Pauline Bewick – whose mother, Harry Bewick, was an equally unconventional, free-spirited resident on Frankfort Avenue when Sheila taught child art there – remembers Sheila as a tiny crusader covered in flour hurled at her by an outraged citizen after Sheila took part in a protest march. The poet Paul Durcan attended her innovative child art classes, which started his passionate love for paintings. In the preface to his acclaimed book, *Crazy about Women* – a collection of poems all written in response to paintings displayed in the National Gallery of Ireland – he wrote: '*The origins of this book ... go back to winter nights in Dublin in the early 1950s when my mother used to take me one night a week for yet another magic assignation with Sheila Fitzgerald. Sheila Fitzgerald was a painter who gave classes in her home in Frankfort Avenue. To these two women – Sheila Durcan and Sheila Fitzgerald – I owe my lifelong obsession with picture-making.*'

Young artists like Camille Souter and Barbara Warren found lodgings in Sheila's home; the walls covered in paintings by children

– sometimes on whitewashed sheets of newspaper when Sheila couldn't afford blank sheets. *An Ark of Light* explores Sheila's life from the time that she had the courage to separate from an unhappy marriage and start out on a quest that was both physical and spiritual: to strip away the veneer of complexity and strive – despite tragedies and setbacks – to grasp the joy at the core of life.

Painting and sketching were Sheila's childhood passions. The family's Visitors Book shows people crowding in to share their home in Donegal. Cousins or friends or local children who felt free to play tennis in the garden or were encouraged to visit the coach house, where Sheila had her studio, to try their hand at watercolours.

Her father – a pacifist who supported Home Rule – was a utopian barrister who often defended locals without seeking payment. His passion was composing music. He loved Walt Whitman and carried *Leaves of Grass* in his pocket on family walks. Occasionally he anonymously contributed to 'An Irishman's Diary' in *The Irish Times*.

His wife, Sibyl, suffered from arthritis but loved to garden and paint. Like many upper-class women, she was fascinated by mysticism. Household decisions often fell to her eldest daughter, Sheila's sister. When the IRA stole the family car during the War of Independence, it was Sheila's sister who visited the cottage where the local IRA were based to seek its return. Startled volunteers played her protestant hymns on a gramophone until their commander returned and handed back the car. The IRA came back one night to commandeer two bicycles, but put away their guns after Mrs Goold-Verschoyle exclaimed how she hated the sight of weapons. It helped that they were related to the rebel Countess Markievicz, although some Northern cousins were Orangemen. Sheila recalled writing poems in support of the IRA and her autograph book suggests similar Nationalist sympathies by other siblings. The family looked forward to playing their role in a new Ireland, not realising that the new Ireland envisaged no role for them.

But the outside world intruded on Sheila's paradise. Her sketchbook ended abruptly. On the final page she wrote: 'I stopped after the day two young men came down from the mountain ... the arrival of these strangers brought the more complex world into our small oasis ... (and) heralded the time to grow up.' Those two young men included the husband she married. I had always longed to know more about her life after those drawings stop. Sheila often expressed her desire to write her own life story. Yet I never realised how seriously she desired to be a writer until, after her death, I unearthed a very old passport of hers, in which she listed her occupation as 'writer'. A tattered envelope listed stories she had written and comments from various editors who rejected them. She was at an age when most people's lives seem settled into fixed routines when applying for that passport, travelling cheaply through Spain and Morocco, trying to write and engage with new ideas and people. Her notebook from that time is filled more with quotations from mystics than with her own thoughts. Perhaps, as when studying painting in London's Slade School almost a half century before, she found that the more she tried to write the less she actually could.

In 1985, shortly after her sketchbook of drawings was published, I was in her caravan when a local woman told Sheila that her elderly mother couldn't understand Sheila's book. It wasn't the drawings, the woman explained: what baffled her mother was that Sheila didn't dress in black and live out her life in mourning; that she possessed the audacity to still embrace happiness. Sheila's happiness came from not hiding from grief but refusing to be conquered by it. It wasn't the simple unthinking happiness of a child, but a hard-won happiness. She was happy not because of life but in spite of everything life had stolen from her.

By 1992, when she was in her eighty-ninth year, it seemed unlikely that she would ever get around to writing the memoir that she always talked about writing. Just before my second son was born, I travelled to Wexford and we discussed the idea that one day I would write a novel based on her life. Sheila preferred a form of inter-linking vignettes, with names being changed, certain facts blurred to be less recognisable and the leaving out of some matters that are not included in this novel.

Over several nights, we sat up in her caravan, making recordings in which she discussed aspects of her life which I knew and experiences that were new to me. I never listened to her tapes during her lifetime but I treasure the memories of the evenings we spent talking, reminiscent of my early visits to The Ark as a teenager. After she died in 2000, I hesitated to attempt to write a novel, knowing that I could never capture her unique essence or tell the essential truth of her story in the way that Sheila would have done. There was also the problem of what was the 'essential truth'. Denis (Thomas in this novel), her middle brother who moved to South Africa and was Sheila's rock, regarded parts of *A Donegal Summer* as inaccurate because – as a well-respected member of the Donegal Historical Society – he remembered their childhood differently.

Whose truth could I tell? If Sheila's impressionistic memories contained inaccuracies on one level, then a literal historian's logic might recreate a reality that Sheila could not identify with, because in most families siblings often recall the same events differently, depending on their age at the time or level of emotional involvement. I struggled with this dilemma and with occasionally discovering facts that ran contrary to Sheila's stories. This was partly because it was not in her nature to speak ill of anyone, even her husband who, as I only later discovered, had left their children out of his will.

A year after Sheila's death, I unearthed the tapes and played them. Because she found aspects of nursing home life difficult, some of my final visits to see her had been distressing. But listening to these tapes in private allowed me to reconnect with Sheila when she was still in good health and spirits, even at eighty-nine and then, through the stories she told me, to connect her with her at the ages of fifty-nine and thirty-nine and nineteen. Initially, I tried to tell each story exactly as told to me, but taken out of a conversational context, her words did not form a coherent narrative. After two years of writing, I needed to start again, this time first and foremost as a novelist and not a biographer, taking for courage and guidance a sentence by Sheila on the tapes about how she admired artists who had the courage to take reality and create something new and different from it.

Five years after her death, I published a novel based on the first half of her life, entitled *The Family on Paradise Pier*. Like in this new standalone novel, it deliberately played with some aspects of reality. I changed the first names of each family member to show that my representations of them were subjective recreations, shaped in my imagination. But I retained the family name because the Goold-Verschoyle children were too unique to be any other family. Likewise I kept the surname of the famous Fitzgerald family of Mayo into which she married, although again I have changed the Christian names of her husband and children to show that this is my fictional recreation of them, as described to me by someone who still felt their loss as keenly in old age as when they died. While the majority of these stories are true, down to the touch of her son's old jumper bursting her dam of grief in 1966, all letters quoted in this book are in my words and not theirs.

The Family on Paradise Pier was set in Donegal and Mayo but also in Moscow and Spain as it followed not just Sheila's early years, but the complex lives of two of her brothers. By 2005 I also already had a first draft written of *An Ark of Light*. This novel is different and completely independent from the first book in that, while *Paradise Pier* exploded the political tensions and turmoil in which her brothers' immersed themselves, *An Ark of Light* is a quieter and more solitary book, focused purely on Sheila herself. It tries to tell her story in her latter decades, when she was no longer part of a large boisterous family but needed to make a new life and find a new sense of purpose, as a separated wife in a society that did not recognise divorce and also as the mother of a gay man in those decades when very real dangers lurked everywhere for lesbian, gay, bisexual and transgender people, who had to live within two worlds at once.

During part of the period in which I wrote my final draft of *An Ark of Light*, I was the first ever Writer in Residence at the National Museum of Ireland, based both in Collins Barracks in Dublin, which houses their Decorative Arts and History collections, and in Turlough Park in Turlough, Co. Mayo – the mansion in which Sheila's in-laws lived and which plays a role in this novel. I was blessed by the great support of the staff of these two institutions. It was a privilege to be able to draw inspiration from the superb national collections housed in Turlough Park and to be allowed to spend time writing and conducting workshops in the stately rooms which Sheila would have visited so often as a young mother. I am no historian, and so I would direct readers seeking a factual account of the Fitzgerald family in Turlough to an excellent book, *Turlough Park and the Fitzgeralds* by Patrick Butler, a fine historian and one of the last people to live in that house before it became a national museum.

Now, finally, eighteen years on from her death; a quarter of a century after we sat together late at night in The Ark to make tape-recordings about her life, and more than forty years since the first night when I sat in her caravan listening to her tell me the stories that form the basis of this novel, this is my attempt to provide a fictional account of the second half of Sheila's remarkable life. Some of it is based exactly on her own words when describing certain experiences, some sections are deliberately fictionalised, when I need to fill in gaps where not even Sheila had a full knowledge of what occurred to people she loved. Some characters are closely based on people she told me about, whereas other are composites of various people who touched her life. It is not my task as a novelist to say who is who, because in the end this novel is a work of imaginative fiction based on one woman's memories.

While fiction can never tell the full truth, perhaps it can tell a different but equally important truth. I make no claims to fully know exactly who Sheila Fitzgerald was at these different stages of her life, no more than I can even claim to fully know myself. To write a book like this is to feel judged by the living and the dead and I have no way of knowing if I will ever know the verdict of the latter. I just hope that I have honoured her instruction to take the outline of her life and craft something new from it. I also hope I have done justice to the people close to her about whom she spoke with such warmth.

Having spent thirteen years living with this manuscript, I feel it is time to publish it. I hope that, in my fictional Eva Fitzgerald, I have captured something of how she played a huge part in shaping me into the person I am now, and how she inspired so many people whom she came across in different countries and different decades. On the afternoon in 2000, when the staff at Glasnevin crematorium were baffled by the arrival of a white van from Wexford, Sheila's colourful, handmade coffin looked like a small boat that would cause only the barest ripple. Only now, as the years pass, do her friends realise how that ripple has spread out across her lifetime to touch distant shores and how it still keeps moving on its own course, long after many of the seemingly great waves of her time have petered out. I thank her for the great gift of her friendship.

Dermot Bolger
Dublin, 3rd July 2018